"THIS INGENIOUS AUTHOR TAKES YOU BEYOND *REBECCA*, BEYOND THE BRONTËAN WORLD OF *JANE EYRE* AND *WUTHERING HEIGHTS*, INTO A STATE OF MIND YOU'VE QUITE LIKELY NEVER DARED BEFORE . . . SHE SUCCEEDS BRILLIANTLY."

—*Tulsa, Oklahoma, World*

WAKEFIELD HALL
Francesca Stanfill

"Drenched in opulent descriptions of the rich and famous, Stanfill's novel is an entertaining, spellbinding tour de force."

—*Booklist*

"Francesca Stanfill guides us elegantly through a labyrinth of deceit to a totally surprising truth."

—Dominick Dunne

"Wittily imitating classic gothic masterpieces, Stanfill takes a Brontëan heroine and puts her in a Tom Wolfe-ish New York setting—where 'identity is telegraphed by the names of the corporations or one's position on the *Forbes* list.' A splendidly unabashed postmodern updating of the genre—complete with the requisite foreshadowing, sinister characters, and extravagant settings."

—*Kirkus Reviews*

Please turn the page for more extraordinary acclaim . . .

WAKEFIELD HALL

WAKEFIELD HALL

Francesca Stanfill

A Dell Book

Published by
Dell Publishing
a division of
Bantam Doubleday Dell Publishing Group, Inc.
1540 Broadway
New York, New York 10036

Frontispiece: Ellen Terry as Lady Macbeth by John Singer Sargent, Tate Gallery, London

ISBN: 0-440-21788-1

Reprinted by arrangement with Villard Books

Printed in the United States of America

Published simultaneously in Canada

May 1994

10 9 8 7 6 5 4 3 2 1

OPM

FOR PETER

June 14, 1986

I would have arrived much earlier if I hadn't lost my way three times. What a strange road it was to Wakefield Hall! More than once I'd been tempted to turn back, certain that the twisting lane, with its sudden pitches and misleading signs, could not possibly be right. It was all the more bewildering as the directions had seemed so explicit.

Shortly before noon I came to the walls encircling the estate, to a gabled carriage house next, and finally to the entrance—very tall, very grand, in black wrought iron. I stopped the car, relishing the silence for a moment as I caught my breath. A slight breeze blew, ruffling the trees and blowing my hair about my face.

Double gates loomed before me, their massive stone posts

carved with a pattern not easy to decipher: arrows entwined by lilies, it seemed. For many moments I sat quite still, gazing at the motif embedded in the stone—it was carved in such a way that the serpentine flowers appeared strangely animated and powerful. Then I got out of the car and stepped forward, toward the speaker, to announce myself.

Only at that instant, with a peculiar rush of sense-memory, did I realize how many times I had imagined arriving here—how many times, since first meeting Joanna Eakins on that summer afternoon, I had visualized the road, the gate, the house itself. I tried to remember whether, in my fantasies, the gate had opened to me; it seemed it had. Yet now I felt almost intimidated, hesitant to say my name and enter.

I pressed the bell again and once more announced myself. The gates opened; I drove through.

At first the landscape seemed barely cultivated—meadows of wildflowers that gradually gave way to fields of blue iris. An allée of immense maple trees followed, their green-tinged limbs twisting upward to form a canopy of heavy branches. I remember how cool it was as I drove beneath them, a respite from the unseasonably warm June sun.

At last, in the distance, I glimpsed Wakefield Hall. With its august proportions and columned portico, it was startling in its Englishness (this being Massachusetts, after all!). To the left, down a sloping lawn, I saw a trio of weeping willows where several people were gathered—having drinks before lunch, it seemed. A Saturday ritual, perhaps, unchanged since Joanna Eakins's death.

I glanced into the visor mirror, wiped some dust from my cheek, and ran a brush through my hair. Then I took out my compact and fixed my lipstick, thinking how pale I looked in the stark noon light, and how disheveled, for my linen skirt was very creased.

I got out of the car and walked up the stone steps to the entrance. A slender, dark-haired young woman approached, her face partly obscured by sunglasses. Evidently she had just returned from riding, for she was wearing boots and jodhpurs, both of which caked with dirt; her cheeks looked flushed. Clutched in her left hand was a riding crop that she flicked against one thigh. She was small, but so perfectly proportioned that, at least from a distance, she appeared taller. There was a brittle elegance about her, an aura of command, all the more striking in someone so dainty. We were about the same age, I guessed.

"Rosalind Bennett," she announced, extending her hand. "Joanna Cassel's—or should I say Joanna Eakins's—stepdaughter."

She took off her sunglasses and fixed her dark, almond-shaped eyes on me, the next instant wiping her perspiring brow with a red kerchief. Her fine, almost Florentine face, with its high forehead and long, graceful brow was marred by a purplish bruise on one temple—from a recent riding accident, I assumed. I noticed a slight flaccidity to her skin, particularly under the chin, the kind that comes from having suddenly lost a great deal of weight.

She continued to examine me, one hand with sunglasses still on her hip.

"Elisabeth Rowan," I replied.

"Of course." She paused, as if her thoughts had momentarily wandered. But then, just as quickly, she focused on me again. "No problem getting here?" she asked.

I said lightly enough that I had gotten lost, though in fact losing my way had disturbed me, for I had always prided myself on my sense of direction, on being the sort of person strangers stopped in the street.

Rosalind merely continued to examine me in her cool, implacable way before remarking, "But you don't look any the worse for wear." With another flick of her crop, she said, "I'll show you to the house," and motioned me to follow her. "Then we'll get your things. You must be tired—" she looked at me intently again, "thirsty."

I followed her up the wide steps, banked with huge terra cotta pots spilling with purple primroses, and then along the east facade to the formal Italianate terrace, its stone balustrade punctuated with classical statues of armless nymphs and helmet-clad warriors. From this vantage point my eye encompassed the whole splendid vista, half familiar to me then, for I had seen it in photographs. Four sets of broad shallow steps led to the vast ornamental pool of water in the distance, its surface trembling with the reflection of flowering azaleas in surreal, variegated purples, its oval shape guarded by a pair of statues of Pegasus that led one's eyes further, to the central Triton fountain. Towering spruces and hemlocks lent their blue-green to the palette of this ravishing landscape, which seemed to extend almost endlessly to the high, rounded shapes of the Berkshire hills in the distance.

"So—what do you think?" she asked, interrupting my reverie.

"It's even more beautiful than I'd imagined," I carefully replied. "More beautiful than the photographs."

"Well, it's all Joanna's creation, this," she said perfunctorily. "No one could deny that." There was a distinctly proprietary edge to her voice, however, for she was clearly very proud of Wakefield Hall. Then, with another flick of her crop: "Have you got any idea of the slant of the book you want to write?"

I said I hadn't—which wasn't quite true—and that I had merely come to discuss the possibility of writing the biography of her stepmother, Joanna Eakins.

"I see—a biographer in search of an actress," she murmured, mulling this over. "You should know that I'm not exactly enthusiastic about the idea of a book on Joanna." Then, more sharply: "You should also know that this is very difficult for David."

"I can understand your father's feelings."

"He isn't my real father," she replied, with an exasperated glance. "I'm Joanna's stepdaughter by a previous marriage. My own mother and father died years ago. Joanna just sort of kept me on." She paused before continuing in her staccato way: "But I'm very close to David. And I can tell you this is damn difficult for him. Damn difficult for everyone, Joanna's dying like that."

"You were close to Joanna, then?"

"As close as anyone *could* be," she replied, almost imperceptibly raising her brow. "We had our own relationship." A pause before she flicked her riding crop again, newly impatient. "Where are your things?"

"Still in my car," I told her.

"Let's go get them."

We walked back across the terrace and down the steps, toward my car. All the while I wondered what to make of her brusqueness, and why it was she who, like some dark, unnerving archangel, seemed to have been appointed my guide.

A tall, balding man with pallid eyes and an impeccably cut black jacket—the houseman, I assumed—had preceded us and stood rather stiffly by my car.

"This is Miss Rowan, Kurt," Rosalind said, barely glancing at me. I felt the butler's practiced eye assessing my car, my clothes, and—as I searched for the car key to open the trunk —my handbag. I could feel Rosalind's curious gaze as well. I think she had noticed my sapphire ring and my expensive luggage, neither of which was the sort one would associate with a writer or journalist. Both had been presents from my lover.

Kurt took my bags and disappeared with them into the house.

I looked about, still expecting to see David Cassel, for it was he who had invited me here, after all, to speak with him about the possibility of writing the authorized biography of his late wife. I noticed that the people gathered near the stand of weeping willows had vanished, and proceeded to ask where Cassel was. "David always stays in his study until early afternoon," Rosalind said matter-of-factly. "He'll meet with you after lunch."

She plucked a flower from one of the stone urns that lined the steps, crushing the purple blossom in her hand. "Let's go," she announced, motioning to me to follow her up the steps to the portico. She stamped the dirt off her boots, set down her crop on a nearby bench, and led me inside.

Through the vast entrance we went, moving from the bright noon sun into a serene interior whose filtered light seemed to have been wrested from another country—England, say, or northern Italy. It was a severe but not unwelcoming space of fine detail and proportion. An Adam-style frieze ran below the vaulted ceiling, above the pale ocher walls, which were punctuated, at each corner, by fluted columns whose capitals were picked out in gold. The cool stone floor seemed to mute the sound of my footsteps as I walked tentatively to the left, toward a great marble console overhung with a giltwood mirror that reflected white roses in huge blue-and-white porcelain vases, and, beyond, the massive spiraling staircase.

Suddenly, I was aware that someone else had entered: the houseman, Kurt. He handed Rosalind a slip of paper. "Mrs. von Shouse called," he said quietly. "She asked that you call her back."

I watched Rosalind's face as she perused the message, her brow furrowed. "What time did she call?" she finally asked, looking up.

"An hour ago. While you were riding," he replied.

"Did you say Mr. Cassel was in?"

"Yes," he said, nodding.

"Did she give you any idea . . ."

They exchanged glances. "I'm afraid not."

"Then I guess I should go find him," Rosalind said almost to herself as she distractedly slipped the paper into the pocket of her breeches.

Kurt excused himself and left. Still curious about the message, I continued to observe Rosalind's face: her fleeting expression of preoccupation, even consternation, had already been replaced by her customary severity. "Come on—I suppose you want to see the rest of the house," she said as I followed her. "The drawing room next."

We passed through two great double doors to an immense

rectangular room facing the wide terrace, through whose vast windows, hung with weighty gray-green curtains, the summer sky entered. It was a comfortable room but also, perhaps because of the quality and scale of its furniture and objects, a daunting one. The tufted sofas looked formidable; antique busts stared from niches carved like seashells. Stately photographs, framed in silver, enhanced the aura of almost impersonal formality: Joanna Eakins, in evening dress, with Queen Elizabeth, with John F. Kennedy, with Lyndon Johnson.

Rosalind began to tell me the history of the house. "Wakefield was built just before the turn of the century," she began. "The original owners were Anglophiles who wanted to create their own little England here. A proper English country house near Lenox, Mass.! Of course, it changed a lot after Joanna bought it—when she married David."

I asked how the house had changed. "It wasn't nearly as polished," she replied, after hesitating a moment. "Actually, it was in rotten shape—neglected for years." Her hands in the pockets of her breeches, she strode restlessly about the room, stopping for an instant to take an elastic band from her pocket and twist her long hair into a ponytail. I remember looking at her in profile, struck by the effect of the suddenly severe hair, which almost lent her the look of a Renaissance youth and thus reinforced her aura of enigmatic sexuality.

"Maybe it took an outsider to bring it all together," she continued in a tone that, for her, passed for contemplativeness. "At least that's what Joanna did. With a lot of blood, sweat, and tears, of course!" Then, abruptly, she commanded: "This way," once more motioning me to follow her.

We reached a corridor that led to a small octagonal library arranged in distinctly feminine colors—pale blue, mauve, and *bois de rose*. Very much a European woman's room, with delicate furniture, clusters of pink peonies, and flower-patterned chintz curtains that framed a graceful bay window looking out to a formal rose garden.

"This was Joanna's room," Rosalind said matter-of-factly.

"Her study. Everything has been left as it was before her death—that's how David wanted it."

I looked around in silence for a moment, my eyes drawn to a small needlepoint pillow on a sofa, embroidered with *Je Ne Regrette Rien*; then to a chess set; and finally to a collection of antique hourglasses that lined the shelves on either side of the fireplace, their fragile, undulating surfaces clouded by time.

I walked to a table with an impressive array of portrait miniatures. "And these?" I asked, turning to Rosalind.

"Joanna's collection of Elizabethan miniatures. You know —Shakespeare and all of that."

"Was Joanna a patient person?" I asked, glancing again at the hourglasses.

"Only when she chose to be," she replied with a tight smile.

I walked to the desk before the bay window, struck by the variety of writing paper arranged on top, all in pale gray and engraved with black-violet lettering: JOANNA EAKINS, JOANNA EAKINS CASSEL, one with the initials J E C, and lastly, a version simply with JOANNA. Observing me, Rosalind said, her face with an odd detached look, "It's weird, isn't it? She had so many names, it's as if she had none."

A breeze blew the curtains. I felt even more keenly the delicate voluptuousness of the room, the almost mournful quality of its hyacinthine colors. But it was its meticulousness that I noticed and commented upon to Rosalind.

"She was nothing if not meticulous," she grudgingly admitted, flipping through a copy of *Country Life*. "An admirable enough quality, I guess." Then, beneath her breath: "God knows I wasn't born with it! Except maybe in my work—"

I looked at Rosalind's ethereal pre-Raphaelite face and tried to guess her line of work—photographer? painter?— before finally inquiring what she did.

"Bond trader," she said, as if she were accustomed to measuring the degree of surprise this provoked. "Bond trader," she said again. "Goldman, Sachs."

I asked how long she had worked at the investment bank. "Since I got out of business school. Harvard." She took an apple from a porcelain bowl near the writing table and began to crunch into it. "Not a profession Joanna understood . . . on the other hand, I have to hand it to Joanna—she did admire my ability to make money." Another raucous bite into the apple. "It must have been hard for her to have had a stepdaughter who wasn't a good housekeeper!" Wiping her mouth with the side of her hand, she tossed the remains of the apple core into a wastebasket. "Still, I've got to admit that I'm the first one to enjoy the house while I'm here. The funny thing is that Joanna never used to be so orderly. In her previous life, when she was acting, I don't remember her that way at all." She glanced at her black digital watch. "I'd better find David and tell him you're here. Then I'll meet you by the stairs. You'd like to go to your room before lunch, wouldn't you?" Yes, I said. She left the room, the purposeful sound of her steps echoing through the corridor.

I couldn't help lingering, fascinated by what seemed to be the apparent lack of mementos from what Rosalind had called Joanna's "previous life"—an understated way, indeed, of describing her stepmother's brilliant career as a classical stage actress. Nearly hidden in one corner was the famous cover of *Time*, from the fifties, depicting Joanna Eakins as a youthful, lascivious Lady Macbeth—an image that seemed so at odds with that of Joanna Cassel, mistress of this idyllic place.

In another corner, resting between two diminuitive black porcelain sphinxes, were photographs of Joanna in some of her most famous roles—Hedda Gabler, Cleopatra, Desdemona, Medea. There were photographs of family and friends as well: David Cassel, Wall Street lion, receiving an honorary degree; Rosalind as a child, with plump cheeks and a pinafore; and a young Joanna, in slacks, standing by the arched door of a medieval tower.

I walked to the bookshelves next, feeling a surge of intense curiosity as I did so, for I have always been guilty of judging people by their books. The volumes here were carefully arranged by category: There was an entire section devoted to eighteenth- and nineteenth-century Gothic novels, for instance, one shelf lined with leatherbound editions of *Frankenstein;* below these were arranged volume after volume of critical interpretations of Mary Shelley's famous novel. The next bookcase was devoted to drama—Chekhov, Ibsen, and Greek tragedy. Relevant critical studies, arranged by subject and author, stood on the shelves below. I picked up *The Greeks and the Irrational,* glancing at its chapter headings before bending down to examine the last three shelves.

There I discovered book after book on labyrinths, garden mazes, and mythology. One such volume, much taller and thicker than the rest, stood out: *Labyrinths Through the Ages.* It was bound in rich green leather, its gilt-edged pages marked with long strips of paper. I picked it up and leafed through it, noting how certain terms in the glossary had been singled out: among them, *Black hole* ("A maze situation which one can get into, but not get out of"), and its opposite, *White hole.* I continued to scan both the thick, beautifully illustrated pages and the many notes inserted between them, written in an angular, slanted hand: "Idea for gate"; "Discuss grid with LB"; "Raised pavilion—ask Desmond to send photos"; and "NB: Central tower with twin staircases and statue of Athena" (this, by the illustration of the Italian hedge maze at Stra). How thrilling to see Joanna's own notations; each seemed a clue to her personality—as if, within my hands, the book itself had become a labyrinth.

I came to the dog-eared chapter devoted to English mazes: Blenheim, Hampton Court, Hever Castle, Leeds Castle, Longleat, Somerleyton. At that point there seemed to be a gap, a place where the rest of the section had been ripped out —and carelessly, too, for the ragged, tantalizing edges of those missing pages still remained. I reluctantly closed the book and put it down, wondering what she had chosen to tear out, and why.

I stood up, inspecting the next bookcase, which contained the most comprehensive section—not surprisingly, given the thrust of Joanna's career—on Shakespeare. I had never seen such an extensive private collection of rare editions—illustrated nineteenth-century volumes side by side with fragile eighteenth-century texts. But it was the staggering range of critical studies that fascinated me even more. My eyes scanned shelf after shelf of the scholarly titles: *Shakespeare and the Nature of Women*; *Shakespeare's Romances*; *Renaissance Cryptology*; *Shakespeare and the Goddess of Complete Being*; *The Girlhood of Shakespeare's Heroines*; *The Garden in Shakespeare*; *The Crown of Life*. An immense volume with a glossy deep green cover—*A Complete Concordance to Shakespeare*—dominated the top shelf.

Directly beneath it, to the right, stood contemporary editions of *The Arden Shakespeare*—prompt copies, I assumed, which Joanna Eakins had used in rehearsal.

I examined a copy of *Macbeth* that seemed particularly well-worn—the frontispiece, first, with Joanna Eakins's large, distinctive signature. I noticed the immense capitals, the rhythmic spaces between the disconnected lower-case letters —the stylized signature of an artist. Next, I leafed through *As You Like It*, *Antony and Cleopatra*, and *Hamlet*, all of which were crammed with Joanna's scribblings (stage directions, nuances of tone and theme).

I slowly replaced *Hamlet* on the shelf before picking up *King Lear*. *Lear* was relatively free of notations, though the lines of Cordelia, whose part she had played, were noted with a blue pencil.

I stopped in the midst of the first act. One line stood out, a line that Joanna had not only marked with a star, but thickly underlined in red as well. It was not a line that belonged to Cordelia, but to Lear himself, strangely—a line that reverberated in my mind as I closed the book and left to join Rosalind: "Who is it that can tell me who I am?"

2

Rosalind was waiting impatiently for me by the steps. "Ready?" she said. We turned down a long, wide corridor, past walls hung with eighteenth-century portraits and gauzy pastoral landscapes, until we came to an imposing pair of doors with heavy ram-shaped brass knobs. Turning to me as she opened them, Rosalind said, "I hope this will be all right."

No doubt I gasped at my first glimpse of the room, for it was undoubtedly one of the most beautiful I had ever seen— surely the most beautiful I had ever slept in. The panels of the larkspur-blue walls were painted with trellises entwined with roses, and the great canopy bed hung with fold upon fold of subtly patterned silk; a dressing table, to one side, glowed with red enameled objects. The ceiling was very high, and the heavily curtained windows immense. There were new magazines scattered about, and, on the small table before the marble fireplace, a plate of flawless peaches with a silver knife and linen napkin.

Suddenly, everything about my life in New York seemed unreal and distant—my apartment in the city, with its claustral light; the tension of the deadlines at *The Wall Street Journal*; and my love affair with Jack—all fallen away from me like a half-forgotten nightmare—as if on entering this room, I had been bestowed a gift, however tentative: a gift of peace, and order, and calm.

I felt an impulse to tell Rosalind how happy I felt, but then restrained myself—she would think it ridiculous, no doubt. I felt a sudden twinge of jealousy.

"You're not at all what I expected," she remarked with a small preoccupied smile. "David will be surprised."

"Will he? Why?"

"You're more glamorous than I'd thought you'd be—at least from reading your articles in the *Journal*."

"I suppose that's a compliment—"

"Not that I read the 'Leisure and Arts' page a whole lot," she seemed compelled to interject.

"I wouldn't expect you would," I replied, restraining a smile.

The next moment she continued almost officiously: "I've done my own research, you see."

"Have you?"

"Your bio, I mean. Born in Paris. Father worked in the State Department. Childhood partly spent in Europe—" She looked up with an ironic, slightly triumphant smile. "Should I go on?"

"Not for my benefit," I replied curtly, irritated by her tone. "I know the facts." I snapped open my suitcase. "And you've given my résumé to your stepfather, I suppose?"

"No. Not yet. He'll make up his own mind." I continued

to feel the pressure of her assessing eye. "Nice luggage," she finally said.

"Thanks." Our eyes met. "It was a present."

She seemed on the verge of a quip, but then refrained. "Did you ever meet Joanna?"

"Once," I said. "Outside London, last summer. She was staying with someone I knew. I was invited to lunch—I'd always admired her as an actress. I'd always followed her career."

"And what did you think of her?"

"She wasn't nearly as tall as I'd expected," I replied, choosing my words carefully. "I'd always imagined her as statuesque."

"People often say that—about her height, I mean. There were moments when I'd think of her as being tall and others when she seemed so *little*. It all depended on her sense of self, I guess. . . . Weird, isn't it?" She looked at her watch. "It's almost one—we should go down to lunch soon."

She asked whether I would like a maid to come and help me unpack. I said no, for I had brought very little with me. I would be downstairs in fifteen minutes, I told her, and watched as the doors slowly closed behind her.

I no longer felt tired but restless, full of nervous energy. Walking to the window, I gazed at the expanse of lawn, trying to sort through my impressions—the atmosphere of the house itself, Rosalind's coolness, the enigmatic exchange between her and the houseman about the telephone message.

Again I thought of meeting Joanna in London on that summer afternoon last June. I had been reluctant to share my real impression with Rosalind—somehow it was too fragile for me to entrust with someone so caustic. It seemed necessary, rather, to keep it intact before proceeding with Joanna Eakins's story.

I had arrived early that day, and was led by my host

through the garden to a gazebo, its columns thick with climbing roses; inside it was cool and fragrant, the light dim, so that the reclining figure on the long, low bench was half hidden in the shadows. An open book lay on the floor, a half-empty glass of water near it. Joanna Eakins was sleeping.

Perhaps it was her sleeping that lent her expression a certain sweetness that seemed almost out of keeping in a woman of her age. Her mouth was slightly parted, her head turned toward the shadows, making her short, full hair appear very dark. I could see the precise makeup and the narrow line that had been carefully drawn above her lashes. There was no mistaking the face, yet somehow I had expected it to be more familiar. It was strong, a touch of the Slavic about the eyes and high cheekbones—a face that lent itself to transformation.

A moment later she awoke, gazing at me with startling intensity, as if a phantom had appeared before her.

She sat up, both hands touching her temples—I remember noticing the contrast between her skin, which was very fair, and her eyes, which were very dark. "My book," she said, confused. "Where is it?" A moment later, the book having been retrieved, she turned to me with the smile of a Greek kouros—carved, archaic, as charming as it was inwardly distant. I told her how happy I was to meet her and how much I'd admired her on the stage, for I had seen her perform once —as Shakespeare's Cleopatra. I'm sure I rambled on, but she was gracious and politely thanked me, even going so far as to recall some anecdotes from that famous production. I would have asked her question after question just to hear that marvelous voice! The voice alone would have confirmed that she had been an actress, for the enunciation was so clear, the emphases so dramatic; it was a voice of concealed power, a seductive voice—a matchless instrument for her self-containment.

She asked where I lived, where I had gone to college, and how long I had worked for the *Journal*. I felt her absorbing every detail of my clothes, and face, and mannerisms; she laughingly confessed to a love of jewelry, and admired the charm bracelet I always wore. It was at that moment that I fully realized the attention to detail for which she was famous—I felt as if she were studying me in preparation to play a part.

Now I had arrived at the house she had created, the house where she had died. I walked restlessly about, sitting on the bed for a moment and glancing at the table beside me, with its vase of sweet william, art deco clock, carafe of water, and list of household telephone numbers indicating the kitchen, drawing room, staff room. And then I moved to the desk, with its pens and writing paper engraved with a tiny, beautifully colored rendering of Wakefield Hall.

But it was time to get ready. I took a seat before the dressing table to fix my makeup, but not without that shiver of expectancy that always preceded my glance into the mirror. I ran my fingers through my hair; I had cut it several months before, shortly after my father's death. How bitter and bereft I had felt—and how guilty—to shear the mass of chestnut hair my father loved. Still gazing into the mirror, I suddenly recalled his describing me as having "Yorkshire coloring"—pale skin, glint of red in the hair, deep gray-blue eyes not unlike his own. I hastily powdered my nose and applied some lipstick, barely able to face my own reflection.

To one side stood an assortment of perfumes in antique crystal and silver bottles. I opened one and, drawn to its exotic scent of jasmine and rose, splashed the perfume on my wrists and throat before I descended the staircase to go to lunch.

3

After lunch, Kurt showed me to the pavilion where I was to meet David Cassel. Set apart from the main house, its walls were trailed with ivy, the entrance flanked with tall arbor vitae and low, severely cut yews.

I found myself alone in a spacious room of leather, dark wood, and burnished colors, which had the feeling of an Edwardian gentleman's retreat; the aura was enhanced by the imposing Victorian furniture and by several impressive black-and-white photographs, on tables, of a rugged David Cassel on safari with his trophies (lion, leopard, and buffalo). Souvenirs of Cassel's well-known passion, as a younger man at least, for big-game hunting, I assumed.

The paneled walls were covered with elegant bookshelves

—the reason, I also assumed, that this was known as Cassel's "library," though I would not necessarily have given the room that name; there was something about the extreme order of these books that led me to think they had seldom been picked up or consulted, that they had been chosen by someone else. Real libraries have a well-thumbed-through look about them.

Splendid paintings hung between the bookshelves—paintings that comprised part of David Cassel's renowned collection of Italian art: several views of Venice by Canaletto, as well as a beautiful pair of the rarer English landscapes. Along the wall to the right, opposite the fireplace, stood a tall glass cabinet lined with antiquities—vacant-eyed Greek heads, graceful statuettes, and several lovely terra cotta figurines of whose origin and century I was not certain.

I continued to glance from time to time at the door, expecting Cassel to enter. I was excited rather than nervous, for my education and upbringing had well equipped me to deal with powerful men. Besides, I had always forced myself to do what I feared most.

I began once more to review mentally what I had learned about Cassel from others and from his lengthy entry in *Who's Who*. He was a complex figure in the New York establishment, to be sure, the venerated head of one of Wall Street's oldest and most successful investment banks, Bernham, Worth Brothers—a firm that had withstood decades of change and that had, even in the eighties, maintained its formidable reputation.

Cassel himself was born near Hamburg in 1912 to a Jewish family that had the foresight to leave before the Second World War, then had eventually settled in New York. A distant relative of the founders of Bernham, Worth, he had begun his career as an errand boy, working his way up until, in the mid-sixties, he was made chairman of the firm. He was also known as a longtime supporter of the Democratic party, a friend and confidant of John Kennedy and Lyndon Johnson. As for his personal life: Married three times, including to

Joanna, he had only one child, a son from his first marriage—
an estranged son, I'd been told, of whom he seldom spoke.
To some extent it was the scandal surrounding his marriage
to Joanna that had thrust him into the public eye, for he had
left his second wife to marry her.

I heard the door open and saw David Cassel enter, a trim,
slightly bent figure resting on a walking stick and ceremoni-
ously followed by the hovering Kurt. I introduced myself and
shook hands, thinking how much more startlingly attractive
and virile he was in person. Photographs did not capture the
barely suppressed restlessness of his eyes, the strong lines of
his dispassionate mouth—the palpable sense of intelligence,
controlled energy, and efficiency. He was a man of medium
height whose sinewy looks seemed to have succumbed only
recently to old age (a slight suggestion of a paunch was almost successfully concealed by his beautifully cut tweed
jacket).

"Damn it," he said as he entered the room, chafing against
the constraint of the walking stick. He looked at me hard.
"Good to meet you, Miss Rowan. No problem finding the
place?"

I reiterated what I had told Rosalind—that I had gotten
lost. "But I'm very glad to be here and to finally meet you. It
was kind of you to invite me to spend the night."

"I couldn't ask you to come all the way to Massachusetts,
Miss Rowan, and expect you to go back the same day."

"Even so—thank you." I paused, adding, "Please call me
Elisabeth."

A charming smile indicated his consent. "I'm only sorry
that you've come here for this reason, Elisabeth," he went on
to say, as if he were not quite concentrating on my responses,
"that you never saw the house when Joanna was alive."

He looked around for Kurt, who, already sensing what his
employer wanted, helped him to a large leather armchair
before the fireplace. Cassel asked me to take a seat opposite;
as I did so, he turned to Kurt and said perfunctorily, in a

voice that had assumed a deeper register, "You can go now.
I'll ring you when I'm ready."

He put down his walking stick with exasperated impatience. "Had a fall on a shoot this spring," he told me, settling in his chair. "North of England." His eyes darted from
his injured leg to me and back again: "There's nothing to
recommend about getting old, Elisabeth. I suggest you avoid
it." He smiled in an avuncular way that was not without a
touch of flirtatiousness.

After a slight pause, he began to speak, hammering out
the sentences in a businesslike way.

"As you will undoubtedly learn, Elisabeth, I'm not an evasive man. Let's waste no time in getting to the matter at
hand. I am also—as you have undoubtedly heard—a very
private man. The idea that I would authorize a biography of
my late wife does not, as you can imagine, come easily to
me."

"I realize—"

"Even so," he continued, "I have decided to go ahead with
this for several specific reasons. The first, and the most important, is that Joanna liked your writing. In fact, a year or so
before her death, she herself brought up your name . . . I
think you had written her asking for an interview—is that
correct? She told me that if there ever was talk of a biography, she would like you to write it. She liked your 'turn of
mind,' I think she said."

That Joanna Eakins should have thought of me to write
her biography was astounding. "I had no idea . . ."

"There's no reason why you should have," he answered.
"But no doubt you understand, Elisabeth, my wish to honor
my late wife's request. It is not an easy thing to ignore."
Grief edged his voice; I felt for him.

"Joanna meant a great deal to me," he continued. "More
than anyone will ever know. My life since has been . . ." He
paused, grappling with emotion; then he resumed his vigor-
ous tone. "The second reason to cooperate is that a biography seems inevitable. Even Joanna herself knew that. For

that reason, after her death, I was not at all surprised to find that she had actually left a box of photographs and personal papers which she had marked 'To my biographer.'" He recounted this last, eerie detail so matter-of-factly that I was more struck by his manner than by the idea of Joanna herself helping to organize her own posthumous portrait.

"Since the death of my late wife," he continued, "I've received calls from many publishers and other writers. I would rather Joanna's biography be done by someone capable of producing a distinguished book. And I would rather have some sway over the matter."

"Sway," I noted he had said, not "control."

"Third," he continued, "I have reviewed your writing—your pieces for the *Journal* and your obituary on Joanna, which was, I think, the most astute of the articles written after her death. I have come to the conclusion that you would be capable of writing a thoughtful book, Elisabeth."

I remember noticing the way he constantly repeated my name—a habit I had sometimes observed in those who have difficulty with intimacy. "You never met Joanna?" he asked next, leaning forward slightly.

"Yes," I replied. "About a year ago, in London. But only briefly."

He glanced at the floor. "She was not—" he faltered, his jutting brow furrowing, "very well then, you know."

A moment passed. "I understand you were born in Paris," he said.

"Yes," I answered, remembering Rosalind's brisk rendition of my résumé.

"Your father was a diplomat, is that correct?"

I indicated it was.

"An honorable profession," he said, almost to himself. "Even though there's no money in it." Then, with renewed scrutiny: "And you grew up in—"

"I've lived in many places," I interjected, going on to mention London and Bonn.

"And you went from Europe to boarding school, I understand."

I nodded, mentioning the boarding school in the Northeast I had attended and the name of my college, both of which seemed to meet with his approval.

"And you began to work for the *Journal*—when?"

"Right after college."

"Always writing on the arts, on theater?"

"No. At the beginning I wrote about everything from—"

He interrupted me: "And you're now—" His eyes narrowed as he attempted to calculate my age.

"Thirty-one."

"And you'd be able to find time to write this book?"

I told him I had already discussed the possibility of taking a six-month leave from my job and that it did not appear to be a problem.

"And your publisher—what kind of commitment do you have from your publisher?"

"It's up to me," I said. "My agent has told me that should I go ahead with book, I would most likely get a good advance."

"Good man, Lewis Eckhardt," he said, mentioning the head of the publishing house that had expressed interest in the book. "Know him well," he added. "Comes to my house for dinner."

"Mr. Cassel," I said after a moment. "Now I would like to ask you some questions."

"Ask away, Elisabeth."

"You are, from what I understand, the executor of your late wife's estate."

"Correct."

"Tell me exactly what you would give me access to—papers, letters, journals?"

"I have no letters, since Joanna and I never corresponded. My own letter writing is, as you can imagine, restricted to business." He cleared his throat before continuing: "I would give you access to everything—memorabilia, photographs—

all of which is in my possession, and over which, as the
executor of her estate, I have legal control. Including, of
course, the right to permit you to quote from Joanna's letters
to others, should that question arise. I would give you access
to the memorabilia she herself designated for her biographer.
No journals, as Joanna never kept one. I would encourage
those whom I know, and whom Joanna knew, to speak with
you. I myself would agree to answer your questions—questions submitted to me in advance, in writing, and which we
can discuss when I see fit. And I would permit you, as part of
your research, to return to Wakefield, where—assuming you
cleared it with me first—you would have permission to speak
with members of the staff." He paused, his hand tightening
around the handle of his walking stick. "That is what I am
prepared to do. No more, no less." Then, as if possessed by a
sudden impatience: "I think you should think about all of
this, Elisabeth, and give me your answer by the end of the
week. Should you decide not to do the book, I will, of course,
speak to another writer. But you are my first choice."

I thanked him and, feeling we had momentarily exhausted
the subject, began to speak of other things, including a recent front-page story in the *Journal* about the Wall Street
boom. All the while, however, I continued to be stupefied by
what Cassel had disclosed to me: that Joanna Eakins had left
a folder marked for her biographer, that she had known my
writing, and that she had, in fact, suggested I write her posthumous biography.

But it was Wakefield we were discussing now. "Rosalind
gave me a tour," I said. "She seems very proud of the house."

"She is, very."

I asked where his son lived.

He seemed uncomfortable. "Ketchum, Idaho," he said
with visible disdain. "Ski instructor and part-time carpenter.
Not exactly what I would have hoped for. But life is full of
surprises, children being the most unpredictable part of all."

"And Rosalind is your stepdaughter—Joanna's stepdaughter by a previous marriage?"

"That's right. Her own mother was killed in a plane crash when she was a kid. Her father was a surgeon—Joanna's first husband. English. After he died, Joanna continued to take care of her. Rosalind and I get on very well, thank God."

I did not reveal what I was thinking—that Rosalind seemed like a surrogate son to him. There was her work at Goldman, Sachs, which he had undoubtedly encouraged, her protective way of speaking of her stepfather, and her attitude toward Wakefield. I wondered whether Rosalind would inherit the house.

He began to stand up; so did I.

"Your paintings are beautiful," I said, turning to him. "It's thrilling to see them here."

He seemed to find it surprising that I was "interested in pictures," as he put it.

"My mother came from a family of artists," I said, trying to keep up the conversation. "She was a portrait painter."

He asked her name.

"Claire Hartwick."

"Still painting?"

"No," I replied somewhat reticently, explaining that she had died years ago, when I was two.

"I see," he said in a softer voice, "but she left you with a love of art . . ."

"Yes—my father did, as well."

He gave me another appraising glance before proceeding to tell me about each painting—where and when he had acquired it. As he did so I was struck by his obvious passion for his collection, a passion that surpassed the mere pride in acquisition I had expected. "Bought my first picture when I was sixteen," he said, "and I haven't stopped since. Of course it helped when I made some money." He stopped, gazing at one of the Canalettos. "Though it doesn't seem like much money compared to what they're making now!"

The edge of bitterness in his voice took me aback. "And these," I said the next moment, pointing to the terra cotta figurines of women in the cabinet of antiquities. "Where are they from?"

"Southern Italy," he said, opening the cabinet and taking one out, so that his large hand engulfed the slender figurine. "They were made as funerary figures—eighth century B.C. This one's damn good—you can still see almost all the original painting. Look."

Fixing his eyes on me in a way I found almost disturbingly intent, he handed over the statuette. Time had eroded the folds of her toga and rendered her stylized expression even more inscrutable, yet her features were remarkably untouched by the intervening centuries.

I returned the statuette to David, who replaced it on the shelf before closing the cabinet door. He walked to the telephone and rang for Kurt, his eyes still fixed on me. "I know this is an important decision for you, Elisabeth," he said, putting down the receiver. "If you have any more questions, we can talk tomorrow morning."

"I've already made up my mind," I replied. "I want to do the book."

He shot me a mildly appraising look. "Decisive. Good. I like that." He offered his hand. "Let's shake hands in a deal, then!"

We did so.

Kurt appeared, lending his arm to Cassel. We began to make our way toward the main house, walking in silence along the wide brick path shaded with gentle afternoon light, and eventually passing an allée of pear trees, the herb-planted "Shakespeare garden" ("Joanna's idea, obviously," Cassel noted), and the all-green garden ("the *giardino di verdura*, Joanna used to call it"). No one was about, save for a few gardeners tending rose bushes and pruning trees. Perhaps it was the stillness that made me think of Joanna's death, nine months before. I wondered where, amid this property, she had been buried.

We walked through a long arbor densely covered with gnarled, twisting branches of purple wisteria and then, after a moment, arrived at a high white gothic-style gate flanked by tall, obelisk-shaped hedges. I asked whether this was the entrance to another garden. "No," replied Cassel. "This is the maze—the maze that Joanna designed." With a certain forced heartiness, he added, "Took us years to complete."

And then, my cheeks reddening, I realized: This was where she had died. This was the place where she had been discovered, dead of heart failure, on that September morning.

I returned to the house, so preoccupied with the discussion with David Cassel that I barely acknowledged Kurt as I entered. I closed the door to my room and sat down before the writing table, idly fingering my charm bracelet as I gazed at the marquetry floor: its pattern of overlapping circles pierced with rondels of flowers spun before me. The idea that Joanna Eakins knew my work and had in fact singled me out as a possible biographer continued to astonish me.

I heard a knocking at the door: Olga, the white-haired housekeeper, with her chignon of coiled braids.

"Is there anything I can do for you, Miss Rowan?" she asked with an eager smile. "I thought you might want to have your dress pressed. For dinner."

"Thank you, but it isn't necessary," I replied, wondering whether I should have indeed brought a dress for dinner.

"Maybe you'd like a cup of tea, then?" she said. "It's something of a custom here at Wakefield—tea in the afternoon, that is." She paused. "The late Mrs. Cassel always liked our guests to be offered tea."

"The late Mrs. Cassel"—I remember how that phrase hovered in my mind and how it conjured up a being quite apart from the Joanna Eakins of my imagination. "No, thank you," I replied. "I think I'll just read. Take a nap."

"As you like, Miss Rowan."

The door closed.

I stood up and went to my suitcase, taking out the clothes I had brought for dinner. Then I walked to the immense windows, their tasseled valances and curtains embroidered with the same *trompe l'oeil* trellis pattern as the walls. I felt very tired suddenly, as if the achievement of what I had so long wanted—the authorization to write the biography of Joanna Eakins—had depleted me. I pulled the heavy curtains, extinguishing the late-afternoon light and silencing the sounds from outside. I wanted to sleep.

A knocking at the door awakened me. I had no sense of time, for the room was so dark it might have been midnight. I wondered how long I had slept. I looked at the clock—it had been an hour, no more. Yet it seemed longer, much longer. I felt warm, disoriented, loath to move.

"Are you up?" Rosalind said, a dark figure at the door. She moved toward me. "Dinner's at eight—I just came to tell you."

I turned on the light. "I was very tired," I said almost guiltily, stepping out of bed and searching for my slippers.

"The country air," she said brusquely, glancing at the chair where I had placed my dinner outfit—a pair of linen pants and a silk sweater. "For tonight?" she asked, turning to me; her voice was pleasant enough, but her eyes were disingenuous, even scornful.

"I hope that's all right," I said.

"We dress for dinner. Especially on Saturday."

"No one told me that."

"Someone screwed up, then." She paused, her hands at her waist. "I'll have to find something for you to wear. Shouldn't be hard, in this house." She cast me an appraising glance. "You're a lot taller than I am, but in a long skirt it shouldn't matter much."

"I'm really quite happy to wear what I brought."

"Go ahead, then," she answered in her most sardonic voice. "Make a bad impression on David, if that's what you want." She turned and began to walk toward the door.

"Well, if you really don't mind lending me something . . ."

"No problem. I'll be back in a few minutes."

I glimpsed a flash of red silk in her hands when she returned. Moving toward me, she held up a full gathered skirt and a blouson top, both of which were trimmed with intricately embroidered black satin ribbon.

"I thought this'd be okay," said Rosalind, almost amiably. "The color, with your hair."

The outfit barely fit: the length, on me, was mid-calf, and the waist of the skirt too small. "You've got a pretty tiny waist," I told her as I tried unsuccessfully to close the zipper of my "borrowed robes," as I jokingly called them.

"I didn't promise perfection."

I took a gold belt from my suitcase and wrapped it around my waist so that it hid the gaping hooks and eyes at the waist. "How's that?" I asked, turning around.

"Not bad."

I took a few steps before the mirror, turning carefully and standing very straight, realizing only after a few moments that I needed shoes, for none of mine was suitable.

"Black silk?" Rosalind asked. "Or gold?"

Once again she returned, this time with a delicate pair of evening shoes crisscrossed with gold and silver. They were only slightly too small.

"Now," she said, scrutinizing the effect, "the last thing: earrings." She took a small velvet box from her pocket; it sprang open to reveal a pair of diamond earrings shaped like calla lilies, with pistils of rubies. There was something marvelous and nervous about them, the diamonds so brilliant that the stones seemed to quiver.

"Go on," she said impatiently. "Try them on."

The earrings were almost painfully heavy but undeniably beautiful. Still looking at my reflection in the mirror, I couldn't resist asking Rosalind: "Where did you get them?"

"From Joanna," she replied offhandedly. "A present from one of her lovers."

* * *

I returned from dinner intoxicated and angry—how naive I had been to have so willingly gone along with Rosalind's offer to lend me clothes! Even now I can hardly recall without humiliation the terrible moment when, after noticing David Cassel's coolness to me during the dinner, I realized what had happened: Rosalind had lent me a dress that had belonged to Joanna. Cassel himself was too much of a gentleman to mention it—it was only his discomfiture I had felt, the way he had avoided looking at me, even speaking to me, during dinner. Afterward, while I was in the powder room fixing my lipstick, Jan Wilkinson, another guest, had glanced at me and said, "Funny—Joanna had a dress rather like that once." Her eyes narrowed as she scrutinized me: "But hers was full-length, I'm sure."

I remember standing before the mirror, color flushing my throat and face, being so hideously embarrassed that I could hardly speak. "Did she, then," I stammered, feeling unutterably stupid that I should have gone along with Rosalind's wicked joke. "What a coincidence."

I had forced myself to return to the library, barely able to face David Cassel, let alone Rosalind, who sat on the sofa stroking her cat, looking for all the world like Leonardo's *Girl with an Ermine*. Finally, I caught her eye: She knew I knew, for her smile was not without a hint of spite. The rest of the evening I forced myself to ignore her, knowing it would be foolish to antagonize a crucial source.

I took off the dress and shoes, my head throbbing with a migraine as I continued to dwell on the dinner: the reflection of the tall flickering candles upon the gleaming table, the savory food, the perfection of the silver and the damask napkins; the strange reality of the Saturday-night ritual at which, in my "borrowed robes," I had felt so much the foreigner.

I went into the bathroom to take off my makeup, scrubbing my face so vigorously that my skin felt raw. The bed had been turned down, my nightgown arranged upon it in a facsimile of a female shape, and a carafe of water placed on the bedtable. I looked at the card with the household numbers, recalling how David Cassel had told me to call Olga, the housekeeper, if I needed anything at all.

I lay in bed unable to relax, unable to cast aside the faces and voices of the evening. Rosalind, sitting at one end of the long table, elegantly dressed in deep blue, an aureole of dark hair around her oval face—a bond trader with the features of a Madonna. With what unexpected tenderness she had treated her stepfather! And then David himself, attending to the guests—among them Patrick Rossiter, the English director and Joanna's first mentor, with his avian profile and scent of sandalwood cologne. "The boy next door," he had jokingly called himself (he owned a house down the road, it seemed); a gossip and thwarted storyteller with a gift for simulating intimacy. I remember noticing that Rosalind seemed inordinately fond of Rossiter, though that did not prevent her from mercilessly teasing him about his effete ways and unabashed snobbism. Rossiter had clearly felt compelled to amuse us all (and, indeed, he had succeeded). He had brought his houseguests with him—the horsey Jan Wilkinson and an art dealer, a glowering Frenchman with pitted face, bow tie, and trenchant observations of New York's New Rich.

I continued to toss about in bed, my head still throbbing, as I conjured up those faces, wondering all the while whether there was any significance in the fact that Joanna's name had never once been mentioned during dinner.

The clock in the corridor chimed midnight; the shrill sound of curtains being drawn in a distant room briefly interrupted the silence; the quiet of the house intensified. It was only after another restless hour, and another chiming of the clock, that I finally felt myself falling asleep.

Several hours later I awoke, my head spinning, every limb aching: nausea swept over me in waves, leaving me frightened, confused, with barely enough strength to lift up my head, my sense of isolation heightened by the silence of the house.

How long had I lain like this? Afterward I would wonder, for it had seemed like hours. Finally, in the midst of this darkness and deathly silence, I managed to sit up and ring the bell.

A knocking at the door: the housekeeper, her waist-length braid unraveled. I was so ill that I could barely articulate what was wrong. In a moment she was at my side, her hand on my fiery forehead.

"You've a fever," she said. "A high one, too. How long have you been like this?"

I told her I wasn't certain, only that I had been feeling slightly light-headed after dinner.

She pulled up a chair, drawing her robe around her, and placed her hand lightly on my shoulder. The nausea had mounted, and I wanted to wretch. She held my hand tightly. Through the dim light I concentrated on her profile—sharp, etched with lines—and her unwavering eyes.

By morning, the nausea began to subside. But the weakness remained, and I was told that I should not leave that afternoon, as I had planned, but remain at Wakefield Hall for at least another day.

4

I was trying to sleep, my head still aching from fever, when, later that day, I heard a knocking at the door. It was Patrick Rossiter, whom I had met at dinner the previous night. His tweed jacket and pocket handkerchief would, on anyone else, have appeared rather casual, but not on him, strangely: he was too much the urban animal, with his air of perfect arrangement, even in this pastoral setting.

"Awfully bad luck, this," he said, pulling up a chair and making himself comfortable in a series of small, fretful movements. He was almost bald and very fair, with the thin freckled skin of a redhead. "A flu—in June!" he continued, fanning himself with a magazine. "This is a first for Wakefield, indeed. Normally, this place restores one to health!" He looked at me carefully, almost suspiciously, as if he were about to ask the most intimate of questions, only to come out with, "You *do* take vitamins, don't you?"

I told him I did—which wasn't true—and then tried to change the subject, for I felt guilty and embarrassed that I should have fallen ill here, on this beautiful weekend, in this idyllic setting. "What's Rosalind doing?" I asked, trying to deflect the attention from myself.

"Rosalind has gone riding," he said, lighting a cigarette and neatly crossing his long legs before looking at me askance: "The idea of obsessing on a horse! It boggles the imagination—but mind you, I *loathe* animals. Always have. It is perhaps my only un-Anglo-Saxon characteristic." He continued to smoke, smiling rakishly as he gazed past the bed, and giving me, meantime, a chance to study his face. His features were at once profoundly ugly and aristocratic—beaklike malformed nose, close-set eyes, thin narrow mouth. I thought to myself that I had never met anyone who looked so overtly wicked and yet who, on closer inspection, seemed so disappointingly harmless.

"And you—you must remain here for several more days, I'm told," he continued, looking at me with renewed interest. "Whether that is good or bad luck I'm not sure. Good for your mission, I suppose." He smiled devilishly.

I returned his smile, sensing his mood to chat. "You knew Joanna for many years, I gather."

"I should say. Since she was a very young woman, in London," he said, settling back into his chair. He sighed in his dramatic, Gielgudian way. "What an *untidy* life she had!"

I sat up in bed, searching for the cool part of the pillows and hoping that he would continue. "I've been fascinated by Joanna Eakins for years," I told him. "For whatever reason, I've always dreamt of writing her biography."

" 'O reason not the need!' " he exclaimed, quoting from *King Lear.* I laughed, which seemed to please him. "One couldn't help being fascinated by her," he said, one elbow propped in his other hand. "You're not the first, dear girl, not by any means. The curious thing is that she really changed so little over the years, despite all of this—" Here he waved his hands about, a grandiose gesture meant to encompass all the splendor of Wakefield Hall. "Yes, the curious thing is at once the number of lives she shed, since I first met her, and the fact that she really changed so little. A lass of infinite variety —still driven, still too easily seduced by beauty. Ruthless too, of course, and essentially amoral. Like most artists." His gaze drifted; his expression became almost mournful.

"When did you first meet her?" I asked after a moment, intrigued by his sudden pensiveness.

"When she was eighteen," he said, focusing on me again.

"And how do you remember her?"

"Lovely. Quite shy and yet quite brazen. A curious combination, of course, but one that I have often remarked in the best actresses."

"And she'd come to you looking for work?"

"Yes. We were casting *Coriolanus* at the time, and we needed a Virgilia. Joanna was young, she was inexperienced, but there was a *demanding* quality about her on the stage that was remarkable." He paused for a moment, as if feeling it necessary to explain himself. "When I say demanding, I mean that quality of truly great actors—that werewolf change that seemed to occur the moment she set foot on-stage. The inner spotlight upon the self, that sense of nearly exhausting the audience by her very presence." He paused, still smoking contemplatively. "And then she had the most curious quality of all—she simply made one want to cry." He cleared his throat. "Needless to say, she got the part."

"And you'd never seen her before?"

"No, never." A pause. "No, that isn't quite right—I had seen her once, actually, when I was visiting RADA. Some sort of end-of-term exercise, as I recall."

Patrick continued to smoke, his chin uptilted after each puff, his watery blue eyes fixed elsewhere. Finally, he said, "The truly remarkable thing about Joanna, given her background, is that she knew what she did at *eighteen*. She had a rare perception of Shakespeare, you see, and yet one that seemed to be almost entirely intuitive. Minerva-like, born full-blown! Very rare indeed. A way of delving into the text and then of perceiving the whole—the rhythm of the scenes, the way they cut and flow into one another—a knowledge, an instinct, that was uncanny. Which words to emphasize, what was juicy and what was not. When the staccato, when the legato, when the attack—that sort of thing. The way to use the voice to interpret inner feeling. No one had *taught* her this, presumably." He gave a deep sigh and indulged in a moment of reverie, after which he fidgeted a bit and attempted to change the subject by asking about my job at the *Journal*. But he had ventured too far now to turn back, and I think he realized it.

"And Rosalind?" I asked. "You've known her a long time as well . . ."

"Of course." He put out his cigarette. "Since she was very little. Since she was six."

"And she was close to Joanna?"

"That's not the word I would use, no. I think Joanna felt Rosalind was a duty she could not ignore. A responsibility. And Rosalind is not exactly an easy character, as you may already have guessed." A pause. "All that aside, I'm really quite fond of her. And she of me, I like to think—"

I thought of the conspiratorial looks the two had exchanged at the dinner table. "And Rosalind's mother?" I asked after a moment.

"I don't know much about her, except that she died when Rosalind was little."

So that was something that Rosalind and I had in common, I thought to myself. "And Rosalind's father?"

"Teddy Bennett. A widower. A neurosurgeon—brilliant, volatile. In some ways too much like Joanna for their marriage ever to have worked. Mercifully for her, he died not too long after they were married. And then Joanna met David in New York—and David left his wife to marry her. Lord, what a scandal that was!" He made a little clucking noise which indicated that the idea of scandal was not, to him at least, without its own deliciousness.

"And Rosalind has become very close to David," I ventured again.

"Ah, yes. Yes indeed. She's closer to him than his own child—his own son has been a great disappointment to him, you know. I think he has disinherited him, actually. It's Rosalind who will most likely inherit Wakefield. In any event, Rosalind and David are rather alike in some ways—difficult to know, the two of them. Very bright, very cunning."

"And David's relationship with Joanna?"

I noticed his slight hesitation in answering. "He was very decent to her," he said. "Very proud, especially at the beginning, when she was still acting—"

I reflected on the word he had chosen: *decent*. "Who else was close to Joanna? Friends, family?"

"Her own family not at all. She never spoke of them. As for friends . . . myself, of course." He paused, and then, somewhat reluctantly, added, "And I suppose one would have to say Christina von Shouse."

The name was vaguely familiar to me from New York, though I remembered it was the same name that had been mentioned the day before to Rosalind—the telephone message that seemed to have unsettled her. "And this Christina von Shouse," I asked. "Who is she exactly?"

"A woman about town," he said with marked deliberateness. "A woman with a wonderful eye. A dangerous eye. Jewelry, furniture, that sort of thing—she has made a career of it."

"And she's European?"

"I think not. She's . . ." He paused, wrinkling his nose. ". . . she's from Iraq—or is it Iran? One of those dusty Arab countries, at any rate."

I began to laugh. "You don't like her, I take it."

"Perceptive of you, my dear!" he replied, one eyebrow raised slightly and his voice, for the first time, transparently caustic. "I simply think that Joanna's life would have been less complex, shall we say, without her. I don't think Christina was a particularly good influence. She brought out every

one of Joanna's worst insecurities—reveled in them, actually
—because they suited her purpose. It was all the more dangerous because Christina had such a gift for making herself
indispensable—to Joanna and even, eventually, to David."

"They had known each other a long time?"

"For years—from England. They had met at Thistleton—a
famous house in Hampshire that still belongs to Desmond
Kerrith. Christina was Lord Kerrith's social secretary at the
time—an exalted one at that. Whether she was in fact rather
more than his secretary, no one was quite certain. All too
complicated, I must confess." His expression was fleetingly
suggestive of salaciousness, but it quickly vanished as he
paused, as if he were pondering the entanglements of that
other life. "But then Joanna came into the picture—vis-à-vis
Desmond, that is—and the two women, despite their wari-
ness of each other at first, became fast friends. They shared
certain passions, of course—the theater and Shakespeare—
and I suppose one might say that each had a quality which
the other lacked, and admired."

"Which were . . ."

"Christina worshiped Joanna's talent, of course, and
Joanna admired Christina's worldly ways—her taste, her considerable organizational skills: furniture, dinner parties,
housekeeping—that sort of thing. They would spend quite a
lot of time together, the two friends, in the tower-library at
the edge of the maze of Thistleton. A rather famous maze,
by the way—perhaps you've heard of it? In any event, Joanna
claimed until the end of her life that the library at Thistleton
was her favorite place on earth. Christina would often help
Joanna learn her lines, would prompt her for the great Shakespearean parts—for Cleopatra, I think, and for the last run of
Macbeth, of course." He paused, leaning back and lighting
another cigarette, and then, as if galvanized by a particularly
vivid memory, said, "About that time—this was 'fifty-three
—Desmond gave a fancy dress ball. I remember how the two
of them—Joanna and Christina, that is—appeared in costume together. What a sight they were, arm in arm, at the

top of that splendid staircase, with the tapestries lit by masses of flickering candles! Joanna as Saint Joan, clanking down the steps in a bogus suit of armor—furnished by Motley, no doubt—and Christina as Lady Macbeth, in the costume and wig that Joanna had lent her, the very costume Joanna had worn in the famous Old Vic production and which she'd always kept, among other costumes, in the tower by the maze. How we—the astounded audience—laughed! And how pleased that bizarre duo was by the effect of their appearance. But most of all I remember Joanna announcing in glorious mock stentorian tones, 'Let all ye tremble before us—for here we stand, the saint and the madwoman!' "

His smile had vanished, as if he were disengaging himself from the grip of that image. "Yes," he said, continuing to ruminate. "Christina is a luxurious person, in the true sense of the word, perhaps the worldliest woman I have ever known. The pity is that no one seemed able to wrest Joanna from her. Or vice versa." He leaned closer to me, "You see, in the end, Christina is everything *manqué*—she never succeeded as an artist, or even as a society woman of the wealth and position she would have liked. She never even succeeded as a mother . . ." He paused, explaining in a staccato voice, "Her daughter committed suicide when she was about twenty."

Again he stopped, his expression distant and yet focused, as if he were reenacting that moment. "I think that was the only time when Christina turned to Joanna for solace—after the daughter's suicide, that is. Until then, it had always been Joanna who leaned on Christina in moments of crisis." He stopped, sighing deeply. "In moments of crisis, enter Christina von Shouse. And *exeunt* all reason and sanity. Christina is not exactly gifted with the milk of human kindness, shall we say."

I smiled to myself at the way he had paraphrased *Macbeth* and at his habit of interjecting his speech with quotes from Shakespeare in general. But it was the description of Christina von Shouse that I found most intriguing. "Is she a truly intelligent woman," I asked, "or is she just shrewd?" I had lived long enough in New York to know the difference.

"An excellent question," he said, pronouncing each syllable precisely; his eyes were fixed on my own as he continued smoking. "She *is* intelligent, but let's just say that hers is an intelligence which has never found its proper outlet. She would have liked to be an artist, I think, an artist of note. But she lacked the discipline—and of course the talent, the artistic obsession."

He paused; I sensed him reflecting on the past. "When Joanna was acting, there would have been no need for a Christina von Shouse. There would have been other ways to banish whatever ghost pursued her. But once she could no longer act—well, other things became paramount. It was Christina who introduced her to the world that had always attracted Joanna—the world of wealth, the world of the *beau monde*. David Cassel's world." He sighed deeply. "A fatal mistake for any artist to become entranced with that world!"

"And what was it that Joanna sought from Christina von Shouse?"

"If only I knew! Someone to soothe her, to convince her that it was all destiny, fate—her past mistakes, the inability to conquer stage fright—that it was all beyond her own control.

"It was her influence on Joanna that so alarmed and infuriated me at the end of her life, you must understand," he continued, his voice low and urgent. "That she should have heeded Christina's advice above mine, even above David's, above anyone else's of reason! It was unbearable to watch, simply unbearable, to watch the end of Joanna's life unfold in such a piteous fashion . . ." Looking beyond the bed toward the heavily draped windows, he murmured, "That it should have come to this!" He shook his head slowly, his eyes, with their expression of grief, meeting mine: "If you had only known Joanna then, when she was a very young woman! She was *remarkable*."

"Tell me," I urged him quietly. "Tell me what she was like."

5

W hat struck me about her first, apart from her extraordinary presence on the stage, was the assurance she radiated," Patrick continued. "That, and the quality of her voice. Untutored, of course, and without the training it subsequently received. Her voice was singular, with—" here he groped for the right word, "—an otherworldly quality about it, an ability to project with enormous range and urgency. She had a way of using her eyes to great advantage as well, an almost erotic way of communicating with every member of the audience. Very like Larry Olivier in that regard." He shrugged, and took a last deep drag on his cigarette before extinguishing it. "One sensed that she was a chameleon with enormous potential, that there were so many people within her trying to get out!

"This is what struck me, you see—much more than her looks. She was pretty, but with none of the elegance she later achieved. There was a strength about her face—that beguiling, almost Russian look about the eyes and cheekbones; the slight flatness of the nose. But she needed to learn to make the most of her features. There was something wrong about them here—" he pointed to his forehead, "—and there," then to the bridge of his nose.

Perhaps I looked puzzled, for he quickly added, "Her forehead was too low. I had her change it. That made an extraordinary difference. She was clever enough to sense that something had been wrong in the proportions, but hadn't been able to pinpoint it. And then I had her dye her hair, so that it was dark, almost black, a contrast to her skin." Clearly, he reveled in the role of Pygmalion, for I could feel his visceral, almost voluptuous pleasure in the changes he had led Joanna to make, his delight in the image he had thrust upon her.

I asked what had happened after the production of *Coriolanus*. "It was a success, and her part did not go unnoticed by the critics. Small mentions in the papers, but very fine ones."

"And you came to know her better?"

"Much better. I took her under my wing, as it were. Her voice needed work—she needed to eliminate that slightly nasal twinge, the occasional wrong emphasis here and there.

"And then she needed to know how to *live*, how to conduct herself," he continued, pausing to light another cigarette in his flamboyant way. "There was no one to teach her this, since her mother was in America. I wonder, looking back, how Joanna managed to survive. She was painfully thin and pale, of course, when I first met her." He smiled to himself, as if struck by a particularly pleasant recollection. "Not long after that first audition, I took her to tea at the Savoy and watched her gobble up platters of tea sandwiches, biscuits, and smoked salmon. I remember her turning to me with a charmingly sated look and saying, 'How delicious! I could *live* on smoked salmon.' " His voice assumed a nanny-ish tone: " 'Then you must be a good girl and work very hard,' I told her.

"She was living in a horrid cold-water flat at the time," he continued. "And I have seen some fairly dreadful ones, as you can imagine! There are moments when I look around Wakefield . . . it seems incredible to imagine where she was living when I first met her. There were creaking stairs that led to her apartment on the top floor, as I recall, and a light that gave one just enough time to reach the top. God knows who else lived there—sinister types, to say the least! Curious how distinctly I remember Joanna's beastly room. It was tiny, with cracks in the walls, which she had tried to cover over with newspaper stories on the reigning stars of the day—Gielgud, Peggy Ashcroft, Ralph Richardson. A cotlike bed with a thin blanket, and on her bedside locker, a framed photograph of the Oliviers. One window high up, and a sink, in the corner, where mushrooms had sprouted on the mildewed wall beneath it.

"I suppose I am old-fashioned enough to assume that an actress must develop a persona, an aura about her, that will permeate every aspect of her life. In short, she needed to forget where she was from if she was ever to achieve any-thing, anything at all—not only as an actress, you see, but as a *woman*." He shifted in the armchair slightly, whisking some dust from his trousers and fidgeting with his jacket. "You think me a snob," he said. "I am not, you know. Not really. At least not in the way you think." Then he added, in a cold, amused way, "You are wondering what was in it—what was in it for me, aren't you?"

I knew it was hopeless to dissemble. "Yes, I suppose I do wonder why you would have chosen to be her sponsor."

"Not a question of the old casting couch routine, at least," he replied with another of his devilish smiles. "Hardly that!"

"That really hadn't occurred to me," I said, smiling to myself at the unlikely thought.

"It was her *talent*," he said, leaning toward me. "A gift

that seemed to come from nowhere—a gift that had never been nurtured. Do you know how rare it is to come upon such a talent? She was obsessed with excellence, you see, in every form: in being the best she could, in speaking well and moving well and understanding how plays were constructed, how to make them live! In this we had a certain kinship—our love of Shakespeare and the classics and a love of beauty in all its aspects. I had already begun my ascent, you see. I had made my name. Her journey had only just begun."

"Tell me about the *Macbeth*."

"I begged them to let her try the part. It was of course unthinkable at the time—this was 1950—for such a young woman to attempt it. But with her new voice and black hair —let's give it a try, I thought. Instinctively, she understood the play. The moment I heard her read the first speech, I knew she had it. *Too* extraordinary, that power she had, for one so young!

"It was the first reading, in a cold damp room, in February. Everyone drinking tea, nervous, smoking. Everyone playing it quite safe, as actors tend to at that stage. I had expected Joanna, too, to be reticent—not to give it her all. Not yet. But she surprised us all with a reading that was chillingly well formed, clearly developed. There was something infinitely moving about seeing this young woman there, in her plain clothes, the whiteness of her skin, and her dark hair, the wildness in her eyes! In one fell stroke she had got it right: the layers of self-delusion, the mask of the feminine, seductive wife, the passionate, practical woman beneath it. The erotic bond between this young woman and Macbeth—it seemed right, it seemed totally believable and compelling. She did not come across as a shrew, you see, the way all too many Lady Macbeths tend to. Not at all. It was much, much more.

"That was the role that changed her life," he continued rather matter-of-factly. "I remember how we stayed up throughout the night to see the newspapers that morning. And of course the moment we read Ken Tynan's review—

well, it was beyond anything we might have dreamt of! One of Ken's very few encomiums—a review which made her famous overnight. Nothing was the same from that moment on: Journalists pursued her; suddenly she was in demand for one role, for another. For comedy as well, for she had a great comic gift, you know—something one tends to forget, for later in her career she became famous for the great tragic roles. And for Chekhov, of course.

"But I was talking about those early days in London, and very exciting days they were. One saw Joanna everywhere—at the best restaurants, the best dinners. It was all the more remarkable because she was so young. Just twenty years old! If only she had been as experienced in life as she was on-stage."

A knocking at the door interrupted him. It was Olga, the housekeeper, her eyes darting to Patrick with a slightly wary, almost exasperated expression.

"How are you feeling, Miss Rowan?" she asked, approaching the bed. "You do look better, thank goodness." She plumped the pillows a bit and asked whether I wanted something to eat or some tea. I said not.

"Mr. Rossiter is wearing you out with his stories, I think," she said, making no attempt to hide her disapproval.

"As you know, Olga, the sound of my voice is music to my ears," he replied with an impish glance in my direction.

"He has made the time pass very quickly," I added, restraining my laughter when I noticed Olga's irritated expression.

"I'm sure," she said almost reproachfully. She moved about the room, smoothing the coverlet and removing a vase of drooping roses before she drew open the curtains. "Rosalind asked me to tell you she would be here before dinner," she said, standing by the door.

"And Mr. Cassel?" I asked.

"He's already gone to New York." A pause. "There's nothing I can do for you then, Miss Rowan?"

I shook my head and thanked her.

"You must let her rest," Olga said reprovingly to Patrick.

"Yes, of course," he said, getting up and playfully assuming the expression of a chastised child. "Of course."

The two left, closing the door quietly and leaving me to wonder what the last glance between them had meant.

6

I fell asleep soon afterward and dreamt of a multitude of rooms and houses, all labyrinthine, unfamiliar. One house was strict and white and stood by the edge of a deserted street. It had been inhabited once, but no longer—the occupants had fled, leaving their belongings, all in perfect order, to me. Beds and furniture, sleek and unembellished, things others would like. But I knew I would never become accustomed to the whiteness and silence of this place, a realization that filled me with guilt, and with a longing to escape . . .

The fever had broken by the time I awoke, leaving me cool and spent, my throat parched, my nightgown soaked with sweat. I sat up and sipped some water, looking around the room, then out the windows. The light was dusky—it was almost seven o'clock. A slight breeze had come up, and with it the rustling of trees.

I stood up unsteadily and walked to the writing table by the fireplace, gazing at the paper and pens, and then to the low bookcase between the windows, my fingers running across the leather and gilt spines of the books—nineteenth-century novels, mostly (though I recall some books by Nabokov as well—*The Vane Sisters* among them). There was a collection of Tolstoy, another of Thomas Hardy. I picked up *Far From the Madding Crowd* and opened it, intrigued by the ornate bookplate inside: EX LIBRIS THISTLETON, engraved with a crest of twin unicorns before a maze in which Theseus was depicted fighting the minotaur. Unfurled beneath was a motto that my grade-school Latin did not equip me to translate: "*Intellectus merces est cognitio.*"

Turning to the frontispiece, I found an inscription, written in a strong jagged hand with thick black ink: "To darling Joanna, this souvenir of a weekend in Dorset—Desmond." I wondered whether the book was marked, whether there was something of a talisman about it, and thumbed through the pages, looking in vain for underlined passages or notes written in the margins. It was only at the end, within the last chapter, that I found some dried flowers, now a faded crimson, that had been pressed into the pages and that crumbled at my touch.

I returned to bed and placed the book near me on the covers, still wondering about the inscription and about Thistleton, the house in England with the famous maze that Patrick Rossiter had described earlier that morning.

Perhaps it was the discovery of the book that had made me hungry suddenly. I picked up the telephone, dialed the appropriate number, and asked if I might have some tea and sandwiches.

Minutes later, the butler appeared at the door. He had brought me much more than I had asked for—a pyramid of tiny sandwiches and an orange cake; china pots with tea, hot water, and milk, accompanied by a plate of lemon slices pierced with fragrant cloves—all of which shone like a still life on the silver tray.

He had only just left when I heard a knocking at the door: Rosalind, in black pants and sweater.

"So—how's the biographer?" she asked, striding toward me. I felt her eyes examining my silk robe, with its monogram of intertwined *E*'s—a present from my lover.

"Much better, thanks," I said coolly enough, thinking of Joanna's dress. I wondered at the spiteful mind that would pull such a prank, and was on the verge of saying something to that effect, but decided against it. "I'm sorry about this," I said, smoothing the sheet. "I can hardly remember being so sick."

"No need to apologize." She sat down on the settee at the end of the bed, curling her feet beneath her—an androgynous odalisque in black.

"I should be able to leave tomorrow," I said.

"Not according to the doctor. He said you should stay another day before driving home. Get some fresh air."

"Then I'll have time to go through the maze," I said with a slight smile. "Tomorrow."

"I'll take you through if you want." Perhaps my expression revealed my reluctance to consider Rosalind as a guide, for she quickly added: "Or maybe you'd like to go alone."

"I've always liked challenges."

She cocked her head, observing me: "Good. So do I." She had noticed the copy of *Far From the Madding Crowd* that lay on the night table. "You've been reading," she said, picking it up and glancing at the bookplate. "Joanna and her books," she remarked contemptuously before tossing it on the bed.

"This house, Thistleton—"

"Part of Joanna's English period. I'm sure Patrick has already given you an earful about that."

"He helped keep my mind off being sick," I said, watching her reaction.

"No doubt," came the tart reply.

She stretched her legs and stood up before announcing: "I should go to dinner." The next moment she leaned against the double doors and looked at me—a small, slim figure in black, with nervous hands and an aureole of wavy hair.

"We'll do the maze tomorrow," she announced with a decisive glance; I heard the door shut resoundingly behind her.

7

I felt much better the next morning, and curiously cleansed. I got dressed, called for some breakfast, and read the note that had been placed on my tray, written in Rosalind's spidery hand: "We'll have lunch today at 12:30 on the terrace—Patrick's joining us. We'll do the maze afterward, if you're up to it. Ciao, Rosalind." Moments later I descended the wide staircase and passed through the entrance hall, to the portico.

I walked across the lawn toward the gardens, increasingly preoccupied, however, as I began to reflect on Patrick Rossiter's stories: the account of Joanna's early fame, the role of the English house Thistleton in her life, and her relationship with Christina von Shouse.

I passed Cassel's library pavilion and then, moments later, the formal rose garden. I remember the thorny bushes with their still tentative flowers and how the plants themselves were rooted in carefully defined plots. For half an hour or so I continued at least ostensibly to amble, although in retrospect I realize my walk had a goal, however subliminal: the maze.

Once again I walked through the arbor, with its pendulous purple wisteria, until I came to the gate to the maze. I stood awhile before the high gothic portal, wondering whether I should enter and try my luck. Yet even as I felt my hand pulling the latch, something made me hesitate—a surge of fear and anxiety so crippling that my veins ran ice-cold and my limbs felt queer and immobile. Moments later, when I resumed breathing normally again, I glanced at my watch—my father's gold watch, which I wore on a chain around my neck—only to find that *the watch had simply stopped.*

The next instant, having somewhat recovered my equilibrium, I felt my hand withdraw from the latch, and continuing to stand quite still, I tried to analyze what had happened. At bottom I recognized a familiar murky anxiety, all the more primordial and gripping because I did not know its origin. It was the fear of being lost, of being abandoned and incommunicate, a terror that seemed to have intensified since my father's death.

I turned from the gate and began to walk swiftly toward the house.

The French doors of the dining room opened onto the main terrace, where a table had been set for lunch. Patrick Rossiter stood at a distance, his back to me, a drink in one hand as he gazed at the hills beyond.

I said hello and approached him. He wore a blue seersucker suit and striped bow tie, which enhanced the eccentric, donnish aura of his storklike figure.

"You look like quite another creature," he said approv-

ingly, doffing his wire-rimmed, owlish sunglasses as he in-
spected me. "Healthy and well again. You'd like a drink, I'm
sure—" he began to look for the butler, Kurt, "—or perhaps
you don't drink when you're on duty, so to speak."

I returned his wry smile and told him I would, in fact, very
much like a drink. The next moment Kurt appeared; I asked
him for a glass of white wine, which he brought moments
later.

"Ravishing day," Patrick said, his eyes returning to the
clear, placid sky. "Pity David had to go to New York."

I took a sip of the ice-cold, dry white wine. "He works
hard, I take it."

"Bernham, Worth is his life—always has been."

I asked where Rosalind was: "I thought she was joining
us."

"I'm afraid not. She's on the phone, apparently, with her
office. I'm to play host. She said she'd meet you by the pool,
around four."

Kurt returned to announce that lunch was ready. We sat
down at the table, which was covered with a thick snowy
cloth. Unfolding my napkin, I wondered whether Patrick
would be as talkative as he had been the day before; I feared
he wouldn't—the dimly lit sickroom had lent itself to a se-
ancelike atmosphere in a way that the forthright light of a
radiant June afternoon did not.

Cold salmon was presented, aromatic with dill and accompanied by lemons cut to resemble baskets filled with parsley
(queer how the mind recalls those inconsequential details);
then delicate, savory vegetables. I served myself, ravenously
hungry suddenly, and watched as Patrick did the same, marveling at his abundant helpings (gluttony in the immaculate
has always fascinated me). I remember being struck by his
fair, freckled hands, translucent as onionskin, and how much
older they looked than his face.

I had already decided not to question him directly about
Joanna, at least not at that instant. I mentioned the maze

instead and the fact that I had considered going through it before lunch.

"Lucky for me that you didn't, my dear," he said at once, looking with gusto at his plate. "You wouldn't be with me now, enjoying this heavenly salmon!"

"I've always had a very good sense of direction," I announced rather proudly.

"I'm sure you do, dear girl," he replied with a sidelong glance as he extracted a salmon bone from his mouth. "And it's quite true, of course, that the maze here is not as difficult as Thistleton's. *Too* treacherous, that one! Joanna was mad for it, of course, and wanted to replicate it here. But there, at least, good sense got the best of her."

"Rosalind has offered to take me through later."

"Has she, then?" He raised his brows, as if amused by the idea. "Funny, I've never thought of Rosalind as the Ariadne type." He smiled slyly. "But stranger things have happened—" A pale green dill sauce for the salmon was being offered; he took a generous helping. "Greedy bloke I am," he murmured as he focused on the fish. "But I *do* adore salmon."

I sipped my wine, watching him eat. "Has there always been a maze here at Wakefield?"

"Yes, but very little of it existed by the time David and Joanna bought the house. The original was a rather simple affair. It was Joanna's idea to resurrect it and enlarge upon it."

I suddenly remembered the labyrinth book in Joanna's study, with its missing pages on English mazes. "So the maze here," I asked, "was inspired by the one at Thistleton?"

"Yes, yes of course—I thought you knew that. The maze at Thistleton is very famous. Very famous indeed, though there were years during the war when it was completely neglected, even vandalized." By his sly pause I sensed the love of intrigue, of storytelling, that he had demonstrated the previous day. "The maze at Thistleton always had a classical statue as its goal, though the original was destroyed during the war," he continued. "After Joanna met Desmond Kerrith—after they began their rather intense affair, I should say—she encouraged him to replace it with another. It was Joanna's idea that a maze should always have a goal—something to move toward, something to discover, something hidden. A rather romantic notion, no doubt—" he shrugged, "but then there was that side of her."

"And the statue?"

"A new statue was commissioned, one modeled precisely after Joanna." He sipped his wine, one brow raised as he set down his glass: "A fact which did not entirely please the mistress of the house, I might add."

"Desmond Kerrith was married, then?" I interjected, more than a little surprised.

"Yes, yes of course," he replied, as if astonished that I should even ask the question. "On the other hand, Sibyl—Lady Kerrith, that is—was an immensely practical girl. No witless wife she! I remember her saying that it was better Joanna remain at Thistleton as a statue than as Desmond's wife." He paused to scrape up the last bits of his salmon, washing them down with another gulp of wine. "She had a let-him-get-it-out-of-his-system approach to marriage, did Sibyl. A not unsensible attitude, I might add."

"And then the statue was sculpted," I ventured, still smiling at his offhand manner as I leaned forward, eager for him to continue.

"Yes. Absolutely." He discreetly lowered his voice at the approach of Kurt, as he had done throughout the lunch. "But Desmond very cleverly let Joanna decide *which* goddess she would choose. I remember sitting with her one day at tea at Thistleton, under a splendid oak tree, as she leafed through a book on mythology. I, of course, suggested she choose Demeter—goddess of fertility, the crops, lovely basket, etcetera, etcetera. But Joanna would have nothing to do with the idea. 'Athena's the one who always gets you through,' she told me imperiously. 'Demeter never.' And so Athena it was."

"Sprung full-blown from the head of Zeus," I added quietly.

"A lady without origins. *Exactly*."

I remember how, at that very moment, I had a sudden vivid recollection of a colored picture from a favorite childhood book—Athena, goddess of wisdom, bursting fully armed from the splitting skull of her father, Zeus.

"Not long afterward," he continued, "Joanna was sent to a studio where she patiently posed for hours, draped in a classical dress which was soaked with plaster to achieve the right effect. Cecil Beaton even came to snap a few shots, as I recall. A model was made, and the statue carved with exactly Joanna's features. Eventually, it was set in the center of the maze at Thistleton, where it still stands today."

I lingered on this last anecdote as dessert was brought—a rich hazelnut cake, accompanied by strawberries, of which I took a large helping. (I have always had a terrible sweet tooth.) "And Joanna continued to go to Thistleton," I said, looking up at him as I savored the delicious cake.

"Yes of course. She would spend hours in the maze, sitting by the statue, often learning her lines there or in the tower. She learned Rosalind that way—*As You Like It*, of course. She was marvelous in the part—sublime. One of her early famous roles."

"Funny that her stepdaughter should have the same name," I said almost to myself.

"Yes, isn't it? Joanna thought so too. 'My Shakespearean stepdaughter,' she'd say. Not unconscious of the irony, I might add—our Rosalind is not exactly a creature of the Forest of Arden, is she then?" He took out a cigarette, lighting it in his theatrical fashion.

A moment passed as I absentmindedly finished the last bits of cake. "Did you know that Joanna left a packet of memorabilia to be opened after her death?" I asked him, watching as he engulfed his strawberries in whipped cream. "And that she actually marked it 'To my biographer'?"

For the first time my words seemed to have unsettled him.

"Did she, then?" he asked, almost *sotto voce*. "How very strange."

Kurt approached, brandishing a tray with coffee. "We'll have it over there, please," Patrick said, motioning to some chairs set by the edge of the terrace and tossing his napkin onto the table. I stood up and followed. After we sat down, Kurt, who had poured the coffee, left to clear the lunch table.

Cup in hand, I gazed at the rounded green shapes of the Berkshire hills in the distance and at the oval pool below, glistening with reflections of formidable trees and purple azaleas. My thoughts had wandered—to Thistleton, to the bookplate engraved with the maze, and to the copy of *Far From the Madding Crowd* that I had found in my room.

"Tell me more about Thistleton," I said, turning to Patrick, who had begun to sun himself, "and about Joanna's affair with Desmond Kerrith."

He drew his chair a bit closer with such obvious relish at the prospect of telling another story that I had to restrain myself from smiling. "Desmond was exceedingly well known in those days—much older than Joanna," he began, "the man who showed her the ways of the world. Rather university-of-life-ish—yes, I suppose that's the best way to put it. I'd known Desmond for years, and actually introduced him to Joanna, never suspecting that they would become lovers—or did I? He was in his late forties, you see, and she was only twenty. A young twenty at that, despite her early stardom."

He paused for a moment, lighting another cigarette, his eyes following the progress of the whorling smoke. "He was a collector, Desmond was. Of people, of art, of knowledge, of the famous. A dark, handsome man, with a large head, brooding eyes, and the curious ruthlessness of those who have never really worked—though he was involved with politics at the time and a close friend of Winston Churchill's. The sort of man who once remarked to me, 'One of the great inconveniences of marriage is the fact that it means finding a new mistress.'

"His house—Thistleton, in Hampshire—was very famous. He had invited Joanna and me for the weekend. His house parties were legendary—always a remarkable mix of people, always marvelous food, even then, not long after the war. And of course the house itself was ravishing. Simply the most beautiful country house I've ever seen. It was built at the end of the eighteenth century and surrounded by a park that had been transformed over the years—originally by Capability Brown, then by Repton—into an arcadian paradise. One would go for a walk and discover a walled garden or a Roman bridge or a tower built to resemble the remnant of medieval ruins."

He sighed deeply as if assailed by those memories. "I had been there before, of course, and had noticed that there was invariably one new celebrity among the established names. I suppose that was the slot which Joanna filled that weekend." He stopped for a moment, flicking some ashes away. "Desmond thrived on celebrity, you see. No, it was more than that —it excited him beyond words to look about his table and know that *these famous faces were his friends*. His attraction to Joanna surely was partly based on that—he admired her acting immensely. She was the darling of London after *Macbeth*, you must remember, and much praised and talked about. The fact that she was cloaked by fame made her *acceptable*.

"It was a weekend in June, unnaturally hot, as I recall. We'd driven up from London in a little red Jag of which I was particularly fond. I had gone to fetch Joanna at her flat and was actually quite horrified when she appeared at the door. It makes me laugh to think of it now. She had several enormous valises with her and was quite tarted up, with a garish printed dress and a preposterous hat. For the first time in her life she had a bit of money, you see, and she was spending it frantically. Her taste at that time was lamentable! I remember wondering whether I ought to ask her to change, but decided against it. I simply piled her bags into the car and set off.

"I will never forget Joanna's eyes when, at last, after passing the high park wall overhung with ivy and the stables and the glistening lake encircled by rare trees, we arrived at Thistleton. Joanna turned to me and said—I shall never forget her eyes—'I thought places like this only existed in the cinema!' Desmond was summoned, greeted us, and took us around to meet his guests, all of whom were strangers to Joanna.

"It was, as I remember, quite a titled group, with an influx of the fast Kenyan set that had always amused Desmond. Joanna was regarded with some curiosity by the others—partly because of her unsuitable clothes, I suppose. And she was very young, of course, and very pretty, with her short dark hair and wild eyes. Pretty but not yet beautiful—she was still too conscious of how others perceived her to radiate real beauty.

"As I mentioned, it was terribly hot that weekend, and when we arrived, late morning, several of the guests were around the swimming pool. Vivian Stanley, as I recall, doing her version of laps—perfectly made up face, neck hung with diamonds. She was quite a femme fatale in those days, with a bizarre history of lapsed marriages, the last of which was to a great landowner from Nairobi. I remember her slightly mocking expression as we appeared, and hoped Joanna would not notice it.

"Desmond asked Joanna if she wouldn't like to take a swim. I remember how touching it was when she hesitated before answering, 'Thank you, but I don't know how to swim.'" Patrick looked wistful suddenly. "Perhaps it was at that moment that Desmond fell in love with her? I've often wondered. But he told her that it didn't matter, and asked if she would like to learn. He had Christina Assante, his secretary—now Christina von Shouse, as I told you—find someone to teach her."

"And they soon became lovers?" I asked.

"Yes of course," he replied dismissively, as if my question had been unspeakably naive. "But their relationship as it evolved was complex, composed of many elements, the most critical of which was his ability to *teach her*—to fulfill her notion of being accomplished. And to show her the world. A very nineteenth-century idea, no? He taught her what to wear and how to speak and how to conduct herself within his world. That is not to say there still weren't lapses, of course." He smiled ruefully. "One night at dinner at Thistleton, when dessert was being served—profiteroles surrounded by chocolate sauce—Joanna began to scrape the tray rather too energetically, after helping herself. I shall never forget the look of the butler, with his white gloves and arched brow, as he said to her pointedly, 'There is more sauce coming, madam.' " Patrick laughed, cradling one elbow in his hand.

"And Joanna learned quickly?" I asked.

"Oh yes, very, as she always did—so much of their relationship was predicated on her being able to meet the goals he would set for her. Which she did—astoundingly well. They traveled together as well. Europe was still recovering from the war then, but even so he took her everywhere— Venice, Tuscany, the south of France, to Scotland, where he had an estate called Lochmoor on the North Sea, where she would walk the moors and watch him shoot. He had her learn to ride, to fish for salmon in his streams, and to speak French. He gave her books—Dickens, Thackeray, the Brontës —and in doing so he opened up another world to her."

Patrick looked at me intently. "You see, their relationship was not—as some undoubtedly saw it—that of a lecherous rich older man and an ambitious younger woman. At its core was the complicity of two hungry minds, the meeting of two sensuous intellects.

"Joanna wanted desperately to be his wife, but of course that was impossible." Another amused glance in my direction. "This was England, after all! Desmond's wife was a rather shrewd creature, as I mentioned before—Sibyl, she was called. Striking looks, frigidly elegant. The one passion she and Desmond shared was shooting—in Scotland, in Africa. She knew very well of Desmond's affair with Joanna and did not find it totally unwelcome. In a sense it freed her to travel and to live as she chose, with her own companions, her own set of friends, her own lovers. She never saw it as a threat.

"But Joanna, of course, was naive—naive enough to think there was a chance he would leave his wife to marry her, naive enough to think that it was she, Joanna, who would triumph! Inevitably, after a year or so, the affair began to be tinged with nervousness and gamesmanship—when the bloom of newness has worn off and the future, not ardor, becomes the issue.

"It was about the time that Desmond took Joanna to Kenya on safari that one really began to feel the tension between them. January of 'fifty-three, as I recall. Joanna had by that time become a rather good shot—or at least sufficiently good not to embarrass Desmond, who prized that sort of thing. Kenya was great fun in those days, more amusing than England at the time, with a certain madness and strangeness about it.

"At first the trip went very well. Joanna was enchanted by the landscape and the luxury of our camp, set in the midst of that intimidating, endless land. We had every conceivable convenience—but then of course one expected no less with Desmond. Sleeping tents, dining tents, even a writing tent, as I recall, with a handsome Victorian desk! Marvelous food, the best wine. The young guide was called Bret. Tall, very handsome, and of course considerably younger than Desmond. From the start he had been eying Joanna, was curious about the relationship between her and this older man." Then, as an aside to me, he added, "In those days there was still some sense of decorum, you see. And Desmond had a curiously prudish side—hence, separate tents for everyone.

"One night the inevitable discussion about marriage must have taken place between Desmond and Joanna—even I could hear the echo of harsh words from my tent. Joanna appeared at breakfast with puffy eyes and a cool, slightly defiant air, baiting Desmond by her extra attentiveness to

Bret, flirting with him, being coy. It was maddening to Desmond, though he did his best, for a while a least, not to show it.

"Not much later during the trip, Desmond must have made her understand that there was not even the remotest possibility that he would marry her, a revelation that seemed inwardly to transform her. She became more brilliantly beautiful, with a hard, angry look in her eye and a steely, ruthless way of shooting. They would track buffalo and antelope and she would accompany them, walking in the frightful sun for endless hours, until her feet and hands bled. I shall never forget watching them as they set off one evening at dusk to hunt lion—Joanna in her khaki skirt and wide-brimmed hat, clutching her gun, Desmond and Bret walking behind her, and the black tracker scanning the bush.

"I'm not certain when she began to sleep with Bret—midway through the safari, I should think. One would never have known from Desmond, in any event. It was one night in the Masai Mara when Joanna appeared at the drinks hour that I suddenly realized that she had crossed the moat, as it were. She looked ravishing, relaxed, with the inner satisfaction and peace of those who have taken their revenge. She wore a white blouse and a long slim skirt, her figure lean, her skin tawny from the sun and exercise.

"I've no idea whether she continued to sleep with Desmond as well. I suspect she continued to sleep with them both—it would not have been unlike her."

I noticed how his expression had darkened, and fearing he would draw back, I asked: "And then, after Kenya, what happened?"

"After we returned to London the tension between them —between Joanna and Desmond, that is—mounted to the point where it was awkward, very difficult indeed, to have a civilized dinner with them. She would taunt him; he would retreat. She became frightfully insecure and nervous, changing her clothes, her hair, her makeup, even her voice, with alarming frequency.

"Then came the turning point—" His glance was ominous. "Joanna learned she was pregnant and told Desmond that he was shortly to become the father of their child. He was enraged and urged her—*commanded* her, rather—to terminate the pregnancy. But she would not. She merely became more obstinate, more defiant, as if having the child were still another act of revenge.

"I told her that child or no, he would never marry her, that having the child would be disastrous for her career—this was the mid-fifties, after all—and that it was only foolishness and masochism on her part to have let it come to this point. She must be sensible and end the episode quietly, I said. 'You are living in another world!' I remember saying to her, in exasperation. 'I know,' she replied, with an eerie look. 'That is my greatest strength.' I continued to try to convince her, only to have the discussions end with bitter tears and her refusal to have an abortion—refusals of such vehemence and passion that I never dared bring up the subject again.

"Her decision revolted Desmond, although I suspect the notion of a child was not nearly so repellent to him as the prospect of the *changes within Joanna*. That she would no longer be the slightly girlish, seductive companion of the past two years but womanly suddenly, womanly in a way he did not like. And when indeed her body began to change— when her waist thickened and her features coarsened from the excess weight—he was clearly repelled. This petrified her, as if she had suddenly come to the edge of a cliff and was forced to leap. By then it was too late for her not to go through with it.

"She cancelled her engagements for those months, claiming illness, and left for Scotland, to Desmond's estate."

He lowered his voice. "Finally, the day came—a terrible day, for the child was stillborn. I was with her—or I should say I was waiting for her as she was wheeled out of that room —that room with its greenish light and frightening apparatus. She looked so dazed, so spent, her skin with an awful transparent blueness about it—"

I interrupted him. "It was a—"

"A boy," he replied. "A boy. . . . It took her quite a while to recover. It was months, in fact, before she seemed outwardly to be herself again, for the idea that she had lost this *son*—" He shook his head as if struggling to dispel a nightmare. "I was desperately concerned about her, and was relieved, yet puzzled, to find her so distant from the experience. It was as if she had never had a child at all. Life returned to normal, at least ostensibly. Desmond resumed his visits; a year passed; she never referred to the event again. Neither, of course, did he.

"She returned to work that September—in fifty-five—the beginning of the season. At first she seemed her old self, if subdued, but gradually I began to discern signs of a severe depression. Absent gaze, total lack of interest in her surroundings, alarming thinness. It was in her eyes, which seemed to be constantly preoccupied and devoid of life, and in her voice, which at least offstage had lost its rich and vibrant timbre, that I noticed it the most. She was clearly disturbed and yet, mercifully, she still managed to work. I suppose the only thing that really saved her, ultimately, *was* her work. She told me once about that time, 'There are moments when I think that I won't be able to overcome myself enough to walk across the stage, that I won't be able to summon the energy, the voice—I fear most of all that the audience won't even know I'm there! But then you see the second after I walk on, before the footlights, quite another being takes over me, and I *am* able to do it!' She played Miranda in *The Tempest* that season, and Masha in *Three Sisters*. And it is interesting that even the critics seemed to have detected some subtle change within her, for her reviews almost uniformly reflected a new, deeper sense of respect. I remember how Ken Tynan noticed it and wrote a really marvelous appraisal of her Masha—and then, the following season, of her Clytemnestra in *Ipighenia*. I suppose there was also a part of her which realized, as I did, that the hurt had somehow been necessary to her work, that the suffering had been beneficial.

"Still, the depression continued, deepened, began to intrude on every aspect of her life." He paused, his thoughts turned inward, as if he were held in thrall by one particular recollection. "It is one morning that I remember so vividly, with an awful aching sharpness, a year or so after the birth of the child. I was directing Joanna in a double bill that season, and a rather difficult one at that—Rosalind in *As You Like It*, and as Medea. The daughter in one, the wife and mother in the other. I had chosen the Euripides partly because it was such a marvelous way to showcase Joanna—a logical successor to her Lady Macbeth. She had come to be fascinated by the Greeks.

"She had had a great success as Clytemnestra a year or so before, as I mentioned, in a superb modern-dress production of *Ipighenia*. Very Third Reich, actually. This was after the war, of course, and Nuremberg was very much on everyone's mind—private conscience versus public duty, so to speak. She was simply unforgettable in the scene where she pleads with Agamemnon not to sacrifice their child. A young, quite moving Clytemnestra she was, though the part had caused her some anxiety."

"Why?"

He paused, as if reluctant to answer. "Because she could not cry on cue," he said slowly, furrowing his brow. "She envied other actors that ability—Gielgud, most of all. But she never learned to, and it troubled her, as if it were a failure of discipline or technique—"

"Or nerve," I suggested quietly.

"No," he admonished me. "Not that at all."

"The *Medea*," I said, prodding him.

He lit another cigarette. "We had had, Joanna and I, rather an intense relationship during rehearsals that season. It had always been so, but . . ."

"Go on."

"She had come to depend on me almost . . ." he hesitated again, ". . . almost *unhealthily* for one of her talent. She would ring me up in the middle of the night to ask about the delivery of a line or a question about a character's motivation. This was not totally out of the ordinary. I had always been aware of her tendency to intellectualize the more she feared a part, as a means of avoiding the difficult emotional work. I had been very patient, very understanding in my role of midwife so to speak, especially in the light of the painful affair with Desmond and the loss of the child. But there came a moment when I had to distance myself for her own good—when we moved from the rather more intimate ambience of the rehearsal room to the theater itself. Joanna had always found this a more difficult transition than most actors —the separation from the director, that is. I had prided myself that it was because of our special rapport. But no, I think that crucial step in bringing to birth a new character was simply painful for her. She would alternately cling to me, then be deeply resentful.

"In rehearsal, as Rosalind in the Shakespeare, she was superb—no one has been a more sprightly or touching Rosalind than Joanna, striding the stage in her hose and doublet! But even there I began to see a change—the fear of forgetting her lines or a cue. An almost unnatural calm would come over her as she waited to go onstage—

"The day I remember so vividly was a Saturday in early spring, a week before the final dress rehearsal. We had rehearsed *As You Like It* in the morning with the company. Joanna had asked me to stay and work with her, alone, on the difficult scenes of *Medea*, in the afternoon. Christina was at the theater as well—the two had become rather close, as I've mentioned. Christina would prompt Joanna with her lines or, during that period at least, help with her rehearsal costumes and props. Joanna's dresser had fallen ill, as I recall.

"The three of us had a bite to eat after the Shakespeare runthrough. I remember Joanna ate nothing, that she complained—as she had during that period—of nausea, of dizziness, of fatigue. I didn't think much of it, quite honestly, because doing the two plays running back to back was of course taxing. We returned to the theater, and Joanna to her dressing room, where she changed into the long purple gown she used for rehearsals of *Medea*. We were to run through that most difficult of scenes, the scene where Medea appears, carrying the children, her children, she has killed.

"I sat in the darkened theater and spoke Jason's lines, waiting for Joanna. I waited and waited—perhaps five minutes or so—before Joanna finally staggered onto the stage. And then I waited once more—an eon, it seemed—for her to speak. She stood up, her expression harrowing, and mumbled a few words. Then she stopped, as if frozen in terror, and crumpled to the ground. I waited again, but still she was silent. Finally, I climbed up to the stage and knelt down to speak with her. She looked at me bizarrely and said, shaking her head, 'I can't do this—I don't know if I can speak. The words. My memory. The two don't—' she paused, '—*mesh.*' To this day I remember precisely how eerily she pronounced that word—*mesh*—almost hissing it, and how it alarmed me. Then she looked out to the darkened theater and dug her fingers into my hand. 'Out there,' she said with frightened eyes. 'They look hungry tonight. They'll eat me up.' I continued to hold her hand and reassure her that there was no one out there, no one in the audience, no one for her to be frightened of. I called to Christina, who had been waiting in the wings. She hurried over, as startled as I, and the two of us helped Joanna back to her dressing room. 'My legs are stiff,' Joanna repeated again and again in that queer voice. 'My legs.'

"We went to her dressing room. Christina helped her out of the long dress and into a robe. I remember that Christina was angry, that she looked at me and said in that accusing voice of hers, 'Don't you see—the two plays together, it's too much of a strain. You were wrong even to suggest it.' I told her this was nonsense, that Joanna had managed far more difficult seasons—but to this she was silent, a way of rebuking me, I suppose. I remember Christina kneeling by the trunk with the rehearsal costumes as she put away the trousers for Rosalind, the gown for Medea, how methodically she folded them. I pulled up a chair to the couch where Joanna lay and took her hand; we began to talk. 'I can't do it,' she murmured. 'The words, the words—' " I explained to her that all actors experience attacks of stage fright. Only the talentless never do. A truly splendid performance is the result of rushing headlong into danger, isn't it, finally? She merely smiled in that listless, disconcerting way. At this point I stood up, feeling I could do no more. Christina, who had made Joanna a cup of tea, took my place.

"I paced about a few minutes, unsure whether to leave or stay. It was only then that I noticed how Joanna's dressing room had been transformed. How cluttered, almost homelike it had become. It was filled with books and objects from Joanna's apartment—pillows, photographs, jewelry. The jewelry I rather disapproved of, I might add, from men, from her admirers. But most of all I noticed the walls, which were covered in mirrors of all styles and shapes. I asked Christina about this. 'She *insists* upon it,' she told me. 'During the day she covers them with scarves, but as the performance draws near, the scarves come off.'

"The following Monday we resumed rehearsals. I tried my best not to show my own nervousness, my fear that Joanna would suffer a relapse of this strange siege. She did continue, of course, and made it through both plays in bravura performances, but at great personal cost. In *Medea* especially, the suffering, the fear of forgetting her lines, her fear that the audience would be *indifferent*—all of this was acute. Many nights she experienced nausea—it was necessary to keep a bucket in the wings in the event she vomited."

He paused, his hand to his temple, his brow furrowed. "Something else occurred during this run," he began. "Joanna simply could not be onstage alone without knowing that someone she knew and trusted stood in the wings— myself or a fellow actor. Or Christina. She came, during that time, to rely quite heavily on Christina—Christina to help her with the costumes, Christina to prompt her on the lines . . ." He gave a sad sigh and shook his head, murmuring, "Christina was always there." Then, directly to me: "And Desmond Kerrith, but only rarely."

I asked whether Desmond Kerrith had encouraged the friendship between the two women.

"At the beginning, very much so," he replied. "Partly because it seemed to absolve him of responsibility, I suppose. Christina would be there if he chose not to be. Desmond would come to watch Joanna perform, but never told her when he did. For it became quite apparent that his presence could trigger the stage fright."

"And so," I said, "the relationship between Joanna and Desmond had by that time ended . . ."

"As *lovers*, yes. The deathknell of their passion was of course the pregnancy. That he had seen her bear his child closed like an iron gate across the physical part of their relationship. They still continued to see one another, but as *friends*, friends who knew each other's foibles and idiosyncracies. Joanna began to turn to him for advice on her career—what role to play, the approach to a play—almost as much, or indeed as much, as she had to me. Occasionally, I felt a slight jealousy in that regard—that had been my domain, after all! But it touched me that Desmond was so proud of her career, so proud of her artistry, even though he no longer desired her as a mistress.

"Desmond grew restless. The excuses began. He was seen with his wife more frequently. He traveled abroad—alone, he said, but doubtless accompanied by some beautiful woman. About this Joanna was philosophical, or at least seemed so. She was almost amused by his philanderings. 'That's Desmond,' she would say. 'I would never expect him to behave otherwise!' Whether she actually believed this or whether this was a brave front, I never knew—for there was a part of Joanna that I never knew. I suspect it could only have hurt her.

"I ran into him about this time in Monte Carlo once, in

the casino. With him was a dark Mediterranean beauty, extremely poised and graceful. We said hello, had a drink. I remember the instant when, looking at her as she held the chips, I saw a number tatooed on her arm—the number from a concentration camp. It was so strange! That sublime face, that ugly number seared into her flesh! I shall never forget it." He shook his head.

"What happened to him since?" I asked.

"He is an old man now," replied Patrick with a sigh. "An old man confined to the rooms at Thistleton that paying visitors never see. He had a stroke not long after Joanna died. There are moments when he is lucid, others when he is not. An old man in a wheelchair, surrounded by nurses, dogs, and yellowing copies of *The Economist* and *Apollo.* I had tea with him earlier this year and came away unutterably depressed, although I was told he was in relatively good form that day. He asked about Joanna, of course—it seems not to have penetrated his consciousness that she is dead. Pathetic, isn't it? 'She hasn't written me for ages,' he told me in a pitiful, querulous voice." Then, leaning forward, Patrick added, "You see, she continued to write him for years afterward, until the end of her life, telling him her news or about books she had read, exhibitions she had seen." A pause. "Perhaps you didn't know that letter writing was one of her passions. 'All the joys of intimacy without all the other nuisances!' was how she once described it." He looked wistful as he added, "I rather think Desmond had come to a point where he lived for her letters.

"But I've gotten away from my story—where were we? Yes . . . She continued to work very hard, exhausting herself by the end of the season. Going out a great deal, much too much. She saw many men, men she sensed I would probably disapprove of. The following year she bought a new flat, with a lovely small garden. She was very keen on decorating it, all with Christina's help, I think. A good sign, it seemed to me. 'Teach me about furniture,' she would say to me, and so I did, taking her about to the auction houses and antiques shops—at first heartened by her interest, then alarmed by her reckless spending. Clothes, objects, furs, paintings—her life seemed glutted suddenly by the lot. I cautioned her against it—thinking, in my puritanical way, that this acquisitiveness was somehow not suitable for an artist, but knowing all the while that there was within her an ungovernable possessive strain. And that she longed for roots, even as she seemed to fight them! Everything about her seemed to be tinged with a dangerous *excessiveness*." He paused reflectively. "In retrospect, I blame a great deal of this on Christina's influence."

"They were about the same age?"

"Yes, though Christina appeared considerably older." He paused to light another cigarette, shielding its flame from the breeze that had come up—a gesture I had come to recognize as signaling a new twist in his recollections. "Christina had always worshiped the theatre, and artists in general—so they had this in common, you see, and other things as well.

"I had encouraged their friendship initially, thinking it would be beneficial, that it would somehow bring some order to Joanna's life. And I was right, as it turned out. Joanna seemed to take possession of herself again—her house was better run, her clothes taken care of, her agenda organized. Joanna began to have small dinners—quite *simpatico*, really —for Christina had found someone to cook occasionally. And it became quite the thing, within the company, to attend those suppers."

Then he stopped abruptly, looking troubled for the first time, as if he were wrestling with another disturbing memory. I said nothing, only praying he would continue—which he did, finally, in a quiet, intense voice. "At the end of one such evening, Joanna asked me to go upstairs with her, ostensibly to see a Regency chair she had just purchased. But when we entered her bedroom, she closed the door behind her in such a dramatic way that I nearly began to laugh. It was then I realized something was wrong: She stood with her back pressed against the door, her face white and full of pain.

'Patrick, I'm suffering from such guilt, I can't bear to live with myself any longer!' she said in a choked voice. I asked what it was that could possibly have brought this on. She lit a cigarette and paced the room, then sat on the bed, twisting her hands as she looked up at me. 'Do you see that trunk?' she said, motioning to an antique leather case to one side of the room. Then, in a voice so low that I could barely hear her, she said, 'Inside it there are letters.' I looked puzzled. 'Letters from my mother,' she continued. 'That you've saved?' I asked. 'Oh no! Letters that I've never opened!' she cried. 'For years she has been writing to me, and I haven't been able to bring myself to read them, to even acknowledge them. And now *look* how they've mounted up—' She flung open the trunk so I could see how, inside, it was filled with letters and more letters. 'How awful I am! But I don't need *her* to make me feel guiltier!' Joanna's voice rang with such passionate self-hate that it took me aback. "I haven't seen her for many years, you know. She lives in America. The last time she visited I was at RADA. And then after she returned to the States, she began to write me more frequently—when I was in Scotland. And after Scotland . . .' "

Patrick shook his head slightly, his eyes seemingly focused on a distant object. "I shall never forget her expression then —her face drained of color, her eyes haunted. Finally, Joanna said to me, 'You must understand, Patrick. As long as I can remember, I've been trying to invent another mother!' I tried to calm her down, and told her, after a moment, that it was very simple—steel herself and read the letters and then respond, if she could find the courage. But she told me she would never find the courage, that it had gone too far to turn back. That she must simply rid them from her life. I cautioned her against it, but it was too late. She had begun to fling the letters into the fire, mesmerized as she watched them turn into smoke and ashes. It was only with the greatest difficulty that I was able to restrain her from destroying them all."

He stopped; a disquieting silence pressed upon us as I dwelled on that last chilling image.

It was Patrick who finally broke the silence and said, in a disarmingly casual voice, "But you are looking tired, dear girl. Perhaps I should go and leave you in peace? I've talked your ear off, I know." He glanced at his watch, adding, "You're to meet Rosalind any moment, and I ought to return home." He stood up, crushed out his cigarette, and muttered, "Houseguests and the usual country house imbroglio. They must be wondering where on earth I've gone!"

Together we walked across the terrace, toward the french doors, through the house, and then down the grand stone steps of the portico toward his car, a vintage black Bentley. We said goodbye. I stood on the steps, still feeling preoccupied by Patrick's recollections and vaguely melancholy at his departure. He climbed into the car and started the motor. I had begun to walk slowly up the steps to the house when he poked his head through the window, as if reluctant to leave without a final, witty exiting line: " 'Once more unto the breach,' " he exclaimed; and then, with a saucy wave, he left.

8

It had grown very warm, still unseasonably hot, after lunch. After saying goodbye to Rossiter, I returned to my room, ostensibly to take an aspirin, though I also intended to make a few notes.

The bedroom had reassumed its immaculate persona: the linens were fresh, the pillows cool and creaseless. I lay down for a moment, thinking of Rossiter's stories as I gazed at the spinning pattern of the marquetry floor: Joanna paralyzed by stage fright; the dressing-room mirrors covered with scarves; the tower at the edge of Thistleton's medieval "ruins" . . .

Minutes later, I went downstairs to look for Kurt; he had offered to show me to the pool, where I was to meet Rosalind.

* * *

The swimming pool and its pavilion were, as it turned out, some distance from the house. I remember following Kurt's tall leaden figure, encased in a white jacket, along the brick paths to the rose garden and from there, through the arbor of wisteria, toward the gate to the maze.

We came to an elegant pavilion, similar to Cassel's library, which faced a long pool of dark green water, encased by a white trellislike fence trailing with ivy and white roses. A statue of a toga-clad lady in the Hellenistic style stood guard at one end of the pool, her face with the pretty, quasi-androgynous features associated with timeless beauty. Her left hand was almost all intact, but her fragmented right forearm, which was raised, had not survived the centuries, and its position suggested that she had once been holding something—something awful, from the glinty expression in her eyes. I wondered whether this was a depiction of Judith and whether she had once held the severed stone head of Holofernes.

Rosalind was swimming, her arms rhythmically surfacing above the water as she completed lap after lap. Only after a long while did she stop and acknowledge me, her small oval face, with its dark, uptilted eyes, poised above water as she did a strong, precise breaststroke.

"Coming in?" was all she asked, continuing to swim, her black hair streaming behind her.

"Not today," I replied. "Normally, I'd love to, but the flu . . ."

"Do whatever you want. But I've got to finish my laps."

I reminded her that she'd offered to show me through the maze.

"Did I?" Her mouth formed that familiar, slightly caustic smile. "Well, I wouldn't want the biographer to call me unreliable, would I?" Her arms continued to pulse through the water. "We'll do it when I'm finished."

I walked to the edge of the pool, tempted to go in; it was

hot, the water looked inviting, and I loved to swim. Still feeling enervated, I decided against it, however, and stretched out on a chaise longue instead. All was silent, save for the sound of Rosalind sluicing through the water. I began to daydream, staring at the undulating refractions within the water: I thought of a dream, recurrent since childhood, of a northern sea and cliffs and a wound that left a trail of blood in the surf, then fleetingly of David Cassel, and finally of Jack and the last time we'd made love. Inwardly, I shivered, overcome with erotic longing for him. I wondered where he was at that moment. . . . With his wife and family in East Hampton, most likely . . .

I glanced at Rosalind as she climbed out of the pool—her slim-hipped, boyish figure was one which, before meeting Jack, I might have envied.

"How was lunch?" she asked, vigorously drying herself with a towel.

"Delicious. Thank you."

She rubbed some oil onto her legs with hard, smooth strokes. Observing her and the compulsive way she swam, I wondered again whether she had once been plump.

"And Patrick?" she asked, finally looking up.

I answered carefully: "As entertaining as ever."

She smiled drily, wiping her hands on the towel. "He loves to dish, all right," she said, lying down on a chaise. "Always has. But he's basically harmless. Gossip is what he barters. It's how he maintains his keep—like a lot of people in New York."

I smiled. "And you're *not* interested in gossip?"

"Not really. Facts and numbers are more my thing." With a sharp glance, she added, "I've learned when to talk and when not to talk. I guess you could say that's true. It's one of the many lessons David has taught me."

"And which stands you in good stead in your work."

"Correct."

"And you're very good at your work, I'm sure."

"We all have to make a living."

"And you've done very well," I ventured, easily able to imagine Rosalind in the brutal world of Wall Street.

"Compared to some, sure."

Shadows had encroached on the shallow end, the part guarded by the statue. I looked at the fractured stone figure and asked Rosalind where it was from and whether it was meant to be the ancient Judith.

"How the hell would *I* know?" she replied. "I'm not exactly an art historian. That was Joanna's bag. I don't have much of a feeling for the antique. Never have." She glanced at the statue. "David was never wild about it, that much I do know."

I continued to look at the statue, struck by the way Rosalind had rebuffed my question, though by this time I was accustomed to her belligerence, even her hostility. It was almost five o'clock. I stood up, glanced at my watch and, thinking again of the maze, I reminded Rosalind that it was getting late, and she had offered to take me through it.

"Okay, okay," she remarked, raising one brow. She stood and stretched, yawning loudly before wrapping a towel sarong-style around her purple tank suit: "I'll go change." Once more I remember noticing how much smaller she was than I, though there was a fierceness about her that seemed to absolve her of all daintiness.

I followed her into the pool house, its walls crisscrossed with dark beams, its walls covered with architectural drawings of Victorian gazebos. Rosalind's clothes lay in a heap on a bench.

She went into the bathroom to shower; the sound of pounding water reverberated. After a while she emerged, towel in hand, affecting, it seemed to me, an almost aggressive obliviousness to her own nudity.

It was then I noticed the large, distinct scar on her lower abdomen, above her pubic hair—a thick, reddish scar that had an unpleasant freshness about it upon her fair skin. I remember quickly averting my gaze from it: Rosalind noticed my repulsion.

"Not a pretty sight, is it?" she asked in a curiously dispassionate voice as she slipped on a pair of black jeans. "I had a little problem last year," she went on, her tone clipped, even clinical. "Had a hysterectomy." She began to slip a black T-shirt over her head.

I said something about being sorry.

"Why?" she asked, almost reproachfully. "I never wanted a family, so this sort of killed two birds with one stone." She pulled a comb through her tangled wet hair as she looked into a mirror. "*You* do, don't you?" she asked me with a sidelong glance. "Want kids, I mean."

"Why do you say that?" I asked coolly enough, though her remark perturbed me—I longed to have a child, in fact.

"You can always tell women who want children," she replied, still focusing on her reflection. She took a lipstick from her pocket and began to outline her mouth in dark red.

"*How* can you tell?" I asked, watching her.

"Don't know, but you just can. It's a kind of . . ." here she faltered, only to add, with scathing precision, ". . . *weakness*, I guess you'd call it. Though some people might call it tenderness." She blotted the lipstick in such a way that the dark, ruptured imprint of her mouth lay on the discarded tissue. "It must be humiliating to go through all of that—childbirth, I mean." And then, vehemently, with a shudder: "Thank God I won't ever have to."

The harsh sound of the word she had chosen, *humiliating*, lingered in my mind. "Do you think Joanna ever wanted a child?" I asked.

"Maybe for one brief crazed moment."

"Why crazed?"

"Because I don't think she was exactly made for motherhood."

"Explain—"

"She lived to please men, and only men. And for herself, and her own ambitions. I don't think there was room in her world for a child, that's all." She paused. "And *I* should know—I was her stepdaughter, after all."

"And she never spent time with you?"

"Only when she couldn't avoid it," she said, a trace of bitterness momentarily shattering her chilling aura of self-sufficiency. For the first time, Rosalind had not quite succeeded in concealing her hurt.

The heat had subsided by the time we reached the gate to the maze.

"The trick," said Rosalind, her hand on the latch, "is to keep turning right three times, then left three times." I heard the gate close; we were inside. There was an eerie, universe-eradicating quality to the light, as if it had been permeated by the color of the high green hedges. I took a deep breath, inhaling the pungent, almost medicinal smell of boxwood.

Rosalind led the way along the smooth gravel paths, turning right, then right again. I remember the disturbing feeling that even then, on a blissful summer afternoon, accompanied by someone acquainted with the way, the maze was forbidding. Each time I thought I knew the way I was mistaken; each time I thought we had approached the center I was wrong.

Three times left . . . I began to feel that terrible familiar anxiety, the onset of vertigo. My heart began to pound, I began to sweat, I felt the hedges closing in on me; I leaned against the prickly surface, closing my eyes for a moment.

When I opened them, Rosalind was gone.

"Rosalind!" I called. "Rosalind!"

I cried out again and again, searching for the slim figure in black; but all around me was utter quiet and emptiness.

I raced to one end of a path and then to the other. I had no idea which direction I had taken, how far from the outer ring I had wandered. At last I came to an opening with a stone statue enclosed in an octagon. The statue was a cousin to the Judith, but far more frightening—her mouth gaped, her frantic eyes stared, her handless arms reached out imploringly toward me.

I turned away, running down another path until I came to another "room" with another statue—this one with intricately carved robes, clutched hands, and a vacant gaze . . .

"Rosalind!" I screamed. "Rosalind!"

From the distance I heard a voice calling, "Elisabeth, where are you?"

I ran in the direction of the voice. It was then, as I turned left, that I glimpsed something else: a fleeting figure in red, man or woman I was not certain. I froze. "Elisabeth," I heard the voice calling again. "Elisabeth!" I thought, but was not completely sure, that the voice belonged to Rosalind. I staggered left, then left again, until I came to the first statue: the lady without hands.

I heard the sound of steps and turned around, my heart pounding. Rosalind emerged from the hedges, an exasperated smile on her face. "Where the hell were you?" she asked.

"I got lost."

"So much for your famous sense of direction."

I tried to collect myself, and said, "I saw someone else—someone in red."

"Man? Woman?"

"I'm not sure."

She looked at me askance, almost amused. "Pretty damn unlikely."

I repeated what I'd said: the glimpse of red through the hedges. "There was someone else in here with us."

"I think you'd better rest, catch your breath."

I sat down on the bench nearby, its sides fashioned like tangled branches.

Rosalind, standing before the statue, continued to watch me. "You've been sick," she said.

I nodded halfheartedly, trying to focus on the maze. "So this—" I pointed to the stone figure, "must be another of Joanna's antique statues."

"It's not antique at all," came the severe reply. "She had it made—you know, to *look* antique."

"I see."

"Typical of Joanna."

"In what way?"

She shrugged, kicking at the gravel beneath her feet.

"And she'd come here often?" I asked after a moment.

"Often enough." This, with a wary glance.

I remembered Patrick's stories about Joanna and the maze at Thistleton: "And she'd come here to learn her lines as well?"

"There *were* no more lines to learn here," she replied. "Not by the time Joanna came to Wakefield. She'd given up acting."

"Of course," I murmured, noting the vehemence of her reaction.

Rosalind continued to walk about, glancing from me to the statue: "By that time other things had begun to obsess her."

"What other things?"

Her smile was private and bitter. "That's *your* job, isn't it, Elisabeth? To find out, I mean." She shot me another cold, assessing glance, her hands on her waist. "We'd better head back."

Through the winding tunnels of yews we walked, finally returning to the gate where we had started, though the place looked unfamiliar to me then.

The gate closed with a sharp sound; together we made our way toward the house.

The following morning, I returned to New York.

9

July 1, 1986
Tuesday

The day after I returned to work, I was told I could not use the expression *rara avis*. It is not "our style"; it is considered pretentious. This discussion followed an earlier session in which my copy was mutilated with cross-outs, deletions, and acerbic comments from my editor belittling what he called my "love affair" with Latinisms and foreign expressions. I should have taken this with equanimity, I suppose, but I've never been able to feel anything calmly—least of all an assault on my own voice.

I later confronted my editor so forcefully that he agreed to reconsider the changes he had made. I returned to my desk feeling immeasurably calmer and resolute, yet more doubtful than ever of being able to conform to this school of writing by consensus. No wonder I returned to my book on Joanna with such relief! No wonder I longed for September, when I would begin my six-month leave to research the book.

Only a week had passed since my visit to Wakefield Hall: It seemed like a dream, queer and hallucinatory, yet with all a dream's vivid and enduring reality—a reality I longed, not unfearfully, to reenter. Wakefield had not left my thoughts: sitting at my desk or lying in bed at night, I would reenact my arrival at the house countless times—once more walking through its rooms, meeting David Cassel, and guiltily leafing through Joanna's books, like one slitting open forbidden letters. I wondered even more obsessively who Joanna really was —whether all the clues to her mysterious life remained for me to unearth.

In the meantime I had returned to New York, and to my double life, with all its idiosyncrasies, routines, and clandestine pleasures; to my apartment, with its view of concrete, brick, and glass; to my job at the *Journal*; and to my love affair, three years old now, with a married man. Three years together, Jack and I!

Until I met Jack, I had thought of myself as a bluestocking: the disciplined, cerebral being I had to some extent crafted for my father (for his approval meant the world to me) had given way to another being, at once a twin and stranger, for whom the idea of submission, abhorrent to me in every other realm, had taken on another cast. If to submit gave pleasure, and if in giving pleasure there was a kind of power, then surely what I had been taught to think demeaning could not be so—at least in bed. It was this mesmerizing revelation—the circular power of my own submission— which Jack had awakened with a violence I still remember with a shudder.

Nothing in my education or in my upbringing had prepared me for this—for men, for love, for life. At school and college, I had been taught by those priestesses of reason to think of life (and even love!) in terms of the rational and just. Only later would I see the pitiful inadequacy of those well-meaning theories before the *chiaroscuro* theater of sex. What good was reason when, engulfed in the arms of my lover, all I yearned to hear was this: "I want you. I need you." At such moments, I would willingly have surrendered all that had previously defined me—my work, my intellectual acumen—for him to repeat those words, mantralike, which seemed to rescue me from some unspeakable fate.

Inebriated with his attention, I had mistakenly thought at the beginning that this would suffice. I did not permit myself to wonder whether there might come a point when I would live with him openly, share his home, feel his body entwined with mine when I awoke. I succeeded in convincing myself that I found his consideration for his family—his wife, his children—heartening. But gradually, I came to resent them bitterly; I wished they had never existed. I would look at him from across a table or a room or as he slept and, overwhelmed by a wave of possessiveness, I would whisper, fiercely, *"He's mine."*

But he was *not* mine. He had a wife he respected and four daughters he deeply loved. They lived in Greenwich, I in New York. Jack did not seem discontent with this arrangement, while I—"Reader, I married him," I longed to cry! Yet marriage within the next two years was out of the question, he would tell me. Why? Money is freedom, he would tell me. But it was money, after all, that bound him to the life that kept him from me; money that tied him to his wife; and money that had made him so visible in New York and so eager for a place in the society which, not so long ago, had virtually shunned him.

There *was* freedom in money, I had discovered, but loneliness too. It struck me most keenly when I returned to the silence of my apartment each evening after work. The rooms were still and deserted, the kitchen empty, cushions, books, and towels all in perfect order.

Perfect order is a seduction in itself: Surely it was what I found so inebriating about Wakefield Hall—the beauty and order of those faultlessly appointed rooms, with their thick,

luxurious curtains, immortal flowers, and wax-scented antiques. Within that sphere of flawless domestic order there
seemed no place for the loneliness and inner chaos I would
feel upon returning to rooms of my own creation. Wakefield
seemed to obliterate all I would rather forget: the frustra-
tions of my job, the anxieties of living in this city, with its
filthy streets and convoluted relationships—but most of all
the hurt and suppressed longings of my liaison with Jack.

How I longed to have a child! Black, barren moods engulfed me after visiting friends who lay in maternity wards,
exhausted and ecstatic from having given birth. Dazed with
envy, I would press my face against the windows of hospital
nurseries, gazing at rows of swaddled babies, wishing one
were mine! "I can deny you nothing," he had said to me
once, his words an eerie echo of Othello's. When I laughingly countered, "What—is my name Desdemona?" he simply had no idea what I was talking about. "Enjoy what we
have together," he would tell me. "Live from day to day."

But there was other advice that reverberated in my mind
—my father's, most of all. Not a single day passed when I did
not think of his last letter, written on my birthday, March 3,
just eight days before his death; the nightmare of that last
call and the telegram from his doctors; the terrifying trip to
Geneva.

I unfolded the letter now, as I had countless times—three
sheets of pale blue onionskin paper, the kind he had always
used, covered with his angular handwriting in black ink,
handwriting, once methodical, gone awkward and disjointed
with his illness. His handwriting alone—its sudden surges
and uncontrolled quality—brought me to tears; it was un-
recognizable. And yet I knew the voice to be his.

Dear Lilbet [that is what he'd always called me],

I think of you today, on your thirty-first birthday,
with love and pride. Yet I admit to worrying about you
constantly, now that I am so far away; that you are
alone, and lonely, and that—with my illness—I may

never see you again. The hardest words a father who loves his daughter could ever set down on paper—especially on her birthday! It is the disarray of your life which concerns me and the career which seems to have consumed you to the extent that you have neglected to forge a satisfying personal life.

And now you talk of taking on a book on Joanna Eakins! I have discussed this with you at length; you know my feelings. I wonder at the appropriateness of your subject and—most of all—at your embarking on this at a moment when *you should be concerned most of all with getting your life in order.* [This, in a shaky hand, he had underlined.] You talk of children—but when? You talk of a home and family—but when? The book on Joanna Eakins—the time commitment it involves, the burden of that research—would only seem to distance you even further from other, and I think more important, life goals.

I am just as concerned about the inevitable involvement with David Cassel. I have heard he is a difficult man, one who is committed to protecting his—and his late wife's—privacy and reputation. I have banker friends here, in Geneva, who have dealt with him in the past. All describe him as a man who cannot surrender control, a man who, when even remotely challenged, can be ruthless. Even if you could convince him to cooperate (and I think that doubtful), that would be no guarantee of your success, nor would it mean that the work would assume a greater depth and ease. There have been other moments in your life when you have used your obsessiveness to good advantage; but now I fear for you.

Please consider what I have said. I don't mean to sound like a caviling, overprotective father. You are thirty-one—free to follow your own desires and ambitions. I only urge you, before setting forth on this route, to reexamine your future, your goals, your notion of ultimate happiness.

Never forget—or fail to understand—how much I love you, how much my birthday girl is in my thoughts, and how much I look forward to your next visit.

Happy birthday, dearest Elisabeth!

His shaky signature next; then a short postscript in which, with his characteristic understatement, he advised me of his condition, minimizing its seriousness and thanking me for a package of new books I had recently sent.

I did not possess—nor did it seem possible that I would ever possess—anything more painful than those three sheets of paper. When two days later I reached Geneva, when I glimpsed the ashen face of the embassy's representative, I knew I had come too late. My father had already descended into a coma; he would never again speak; he would never again recognize me or know that yes, I had come to hold his hand! His head, gaunt and diaphanous, lay upon the pillow as if it did not quite belong to the bundle wrapped in the white sheets below. I remember the murmur of the well-meaning nurses that had accompanied the noiseless—yet to me deafening—drip of the intravenous. Arrows faintly moving in the hospital machinery; the stain of his blood on a hospital blanket.

Looking around that room, I had tried, with all the egocentricity of one confronting an invalid, to escape my own pain; tried to memorize that last room of his life. Books I had sent him, neatly stacked, with my note on top; his favorite photograph of me in a silver frame. The nurse had squeezed my hand and tried to comfort me, a gesture I had at once longed for and angrily rejected—what can one say to a child who comes too late? What words can possibly suffice —and why did no one understand that? What doctor's analysis could possibly have made the memory of that day, and of those last days, less smitingly painful? I had missed his last words; I was not there to hold his hand when he said goodbye to the world as he knew it: *I, his only child, had failed him.*

When they buried him on that windy March afternoon, my aching sense of loss only became more intense. And yet it was a pain not untouched, guiltily, by relief—for he, the most moral of men, would never know of his daughter's affair with a married man; my father would never learn of the clandestine passion of my life, *and I was glad of it.* What would my father have thought, what would he have said, if he had learned of those things? Was it better that he had died before coming upon that most bitter discovery of all? There: I have said it. I have formulated the words that any daughter who loved her father would dread to acknowledge she was even capable of thinking.

No wonder, then, that I rushed to escape into the world of my book—the world of Joanna Eakins Cassel and of Wakefield Hall. Unlike the pleasure of his company, it was a world Jack could not take from me, a universe of my own creation. Toward this book he had shown little interest—even, on occasion, a humorous mock jealousy. "The other lover," he had come to call it, saying—rightly—that it obsessed me as a new lover might. I would be lying if I denied that this pleased me in a perverse way. I rather liked the fact that it irked him, that it occasionally took me away from him, that it was inaccessible to him.

I had spent the last few days inquiring about Christina von Shouse. She was one of those women who had achieved the sort of minor urban fame derived from the society columns, where her frequent, and apparently quite interesting, dinners were often noted. Her nationality? Uncertain—but this was not surprising, given the pastless *beau monde* of New York. Some said she was Iraqi, some Lebanese.

Earlier that week I had discovered that my friend Russell Heywood, the jewelry expert at Hutchinson's, the prestigious auction house, knew her quite well. A visible member of New York's substratum of *haute* purveyors, Russell had often attended her *soirées*, it seems: New York had become parure country, after all, and the connoisseurs of such things were sought after and much courted.

I asked Russell to describe Mrs. von Shouse. "A woman reduced to buying her own jewelry," was his cynical appraisal. (Russell, with his professional eye for gems, his international accent, his love of "dish," as he called it, his fascination with the New Rich—his wicked jokes about his role in "cementing the mergers"!) He mentioned that she had telephoned him only recently to inquire about some lots in his upcoming sale; it appears she has a passion for jewelry and Russian furniture. To this he had slyly added, with the special cruelty reserved for those who furnish the speaker with a livelihood: "Her idea of an erotic encounter is to lie down on a Biedermeier commode and have the butler polish her!" When I expressed surprise at his sarcastic tone about a purported friend and client—a woman he dined with every week —he merely shrugged his shoulders and remarked, "This is New York, isn't it?"

How obligingly Russell disclosed *which* lots in the sale she had singled out, even going so far as to evaluate the quality of each. Perhaps she might attend the sale herself, he told me; perhaps it would be worth my while to be there.

I told him I would try and asked the time and date. The following week, he said, on Tuesday, at two o'clock.

10

I returned home from work the next day famished and slightly depressed. It was not so much the pressure of deadlines that had depleted me, but seeing Jack earlier that afternoon at lunch, at the Four Seasons. I had never acknowledged him, of course, nor had he acknowledged me: our pact. Yet his presence had pressed upon me painfully, making me unable to concentrate on my own companion— or, indeed, on anything I'd said. Amid the sea of dark suits all I had seen was my lover.

In the past, Jack had always called after such encounters; on this day he had not. I tore off a piece of French bread and poured myself some white wine, drinking it greedily as I continued to thrash against the constraints of our affair.

The air was thick with heat that night. I kicked off my shoes and walked into the bedroom, thinking all the while of the first time we met. At the Four Seasons, ironically. Jack had been lunching with an old friend of mine from Boston at the same corner banquette, that coveted status seat. I knew his name only slightly: his company, Northtech Communications, and the fortune he had made in cellular telephones and cable television had been written up recently in *Time*. I thought him engaging, but not in any troubling sense (for me the first signal of an incipient attraction).

I had just returned from a holiday in Normandy and Brittany with my fiancé, as I recall.

"Do you speak French?" Jack asked me appraisingly, in a way which suggested that this symbolized another, perhaps more exclusive, world—one which had denied him membership. What I so vividly recall was an edge to his tone that irked me. In response, I said, yes, I spoke French, "and German too." How obnoxious I must have seemed, how insecure! But still I continued to go on. In my zest to keep up the repartee, I subsequently asked the two men whether they had heard this joke: "If you speak more than two languages you're a polyglot," I began. "If you speak two, you're bilingual; and if you speak one, you're American." At this they laughed; we talked a bit more; and then I left the restaurant.

I never really thought of Jack Varady again—or only fleetingly—for I was engaged to another man at the time, a man my father had met, and respected, and whom I thought I loved.

It was not until months later, shortly after Thanksgiving, that I encountered Jack again—this time at the Swissair terminal at the airport in Geneva, where I had been visiting my father. I had spotted him reading the *Financial Times* in the section set apart for first-class passengers, but never considered approaching him. After checking my seat assignment at the desk, I simply took a seat and immersed myself in a book.

A few moments later, I heard someone greet me by name and looked up to find Jack Varady. He asked if I was traveling alone. I said yes. "Then come sit with me," he said. "I'll have your seat changed." I would be lying if I said I wasn't thrilled, but then embarrassment took over, and awkwardness. I said I couldn't possibly sit with him—I had a lot of work to do, I had some books to read. But clearly, none of these excuses sounded convincing: The next moment he interrupted me with a brusque, "You're meeting someone else, then?" No, I wasn't. "Well, for God's sake, why can't you sit with me?"

Finally, with some exasperation at his seeming lack of sensitivity, I told him that if he really insisted on knowing the reason, it was because he had a first-class ticket: Mine was coach. He laughed. So that was all, he said. "Well, that's easily fixable." He told me he'd simply have my ticket "upgraded" and then we would be able to sit together.

I remember inwardly recoiling when he offered this solution: Was it the notion of money changing hands or the word *upgrade?* Even now I am not sure; I only know I felt uncomfortable and that I must have shown it. I thanked him, but said I couldn't possibly accept his changing my ticket (though the notion of being ensconced in first-class luxury was tempting, to be sure.) "Okay," he said, his eyes assuming another, harder glint. "I'll change *my* ticket, and then I'll come and sit with you."

The tickets adjusted, we made our way to the plane and found our places. I put away my hand luggage, but not before taking out two books that would remain with me throughout the flight—emblems of another, higher order that always accompanied me on such journeys.

He had been watching me; when I finally took my seat, he said, "I like your legs." I blushed, but tried not to let him see, merely smoothing my skirt about my knees. His eyes continued to scan my face. "And your mouth," he added, as if he had never quite finished the first sentence.

"What about my mind?" was my arch response, a desperate and clumsy attempt to conceal my delight. "That goes without saying," he said with a charming smile.

He had already guessed the first of many crucial secrets: I

was a tall, studious girl who had never really felt pretty, despite the protestations of others to the contrary.

He began to look for the "stewardess"; his impatience amused me, for he was clearly accustomed to superior service. Finally the flight attendant appeared and asked me, in French, what I would like to drink. A glass of white wine, I responded in French, feeling Jack's eyes upon me as I did so; then she posed the same question to him, in English. A martini straight up, he said.

He had noticed the two books in my lap: *Madame Bovary*, which I was rereading, and *The House of Mirth*. I went on to explain that I was very interested in the life of Edith Wharton, and did he know much about her?

It seemed incredible to me then—and here I must profess to my snobbery, which in retrospect seems almost comical—that he had never really heard of Edith Wharton, or only distantly: He knew that she had written a couple of novels, "and wasn't one called *Erich Fromm?*"

I laughed—I laughed so hard I almost spilled my drink—and when I finally looked up at Jack, I could see that he was angry.

"Oh, don't be offended," I said in my offhand way, sensing he was really miffed. "There's no reason you should know about Edith Wharton." I explained that she had written many novels, "and one of them was *Ethan Frome*. Erich Fromm's a psychologist."

His eyes were hostile; he sipped his drink and picked up his newspaper. Moments passed. Meantime, I stole a few glances at his face: He was very blond, with a face whose planes were devoid of the superfluous. The nose straight, the mouth fine, a purposeful, strong chin; even the gray in his eyes seemed to have resisted any infiltration of colored pigment. I tried, without success, to analyze precisely what rescued his features from mere handsomeness, only to decide later that his was the face of a northern adventurer attracted to exotic realms.

He continued to read the business pages of the *Tribune*

while I tried to focus on the nervous nineteenth-century heroines whose stories lay in my lap. I began to wish I hadn't laughed so hard; I wished he would speak to me.

Lunch arrived, forcing him to abandon his newspaper. He began to eat in silence.

After five minutes or so, I finally looked at him and said: "If you don't like the company and the food, why don't you take your place up in first class? It shouldn't be hard to upgrade your ticket."

"It isn't the *food* that bothers me," he said without looking up.

"Either you sit here sulking for eight hours, or you accept my apology so that we can talk and at least have a pleasant flight." I took a sip of wine, feeling rather pleased with myself.

"An argument well presented," he said, turning to me with a boyish, consenting grin. "Now, tell me about yourself. You're engaged, I see." He had noticed the ring on my left hand. "So who's the lucky man?"

I told him my fiancé's name and mentioned that he was a doctor, an internist. I smile to myself now when I recall how proudly I must have said this, which made me all the more disconcerted when Jack responded, unimpressed, "An internist? Doctors and lawyers—they don't wear very well. Think about it."

I asked him why he had said this. He gazed at me with sudden thoughtfulness: "Because they're not *free*. They're always at the mercy of other people." He paused, sipping his wine once more before adding reassuringly, "But I'm sure this man is terrific. And I'm sure you'll be very happy." He asked me when we would be married. In early March, I told him, in New York. "To you," he said, raising his glass. "To you and your future happiness." Our glasses met.

"Does he speak French and German?" he asked me next. "And is he an expert on Edith Wharton?"

"Only French, not German," I replied, laughing.

"And he's never been married? No children?"

No, I said, this was his first marriage, and mine, and we hoped to have children.

"And your job?"

"I'll always continue to work," I answered confidently. "It's possible to do both."

We had finished lunch by this time and were being served coffee. "And you," I said, turning to him. "You're married, aren't you?"

"Yes. For many years."

"And you have children?"

"Yes. Four girls." He went on to tell me their ages, which ranged from six to twelve.

"Then you should ask *them* about Edith Wharton," I said half in jest. "And your wife—what does she do?"

"My wife, what *does* she do," he said, almost to himself. And then, briskly: "My wife happens to be a great organizer of charity functions. She also spends a lot of time having lunch at the Colony Club. In short, she doesn't work. Does that answer your question?"

At this I felt slightly embarrassed, as I sometimes had when asking Europeans what they "did."

Without my prompting it, he went on to say, "And her French, which is her only foreign language, is minimal." He paused. "You might say she is very American in that respect."

I smiled. So he had remembered my little joke at the Four Seasons. "No," I corrected him. "I said it was very American to speak only *one* language."

"You learned French as a child?"

I nodded. "Hasn't anyone ever tried to teach you French?" I asked after a moment.

"No. Never."

"It isn't so hard."

He looked at me intently. "Maybe you'll teach me one day."

I felt a stab of delight, and panic. "Sure," I said, feigning nonchalance.

He took up his newspaper, the luncheon trays having been

cleared by this time, and resumed reading. I remember a twinge of disappointment as he did so, for I had rather enjoyed his attention, even his teasing: It had felt so good to laugh! Even so, with a certain forced industriousness, I quickly appeared to immerse myself in other things: Lily Bart, my fiancé, my work. But still my thoughts wandered and so, occasionally, did my gaze toward the man who sat beside me, his light eyes scanning the *Tribune*'s business pages with great intensity.

At last, the book in my lap, I turned my head to one side and fell asleep.

When I awoke, I discovered that my head was resting on his shoulder. I started, overcome by the disturbing and yet partly thrilling suspicion that he had been watching me sleeping. "I've been watching over you," he said quietly.

Once again I did not want to acknowledge what my intuition detected—a certain tenderness in his voice. And so I responded in my flippant way, "I find it hard to imagine you in the role of guardian angel."

"Stranger things have happened," was his answer, uttered in a voice that was not in the least jocular. I looked away, ostensibly to search for my handbag. After taking out a small pouch with makeup, I powdered my nose and fixed my lipstick with small, self-conscious gestures until, at last, I felt recovered.

"Where did you grow up?" he asked, still watching me.

"Lots of places," I told him. My father had always been in the State Department, I said, and I had had a rather rootless childhood.

"And your mother?" he asked.

I told him I had never really known my mother, that she had died when I was two.

"And your father never remarried?"

No, I said, never.

Once more I felt the need to deflect the attention to him; I asked where he was from and about his family.

He told me somewhat reticently that he was born in Commack, Long Island, where his father had been a contractor. I continued to probe, albeit gently, and quickly gathered that he was—like so many self-made men of power and achievement—the product of a loving, ambitious mother and a father whose station in life he was driven to surpass.

I asked when he had left his hometown—as soon as he could, he said—and where he went to college. He told me he'd won a scholarship to Dartmouth and that during his four years there he worked to pay for his expenses.

He paused, as if recalling something distant, something he rarely divulged. He had made a college friend from New York, he told me, a friend with some connections who had helped him get a job during the school holidays, working in the coat-check room of El Morocco. With a certain poignancy I imagined him there, at the nightclub, checking the coats of his classmates and their dates, who had come to dance and drink.

"And now you're more successful than all of them," I said.

"Yes," he answered decisively. "But I always knew I would be."

I asked him whether he ever returned to Commack.

"No," he replied in a voice that did not encourage more questions. "Never."

The captain announced that we were approaching New York; minutes later we landed. I said goodbye to Jack at customs and walked through the phalanx of steel doors to find my fiancé waiting.

I was no longer engaged when I next saw Jack. Malaise, restlessness, a final reluctance to be married—doubt had begun to affect my emotions and, ultimately, the relationship with my fiancé. And so I broke off the engagement—ruthlessly, too—leaving my fiancé wounded and bewildered, my father and friends astonished by my sudden leap from love to disaffection. It is not a moment I am proud of, and even now find difficult to discuss—but I was young, with all the callousness of one who had not yet suffered in love.

Not long afterward, on a weekend in February, I impulsively decided to go skiing, thinking I would find some release from confusion and self-loathing. I booked a room at a motel and flew, alone, to Aspen.

The next day, Saturday, I skiied from the moment the lifts opened, hardly stopping for rest or food. Indeed, with each turn, I began to feel more tranquil: the weather was glorious, the snow light and high. And I had never skiied better, pulsing down the fall-line with a fierceness and precision that satisfied me.

I had just descended Ruthie's Run after lunch and was waiting in a lift line when I heard someone—a man—call my name.

I looked around, glimpsed a waving ski pole and, to my astonishment, saw it belonged to Jack Varady. He stood apart from the crowds, in the line reserved for private ski school instructors and their clients. I simply smiled, returned his wave, and resumed waiting.

Minutes later his queue was already at a par with mine (his, of course, was moving considerably faster). "So there you are!" he exclaimed, all the while trying to discern whether I had a partner. Convinced I had none, he said, "Come join us!" The next instant his hand had gripped my arm, and I found myself standing with him and his instructor in the privileged line.

Yet I only felt irritated. He hadn't *asked* whether I had wanted to join him: He had assumed I wanted company whereas, in fact, I had rather enjoyed being alone and had no real desire, that weekend, to ski with anyone else or even to make conversation. Besides, I was an excellent skiier and feared he wasn't.

He had sensed my coolness. "You don't have to ski with us, you know," he said, putting on his large black gloves. "I just thought I'd save you from having to wait so long in that line."

"I was quite happy with the white trash," I said tartly. "Besides, it wasn't such a long wait."

He said nothing, merely poking the snow with his ski pole. "Where's the fiancé?" he ventured sarcastically. "Too busy catching up on Edith Wharton to ski with you?"

It was all I could do to restrain myself from being rude, though my eyes, no doubt, showed my anger. "And your wife?" I retorted. "Where's she? Having tea at the Colony Club?"

"My wife," he said, "only skis cross-country. Downhill, never."

It was our turn to get on the lift. The next moment, our skis swinging beneath us, we were on our way up, across the steep slope, through the trees, to the top of the mountain.

"Where *is* the fiancé?" he asked again insistently.

"There is no more fiancé, if you really must know," came my exasperated answer. "I'm here alone." I turned to look at him directly, grudgingly acknowledging that he looked handsome and golden through the light of my goggles.

My hands felt cold. I asked whether he would hold my poles while I put on mitten liners. He did so, and after returning my poles, he leaned over and zipped up my parka, snapping the collar shut. "You'll catch cold," he said. I looked away.

"Tell me what happened," I heard him say in a softer voice.

"About what?"

"Your fiancé."

"I don't know," I said, stabbing the air with my poles. "I wish I *did* know. But in the end I felt uneasy about the whole thing, so I broke it off."

"And broke his heart," Jack interjected.

"Hearts mend," I responded, with a matter-of-factness that makes me shudder when I recall it. "And in the end it was better for him, I'm sure. I doubt I would have really made him happy."

We rode the rest of the way in silence, passing from the

sun of the slopes through the towering shadows of ever-greens, until it was time to get off the lift. The instructor, Chip, joined us—he was tall, fit and dark, radiating the health of one who has never known ambivalence.

"Come with us—just for a run," Jack urged me. "And then, Miss Garbo, we'll let you be alone all you want."

I reluctantly agreed, and we set off.

I quickly realized that Jack was, in fact, a wonderful skiier: he had a taut, aggressive style, with a faultless way of weaving through the moguls, piercing their tops swiftly and surely as he moved down the fall-line.

At the bottom of the steep, bumpy run, the two men waited for me, watching. Snow flew as I came to a stop. "You're a very good skiier," Jack said. "But then I thought you would be."

"Thanks," I said, adding that it always took me a while to warm up when I ski with strangers.

"We'll go down this one again," he told Chip. "And then up, over to Bell Mountain."

This we swiftly did: up one run, down the steep pitches of Bell Mountain, until the lifts closed. Seldom have I known such a combination of exhaustion and elation; seldom have I felt so keenly the luminous camaraderie of the mountains. In the end it was I who implored the two men to stop—I was thirsty and wanted to have a drink before making our way down the darkening trails.

I recall that moment as among the happiest of my life—how good the icy, foamy beer felt, how radiantly tired my body, and how otherworldly the mountain light of late after-noon, streaming through the wooden window frames.

We parted at the bottom of the mountain, by the bar of Little Nell's—the music was raucous, the crowds predatory. I could hardly hear Jack's last words above the din, though I remember quite vividly how my hand felt in his when we said goodbye. I walked back to my motel carrying my skis, my shoulders aching.

I knew I would not find him the next day, but caught myself scanning the lift lines for him even so.

Two days later, I returned to my office after lunch to find a message from him on my desk.

He invited me to lunch the following week, and I accepted: It seemed to me that one lunch with a married man could not possibly be considered a transgression (though in my heart I had already sinned, and knew it).

We met at a little bistro in the Village, long since defunct; of the food I remember nothing, save for the color and bite of a kir royale. We spoke about my work, as I recall, and the places I had lived—Brussels, Bonn, Geneva—and about books. He had read *Madame Bovary* since our meeting at the Geneva airport and asked me about Flaubert—the story of his life and how he came to write the novel. I told him what I knew and remember being touched by the hungry way he listened, and by the avidity and intelligence of his questions.

The lunch merely confirmed what I had long ago intuited: He was an unhappily married man. He had met his wife long ago, while he was at Dartmouth, she at Pine Manor. They had married very young; they had four daughters; she was an excellent mother. Yet his searching gaze, his voice, his eagerness to touch, revealed that he could not reconcile himself to a passionless life.

It was four o'clock when we parted.

We met again the next week, at another restaurant—a midtown trattoria this time. I was pale, harried, preoccupied, on deadline, overwhelmed by the feeling that I should never have taken the time to leave my office. But when he entered, at one o'clock precisely, my delight in seeing him was so intense that I could not believe I had ever entertained the thought of cancelling the lunch—like a starving person who, coming upon nourishment, realizes only at that moment the full nature of his cravings.

Through our conversation pulsed the subtext of desire: It was difficult to focus on talk when our eyes insisted on engaging in a dialectic of their own—how and when we would sleep together, and where. Yet nothing of that nature was discussed that afternoon.

He held my hand long and tight as we said goodbye. Had he asked me, at that moment, to spend the afternoon with him I would have said yes without question.

He invited me for a drink three nights later, a Friday in late February; he would pick me up at my apartment. I wore a hooded dark green cape and woolen gloves whose fingers had holes I tried to hide.

The limousine had black, obscuring windows; the leather seats were soft, the interior light dim, luxurious. He sat to the right, in a gray suit, his hand resting by the panel of controls. I fleetingly glimpsed the driver's cap.

His hand upon mine, holding it tight; the pressure of his clear blue eyes. "I need you to survive," he said. I looked away, unable to respond, my throat taut, my mind vortexed by desire; I felt his hand, his gaze, again.

"I only want to be with you," I murmured. He took my hand, pressing his lips again and again to my palm.

I drew my hand away and touched his cheek. "Where— shall we go?" I forced myself to ask.

"Anywhere you like."

I mentioned a restaurant on the West Side, not far from Lincoln Center. He pressed a button, opening the screen that separated us from the driver, to whom he gave directions (the seamless locking of the screen in place). We drove down Fifth Avenue, crossing into Central Park. I have a vague recollection of descending through winding tunnels.

"I never thought . . ." I finally said.

"I know," he murmured. "I know."

He took my hair, twisting it in his hand. "I saw you last night at dinner," he said. "The restaurant—"

"I was with a friend."

"He wanted to sleep with you."

"How do you know?"

"Men *do* know."

Blood rose to my cheeks at the thought of these erotic

signals exchanged by men. I looked away, fingering the buttons of my blouse, pretending to look beyond the window.

He drew me close; my hand, within his jacket, across his perfect shirt. I felt the rounded landscape of his muscles, his wide, hard cuffs. He was warm, impatient, his mouth imploring.

The car had stopped: the restaurant.

"Keep driving," he told the driver gruffly. I remember his eyes—pitilessly focused and yet profoundly elsewhere. He had taken off his jacket; I eased beneath him, on the leather seat, frantic for the pressure of his whole body. Yet he would not rush: I remember with what fierce concentration, how slowly and methodically, he undid each button. His hands and mouth were gentle, expert, unrelenting; I arched my back and shuddered; I never wanted it to end.

Hours later: the welcome cool of sheets, the tangling of our bodies upon the bed.

Only at dawn did we finally fall asleep. When, hours later, I awakened, all that remained of him was a note, beside me on the pillow, signed with thick, angular initials.

I, who had always felt that life was elsewhere, was no longer haunted by that feeling: Life existed where Jack did. The shame I had expected to experience, that squalid feeling —this I never knew at the beginning. Indeed it was the very absence of shame which perplexed me and which, much later, was to produce the dreaded modicum of guilt.

In bed he taught me a language that had no name. To call it sex would only cheapen what we knew together; tenderness or loving-kindness might be closer to the mark, but even then I find myself chafing against the lexicon's constraints. Suffice it to say that he taught me a vocabulary of touch and openness I had never before encountered, or even dreamt existed.

I could ask him anything in bed.

I grew accustomed to his sensitivity and utter concentration, but most of all to his restless, exciting presence during the hours of the night: his arm pulling me close to him so that I could feel its rounded, hard muscles; his lips warm and hungry on the back of my neck. No longer did it seem satisfactory to sleep alone, and when I did, the night seemed endless.

I wonder if he ever guessed the extent to which he had affected my life in this regard—indeed, looking back, I realize I was ambivalent about his knowing it.

My love of visiting places off-season intensified with Jack. Paris and Rome in August; and Russia once, in winter, in early February. Indeed, I count that week in Leningrad and Moscow among the halcyon days of my life—never before or since has cold seemed so voluptuous, never had we been so utterly alone.

We had been to many splendid hotels together, Jack and I, but toward none of them do I feel the same affection and longing than for the two threadbare Russian hotels where we stayed and within whose rooms, furnished with the flotsam and jetsam of a vanished imperial era, we spent our happiest moments. In Russia we were, as we had never been before, *truly free*: free to make love all afternoon, free from prying eyes, free to experience a foreign land together.

We visited places the roll of whose names fills me even now with memory and desire: Petrodvorets, Tsarskoye Selo, Ostankino, Peredelkino, Pavlovsk. Palaces of improbable pastel colors rising from the snow; museums that yielded up to us their treasures.

Yet even then I must have sensed how, all too quickly, those Russian days would end. There was a subtle desperation to the way I clutched at souvenirs: the enameled spoons, and the Lomonosov china teacups, painted with half-open walnuts revealing gilded kernels (and which still seem to impart to any liquid a bittersweet taste). But most of all, the bunch of violets which Jack surprised me with one afternoon in cold, flowerless Moscow and whose petals I had kept, pressed between the pages of *Anna Karenina*.

I picked up that book now from the table by my bed, touching the fragile dried flowers preserved within its pages; then I drew it closer still, trying to recover the last vestige of the violets' scent; but none remained. Still thinking of Russia in winter, and of Jack, I slowly closed the book and set it back in place.

11

The following Tuesday, as Russell Heywood had suggested, I attended the jewelry sale at Hutchinson's.

I never doubted Christina von Shouse would be there: It was only curious that I had envisioned her *precisely this way*. She sat in the third row—a woman of a certain age, as the French say, immaculate and very thin, with the juiceless elegance of a particular breed of New York matron. "A woman who has always just missed," Russell had told me, "with the misfortune of having acquired a taste for rubies."

It was a hot July day, with a moody sky and the threat of thunder.

I choose a seat two rows behind her. Dealers were filing in —talking, sipping coffee from paper cups—and telephones were being set up. It was a good sale as they go, but not a splendid one: "Fine" jewelry, not "Important." The most coveted pieces came from the estate of an eccentric widow from Boston, an invalid who had spent her life hoarding jewelry (visions of an old woman propped up in bed, counting brooches and cataloging species of pearls).

Leafing through the pages of the catalog, I glanced up every so often at Christina von Shouse, trying to divine in that face the good friend, the confidante, of Joanna. She looked at no one else, seemingly oblivious to the goings-on around her, studying her catalog and occasionally marking it with decisive strokes. The precision of her look, its very sureness, fascinated me: the polished layers of her short black hair, with its bold frontal streak of gray; the hard sheen of her pearl earrings against the pale, matte skin; the perfectly delineated stamp of dark red lipstick. Her profile, with its high, severe nose, was reminiscent of Piero's twin portrait of the Montefeltros—at once hawklike and incongruously sweet. There was about her an odd mix of girlishness and the strictness of the *belle laide*.

Moments later, glancing at her watch, she stood up, suddenly impatient, her eyes scanning the room; a small-boned, perfectly groomed woman in a red linen suit and a pair of cufflike gold bracelets, her prettily shaped legs and feet fitted with costly black pumps. She left the room for a moment, clutching her catalog with a charmingly anxious look—her posture impeccable, her movements quick, coltish—only to return minutes later to immerse herself in the catalog once more.

At last the sale began. It was only after twenty lots or so that she raised her paddle, which was number seven, for a twisted-pearl-and-diamond bracelet, a bracelet she did not succeed in getting and which fetched almost three times its estimate. I saw an expression of dismay cross her face, only to be replaced seconds later by her habitual calm.

Ten lots later she tried again, this time for a pair of ruby earrings. Still no luck. She shrugged her shoulders almost imperceptibly and put down her paddle once more.

It was a half hour later, perhaps, that the brooch she coveted appeared: an enormous dark butterfly, pavéd in rubies, seemingly caught in mid-flight, its diamonds *en tremblant*. It was French, according to the catalog description, and had most likely been dismantled from the center of a large, elaborate necklace. I could understand why Christina von Shouse had been drawn to the jewel: its scale and colors, its very boldness, suited her perfectly.

The bidding began slowly. At first she sat quite still, her eyes fixed on the podium, the catalog in her lap. At last, after the low end of the estimate had been passed, she raised her hand. Someone in the back of the room—I strained to see who—had begun to bid against her. She bid again, and then again, always bidding against the one other person in the room who was also determined to get the piece—a dealer perhaps, whose bids were placed with a faint nod and whom I still had not been able to identify, or a telephone bidder. Finally, the bidding having surpassed the high end of the estimate by five thousand dollars, I saw Christina von Shouse's hand, with its red lacquer tips, slowly descend; she placed her paddle beside her and shook her head. The sound of the gavel signaled the end of the bidding. She had lost.

I wondered what she would do now and watched her closely.

For many moments she did not look up, but sat quite motionless. Her feet moved slightly; she coughed; with her left hand she smoothed her hair. Then her face assumed a bright, set expression. It was only her smile that was mysterious—indeed, I thought I discerned a suggestion of triumph in it. Peculiar, because she had lost, after all!

Her head high, her expression inscrutable, she stood up to gather her things. Holding her red umbrella and leaving a trace of tuberose perfume in her wake she left.

* * *

It was easier, having seen her, to imagine calling her.

In the meantime, I continued to find out as much as I could about her background. She had worked, as a young woman, in England; in London, she had married a moderately rich man she divorced soon afterward. A second husband, acquired after she had moved to New York—vaguely in the shipping business—left her what is commonly known as "some money" (enough to live on comfortably, but not lavishly, by New York standards). She had one daughter, from the first marriage, who had committed suicide in the late seventies.

Still, it was Patrick Rossiter's words that reverberated in my mind even as I jotted down the facts of this woman's odd life. "Christina is everything *manqué*: artist, mother, scholar." Scholar? I had asked, thinking that seemed incongruous—an aspect of her personality I would never have surmised. Yes, he had replied, adding that she was an intimate friend of Neville Somerfeld, the British publisher, with whom she shared a mania for history. It was Somerfeld who had encouraged her to write some sort of book, the subject of which she had never disclosed, though some thought it had to do with the decorative arts in tsarist Russia. Apparently, she had been working on this book for years. "And it's to do with Russia?" I queried again. Yes, Patrick had reiterated. "That's her obsession. It has been for a long time—long before it became fashionable." To this he had added: "No doubt the money she 'borrowed' from Joanna was used to fund more of her Russian acquisitions. Or her jewelry. You see, she and Joanna shared a passion for jewelry—" he had paused, "—and for secrets."

She was listed as C. von Shouse in the telephone directory; no address. The following Tuesday, about four-thirty, I called her.

A maid with a Spanish accent answered the telephone. "I will see if madam is here," she told me. A long time passed, it seemed, before I heard a new voice on the other end: a low, lilting voice with an elegant accent verging on the English, a younger voice than the one I had anticipated.

She listened while I explained my reason for calling: the book about Joanna; my research; I had heard so much about her and hoped she might "give me some insight into Joanna Eakins." There was a pause. For a second I thought she might refuse to speak with me. But that did not happen. Instead, she said, "You must come see me later this week—for tea. Does four o'clock on Friday suit you? Perfect." I asked her address: 778 Park Avenue. "Until soon, then," she said.

I put down the phone and took a deep breath: I had expected the call to be much more difficult; I had expected her to resist, to ask many more questions (my background, specific areas of Joanna's life we would discuss). Instead, she had acquiesced in an instant, had invited me to meet her so readily that instead of feeling relieved, I felt—at least for an instant—strangely uneasy.

12

Early the following evening I lay in bed, perspiring and half covered with a sheet, while Jack, beside me, spoke with someone in his office on the telephone. Outside, the summer air was heavy, humid, the curtains motionless by open windows. The air-conditioning had broken down, and murky heat had long since penetrated the rooms of my apartment.

I had raced home from the office to meet Jack late that Wednesday, preparing myself for his arrival with the excitement and anxiety that always preceded our assignations— afraid, as I was increasingly, to deprive his eye of stimulus. Into my skin, parched from the summer sun, I had rubbed a rose-scented lotion; from scented drawers I had taken black satin, lace-edged lingerie.

We made love shortly after Jack's arrival. The heat, coupled with the villagelike quiet of the abandoned city, seemed to have quickened desire: even now I recall the shivery pleasure of Jack's tongue, how frenziedly our bodies came together. Afterward, I lay beside him, spent, while he spoke of numbers, contracts, and stipulations in a language I did not always understand—a language so coldly different from the one he had taught me so expertly, and with such erotic tenderness, in bed.

I remember being fascinated by his ability to shift abruptly from world to world; I remember how the ruthless wielding of his power on the telephone excited me, and that, secure in the knowledge that his ruthlessness did not extend to me, I marveled at how he exercised it elsewhere—at his company, Northtech Communications.

He put down the telephone and sat in silence, his eyes distant. Still gazing ahead, he pressed my hand to his lips before murmuring, "I'd better call home." His family was in East Hampton, as they always were in summer, leaving Jack and me the glorious weekdays to ourselves in the hot, deserted city.

He took his robe from the bed, knotting the belt around his waist. "I'll go into the other room," he said, standing near me.

"No. Stay here. Don't leave me."

"It only upsets you," he replied with a knowing glance. "It's better if I go into the other room."

"No, stay here," I repeated, pulling him toward me; it seemed more prudent to listen than to be left with my imaginings.

He sat down reluctantly and dialed the number from the edge of the bed; meantime, I donned a silk kimono and moved to the dressing table before the window, ostensibly to brush my hair.

He spoke with his wife, Alice, and afterward, with infinitely more tenderness, to each of his four daughters. He asked about the girls' tennis and a match at the Maidstone Club; he asked about their riding lessons and whether they had taken the dogs to the vet. I bit my lip and looked down into the distending, mirrored surface of the dressing table, listening with fascination and resentment to the details of this orderly life. I knew, and yet did not want to know, how much Jack loved his children—how much he loved his eldest daughter, Amanda, especially. I wanted this, our life together, to be his one and only universe. I had come to hate the telephone.

His wife came on the line again. He began to speak of their vacation plans, of Mougins, of a house they had rented there, in the south of France, for August.

At last he said goodbye to her and to his daughters.

"Mougins?" I said, turning to him, a grain of anger in my voice. "You never mentioned France."

"I'm sure I did."

"No, you never did."

"It's only for August."

"There are four weeks in August."

"I'll be back and forth," he replied, adding something about the Concorde.

"Why *France?*" I asked bitterly. It was painful to think of him in Mougins without me—I, who loved France so and who always dreamt of being there with him.

"It was Alice's idea," he said, flipping through a magazine. "For the girls. For their French."

"But *I* speak French, too!" I cried in a voice I hardly recognized, the voice of a pleading, needy creature—the voice I had never let my father hear. "You love to hear me speak French."

"Yes," he reassured me. "I do. I do." He held me tight and whispered, "Say something in French to me now."

I pulled away again and resumed my place before the dressing table, my eyes filled with tears, my entire being overwhelmed with the sordid disarray of my life—its clandestine pleasures and futureless delights. "*When* will you tell her about us?" I asked, turning to face him. "When will you take that step?" I sensed him drawing back, as he did increasingly when the Subject came up.

"Only I can make that determination," he said.

A moment passed; I struggled not to be irritated by his verbose language.

"Come here, darling," he said, taking me in his arms, his mouth momentarily stifling my voice.

"I want to be with you always," I murmured. "I love you so much. I want to give you a son."

But here, even as I felt him grow hot and hard, his mouth stopped me from speaking. "Don't ruin what we have together, darling," he whispered between kisses. "Trust me to do what's best, at the time that's right for us both. You know how much I love you. You know the pleasure you give me . . ." He kissed my hair, my eyelids, my cheeks, lulling me to acquiescence. "I've never loved any woman the way I love you." Then: "Trust me. Be with me. I adore you."

Once more I pulled away and sat before the mirror, barely able to focus on my pale, disheveled reflection.

"Let me watch you dress," he said gently. "I love to watch you dress." I felt his mouth upon my nape. "Let me brush your hair." I gazed into the mirror as he did so, feeling the hard strokes of the brush tingling against my scalp as he murmured, "I love your hair. I wish you hadn't cut it." He ran his fingers through my hair, pressing them against my temples as he looked at my reflection in the mirror. "I love the way it feels."

I smiled gratefully, though still tensely at his words, and began to apply some makeup, searching my reflection all the while for a new wrinkle, a new flaw. I ran my hand across my neck, to a small purplish bruise which I proceeded to conceal with powder, and which made me recall other such bruises—in Leningrad, in Brussels—which I had also concealed, with a queer sort of pride, with fur collars or silk scarves. A year before, two years before, this wound, achieved in lust, might have thrilled me. (For others had, with Jack—a graze upon my lower lip and bruises on the small of my back that had meant forsaking certain bathing suits once, in Positano.)

I began to stand up, but his hands, upon my shoulders, held me down. I felt the rigid cold buckle of his belt and, the next moment, his hands, parting the silk folds of my kimono as he caressed my breasts. Bending over to kiss each nipple— stiff at his touch—he finally asked, "Where shall we go to dinner?"

Silently, I disengaged myself and went to choose a dress.

"Where would you like to go to dinner?" I heard him ask again. From the innermost part of the closet I told him I would like French food.

"Anything you want, darling," he said.

13

It was the handle of Christina von Shouse's umbrella—the red umbrella she had carried at Hutchinson's—that I first glimpsed after stepping off the elevator two days later. The handle was carved of ebony to resemble the head of a black swan, its cabochon sapphire eyes peering from a porcelain stand as if to question me and my intentions, and making me recall in that instant its owner's exit from the auction the previous week—how determinedly she had moved, how firmly she had grasped the black swan handle.

Still feeling hot and disheveled from the brutal heat outside, I rang the bell to her apartment.

For many moments no one answered, so I stood alone in the hall, examining the splendid architectural drawings that

lined the walls: Quarenghi's renderings for the tsar's palace at
Tsarkoye Selo, it seemed. Again I thought of Russell Heywood: "She has a passion for Russian history and objects," he
had told me. "Her apartment is unlike any other. Wait—
you'll see."

A maid in a gray uniform finally appeared, opening the
door with a murmured greeting and bowing her head slightly
as I entered. The room where I now found myself—a stark,
decisive foyer with *faux* stone walls—was air conditioned to
an arctic chilliness. I looked around, shivering slightly as I
continued to study the room. An object spot-lit on a pedestal
in the opposite corner caught my eye. I walked toward it,
marveling at the diminutive ivory statue of a warrior figure
rearing on horseback; I wondered whether it, too, was Russian.

Still cold, I clasped my arms about me, waiting.

The maid returned. "Madam will be here in a moment,"
she said, averting her eyes from mine as she led me into the
drawing room.

No doubt I caught my breath as I entered that remarkable
room, a room redolent of Petersburg *luxe*, whose walls were
painted a rich Slavic blue that was strange, deep and foreign.
I suddenly felt out of place in my light summer dress, though
it was July, for I sensed that this was a place that had never
known summers and from which the vicissitudes of weather
and even time had been excluded.

Meantime, I let my eyes wander, trying to grasp all the
details that contributed to the whole. Never had I felt so
keenly that what I had entered was more than a room but a
whole expression of being, its objects—poised on tabletops,
bureaux plats, and consoles—the evidence of experience and
a distinguished eye.

It was a gracefully proportioned though not vast space, its
ceiling dominated by an inset of a moody blue-gray nineteenth-century "sky" with clouds softly lit by a central crystal
chandelier. I continued to walk about, taking in the smooth
barrel shape of the birch chairs, the portraits of stiff Russian

aristocrats, the blood-red of heavy silk curtains against the blue walls and, finally, the quasibarbaric touch of the leopard-patterned carpet that knit together the whole.

Indeed, nothing that my friend Russell Heywood had told me had prepared me for the utter luxuriousness of the room, the richness of its furniture and objects. I remember thinking that Christina von Shouse must have been left a great deal more than just "a little money" (Russell's words) by her husband—but then Russell's concept of "a little money" had changed of late, for he had become all too accustomed to the vast new fortunes of the eighties.

I was still in the throes of this fascinated and absorbed state when Christina von Shouse finally appeared: a small yet powerful presence next to whom I felt rather too tall, awkward, and skimpily dressed. Her clothes were deceptively simple—narrow black skirt and white silk shirt—her only jewelry a strand of large, lustrous gray pearls. Again I was struck by her singular profile, at once delicate and feral, and by the way she radiated self-possession and control, the sort that comes from having known the darker side of life.

Greeting me and shaking my hand, she said with a solid look, "How good to meet you." Then: "You're not at all what I expected. I would have thought you much older from your voice on the telephone. And from your writing." She smiled, the edges of her mouth, precisely lined in matte blue-red lipstick, turning up slightly. "But then life is full of such surprises." Her voice was low, with a hearty vibrato unexpected in such a frail-looking woman. "Come," she said to me. I noticed her hands, with their red-lacquered nails—capable hands adorned with a single heavy gold ring inset with a scarab in carnelian.

She gestured me to follow her to the library. Its deep red walls were offset by the gleam of wood, brass, and striped satin; at its center stood a handsome round table with a remarkable chess set, its antique pawns in Russian costumes. ("One of my great treasures," she pointed out. "Very Tolstoyan, no?") Placed around the table were chairs, their wooden backs carved out in the shape of hearts. "Biedermeier. Very, very rare," she said, aware that I had noticed them, as she touched the back of one such chair. She went on to say that it was her old friend the French antiquaire Madeleine Castaing who had awakened her passion for antiques, and for the Russian style in particular. "Have you never been to the shop of Madame Castaing in Paris?" she asked, watching me so closely that I felt the question to be almost a test. Yes, I replied, I had been there once, and told her I distinctly remembered the eccentric figure of Madame Castaing—an elderly Hamlet in black tights, sitting in a corner of her shop, with its bizarreries and musty nineteenth-century scent. I went on to tell Christina, her eyes still fixed upon me, that it was only then I had truly understood the expression "the secret life of objects."

"The secret life of objects," she murmured, almost to herself. "Ah, that's very good." Then, to me directly: "Yes, that's exactly the way I would describe Mme. Castaing and her shop—" she shot me another appraising look, "its *ambiance*."

I asked whether she restricted her own collecting to Russian works of art. "I don't like to think of my being restricted to any one thing," she said almost reprovingly, admitting that she also "dabbled in" jewelry. "So I suppose one might say I was a collector of Russian works of art and furniture, jewelry, and—" here she paused almost imperceptibly, *"life experience."*

A small writing table stood in one corner, its surface appointed with antique desk accessories in malachite; there were photographs as well, including several of Joanna Eakins —alone, or with Christina von Shouse. I stepped up closely to study one such photograph, a ravishing portrait of a veiled Joanna as Hedda Gabler, by Cecil Beaton. "The privileges of beauty are enormous," murmured Christina, watching me examining it. "Cocteau was right, was he not? What would he have said, I wonder, about the privileges of talent combined with beauty?" Rearranging the position of the photographs, she looked down in such a way that her profile appeared at its most severe. "In my own case, I have had to rely—" she paused, "on other attributes."

She took up another photograph. "Here she was in *Electra*," Christina said. "And here in *Macbeth*, shortly after I first met her. How young she was! I was living in England at the time. Her first great role, and the one which brought her fame overnight. *Look!*" She handed me the haunting photograph, one I had never seen before, which portrayed Joanna as the young, mad Lady Macbeth in the sleepwalking scene, with serpentine dark hair, hollowed cheeks, lascivious mouth, and wild, demented eyes. "Look closely and you will see that she is actually cross-eyed—she played the entire scene that way, so that she might simulate the expression of a mad person. Brilliant, no? It was that stare which clinched the part for her, you see—her green umbrella."

I asked what she meant by "green umbrella."

"That was what Laurence Olivier called the one detail which clinched a role for him and by which he could envision the whole being—face, mannerisms, walk. Joanna worked rather the same way when she was creating a role—physical details were most important to her. I remember when Joanna began to delve into Hedda Gabler, how she seized upon that one seemingly minor detail given by Ibsen—Hedda's thin hair—and from it constructed the entire icy persona. It was—" she paused again, her gaze almost unnervingly intent, "*uncanny*."

I had put down the *Macbeth* photograph by that time; Christina's red-lacquered nail was already pointing to another. "And here she was as Cleopatra—Shakespeare's Cleopatra, of course," she said, turning to me. "She was unforgettable in that role—you can't imagine!" She gave a deep sigh. "It is possible, I suppose, to muddle one's way through other Shakespearean roles, but Cleopatra is not one of them. A bad Cleopatra is simply *ludicrous*. Joanna knew that and was greatly troubled that she wouldn't be able to live up to the part—the shifting moods, the imperiousness, the girlishness, the sensuality. The fiery poetry, most of all! But she succeeded, as she always did. Splendidly. She was perhaps thirty-five or -six when she played Cleopatra—her last great role."

She set the picture back in place and, turning to me once more, spoke with renewed vehemence. "It is so easy to forget what an artist Joanna was as a very young woman! How deeply talented, how brilliant! She used to loathe my having these photographs about—but I have a reverence for artists, you see, never having succeeded in that way myself. Perhaps that is why I have had to settle for *things*, for *acquisitions*." She gave me another of her decisive looks, as if something within her had been concluded, and continued to let me look around the room.

I had noticed many photographs of a young woman with a reticent expression, a young dark-haired woman who resembled a tentative version of Christina. "You are wondering who this is, aren't you?" Christina said rather eagerly, picking up one such photograph and coming closer: "This was my daughter, Alexandra—how pretty she was, wasn't she? She died eight years ago. Joanna was heartbroken. Devastated. Alexandra was rather like a surrogate daughter to her, you see. Joanna adored her, and had encouraged her to become an actress—as I had—when she was a student at Amherst. 'She has that gift,' Joanna would say to me when we would watch Alexandra onstage, 'that ability to make the audience sit up and take note.' Yes, that was just the way she put it. Joanna was eager that Alexandra train for the stage in London, at RADA, as she had done. Had she lived, my daughter would have been a great actress—of that I am sure!"

She handed the picture to me to examine. I remember the intense awkwardness of that moment—the expression of Christina's eyes altered, had become pained and glazed with a somnabulistic remoteness. "Yes, Joanna wanted her to become an actress," she said again. "But then it didn't work out . . ." Her voice trailed off as I set the picture down. The next instant, however, she resumed her customary patina and said, "Come. I'll show you another room, and then we'll sit down and talk."

We turned right, down another corridor whose walls glimmered with Russian icons, until we came to a small ivory-colored room with muted light and charming birch furniture. Devoid of stylish objects and deep colors, almost monastic in feeling, it seemed to have been wrested from another house entirely. Even its light seemed drained of color, with a distinct purity and whiteness about it. "This was where Joanna liked to stay," she said. "It was always her room when she visited me in New York." I could feel her scrutinizing my reaction. "It surprises you, no?" she asked after a moment.

I answered yes, in a way it did: "But perhaps she found it refreshing after the richness of Wakefield," I murmured in response.

"Precisely," she said in her deep voice, rolling the word slightly so that it was resplendent with a certain exoticism. "There was much about Wakefield that was a *catastrophe*, let us be honest."

I looked about the spare white room once more before Christina finally said, "Perhaps it is time for us to sit and talk."

We made our way back to the drawing room, where a tea tray had been set out on a round table that had three marble sphinxes as supports; on the armchair next to it was a black lizard handbag I assumed to be Christina's. She gestured me to sit down.

I asked if she would permit me to record our conversation.

"Of course," she answered. "I would have expected you to do so." I bent over to start the machine, and as I did so, she noticed my charm bracelet, with its amulets in gold and semiprecious stones. "Pretty, your bracelet," she said. "May I see it?" Examining the little charms more closely, she said, "They almost look Russian"; then, with her characteristic authoritativeness: "But of course they aren't."

She sat up quite straight, keen-eyed, her eyes never wavering from mine as she smoothed a volute-shaped curl of black hair around her ear. "You look chilly," she observed. "We ought to get you a sweater." I acquiesced, for I was very cold; she asked the maid to bring me a cardigan. "I don't like warm weather, you see," she told me when a soft black sweater was brought. "I am rather a winter person. The cold suits me— and my lovely furniture—much, much better." She laughed and then, with a sudden intensity, said in a different voice, "Tell me precisely what it is you want to know about Joanna."

"Everything," I told her definitively, even as I smiled.

"Ah," she quietly exclaimed. "That would take more than an afternoon!" She had grown very serious, and I remember noticing that in the light of the drawing room she suddenly looked old, haggard.

"And to whom have you already spoken?" she said, leaning forward to sip some tea, fingering her gray pearls with her other hand.

"To Patrick Rossiter. Not yet to Rosalind or David Cassel."

"Rosalind," she murmured. "You should be careful of Rosalind. And David, too—but that is something you must know already."

"Why?" I asked, curious to hear what she would say.

"Joanna hated him," she said flatly. "Toward the end of her life she had come to despise him—I'm rather surprised I even have to tell you that." For the first time there was a suggestion of derision in her tone—*naive*, she seemed to say. Resuming her implacable expression, she shrugged slightly, smoothing her black hair once more in that precise, characteristic gesture. "But I suppose that was to be expected, after all. It was such a *ferocious*, sexually charged love affair between them at first—it could not possibly have sustained itself. And whatever he had hoped to get from her—from the marriage—he had already achieved, presumably." To this she added after a moment: "No one denies that it was an excellent merger—their marriage, that is to say." She took another sip of her tea, looking up at me with a charming smile. "I hope I haven't shocked you, my dear."

"Not at all," I reassured her, hoping that she actually believed me. "What you have to say is fascinating."

"It is a long time since I have been called fascinating!" She laughed coquettishly. "Although, in my day . . . Alas, that is ancient history now, as they say. Love is a sickness, a *catastrophe*, after all. I have been through the madness once—" she gave a mock shudder, "and that is quite enough. One must go through it once, like measles or chicken pox, and hope to God that it will never reoccur. But you find what I have to say fascinating. What more could one hope for?" She laughed again.

"I assume David Cassel did not treat you well," I finally told her.

"That goes without saying," she answered calmly, but her eyes registered a modicum of surprise that I should have ventured the observation. "But should I have expected otherwise? He is essentially a person without refinement, without culture. He treated me shabbily, wickedly—as he did Joanna in the end. They will tell you she was sick, she was frail—but what they will not tell you is that *she willed herself to death*. The artist and the woman of creativity he had totally succeeded in destroying, you must understand. In her place was a monster of domestic trivia—*a housekeeper, a decorator*." She pronounced the last words with disgust, as if describing the vilest creatures on earth. "So, you see, Joanna had done what he wanted, and in the end he despised her for it. Perhaps you have heard the old proverb, 'Beware of what you want. You may actually get it.' Well?" She raised her eyebrows in a tired, quizzical expression. For the first time she looked almost ugly, her slight frame curiously diminished.

Moments of silence followed. Sensing her introspection, I knew better than to interrupt her thoughts with my own questions. Finally, her attention seemed to return to me, though for a moment her eyes retained a faraway quality. "But the house was beautiful, of course," she said, expressionless.

It was becoming late, and the light cast by the crystal chandelier above us seemed brighter, more intense, and more unreal across the *trompe l'oeil* clouds of the ceiling. I felt queerly excited yet enervated—once again struck by the singularity of this setting and the woman who had created it.

It was her memories of the marriage of David Cassel and Joanna Eakins that interested me, I told her, trying to fill the strained pause in our conversation. I asked her to tell me more.

"Of course," she said amiably; and after reaching into her handbag and peering into the mirror of her gold compact as she powdered her nose with a swansdown puff (a gesture of vanity or self-contempt, I could not ascertain), she called for some fresh tea and, settling back against the tufted green silk of the armchair, began her recollections.

14

You know, of course, that it was an enormous scandal when they met, Christina said, when David left his wife to marry her. There is always a pattern to the wives men choose—in David's case, he had always liked childless, creative women. Women of independent means, usually—not for any venal purposes, mind you, but simply to preserve his freedom. Such women disturbed his life less. An illusion, of course, but what is life without illusion? His previous wife—his second wife—had been a painter. His first [she furrowed her brow] also had artistic inclinations—precisely what, I can't recall. Neither was famous, of course—as Joanna was—not nearly so accomplished. And neither was—as Joanna was—a *gentile*. David Cassel is an example of that strange phenomenon, you must understand—an "Our Crowd" Jew who longed to be a WASP, a Jew who is at heart deeply anti-Semitic, despite all his donations to the appropriate charities.

He has always been motivated by distinguishing himself from the others—the Jews from other places, who have only recently become rich, those whom he views as being provincial and undignified. You know, do you not, how people always find his candor charming, and I have been told by some how amusing and refreshingly frank it is when he says today, "But I've been rich for many years!" There is of course a reason *why* he says that. His wives were always part of that quest to set himself apart from the rest, from the others— from the corporate raiders, the real estate moguls, the new tycoons for whom he has nothing but contempt. His wives were always part of that ambition: to find a woman accomplished, elegant, and *gentile*. The first two qualities he had succeeded in finding, but the last had still managed to elude him. That is, until he discovered Joanna! The fact that he actually fell in love with her was a pleasant detail—pleasant, charming, but not completely *necessary*. David's attitude toward marriage was, for an American, rather European in approach: *Faute de mieux, on couche avec sa femme*.

And so he romanced her in his spectacular way, taking her for a winter's *séjour* at Saint-Moritz, attending Joanna's performances of *Hedda Gabler* night after night, and always escorting her to the most luxurious restaurants afterward—or perhaps ordering meals sent up to his apartment. His taste in art and women, you understand, is matched only by his lust for good food—he is one of those men who could endure the most miserable liaison as long as it continued to provide him with delicious meals!

It did not take Joanna long to succumb to his charms—in that way, she was as impulsive as he was calculating. That is not to say Joanna was so terribly naive: in her career, never, but that is not the same as the affairs of the heart. *Le coeur a ses raisons que la raison ne connaît point*: Pascal said it centuries ago, my dear, and it is still true, alas. Professionally, Joanna had always been clever. God knows she had used enough men in her time—and why not? But David had caught her off guard at a vulnerable moment in her life, at a time when even she had begun to tire a little of her career and of her fame and of seeing men solely for the purpose of advancing her work. As for David—it came as a surprise to him that the physical aspects of love he had always associated with the girls from Madame Claude, and the socially inferior women whom he had always relied upon for life's less exalted purposes [here she smiled], were not wanting in a woman who was also intelligent and refined. I'm sure you must know men like that, my dear—men who never think that the two qualities could possibly coexist!

It was for Joanna the *coup de foudre* that we are all bound to experience at one time or another, some earlier in life, some later: Falling in love is a madness at any age, but never more so than when it occurs as a woman approaches forty! For then it has the quality of the last gasp, after all. And here was a man whom she admired and who, in his world, had matched her in accomplishment. And who was amusing and made her laugh, and—let us not neglect this!—who succeeded in showing her a certain part of life that until then had been curtained off, shall we say.

This surprises you, no doubt, for she had played at passion beautifully. When one thinks of the erotic scenes she had simulated in front of endless audiences! Even her early Lady Macbeth was so chillingly sensual—and of course there was her famous Cleopatra. But you see, in real life—and here you must trust me—*she had simply never known it.*

No, let me correct that—she had known it only once before. But that was long ago, after all, and by the time she met David she was almost forty, and despairing that she would ever be settled in any way. And like so many unfortunate women who come to that point in middle age, she would do anything, anything at all, to grasp it! You cannot imagine how, when this happened, how it turned her life upside down. It was touching, it was *pathetic*, to see this brilliant woman, this artist, reduced to madness, to obsession. Suddenly, there was nothing else in her life but David Cassel and how she would appear to him. Whether he would in some strange way *approve* of her.

I remember one day in particular when Joanna called me to her apartment in a frantic state. I thought something awful had happened—she was in *Hedda Gabler* at the time— but no, it was simply that David Cassel had invited her to lunch and she could not decide what to wear, how to present herself. And so here it began—the preoccupation with clothes, with appearance, with the right mention in the right social column. It took my restraint not to tell her how revolting I thought this was—although ultimately I *would* tell her, and in the end I like to think she was grateful for my advice. She had never really ventured into that world—*his world*— the world of New York society, you see, and fashionable restaurants and the *beau monde* that had always so attracted him and with which he had always surrounded himself. Her days had always been devoted to work, to discipline, to preparing for the performance that night. And now here was a woman who had transfixed audiences in Shakespeare, in Ibsen, in Chekhov, terrified about appearing at La Caravelle for lunch!

One would think she would have been above that, that she would have felt superior: She was famous, she was an artist, she was acquainted with fashionable London society, after all. But no, not at all—that was the pity of it!

But I was recalling the afternoon when she called me, wasn't I? Yes . . . I arrived at her apartment—she was living on Central Park South—to find everything in great chaos, the bed strewn with dresses of every style and color, Joanna without makeup, unable to decide which she should put on: "Tell me," I remember her nearly pleading with me. "What do they wear, the women at these places? How should I look for him?" It was frightening, it was *ridiculous*, to see an artist of her stature reduced to a silly woman who could not decide what dress to put on!

But this was a side of Joanna which David never saw: She was much too clever, and too determined! He saw the enchantress only, for any weaknesses she concealed from him. He took her shooting at an estate he owned, at that time, in Scotland. Shooting was something which rather fascinated her—she had been to Africa years before—the echo of the shots, the ritual, even the carnage. In his younger days David was an avid sportsman, you know—quite a formidable shot. He loved to fish, he loved to be on his boat in the ocean for hours at a time—she suffered from a fearful seasickness, but this, too, she endured for him, forcing herself to accompany him. I myself have a stomach of iron and went with them several times—and there was Joanna violently sick, wretching from seasickness, but always staying below so that *he would never discover what she construed as weakness.* You might think she ceased to accompany him on those fishing trips—but no, not at all! She continued to force herself to go, again and again, vomiting each time until I thought she could withstand no more, until the moment finally came when she had conquered it. She became an expert fisherman—or fisherwoman, I should say!

You must understand that I had the special perspective of having known Joanna and David, separately, for many years. I had met her first in Hampshire one weekend, at the house of a mutual friend—how well I remember her! She had leapt to fame with *Macbeth*, of course. Still, she was young and inexperienced and woefully insecure in—shall we say—worldly matters. We soon came to be close friends. I like to think I was helpful in my small way. I did so admire her talent, and then of course we shared a passion for Shakespeare. I would help her learn her lines, I would advise her on her costumes —as well as the more mundane aspects of her life, the sort of things one would never expect an artist to bother with!

So, you see, I knew her well, long before her first marriage to Teddy Bennett—a neurosurgeon, Rosalind's father. It was

a time when she was drawn to a certain intellectual type of
man—quite unlike David Cassel, needless to say! Like many
essentially cold men, Teddy was fascinated, at least in
women, by the flamboyant; Joanna thrilled to his *sangfroid*.
Curious, no? Their attraction to one another was not without
a hint of mutual voyeurism. I'm quite sure she fell in love
when she first watched him operate—the idea that he could,
quite literally, dissect the mind! And he, of course, was besotted with her acting. Ah yes, how well I remember him in
the audience, riveted by Joanna in *Measure for Measure*. She
played Isabella, of course—an irony that did not escape me,
mind you, for there was more than a touch of Angelo in
Teddy Bennett! The fact that he had admired her first *from
the audience* was a prerequisite for Joanna in matters of the
heart. You must simply take my word for it, my dear: Joanna
could never sleep with a man unless he had seen her first
onstage.

Teddy was a widower—tall, cerebral, with beautiful fingers
and a radiant, ascetic smile. I never really liked him. Rosalind
was small then—perhaps six years old when they married, in
'61 or so. He lived in Eaton Square; I had a small house in
Kensington—Gore Street, actually. I was already married
then—my daughter, Alexandra, was four years old at the
time. We would dine with Joanna and Teddy fairly frequently, although even my first husband—who was in the
import-export business—found Teddy rather tiresome—one
of the few opinions we shared, I realize in retrospect!

I thought the marriage to Teddy a mistake from the beginning and told Joanna so. As it turned out, I was quite right in
my predictions: As so often happens, the very quality that
had attracted one to the other was precisely the thing that
drew them apart—his *sangfroid*, her volatility, that is to say.
After a year or so it evolved into a *mariage blanc*, with Joanna
seeking her pleasures elsewhere.

I continued to see her a great deal, despite the dour influence of Teddy. Then, sadly, things changed: I left for India
with my husband and little daughter. Moved to Bombay,

ghastly place—two infernal years we spent there! But of course I kept in touch with my dear friend. We would ring each other up several times a week; we would correspond. She was a splendid letter writer, as you may have heard. I did my very best to follow her career and managed to get to London whenever possible to see her onstage. Ah, how well I remember that dreadful, provincial period in my life! How I would devour the cultural pages of *The Times* and *The Observer* . . .

It was during my absence that Joanna's career entered its first *rocky* phase—you can only imagine the anguish that this caused me, being so far away! When she performed, she was simply brilliant. Increasingly, though, she would cancel performances, claiming something was not right: a spat with her director or a problem with her health—the bronchitis and respiratory illnesses that had always plagued her. And then something else, equally perplexing, began to trouble her. She began to have a very difficult time memorizing her lines: Often she would resort to transcribing the entire part on paper herself, simply to brand the words on her mind. For those of us who had known her earlier, the idea of her having to do this was simply *unthinkable*. She, who had always been able to learn a role with lightning speed!

But as I think back—as I so often do, my dear—I can see the seeds of those troubles much, much earlier. The season of *Medea* and *As You Like It*—in '55 or so. Patrick Rossiter was there that afternoon as well, the two of us waiting for Joanna to begin. Finally, she staggered onto the stage, only to collapse moments later. At first I thought she was trying a new tack—but then I knew something was wrong, something dreadful had happened: *The words would not come.* And there we were, the two of us, alone with this fragile, incoherent creature! Patrick hadn't a clue what to do—thank God I was there! Even now I shudder each time I recall it—how pale her face, how disjointed the words she finally managed to string together as she looked up helplessly at me! But you see, *I* was there to help her, to hold her hand, soothe her nerves. I hesitate to say this, at the risk of sounding self-serving—*but, you see, I was the only person Joanna ever really trusted.*

Imagine, then, how difficult it must have been for her when I left for India—and how thrilling it was, two years later, when we were reunited. I was divorced by that time and had returned to London with my daughter. Only then did I realize how much I had missed my old friend, had missed reveling in her talent! We met for tea at the Ritz the day after my return. December 9, 1963—yes, I remember everything about it: the jasmine perfume she wore, the blue wool dress from Balmain, the new *coiffure*, the sound of that heavenly voice! She looked lovely, elegant—so different from the insecure young woman in tawdry clothes I had first remembered meeting. We talked and talked, about everything and everyone. It was very late when we left—I remember everyone else was ordering *apéritifs*. She seemed so happy I was back: She took my hand and said, in that searching way of hers, "It will be like the old days again, won't it, Tina?" I reassured her that it *would* be the same, I would be there to help her, though of course it could never quite be the same. We had new lives, new demands, after all. She was married, she had a stepdaughter. I was divorced, I had my darling little Alexandra.

We soon grew close again . . . it was a *lovely* time! Joanna and I would go on walks together, have tea or visit an exhibition on those days she was performing. We would discuss her roles—what approach to take, her costumes. And of course she confided in me, as she did no one else. She would tell me about the men who would come see her in her dressing room—ostensibly as fans, but hoping for much more. You can only *imagine* the men—the powerful men—who would pay court to her! She would imitate them—the seductive lines they fed her, the lavish presents—she would tell me *everything*. Of course she had affairs with many of them. Why not? She was an artist, after all—that was part of her privilege. But these were small matters compared to my con-

cern for her *career*, her talent. I was so completely relieved
that the symptoms of stage fright, and of illness—real or
imaginary—had seemed to abate.

Yes, we were quite inseparable—drawn even closer
through our daughters. Or, in Joanna's case, her stepdaughter. My Alexandra, her Rosalind, were close in age you see. It
must have been difficult for Joanna to watch my own little
girl, who was so much more charming and lovable than the
child she had inherited and whom she tried, unsuccessfully,
to shape. Even then Rosalind was an astonishingly calculating and spiteful eight-year-old, with not the slightest interest
in the playthings of most little girls. I have an enduring
image of her playing for hours with her collection of knights
or with her abacus—those plump little fingers moving rows
of black beads. The fascination, at that early age, with numbers!

But *my* child—my Alexandra—was a creature of fantasy, of
the imagination, a romantic little girl! Rather like Joanna
herself at that age, I liked to think. I remember Joanna turning to me one day when Alexandra was dressed in a fairy
costume, playing a game of make-believe. "If only Rosalind
were like *that!*" she said with a bitter sigh. Almost as if she
were jealous of me—*imagine!*

I would take the girls to the theater whenever possible—I
did so want to enlarge my daughter's world. To the dress
rehearsal of *Midsummer Night's Dream* that winter. A
splendid Edwardian production, with Joanna as Titania. The
three of us, sitting in the darkness, waiting for the curtain to
go up. How wonderful Joanna looked, her neck swathed in
lace! And how entranced my little Alexandra was—she
hardly drew a breath. Rosalind, naturally, looked sour, bored.
I took the children backstage afterward—I remember how
thrilled Joanna was to see us, to see my Alexandra, especially.
She took her on her knee and showed her the makeup
brushes, the jars of greasepaint, the trunk with her costumes.
You can imagine how enthralled my daughter was, what an
impression that visit made on her . . .

Yes, those years in London, the mid-sixties, were full indeed, an exciting time in every way. But they were not without difficulty for Joanna: There was always Teddy's disapproval to contend with, and bitter little Rosalind. Whether these things affected her career, I cannot say with complete certitude—yet how could they have not? She had some glorious successes, of course, but there were rough patches as well. The problem with stage fright did not go away, alas—by '65 or so it had become rather worse. I began to see rumblings of it that winter—her Nina in *The Seagull*. But, you see, there the aura of fear, of tentativeness, rather suited the part—the failed provincial actress—so I did not think much of it. Then came Lulu in that terribly controversial production of *Pandora's Box*. One of those angry young men directed it—his name escapes me at the moment. She had begun to veer from Shakespeare, wanted to stretch her wings with more experimental productions—the influence of Olivier's Archie Rice, no doubt! One might have thought Joanna was perfectly suited to the part. Her Lulu was simply terrifying and defiant in its sexuality, no question; but then she had always excelled in playing sensual, self-destructive creatures—that was what made her Cleopatra, her Lady Macbeth, so marvelous, after all. But the Lulu took its toll on her—the morbid fear of forgetting her lines, the recurrent nightmares, the nausea. She missed rehearsals, she cut her hair terribly short—quite unflattering, I thought. She had become dreadfully thin, preoccupied. I remember the awful tension of the last dress rehearsal—the company's fear that Joanna would simply refuse to go on.

Over the years we had evolved certain little rituals to help us through, Joanna and I—the makeup brushes arranged precisely so, the rouge in a gold pot with her initials always on the right, the dressing gown she had worn since *Macbeth* folded on top of the trunk where she kept her old costumes. How many times we would sift through the trunk, folding those jeweled gowns and capes and mantles, recalling one performance or another! Each afternoon I would cover all the mirrors of her dressing room with scarves; late in the day, we would uncover them together, one by one—it was a way of assessing her state of mind, you see. If she avoided the mirrors—well then, I knew we were in trouble! "You won't let me get away with *anything*, will you, Tina?" she would say.

So, you see, my life was doubly full then: I was *needed*—by my best friend and by my daughter. Joanna absolutely doted on Alexandra—anyone could see it! How she would spoil her, with presents and theater tickets and all sorts of treats. She must have known that the way to my heart was through my daughter—I rather *lived* for her, you must understand!

It was during that very troubled time of *Pandora's Box* that Joanna organized Alexandra's tenth birthday party—in May of '67. What pains she took to set it up in my garden on Gore Street! She had a diminutive stage erected, in the gothic style, all in white and gold. It was exquisitely done—she had spent a fortune on it. There were small gilt chairs for the audience, comprised of children, mostly—Rosalind came, of course—and engraved programs which listed the various "acts." Classic fairy tales, mostly, with Joanna and a few actor friends taking part.

But the most touching moment of all occurred at the beginning, when Joanna stunned us by appearing in white and blue Elizabethan costume, embroidered with *fleur-de-lis*. She assumed the stage herself and began to recite those splendid opening lines of the chorus from *Henry V*: "O, for a muse of fire—." It had always been one of her very favorite speeches from Shakespeare, but never did I—or anyone else who was there that day, even the children who had gathered —feel its magic as keenly as I did that moment when Joanna, in her beautiful clear voice, began to recite the words of the chorus. Her eyes were suddenly intense and bright, her face wondrously alive as she conjured up that "heaven of invention." No one stirred; no one's eyes wavered until she had uttered the last syllable. She had succeeded in communicating what they could not really understand, you see—which is, after all, the essence of Shakespeare! It was an extraordinarily poignant moment. When I think of Joanna, as I invariably do, from day to day—*that* is how I think of her, not as the spectral self she eventually became.

Alexandra's birthday was perhaps the only peaceful moment of that jinxed Lulu period. The next month, Teddy had a massive heart attack—dead in an instant. To Joanna's credit, she behaved quite correctly afterward—toward Teddy's family, toward Rosalind. There were also changes in my own life: I had begun to feel restless, tired of British rigidity and the atrocious climate! I had a new beau as well, a New Yorker, who not much later asked me to marry him; he was a kind, solid sort of person—I thought he would be good to my daughter. I sold my house in Kensington and left for Manhattan. Not without a long soul-searching talk with Joanna, of course—you can imagine how this filled her with trepidation, to think of me on the other side of the Atlantic! I urged her to come to New York, to accept an engagement there as soon as she could, with Rosalind.

All of this I tell you as a prelude to Joanna's meeting David Cassel—the *mise en scène*, so to speak, which you, as a writer, should appreciate! I had met him—David—through my second husband, who was quite a prominent businessman. We got on—what is that expression—like a house on fire, David and I, though I was less than enthusiastic about his wife. Rather a bore, I thought. As it turned out, Joanna came to New York the following spring. There was great excitement about it—she was to do *Hedda Gabler*. Of course I was *thrilled*, and arranged a little dinner for her after the opening night. David Cassel came. I had suspected he might be entranced by her, but even I was surprised by the way it simply *ignited*. There was no other word to describe it. At the end of the evening, they were already in a world of their own— *égoïsme à deux* at its most revolting and extreme. They seemed aware of no one else. I took this with good nature, even though it very nearly ruined my dinner party.

David, of course, was still married—his wife, poor well-meaning creature, was also there. I did feel for her—it was so obvious what had happened: Midway through the dinner, he ignored the wife entirely. But no one ever said life was fair, and in New York, you know, *everyone* is quite available, don't you agree? At least I have always found it so.

Then came the clandestine courtship, then the divorce—a very public divorce, as you know. Really quite a scandal. It was only David's relationship with the publishers of the major newspapers that kept the publicity at a minimum. But then he has never hesitated to exert his power in that way—that's something you should be aware of, my dear. Rosalind stayed with Joanna after her father's death. She was twelve at the time. Joanna, out of guilt, out of some vestige of feeling, continued to take care of her. Joanna was not an ideal stepmother, I'm sure, just as she would not have been an ideal mother.

But I'm rambling, I know. You look impatient. You want me to continue in an orderly way, I can tell by your eyes. Very American, that impatience!

And so, after going through all the messiness that accompanies such things, Joanna and David were married, in 1970. Only a handful of friends came, myself among them. It was a quiet, tasteful ceremony at David's apartment, presided over by a judge he had chosen. It is vivid to me still, that scene—Joanna in the palest green suit, looking peaceful, lovely, the two of them standing in that beautiful drawing room, surrounded by David's extraordinary *quattrocento* paintings and glorious furniture. Some find it ironic, of course, that David has chosen to amass—over a great many years—such a quantity of Italian religious paintings and Old Master drawings. But that is not so surprising, is it, when you know him well? It is part of his removing himself from the rest of the pack, you see; it is part of his compulsion to crush out his background.

You ought to speak to the curators who have worked with him, the art dealers he has trampled over—they, almost more than anyone else, could show you the ruthless side of David Cassel. The hunt, the chase for the perfect object or

painting, was always paramount with him—they will tell you
how he would call in the middle of the night to discuss some
minor flaw in a contemplated purchase. Flaws of any kind
frightened him, you see; and Joanna had succeeded in convincing him that she was *perfect*. It was a role, like any other,
which she adopted when she met David. But roles have a way
of coming to the end of their run. And this was no exception.

She continued to work, although I—who knew her so well
—could tell, for the first time, that her heart was not in it.
The time had come for her to attend to other things, to
setting up her life with David. And of course here he expected a great deal: It would never have occurred to him that
she should not attend on him, as had all the other women in
his life. And if she did not—well, there would always be
others, others in his circle who were bored, others entranced
by his power and money, others who could be bought. He
had always subscribed to the services of Madame Claude,
and it was not long after they were married that he continued to do so.

Again I've wandered a bit—you must understand that it is
hard for me to make these recollections into a tidy bundle!
By this time she was not acting; she had chosen to take a
respite from it all, although many offers had come her way—
in England, at the National, she was asked to do *Macbeth*
again, as I recall. A mature Lady Macbeth this time. Of
course she said no—ostensibly, because she did not want to
leave David, but also because she had a horror of playing a
"menopausal Lady M," as she called her. "At that age she'd
be too old to be ambitious," I remember Joanna saying,
rather wearily—paraphrasing Tynan, of course. There came a
point when she was asked to play what she called the "old
lady" parts in plays where she, as a young actress, had once
had success. Madame Arkadina in *The Seagull*, even Gertrude in *Hamlet*. In the late seventies or so, Visconti wanted
her for the film of *Death in Venice*, the part that eventually
went to Silvana Mangano—they were just the same age and
rather resembled one another, after all. But here again

Joanna refused; besides, the cinema had never attracted her —how could it have had, without the thrill of an audience? "I need to *feel* them there, below me," she'd say. Didn't Ken Tynan once compare Larry Olivier to a "dominating lover"? Well then, my dear, think of Joanna in much the same way!

Yes, she was no longer young—perhaps that was why she set her sights elsewhere, on *temporal* things. She wanted, she *desperately* wanted, a house in the countryside—a house like those she had visited in England. There, of course, she had never been fully accepted; there, she had always been an outsider looking in. Here it would be different: Her husband was a man of power, of influence. And, of course, he was very rich—she could afford almost anything she wanted. They began to look in all the expected places—the North Shore, Newport. Westchester, of course, was out of the question: David associated it with an earlier epoch of his life, with the afternoons at the Century Club and the dreary evenings with his first wife.

Finally, they settled on the Berkshires and the land near Lenox. "I want a heaven of my own invention," I remember her telling me. "Like Thistleton." You have been to Thistleton? No? Ah, well you should go there. I know the owner well—he has remained a close friend. It's really impossible to understand what drove Joanna without going to Thistleton.

It was in the autumn of '71, as I recall, that they first went to Lenox. She fell in love with the landscape there and the town and the history of all the great nineteenth-century houses that had been built in the surrounding area, many of which had fallen into disrepair. And of course the Mount— Edith Wharton's house—had always fascinated her. Nor was it immaterial that the area, the Berkshires, had a name which even *sounded* English. And then there were Tanglewood and the Williamstown Theater Festival—that appealed to her artistic sense, the idea that there would be fellow performers in the area. They looked at several houses, but when they saw Wakefield Hall, there was simply no question they had found their dream. The fact that the name, Wakefield, is actually mentioned in Shakespeare—the battle of Wakefield, in *Henry VI*—yes, even that seemed a good omen! They had found it just in time, in fact, for a developer had recently looked at Wakefield and there had been talk of converting it into a hotel or condominiums or something equally hideous.

David was as enthusiastic as she, for he had come to a point in his life when the idea of being the country squire appealed to him, at least temporarily. In fact, he had little interest in the house, its decoration and so forth. He is quite the urban animal, David, when all is said and done. Even so, he no longer had the same need to go to his office on Wall Street every day—Bernham, Worth would come to Dunsinane, so to speak. A bad pun, I know!

She became immersed in—obsessed is perhaps a more accurate description—Wakefield. The search for the decorator had begun, and then the landscape artist. Philip Thurston, an Englishman, was chosen—a frightful snob if ever there was one, something which appealed to Joanna in a curious way, just as David's money and power appealed to Thurston. But the decorator, that was a difficult quest! Joanna summoned several from New York. She had become rather imperious in this quest, had become used to the money, the private secretaries, people obeying her commands—the seamless, streamlined life of the very rich. It was only later in her life when she would realize the true elegance of thrift, of *savoir faire*. I saw it so clearly, alas. Like so many women who marry rich men, she had developed a curious amnesia about the past—suddenly, it was as if her past had fallen into the sea, had never in fact existed. It had always been thus, it seemed to her. She began to take on that dogmatic tone that such women often assume—this is the best, that is the best—a tone which is meant to pass for real knowledge. I had a talk with her one day and said it must stop, that she was becoming a terrible bore. She listened to me, I like to think.

None of the American interior decorators pleased her. Finally, she decided on the Englishman Simon Gower, who had once worked with John Fowler. And then, as the architect, she chose Lawrence Brandt. You haven't met him yet, I take it? Only once, then? Ah well, that doesn't really count. He is brilliant and ruthless—charming too, of course, when it suits him. Joanna came to adore and respect him—a happy collaboration, really, though I did not always approve of what he did. They were on the same wavelength, you might say, and he got along quite well with Gower. They were an exceptional team—Gower and Brandt—though Larry was quite young then, of course. And even then, drivingly ambitious.

But the difference was really Joanna. Houses and decoration were not her natural forte—at least I have never thought so. But she forced herself to become extremely knowledgeable, forced herself to become an expert in all the domestic minutiae which at other moments in her life had so disinterested her. But of course there was David, and the question of pleasing him. She had, by this time, all but stopped acting. That is not to say she hadn't been offered parts—not at all! But her work, at least ostensibly, had ceased to be the passion of her life: Wakefield, instead, had supplanted it. *Wakefield was all.*

Two crucial events occurred then. The first—and of course you know about this—was the article that appeared in *The New York Times Magazine*, the cover story called "The Unfulfilled Promise of Joanna Eakins." How that morning is seared in my memory! I was staying at the house, and I remember having breakfast in that charming little Edwardian breakfast room with Joanna, and how impatient she was that Sunday morning to read the newspaper and to delve into the crossword puzzles she loved and for which she had a demonic aptitude. "Why hasn't it come yet?" I remember her saying so impatiently, ringing the bell for the butler. Even now, that moment seems so curiously vivid: Joanna, in her dressing gown, and I, sipping my coffee in that little conservatory room. But the newspaper did not come—and finally, after an hour, during which time she had become totally impatient,

David entered. His eyes were dark, preoccupied. I knew something had happened, but I did not immediately associate it with the absent newspaper. Joanna asked what had happened, and finally David, with some reluctance, rang for the butler and asked for it. And then, of course, when we saw the cover of the *Times* magazine—which David could no longer hide from us—well then, we knew the reason!

The story devastated her, it was that simple. Her face went ashen; the light extinguished from her eyes. It wasn't an unfair story, mind you—but no matter. The worst was its effect on Joanna. It took months for her to recover, months for her even to appear in public.

The awful part of this, of course, was that David himself was not unaffected by this event. His wife, in his eyes, was no longer quite the success he had imagined her. The article had tarnished his perception of Joanna. He began, however subtly, to mock her.

By then, of course, the house was quite complete. The gardens had been laid out, the library pavilion finished, the interior work in good order. She then became obsessed with having a child. Early in her life she had lost a child, you see, and she was convinced that she must try again at all cost. This was, let me see, perhaps 1974—she was about forty-two at the time, not the easiest age to become pregnant in the best of circumstances, and in Joanna's case it was especially complicated. Even so, she did finally succeed. But at the same moment she also—strangely, or perhaps not so strangely—embarked on a program of exercise and very long, rigorous walks. "To keep fit," I remember her telling me, "so that I don't become hideous and fat." Why she did this I will never quite understand, for the nausea she experienced in that pregnancy was frightful, alarming. But still she forced herself to walk and walk. On one of these excursions around the property—and the property includes several hundred acres, as you know—she caught cold and suffered a miscarriage not long afterward. She was devastated—grieving, guilty. As she well might have been . . .

Two children, then, she had not succeeded in bringing to birth! First, years before, a boy, and then a girl. This obsessed her, as if it had been her fault, as if she had done this consciously. Willed it, as it were. I told her this was nonsense, but even I could not manage to convince her. And in a sort of madness, she began to think she could communicate with the children she had lost—the first child, particularly. She sought out mediums and psychics and asked me to accompany her to séances, where these charlatans would claim to be able to communicate with the children! It was by far the darkest period of a life that had known its dark periods, I assure you.

David became increasingly impatient, not surprisingly— impatient and scornful. He had married this lovely creature who had not only charmed him onstage but entranced him, at least in the beginning, in what is commonly known as 'real life,' and then she had changed. She no longer acted, no longer had the passion of her work to sustain her, was no longer regarded as a prodigy, and—perhaps this was the deadliest aspect of all—*she was totally dependent on him.* To be a woman of taste, a dreary woman of society, was what she wanted—or thought she wanted! It was the one role that had always eluded her, you see. But it also happened to be the one thing that David did not want her to become.

She had done everything she could to transform Wakefield into a paradise—attended to all the details, organized it so that it seemed to run effortlessly—*and in the end, he only despised her for it.* The house mattered not one whit to him, you see—he preferred Joanna famous, a celebrated actress, not a *hausfrau.* Joanna met this realization with shock, with bewilderment. She couldn't escape, of course, for she had no real money of her own. Her own money had been badly managed, and besides, money of her own making had never really interested her, never seemed totally real. And she had never worked with money in mind—acting was a vocation. She had always acted for the sheer joy of it: 'It's the only way out for me,' she would say. She was an artist! And now David no longer admired her, for she had become like all the other needy women driven for his approval—that is the strange and terrible thing!

I remember one night, at dinner, when the three of us were together and Joanna mentioned a bracelet she had recently bought. David immediately cut in and corrected her, "The bracelet *I* bought for you, Joanna," he told her. And she, instead of responding as she should have—with a sharp retort at his rudeness—merely looked up with those dark, clear eyes and said, "Of course, David. The bracelet *you* bought for me."

She had begun to be terribly anxious about her age— fearful, as ever, of losing her memory and of losing her beauty. She took strange vitamin pills and injections; she would go for weeks eating nothing but fish, claiming it was good for the brain cells. Her dressing table at that time was a mass of cosmetics that promised to restore skin to its youthfulness and to arrest aging. She experimented with her hair, which had never satisfied her—she had always had difficult hair—and thought of changing its color. But I dissuaded her from it.

Finally, to my great relief, Patrick Rossiter persuaded her to play Hermione, the queen in *The Winter's Tale*—it had become one of her favorite Shakespearean plays. "The most mysterious," she always said. At last, I thought, the work would save her! She returned to New York to prepare for the role—a small but memorable one—and was brilliant in the rehearsals, which I was fortunate enough to attend. She had recaptured her old self—wearing little makeup now and no jewelry and the same black dress every day for rehearsal. When she was truly working well, she could not even focus on the way she dressed. But the horrifying thing was that the stage fright had finally tightened its grip upon her. The first night, with that glittering audience, she simply fell apart, unable to remember her lines or her stage directions, vomiting with fear as she waited in the wings—even my presence was not enough to soothe her! The second night was even worse; there was the smell of Scotch on her breath even as she waited in the wings. . . . She was replaced soon afterward by Gwen Hamilton, who was a bit young for the part. Joanna never appeared onstage again.

She went to psychiatrists and all sorts of experts, looking for the secret that would unravel this illness, the stage fright. In her own mind, it was linked somehow to the children she had lost—a strange notion, I always thought, but the mind is a queer place of its own, with its own labyrinths and alleys and dark closed-off corridors. Perhaps the theory was not so ridiculous—and certainly those whom she consulted never were able to help her much or to find other reasons for her being unable to act again before an audience!

David was increasingly disgusted, cutting. There was talk, one night at dinner, of a trip to the south of France to visit friends, and I remember how quick David was to cut in, "Joanna isn't *up to it*," he said. That was always the expression he would come to use—Joanna was not up to it. Entertaining, acting, going to New York, traveling. And gradually, of course, their relationship having evolved in this way, he succeeded in convincing her that she was indeed not up to much of anything. But was it so surprising, really? Their liaison was, from the very beginning, destined to fail—the funereal progression from the *coup de foudre* to the final disenchantment. An eternal phenomenon, no? Their liaison was founded on a passion that was sure to extinguish itself. It was founded, to no small extent, on self-hate and the need to extinguish the real self—not on self-love! It had become a *disaster*—for David, but even more so for Joanna.

15

I wonder if anyone who visited the house ever guessed it, Christina continued. Everything was beautiful, so fastidiously and seemingly effortlessly organized. The irony, of course, was the deadliness of this perfection for Joanna! The more the house was under her control, the less control she had over her own life, her own desires, her own great creative gifts. I think she herself sensed that, you see, but she was incapable, by that time, of doing something about it. Of leaving David. Something had gripped her, gripped her soul and paralyzed it. To this day, I wonder exactly what it was.

It was a dreadful, infernal period: David's affairs were whispered about first, then discussed with much ribaldry, at lunch and dinner. The girls in New York, girls in Paris, girls in

London—the women he propositioned at dinners and called in the middle of the night. (I would give you names, but there—I am being discreet!) Everyone knew, of course, except Joanna—for a time at least, although God knows she must have sensed it. God knows she had suffered enough fulfilling David's, let us say, idiosyncratic sexual demands. When a year or so later she did discover that he was lying to her, that there were other quests to be enjoyed, she was desperately hurt and bewildered, almost shell-shocked. As one incapable of her own distress, one might say . . . Joanna would have appreciated that phrase and agreed with me, no doubt, for Ophelia was one of her very earliest roles, was it not? It was a pity that the role in the Olivier film went to Jean Simmons; I have always thought that Joanna would have been sublime, original! But, alas, the part did not go to her . . .

Meantime, life at Wakefield had assumed its own rhythm. David and Joanna had always had separate bedrooms. He disliked seeing her without makeup—it disconcerted him— and she, too, had become reticent about appearing without the accoutrements of a rich, well-groomed woman. A hairdresser came every evening when she was dressing for dinner, and a makeup artist as well—a habit she had picked up from the duchess of Windsor. Whereas before, when she was acting, she had never fussed very much over her looks, now they seemed to obsess her. The mirror worship was endless. I began to chide her about this, accusing her of becoming tiresome and spoiled. "I have my reputation to maintain, Christina," she would reply. Yet I remember her eyes looked defeated.

They had settled into a period of intense mutual disillusionment—with each other, with each other's friends, but most killingly of all, with each other's career. He had begun to tire of what he called her "childlike personality"—her need to be immersed in another life, the life of a character she was playing onstage. Nor did she continue to be dazzled by his work. It had lost its glamour for her. It seemed like so much crassness—that was the word she used, as I recall—so much manipulation. She did not get along with many of his friends, his colleagues. She had a reverence for real intelligence, for intellect, and had come to think of David's circle, and of David's pleasures, as deeply vulgar and dull.

Even in bed—from what she intimated to me—she was increasingly repulsed by him and by his demands. Their sexual entrancement with each other—the attraction that had fueled their courtship and driven them to marriage—this too was finished. "His idea of pleasure is my idea of humiliation," she told me once, bitterly. She would reveal nothing else about it—nor did it ever even occur to me to inquire what she meant! Still, I have often wondered exactly what she meant and whether her final letter to David—the letter she left him at her death—was partly meant as a measure of retaliation.

And then something else occurred, this when she had studied and learned more about decor, gardens, and objects. She began to question his taste, his eye in art and furniture. A dangerous thing when a woman begins to question a man's taste—I have always thought it bodes ill for the future.

So you see the passionate period, the drunken *égoïsme à deux*—all this had dissipated, and finally they were left with each other, and the house. No children—ah, except for Rosalind, that is. But she was another man's and another woman's daughter, though she would have preferred to have been thought of as David's own. This was not surprising—she had always alternated between love and hate for Joanna, and she had always been mad for power. David epitomized all of that! Rosalind stepped in to fill the gap when the relationship between David and Joanna began to founder. The worst husbands can be the best fathers—or stepfathers—if they are kindred spirits. And David and Rosalind *were* kindred spirits—both hungry for power, both gifted in making money, both unwaveringly secular in their ambitions. Queer, isn't it, because Rosalind looks so angelic! And yet she is a bond trader, of all things.

David's affairs up to this point had been conducted seria-tim with all sorts of women—now this, too, began to change. He took a mistress—a proper mistress, a Frenchwoman, quite young—and they were often seen openly at the Hotel Du Cap. A more conspicuous place to humiliate Joanna he simply could not have chosen. She knew this—as did we all —of course! By then she was at a point past caring. It was so different from the other times, when David's affairs had ac-tually driven Joanna to be wild with jealousy. But by this time Joanna seemed beyond jealousy and self-reproach. She had reconciled herself to her life. She no longer spoke of divorce—she thought of her marriage as a job like any other. Still, I felt her *searching*. Her sexual hunger, which had abated with depression, began to reassert itself. She had flings with other men, younger men whom she knew she would never see again.

Then, at a dinner in New York, she met William Verey, the historian, the Arabist—perhaps you may have heard of him? He was, I admit, an extraordinarily attractive fellow—blond, handsome, an intellectual who spoke innumerable languages . . . How tragic when he was killed last year! Joanna was besotted with Bill, and he with her. He *admired* her intensely —that was no doubt part of it. He was perhaps five years younger than she and at the height of his success, having just published his brilliant study of the Muslim world. She would stay more and more often in the city, at her suite at the Carlyle, and would occasionally visit Bill in Nantucket, where he had a house.

It was not surprising to me that she chose him as a lover, for she could talk with him about things that mattered to her: books, the theater—all the things she had loved and which she had, at least temporarily, cast aside for David. Indeed, Bill almost succeeded in convincing her to return to acting, but at the end Joanna could not get herself to do it. The stage fright—the fear of stage fright, rather—was still too daunting. I remember Bill telling me once—this after her death, for he was a discreet man—how Joanna would often awaken at night, mad with fear that she had forgotten her lines, pursued by nightmares that she was wandering naked and voiceless through a series of rented rooms. It would not take Sigmund Freud to decipher those dreams, would it, my dear? There were other nightmares as well, he told me, others less frequent, though no less terrifying to her—dreams of being alone on an endless road, a child grasping her hand.

For a short time it seemed that the affair with Bill had provided her with a certain tranquility. And it seemed—at least for a moment—to make her stronger, better able to deal with David and his slights. And with Rosalind! Rosalind is a difficult girl—she can be charming, too, of course. I say this knowing all the while that she will do well in New York—she has that toughness, the *sangfroid*, all this coupled with the disarming face! When I first met her, I thought her simply mysterious, but now I know better.

What else can I tell you, my dear? Or have I spoken too much already? About the very last years of Joanna's life I can tell you a little. It is quite unbearably painful for me to speak of it. She and Bill continued to be lovers, and for a while, this seemed to soothe her. There was never any question she would ask David for a divorce. She had discarded everything else, you see—her talent, her acting—and she was now all too accustomed to the money and the luxury! A prisoner in the house she had begged him to buy for her—

There were only two hopeful elements of that dreadful time—Joanna's interest in my own daughter and in the maze at Wakefield. I suppose I should tell you about my daughter first: Joanna and Alexandra's affection for one another had only intensified through the years. "Lend her to me anytime," Joanna would say with a sad laugh. And so, in effect, I did: Alexandra's talent for acting was such that I could not have found a better mentor—nor one who was more encouraging and supportive! All through boarding school, and then through college, Joanna was her greatest fan. She would come to Amherst to see Alexandra in every play—in *Private Lives* one year, in *A Doll's House* another. You can only imagine what a stir this caused, how proud my Alexandra was to have Joanna Eakins visit! Joanna was determined that Alexandra follow in her footsteps, that she go to RADA—"I won't *rest* until I see her there!" she would say. The sour note in this was, of course, Rosalind's jealousy. My Alexandra was talented, charming, and beautiful; Rosalind was—*Rosalind.* Her only defense, I suppose, was her closeness with her stepfather, David. They simply *adored* one another. At Wakefield they were seldom apart, and when David was in the city, he would often have Rosalind come down from Cambridge to go to dinners with him.

So you see how lucky it was for Joanna to have had my own daughter to nurture; and then, as I mentioned, there was her obsession with the maze. It was about that same time she came to be fascinated by the idea of creating a maze on the property—a maze similar to the one she had known at Thistleton, and which I, too, had known as a younger woman. I had also been a friend of the owner's, Desmond Kerrith, you see. Larry Brandt was sent over to Thistleton to study its plan and to devise a maze appropriate for Wakefield. The maze at Thistleton, originally designed by Brown and Repton, was of course a much wilder maze than the one created for Joanna—it had hairpin turns, an almost vertiginous quality. And it had fallen into decay. Joanna's maze, which you've seen, no doubt, is symmetrical and far more contained. When it was first built, she decided it was not elaborate enough—it needed to be more challenging, more intricate. "More *diabolical,*" she'd say, with that mischievous look. She embarked on even more research, again with Larry Brandt. She studied Greek and Roman labyrinths and others, in medieval France, Italy, and England. She became quite a scholar in all sorts of arcane maze lore.

It was partly to continue her research into mazes that she went to London in the summer of 1985. I only recall the date because there was something in that visit that seemed to irreparably change Joanna. Looking back, I struggle to understand what had happened in London, on that trip, that

seemed to alter her life! I suspect it was her visiting friends
there and seeing the theater and fully comprehending the
extent of her unrealized ambitions! Her contemporaries were
still acting—they had acquired a rhythm and purpose to
their lives—and she felt she had discarded all of that for
money, for empty social ambition, to compete in a world
where she had no business competing.

She had developed a sort of mania about this, a jealousy
toward younger actresses. . . . It was not in the least attractive. Something in her had snapped—*à la recherche du temps
perdu*, perhaps, coupled with the knowledge that she had
squandered her quite considerable gifts.

I noticed a harrowing change in her when she returned.
The will to live, to discipline herself, even to exercise (as if
that was the only sense of control over her inner self!)
seemed to have evaporated entirely and was replaced by *a
will to die.* By then it was too late for anyone to help her.
"There is no one in me," I remember her saying toward the
end, when each day, each meal, had become a struggle, a
battleground of discipline: herself against a darker self.

She cut off her friends. She refused to see William Verey.
She seldom came to the city anymore, preferring instead to
lock herself up at Wakefield—her love of privacy having become something of a mania. For a time she seemed obsessed
by revisiting the mediums she had once consulted. But even
that had lost its charm, and I remember once, after a séance
with a certain Madame Stella, that she seemed disgusted.
"That sloppy charlatan," she called her.

She was only fifty-three, you must understand! Thinking
back, I cannot decide whether she looked much younger or
much older. Her eyes, certainly, had taken on a very ancient
look. She seldom wore any of her beautiful clothes anymore,
but had adopted a sort of country uniform: a long black skirt,
black sweater, no jewelry except for a curious bracelet about
her wrist. Nor would she eat—or barely enough to keep the
meekest creature alive! She would subsist on consommé,

made to her specifications, and a bit of fruit or pudding—
that was all.

Wakefield she did not neglect, though—if anything, she
redoubled her efforts to perfect it. Never do I recall it looking
more splendid, each room like a painting of the ideal house
in the countryside. It had become her habit to stay in her
bedroom each morning, tending to the household duties and
writing some letters—she was a marvelous letter writer,
Joanna, when she chose to be. Sometimes she walked and
walked for hours, only returning shortly before dinner. Other
days she never left her room at all. She answered the telephone almost never—even toward the telephone she seemed
to have developed a deep strange fear. Often she would remain in her room the entire day. Other times she set off
around the property, inspecting the maze.

And as you know, that was where they discovered her that
morning—by the gate to the maze. Dead of heart failure,
brought on by malnutrition and by the diet pills she had
come to depend upon. Yes, that was where they found her,
near the maze.

I helped them clear out her things after she died, although
some rooms were kept exactly as they always had been. Her
bedroom has remained the same. Her clothes are still there—
the books and all the paraphernalia of her life. The mauve
octagonal room downstairs, her study—that David left, too,
just as it was during Joanna's life. Her writing papers, her
books, her favorite needlepoint pillows, and the collection of
hourglasses—all left exactly as she had liked them.

In death, David seemed to grant the attention that he had
denied her during a great part of their marriage. Her funeral
was beautiful, every detail meticulously thought out by
David himself. For however much she seemed to have
wanted to embrace death, Joanna had not been able to bring
herself to the point of planning her own funeral. Curious,
because she was such a perfectionist about ritual—it was
among the things she so admired about the English! I have
no love for David Cassel, as you know, but in that regard I

must admit he behaved correctly. Perhaps it was the sense of
Wakefield and its extraordinary perfection that made him
think differently of Joanna after her death. In death, you see,
she achieved the faultlessness, in his eyes at least, that he
had found lacking in her while she lived. Only then did he
speak of her again with admiration.

So many famous people came to her funeral on that autumn afternoon. Both David and the house seemed in their
element—shining, proud, serene. Still, it was not possible for
this to obliterate my memories of the last days of her life—
memories that are almost too painful for me to describe,
even now. Those of a strange mad creature who refused to
eat anything but an allotted amount of broth and who
seemed to have pitted all her anger, all her hatred, against
herself, against David. She who had always feared him so,
now, in the certainty of her impending death, spared no word
against him. She told me in detail how he had, on so many
occasions, humiliated her with his affairs and in other ways
that seemed too traumatic for her to discuss—even with me,
her old friend! How he had torn her down in front of others,
how he had subtly destroyed her sense of self and mocked
her work. I suppose most of this was true, you know—but
even I would not say that it was *all* true. And David, by this
time seeing her so far removed from the enchanting woman
he had once known, began to show a certain pity and tenderness toward her. These overtures she rebuffed. Perhaps she
wanted to be left alone with darling self, so to speak—or
alone with darling *despised* self, I should say.

I think back so often on the last time I saw her. She was
going through old photographs and letters late that afternoon, putting everything in order. "Splendid order!" she said
with a heavy sigh at one point. "There's something morbid
and final about so much order, isn't there, Tina?" She continued to go through her papers and folders until at last,
when all was done, she turned to me and began to reminisce:
"Don't you remember, Tina, when we were at Thistleton
together going over my lines, playing with my costumes—

that old trunk, in the tower, with all my trophies? I'd leave them in a heap on the floor, and you'd always straighten them up, folding them one after the other, so beautifully. You never asked for help, for *anything!* You've always been such a stalwart person." Yes, those were exactly her words. Then she suddenly assumed another voice, the voice I had not heard since she'd played Shakespeare: " 'The crown imperial, the intertissued robe of gold and pearl—' " She stopped, turning to me with a strange look—exactly the look I remembered from that hideous rehearsal when the stage fright first seized her, with *Medea*. " '. . . the intertissued robe of gold and pearl,' " she slowly repeated. "I always thought those were the most beautiful words in the English language. I can't imagine how I could have lived all these years without Shakespeare's words. How I could have cut them out of my life and never been brave enough to acknowledge how much joy they gave me. Or how terrible it was when I could no longer remember them." She glanced around the room—that perfect octagonal room—and said, almost with disgust, "For *this*. For *order*."

She disappeared that night and was found dead the next morning, by the gate to the maze, early in September. I am told she had left a letter for David, a letter to be opened after her death, in which she told him how deeply she hated him and why—you did not know that, then? Yes indeed. It is true. And I have often wondered—as I'm sure you would—how one could possibly cope with that, with the hand twisting up from the grave! I doubt even David, for all his strength, could have remained unscathed by it. And I have often wondered where that letter is, whether it still exists.

Ah, I feel exhausted by these memories. . . . Strange how I feel I have relived those years here, this afternoon! I have talked on and on. . . . There is more I could tell you, but I am simply too tired, my dear, and this has taken longer than I ever dreamt. And good heavens, look at the time—it's already half past six!

16

Christina von Shouse had stopped speaking and sat quite still against the armchair's deep green silk, her hand resting in such a way that I noticed, once again, the carnelian scarab of her massive gold ring.

Even now it is strange how vividly I recall that moment of sudden silence, and the minutiae that seemed to delineate it, wrenching me from the realm of her recollections: the taste of my tea, which had grown cold, and the soft yet deliberate sounds of the table being set for dinner in the room beyond—the sounds of silver, crystal, and porcelain placed upon wood; and her hand, always her hand, with its sturdy veins and massive ring, resting on the arm of her chair. Outside, the thick yellowish light had changed, had become

more translucent, intimating that the torrid heat had subsided, however slightly.

I felt overwhelmed by fatigue suddenly, having listened to
Christina with a dual intensity—scrutinizing her and her
character at the same time I had analyzed her descriptions of
Joanna. There were so many other questions I should have
asked, I realize now, in retrospect—yet another instance
when I have been afflicted with what the French so pictur-
esquely call *l'esprit de l'escalier*. At the time, it was only the
broad strokes of her sketch that I grasped and, in doing so,
the nature of her relationship with Joanna: the artist and the
artist *manqué*, the beauty and the *belle laide*—the latter the
most powerful of all, for strong indeed is the woman who has
confronted the fact that she is not pretty and makes of herself a different sort of creation. Christina had many talents, I
sensed, not the least of which was a seeming lack of self-
absorption—remarkable in this neurotic city!

Looking back, I remember it was her attitude that struck
me—her self-possession, her seeming lack of any inner struggle with her memories. Her thoughts had already turned
elsewhere: to the present; to the dinner she was about to
give; and to me.

"So," she said. "Has this helped you?" She paused. "I have
talked a blue streak, as they say. I have confused you, perhaps."

Not at all, I reassured her, dissembling slightly, for it
seemed better not to indicate how unsettled I was by her
recollections—her account of Joanna's marriage to David
Cassel particularly, but most of all her description of
Joanna's vengeful posthumous letter. I wondered what actually lay at the root of Christina's hatred of David Cassel; but
there would be time enough to find out.

I asked if she would allow me to see the letters Joanna had
written her.

"I'm afraid they no longer exist," she replied with dismay.
"Joanna made me promise I would destroy them."

"Was that a promise Joanna asked of all her friends?" I said, watching her expression.

"That remains to be seen, no?" She raised her brow slightly as she paused, smoothing her hair with her ringed hand. "And you," she said, turning to me with a new vigor, her voice very clear and clipped. "Have you lived long in New York?"

I said I had lived here ten years and had begun working for the *Journal* immediately after graduating from college.

"May I ask your age?" she queried next.

I told her I was thirty-one. "Ah," she murmured. "Only slightly older than my Alexandra would have been." Then: "And you are not married?"

"No," I replied.

"And you never have been?"

"No," I said, slightly irked by her questions.

But she continued to persist, asking me where I was from and where my parents lived; it seemed to her that my family name was familiar. "That would surprise me," I told her with some reticence, adding that my father, Norman Rowan, had died earlier that year.

"The spelling of your first name—unusual for an American."

"I was born in France."

"Of course." A pause. "So you are quite alone in the city, aren't you?" she observed in the same familiar tone; and then, perhaps sensing my reserve, she said almost apologetically, "I hope you don't mind my asking. I'm very *maternal*, you see." I felt her scrutinizing the pearl earrings Jack had given me, instantaneously assessing their value and quality. "So you are alone," she repeated, her eyes continuing their scrutiny. "Not easy, I should think, for a young woman in this city. On the other hand, you have your work. It must be riveting to have such interesting work—a sort of *mission*."

I sensed she wanted me to say more about my own life, but the more she pressed me, the more reticent I felt, merely continuing to gather my things—notebook, pens, tape recorder—as I went on to mention, in a voice that I now remember as being unnecessarily brusque, that I would undoubtably need to speak with her again. "Of course," she said without hesitation. "That goes without saying." She leaned forward to put my teacup and saucer, and then hers, on the tray before us, neatly mopping up some spilled tea with the edge of a linen napkin monogrammed with her large crimson initials. "I assume you'll see Lawrence Brandt as well," she said without looking up.

I said yes, I intended to call him soon to try and make an appointment.

"He will have his own point of view, of course," she said, facing me once more. "And then David has been a very good client of his, so I would counsel you to keep that in mind. He is an interesting man, Lawrence—not easy to know and frightfully ambitious. Joanna liked to describe him as having a 'voluptuous mind.' " There was more than a touch of derision in her voice. "That is a quality I never saw. But it's up to you, of course, to form your own opinion." She paused, adding, "He is a man who has never suffered—a dangerous species, that! But you must know others like him, surely."

I looked at her, unable to conceal my surprise. Looking back, I should have caught this veiled reference to Jack. But I did not realize it then, and merely continued to gather my things, overwhelmed by a sudden desire to flee, to be outside and collect my thoughts.

We stood up, passing through the drawing room and, from there, to the entrance of the stylish pale green dining room—the table set for six, the wood gleaming, the smell of some exquisite dish wafting its way from the kitchen. The whole *mise en scène* of a small summer dinner in the city, perfectly executed: thick, spotless linen napkins, shining flatware in silver and agate, and a set of memorable Russian plates (white porcelain bordered with a design of moiré ribbon entwined with leaves). It seemed characteristic of her that she should have organized this faultless, somewhat formal table in the middle of the summer's heat while others had relaxed their standards.

"You must come to dine one evening," she said, undoubtedly aware of my gaze, perhaps even of my thoughts. "In September, perhaps." Whether she expected more enthusiasm on my part I do not know, for she quickly added, "Although I'm sure you must be very busy."

"Everyone is busy in New York," I answered, grasping my notebook and feeling very much the schoolgirl.

"Yes—busyness is the disease of the city, isn't it?" she said with a sigh. Then, wryly: "I have never lived in a place that lent itself so little to contemplation—or to *real* learning and *real* accomplishment, for that matter."

We came to the entrance hall, its light nocturnal now, its pair of twisted candelabra beckoning to be lit, anticipating the arrival of other visitors, with other agendas. I walked to the diminutive equestrian statue that I had noticed on arriving and asked her whether it, too, was Russian.

"Of course," she answered, with a delight so intense it surprised me. "It is my very favorite, you know! I found it long ago in Paris, in a shop on the quai Voltaire. It's a copy of the wonderful statue in Leningrad of Peter the Great by Falconet—charming, isn't it? For me it brings back so many memories, you must understand!" Her voice became unexpectedly chatty. "Long ago, as a very young woman, I spent several months, in the dead of winter, in Leningrad." She ran her finger across the surface of the diminutive marble figure and then across its base, inscribed with Cyrillic lettering. "I shall never forget it. I had a friend then, a Russian, whom I'd gone to visit. It had begun as a flirt, one might say, and then . . . He was an artist—" She paused, then continued with an almost girlish coyness: "They've a great reverence for artists—the Russians, that is. Perhaps that's why I have always felt such an affinity with them!" She laughed, but it was an interior laugh, a laugh that seemed to evoke her as a much younger woman—almost pretty, even flirtatious. "Yes, a daring thing, wasn't it, to install oneself, a foreigner, in an apartment near the Nevsky Prospekt!" She pronounced the last name with a perfect Slavic accent, savoring each foreign syllable. "I was eighteen. He was considerably older. What he taught me about life—amazing now, to think of it! It was a bitter cold winter. The snow was high, the light of the city was blue and frozen. There was not much food . . . But then June came—and I shall never forget my first glimpse of the Winter Palace at midnight, during the white nights! That dazzling palette of northern colors, and the sky! It was one of the most unforgettable moments of my entire life." She stopped abruptly, as if she had caught herself exhibiting a rare lack of self-discipline, and returned the next instant to the polished self, the unreflective self she had so suavely brandished before.

In a bright, suddenly extroverted voice, her eyes fixed on me, she said, "You have never been to Russia, I take it?"

"Yes," I replied, adding that I had been to Russia earlier that year, in February.

"Ah—you've been there, then, *in winter* as well! The most Russian of seasons. So you know. We have *that* bond, then! It is unforgettable, isn't it, to see those splendid cities in the snow?"

I murmured something vague in response, momentarily unable to focus on her reminiscences: inwardly, I was recalling my own trip to Russia, with Jack—the savage, elegiac cold of Leningrad, the trees heavy with hoarfrost, and the long, dark afternoons we had spent together making love in shabby hotel rooms. I absentmindedly picked up a familiar object from a nearby table, running my hand along its surface—a Lomonosov china teacup painted with half-open walnuts. Jack had bought me a set of such cups from a little shop on the Nevsky Prospekt.

"Well then, you must know," she continued fervently, interrupting my wandering thoughts. "Didn't Russia change your life?"

I paused, overcome by my own memories of Russia. I put

down the teacup. "Yes," I said, lowering my gaze. "Russia made a great impression on me."

"As it did on me as a young woman," she responded emphatically. "Unquestionably, yes. So we have that in common, you see. That, and your fascination for—what was that phrase you used? Ah yes, 'the secret life of objects.'"

She escorted me to the hall outside, with its neoclassic mirror and porcelain vase filled with fragrant tuberoses and freesia. I caught my reflection in the mirror, and remember it was only then that I fully realized how much taller and more robust I was than she.

One last question occurred to me as I pressed the elevator button. "Tell me," I said, turning to her. "You seem to condemn Joanna for her fascination with society, yet you yourself are such a part of all that!"

"True," she concurred, with a knowing smile. "But there is a crucial difference, you see. It does not *matter* to me." The elevator arrived. "Until soon, then," she said with a small precise wave.

The elevator door slowly closed, and I descended.

17

Several weeks passed. Meantime, I continued my investigation, all the while puzzling over my meeting with Christina von Shouse. The seductive unreality of the pseudo-Russian apartment continued to fascinate and disturb me. I would listen to the tape of our conversation late at night—sometimes after speaking on the telephone with Jack —only to realize that the stories, wrenched from the setting where they had been related, seemed more than subtly altered. Yet I could not understand the exact nature of the change or why the setting should have had this incantatory effect. Christina's words seemed strangely intermingled with the colors and objects of her apartment—the blue of lapis

lazuli and the gleam of red satin—as if one element needed
the other in order to exist.

One day Russell Heywood called, curious about my interview with Christina von Shouse. I told him it had gone well,
but that there were several elements I found puzzling; I
asked if he would meet me for lunch the following day. He
immediately agreed, as I had known he would, for there was a
devilish, baroque side of Russell that seemed in keeping with
his taste in jewelry and furniture, his love of intrigue, and his
spicy wit. (Russell on a newly sedate woman who had recently landed an elderly billionaire, for instance: "The more
sluttish prematrimony, the more matronly post-.")

We met the next day at the Corinth Coffee Shop on
Lexington Avenue, not far from Hutchinson's, on a swelter-
ingly hot afternoon, though Russell looked habitually cool
and Byronic, his tall lean figure in a tan summer suit, his
black hair pulled back in its dramatic ponytail. I kissed him
on both cheeks, half jokingly adding that I had never known
anyone from Kansas City—his hometown—"who could so
easily pass as Euro-trash." At this he pretended to be miffed,
but I knew him well enough to know that part of him was
secretly delighted.

I asked whether Christina had succeeded in fetching anything at the jewelry auction I had recently attended.

"No," he replied. "She hasn't bought anything for a long
time. Plays at it, though, like a pro. I think it's become a
game for her. She hasn't a lot of money, you know—never
did." His eyes scanned the menu. We ordered lunch.

"But was there ever a time," I asked, "when she was spending a lot of money—for jewelry, furniture?"

"About seven, eight years ago," he said, looking up. "Before things started to go really high."

Our sandwiches arrived; we began to eat. I mentioned that
I had been rather startled by the luxuriousness of Christina's
apartment, that it seemed excessive for someone who had
been left, as he had put it, "a little money" by a former

husband. "Where do you think the money has been coming from?" I asked.

"No idea," he replied offhandedly, and then, divining something from my expression: "You think someone's been helping her along? Giving her money?"

"Maybe," I mused. I suddenly remembered what Patrick Rossiter had told me weeks before, a detail I had somehow forgotten—that the money Christina had "borrowed" from Joanna was used to fund the former's acquisitions. I asked Russell whether he had ever suspected that Joanna Eakins Cassel may have been supporting Christina's extravagances.

He said it was possible—if unlikely—as they often came to viewings together. "Especially the Russian sales. Some of the jewelry sales, too."

I wondered aloud what could have motivated Joanna to support her friend's luxurious tastes.

"Who knows, in this town? Maybe Christina felt that Joanna owed her one. It's all about power—and gratitude."

"And guilt," I ventured, almost to myself. "Patrick Rossiter told me that Christina and Joanna had a passion for jewelry, and for secrets."

"He *would*, the old queen," Russell retorted.

I laughed. "You don't think he's a reliable source, then?"

"Reliable—yes. But only to a point. Probably has his own ax to grind. But then who doesn't?"

I went on to say that Christina had also mentioned a last, bitter letter that Joanna had supposedly written to David Cassel, which was to have been given him after her death.

"Sure, I've heard that," Russell replied matter-of-factly. "But I've chalked it up to rumor. One of the many rumors making the rounds of Park Avenue."

We finished lunch and stepped outside into the searing heat. I asked whether he was preparing for an upcoming sale.

"For September," he said with a nod, taking my arm. "Important jewelry."

"Not 'Magnificent'?" I teased him.

"No," he replied, a mischievous look in his eyes. "This

happens to be one that even our friend Christina could afford."

When I turned to focus on the architect Lawrence Brandt, I found myself unable to disassociate him from Christina's harsh words. "Be careful of him," she had told me. "He is a man who has never suffered—you must know others like him in New York." "Drivingly ambitious" was the way she had put it, and then, most disturbingly of all, "a destroyer of women." Yet she had also told me that Joanna had described him as having a "voluptuous mind."

It was this last description that I found at once intriguing and unsettling: It seemed at odds with my own first impression of Brandt, for he was not a total stranger to me. I had actually met him some years ago, with Jack, at the inauguration of a building Brandt had designed for Northtech's new offices in Seattle. We had stood together in the frigid December cold with a group of Jack's executives, the wind cutting the edges of the monumental building, I, slightly to the back, in a fur coat Jack had given me. The building itself was powerful and, in its daring reinterpretation of the neoclassic, quite courageous. I remember catching my breath as I stepped inside the singular entrance, with its splendid sweep of steps, its towering columns, and its elegant oval skylights, which vaguely recalled the work of Soane. Jack and Brandt had stood together at a distance from me; Jack, with his light hair, his fair skin ruddy from cold, played host in his jovial way. Next to him, the architect: tall, dark, and arrogant. I remember that his looks unsettled me, as one would be disturbed, upon awakening, by the atmosphere of a dream. Even now, as I struggle to re-create how I first remember Lawrence Brandt, I can only say this, and even then haltingly: Think of a man who is tall and almost ungainly but within whose seemingly discordant, uncompromising features there is a kind of charm—enhanced by his beautiful voice and by his manners. Having said this, I admit I did not like him that afternoon, for I had found him unnervingly cold, subtly dis-approving—too conscious, perhaps, of his talent, intellect, and reputation. Indeed, I remember thinking that even his gentlemanly manners were not born out of true consider-ation but, rather, out of contempt—a way of keeping people at bay.

There had been a lunch in the executive dining room after the short inaugural ceremony. Brandt sat on the opposite side of the table, two places from Jack. I noticed that Brandt did not, as the others did, defer to Jack at all. No doubt Jack found this refreshing, for he respected talent, and Brandt's talent was large. And so the lunch proceeded. I made conver-sation with the gentleman next to me (whose name I do not remember), my gaze escaping all the while to the man who had created the room and the building that contained us. I tried to speak with him at one point, but Brandt said very little in response. By the end of the lunch I concluded that his brilliance as an architect was only matched by his aloof-ness. Most of all I remember how appraisingly, even cyni-cally, he had looked at me as we parted—as if I were wearing a placard around my neck on which someone had written THE SCREW.

I never saw Lawrence Brandt again, though I occasionally read about his work and his career in *The New York Times* or in magazines: a building complex outside of Barcelona; an-other outside Frankfurt; an award he had received at Prince-ton. And then one day, about a year later, I picked up an issue of *Town & Country* that had on its cover a close-up of a blonde with startling aristocratic looks: sapphire-blue eyes with a thick fringe of lashes, the head balanced on a neck that seemed to support it only by an act of legerdemain, delicate bare shoulders, and—unusual for a magazine that tends to hawk such things—no jewelry at all. That she was completely unadorned by gold or precious stones seemed to reiterate the air of confidence in her own beauty which radi-ated from the photograph's subject. I was curious to see whom this classic face belonged to and turned to the cover description inside: It was Isabelle Carpenter Brandt, Lawrence's wife.

And now, nearly two years later, on a Saturday in September, I would meet Brandt to question him about Joanna. I wondered whether his wife would be there and what she would be like. When I had first called his office to set up the appointment, I was told that it would be impossible for me to see him within the next month—he would be traveling here and abroad. I had continued to insist, however, and when the secretary mentioned that he would be at his house in East Hampton one weekend, I suggested that I meet him there. Surely he could spare an hour of his time on a Saturday afternoon! Finally, she acquiesced and the appointment was set.

The following week I went to the morgue at *Time* and then to the research library to read what I could about him in *Who's Who*. Born in St. Louis; educated at Harvard; served in the air force in Vietnam 1969–70; prizes—Pritzker, Prix de Rome. Marriage to Isabelle Carpenter. It was the mention of Vietnam that somewhat surprised me. I would have thought that, being a privileged member of his generation, he would have maneuvered his way out of military service. The fact that he had not intrigued me.

I would drive to Long Island the following weekend, on a Saturday morning, to meet him.

18

It was late afternoon on the third Saturday of September when I found the house of Lawrence Brandt. The weather was glorious, the light with the poignant clarity that accompanies the clean north winds of early autumn. This was the first time I had been to East Hampton that season: My work and the book on Joanna had kept me in the city.

I had left my apartment that morning, thinking I would take a walk on the beach before my appointment with Brandt at four-thirty. I was glad to have set out early, for the turbulent Atlantic never seemed more beautiful than it did that afternoon—the water an icy purplish-blue, the thunderous breakers monumental. I walked and thought, rehearsing the questions I wanted to ask Brandt about Joanna, all the while trying to prevent my thoughts from wandering to Jack, who was with his wife and family in Greenwich.

Jack had a house in East Hampton as well. I had recently seen photographs of it in *Architectural Digest* and remembered with some amusement how Jack had scrutinized the plans and elevations, all the while complaining of the cost of construction: The house had become increasingly complex and extravagant as the building progressed. It suddenly occurred to me that I should try to find the house. I gathered my things, brushed the sand from my feet, and asked a passerby the directions to Further Lane.

The house was not difficult to spot. A sign in florid script with *Belleplage*—the French name insisted upon by Alice Varady—was set conspicuously by the road. I turned into the driveway until I came to the gate and, from that vantage point, scrutinized the house itself—a severe, even sculptural structure of glass and wood linked by a network of curving white rails.

I started the car and drove up the driveway, past a silver sports car I knew to be Jack's. To the left, in the distance, stood a tennis court, the awning of its gray-and-white-striped gazebo fluttering in the wind.

Wind blew, animating the tall beach grass along the dunes of the abandoned house; all else was silent. I walked toward the lacquered white door, surrounded on each side by glass, and peered inside, mesmerized. How many times had I imagined this house—the family warmth and domestic order it represented! Fascinated, I assessed the decor, absorbing each table, chair, and object: a rack with straw hats, a pair of green gardening gloves next to a basket piled with sunglasses, a clutch of bright umbrellas in a brass stand. The rooms were attractively, if conventionally, furnished: a few obligatory antique pieces relieved the eye of the monotony of the serviceable sofas, with their tightly woven wicker frames and smooth white cushions. Everything looked as if it had been eternally set in place—a comfortable, if unsensual, room with an absence of fluidity.

I continued to scrutinize the objects, as if they comprised the pieces of a mosaic depicting the mistress of the house. I knew how Alice Varady loved Belleplage; I pictured her here, inserting her hand into that spotless green glove, taking a pair of sunglasses from the basket, calling to her daughters to come for a walk on the beach. They would stroll along the dunes together, she and her girls, each wearing a protective hat plucked from that rack. Alice was fair-skinned; from these rooms, I gathered she was meticulous; I knew Jack disliked freckles.

I looked to the right, at the broad staircase of bleached wood. To each side of its shallow lower steps stood pair after pair of shoes—women's, girls', and men's—all perfectly arranged. The sight of those sprightly, expectant, well-worn shoes somehow sparked such anger, resentment, and self-disgust within me that I felt nauseated. Shame and confusion overwhelmed me. Here I stood, reduced to the jealous girlfriend, sneaking around my lover's house, my nose pressed quite literally against the glass, unsure whether I wanted to destroy what I saw or seize it for myself.

I covered my face with my hands, then I looked up, gazing at the taunting rooms again, thinking how safe and orderly they were, and yet—and this I realized with a shivery power —how *fragile*. I, the intruder, could choose whether or not Jack's family would continue to live in blissful ignorance or whether I would rip apart that peace. What would I be, generous or vindictive? My head began to pound. I almost felt faint, yet I continued to stand there and stare, driven by a demonic, masochistic curiosity. Again and again I asked myself the same questions: Why has he not left his wife? When will he marry me? And lastly, but no less painfully, would I still be with him if he were not rich? Of those questions only the third seemed instantly answerable . . .

I finally forced myself to look away, turning my back on all the small yet searing evidence of Jack's family life—the life he led apart from ours, the life he had denied me, the life I had not, until that moment, fully visualized.

I began to walk slowly back to my car, looking up only when I heard a voice—a man, the caretaker most likely, dragging a pot of withered geraniums. He wore a white shirt and had a black mustache, was lanky, almost rakish in appearance. "I can help you, miss?" He spoke with a florid Spanish accent. "You look for somebody?"

I stammered that I had lost my way, that I was looking for Ship's Prow Road.

His eyes were suspicious. "The Ship's Prow Road is back there—" he gestured in that direction, "maybe many miles. You go down this road, you turn left, you go a long way to stop sign—"

"I see," I replied, nervously feigning interest in the directions. "Left, you said?" My voice was listless; I remember hearing it almost as a thing apart.

He nodded. I opened the door to my car; he followed.

"This is a pretty house," I said as casually as I could, looking toward the dunes. "It must take a lot of work. To keep it up."

He nodded self-importantly. "Sure," he said. "A lot of work. Y a lot of money." He rubbed his thumb against the middle fingers of one hand, as if to indicate how much.

"Nice family, though?" I looked from him to the house and back again, squinting in the sun.

"Sure, nice. A whole family of girls—" He shrugged, a Latin reconciling himself to a family without sons.

"Daughters, you mean?"

He nodded. "Four girls. I like." Then, proudly: "The señora is cultivated. Is good education."

"That's important," I murmured. "A good education."

He pulled out some cigarettes and offered me one before going on: "You no idea—the little girl, Becky, is hurt one day, on the horse. The señora, she cried like the Magdalena."

I looked away, finding it unbearable to hear more. "So it's

down this road and left and then a long way, till the stop sign," I repeated, finding a strange solace in the directions.

He nodded as I started the car. "*Si* no, you come back. I show you."

"Yes of course. That's very nice of you."

I pulled away and gave a small, seemingly grateful wave. Further Lane stretched before me, a tunnel patched with light. I continued to drive, all the while trying to force myself not to think of Jack's house—of his wife's hats, of the gardening gloves, of the shoes by the staircase, of the furniture and its resolute, polished surfaces. I tried to suppress the rage building within me as I recalled Jack saying so many times, "I can deny you nothing." I tried not to think of him saying, "I need you to survive." I tried not to recall how many times he had painted such a bleak picture of his family life, as I— eager audience—had listened sympathetically; yet that bleakness hardly seemed reflected in the contented rooms I had just seen! I tried not to think of those things, or of my own terrible longing to have a child. Finally, I tried simply not to *think*, and stopped the car by the side of the road to rest my aching head on the wheel. I wanted to cry, but the cathartic tears would not come—only terrible, exhausting feelings of failure, jealousy, and disarray.

I slowly pulled my head up and looked at the clock on the dashboard. It was just quarter past four. The interview with Lawrence Brandt loomed before me.

Trying to suppress my anger and anxiety, I continued to drive until, at last, I came to Ship's Prow Road. The sun was still warm, the grass slightly moist and spongy from a shower that morning.

I turned into a driveway marked by two robust holly trees and drove past a white fence trailed with wild white roses; past a cluster of pines and, finally, to Brandt's house. It seemed, unlike its neighbors, to have no fanciful name— merely a plain white sign that said BRANDT.

The house was a turn-of-the-century shingle-style structure quite unlike others I had seen. I would have been tempted at first to describe its style as being typical of its period and genre, yet on closer inspection I realized there was something distinctive about it. There was nothing quaint or whimsical in its lines: Everywhere one searched for the expected one's eye was drawn to the unconventional. There was a large turret at its center and many different gables and balconies, which, if taken individually, would have seemed completely illogical, even incongruous, yet the total effect was one of harmony and balance. The more I gazed at the house, the more appropriate I thought the name of the road where it stood—Ship's Prow Road—because of the mastlike angles of the roof and the way the porch seemed to surge forward.

I closed the door to my car, alternately trying to dispel the image of Jack's house and the embarrassing memory of meeting Brandt that winter afternoon in Seattle.

Suddenly, I heard the voice of a child. The next instant, this apparition: a small towheaded boy bobbing atop the shoulders of a tall, rangy figure I knew to be Lawrence Brandt; behind them, a bounding black Labrador that barked at my approach. A red-haired woman in a pink uniform—the nanny, I surmised—ran behind them, calling, "Frederick!"

This was not at all the scene I had anticipated: I had envisioned the architect bent over his drafting board, hard at work. And then I thought how strange that no one had mentioned the existence of the child.

They came closer to me, the dog still barking fiercely. "Down, boy!" commanded Brandt. "Down, Dragon!"

I approached them, wary of the snarling and, it seemed to me, aptly named dog, and introduced myself to Brandt. Shaking his hand, I realized from the look of recognition, even disapproval, in his eyes that he did indeed remember me from Seattle. Now I had come in my writer's guise to ask him about Joanna. He would be guarded. Perhaps Cassel had already gotten to him. Or Rosalind.

Avoiding his eyes, I knelt down to say hello to the little

boy. I asked Frederick's age. "Three," said Brandt as I smiled at his son.

The child's cheeks and overalls were smudged with dirt; his eyes bright, inquiring and blue; his hair, warm from the sun, white-blond. I ran my hand across the small curve of his head and felt the silky curls at his nape. This, then, was Brandt's child with the wife I had seen on the magazine cover.

But the next instant, Frederick was all squirms and action; I gave him up, watching as he ran toward the lake. The nanny had given him a stick, which he waved as he veered toward the water. "Duck!" he yelled again and again at the ducks that swam nearby. There was another awkward pause as I stood alone with Brandt, my mind racing, as it sometimes did when I was tense. His son did not in the least resemble him, I thought.

"He's an adorable little boy," I said, standing up and brushing some grass from my skirt. "You must be proud of him."

"Yes," he said thoughtfully, his gaze following the careening child in the distance. I noticed how Brandt's dark brown hair would fall across his face and how he would push it back; I noticed how his rough-hewn features were somewhat at variance with his low, distinguished voice. And then, as if he had only just focused on what I had said about his son, he asked, "Do you think so?" Without waiting for me to respond, he turned to me abruptly, with an almost glowering expression, and said, "Let's go inside. We can talk there."

I followed him to the wide front steps that led to the porch and then through double doors, with mullioned windows, that led into the entrance hall. It was a larger, lighter room than I had expected, masculine in feeling and cerebral in its proportions, colors, textures. To the left stood a massive staircase and to the right, a handsome fireplace whose mantel, carved of oak, was perhaps six feet tall. In the middle of the room stood a round table—primitive in style, as if it had been rescued from a ship.

We passed through another set of heavy oak doors to the main room, a long, high galleried space that seemed to be library, sitting room, and dining room all at once. A spiral staircase led to the upper level, where the walls were entirely lined with books. It was perhaps the most casually elegant room I had ever seen (faded fabrics, generous sofas heaped with pillows), yet no place that was so clearly the product of a refined eye could escape a slightly formal feeling. The whole had a largess that reminded me of Wakefield Hall, yet a strength that set it distinctly apart.

I realized with a start that Brandt was watching me, impatient to begin. He asked me to sit down. Again, I noticed his manners, which were at once formal and brusque, and which hinted of intolerance—the same arrogance I remembered so clearly, and with such discomfiture, from Seattle.

I tried to appear as businesslike as possible and took a seat on one of the two sofas that flanked the fireplace, filling the tense silence by taking out my notebook, pens, tape recorder. (He had raised no objection to my recording our conversation.) He continued to stand, his back to the fireplace, waiting for the first question.

I began by mentioning how remarkable it was to find this sort of room in a house built at the turn of the century. Smiling—at my naiveté, no doubt—he told me that the original did not in the least resemble the place where we now stood: It had taken three rooms, in fact, to create this single space. I fleetingly wondered where his wife was and why there was no sense of her presence here.

There was another strained silence.

I had, by this time in my career, interviewed many people of different professions and walks of life, and was accustomed to the initial gropings and false starts of an interview; yet never had I felt at such a loss for words. Soon, however, my initial embarrassment gave way to irritation—it appeared that Brandt was determined not to make my job any easier. He seemed so condescending that when he finally asked whether I would like something to drink, I heard myself saying no, though I remember my throat was dry.

"I hadn't intended to speak with you," Brandt finally said bluntly. "It was David who persuaded me to. I almost never speak to journalists—"

"I've no desire for you to break your own policy, Mr. Brandt," I retorted, irked by his manner.

"You didn't let me finish," he interjected. "I was about to say that I rarely speak to journalists, but I never doubted I should speak with you." He paused. "And I wanted you to understand that. Please," he said, and then, in the same resigned tone: "Let's begin."

I picked up my pen, looked at him directly, and asked when and how he had come to know Joanna.

"Shortly after she and David bought Wakefield Hall."

"And you had never met her before?"

"No."

"Had you ever seen her onstage?"

"Only once, in *Hedda Gabler*."

"And what do you remember of that?"

"She was unforgettable."

"And how did she come to call you about Wakefield?"

"I'm not sure." He looked out the window impatiently.

"There must have been something of your work that she had admired . . ."

"Yes, I suppose there was—a house outside of San Francisco that I'd designed the previous year."

"This was at what point in your career?"

"The beginning."

"What was it about that house, the one you'd designed, that appealed to her?"

"I don't remember." Then: "It had a large octagonal library—yes, that was it."

I thought of Joanna's octagonal study. "That was the room she singled out?"

"Yes. Octagons fascinated her. That was one of the reasons she was drawn to Wakefield—the octagonal room that she eventually used as her own library." He paused. "I remember that she laughed, even seemed surprised, when I told her that Thomas Jefferson was also obsessed with octagons."

"Do you remember what she said to that?"

"She said she had no idea about Jefferson, that her own fascination had to do with an octagonal tower at a country house she had known in England."

"Thistleton?"

An almost imperceptible pause. "Yes."

"Do you have any idea why octagons fascinated her?"

"Only a general sense."

"Which would be?"

"It's the most ordered shape in architecture," he replied, folding his arms. "It's nondirectional as well, and can be used as a turning point, a farewell, a knuckle in a classical design. It has all the properties of a circle, yet it can also be furnished. A furnishable circle, in other words."

"So you think her fascination had to do with the octagon's properties, as a shape?"

"Partly."

I felt him draw back, and ventured forth again. "This was early in your career, you said—when you were known, from what I understand, as something of an *enfant terrible.*"

"Was I?" He did not look displeased by the description.

"In the sense that your work was controversial."

"It may have been. In those days, I was far more susceptible to criticism."

"And now?"

"Now I don't care about it." He paused before adding, " 'It is easy to sit by the shore and criticize the skill of the navigator.' "

" 'It is easy to sit by the shore *with folded hands,*' " I countered, having recognized the line as Petrarch's.

"I'm glad to see you value accuracy," he remarked wryly.

"I have a passion for details," I replied quietly, taking up my pen before posing the next question: "You had returned a few years before, from Vietnam, before meeting Joanna?"

"Yes."

"And where did your first meeting take place?"

"At the Carlyle Hotel."

"Why the Carlyle?"

"She and David were staying there while their apartment was being renovated."

"And how did she appear to you then?"

"Charming and highly intelligent."

"Nervous?"

"Not particularly." He leaned against the mantel, glancing at me and then, beyond, through the windows.

"And what did she say about Wakefield?" I asked, becoming impatient with his laconic responses.

"That she wanted to turn it into a paradise, like the houses she had seen in England. A highly ordered, man-made paradise."

"Those were her exact words?"

"Yes."

"Did she say anything else—about her ideas for the house?"

"Yes. She had already given it a great deal of thought. She was, in that way, an extremely deliberate person. Nothing was left to chance."

"Can you remember some of her ideas, the feeling she wanted to create?"

"She said she wanted a 'rigorous house,' with an underlying sense of order that would come from its proportions. The geometry of squares, double cubes, and octagons interested her."

"Why, do you think?"

"She once told me that since she no longer had the fantasy of acting, she might as well take refuge in numbers. She had begun to read about the building of gothic cathedrals—the idea of sacred geometry intrigued her."

"What other ideas did she have about the house?"

"She said she wanted a clear division between public and private rooms and that, in general, she disliked rooms that revealed too much of the owner's personality. 'No bourgeois coziness,' she said. What she wanted, at least on the main floor—this I remember clearly—was an elegant and 'challenging' space. Pure decoration interested her much less."

"Did that surprise you?"

"Yes, it did." His smile was private, contained. "I'm usually asked to design a house that's both cozy and grand—two contradictory properties that happen to be fashionable."

"And then what happened? How did you proceed?"

"We made a date to meet—the following Saturday, I think. We drove to the Berkshires together."

"And the house itself—your first impression?"

"It was in extremely bad shape. Only a shell of the original, including the octagonal study, remained. It needed a tremendous amount of reconstruction. It needed to be made coherent. Much that had been done to it in the twenties and thirties had to be destroyed."

"I assume Joanna had other ideas?"

"She was a woman who had studied enough, and seen enough, to know what she wanted. She had a refined eye, an eye that she had consciously trained."

I asked him to explain.

"It was something she developed with a great sense of will, I always felt. It did not come naturally, but with determination. And her determination was formidable, of course."

"Did she talk about her career, about her life?"

"At the outset, very little. By the time I knew her, you must remember, her career had virtually ended."

"The stage fright?"

He paused, furrowing his brow and brushing back his hair with one hand. "So they say," he replied abruptly.

I remember looking down at my lap, tense and almost angry, filled with a reckless desire to challenge him. "And you were never her lover, Mr. Brandt?" I asked him.

"No," he replied quietly. "Never." He was so dignified and subdued in his response that I felt rather embarrassed. "I hope you understand . . ." I began to say.

"Yes, I know." His tone was resigned. "You had to ask that question." He took a seat opposite me, in an armchair, momentarily silent as he leaned forward, his hands clutched.

"I gather she trusted you very much," I ventured after a moment, feeling a slight shift in his attitude. "You were her friend, after all, as well as her architect."

"I hope so," he answered, looking down. "I like to think so."

"And so you knew her, perhaps, in a way others did not."

"Yes, I guess that would be accurate." He looked at me again, the expression in his eyes disconcertingly remote. I felt disheartened, sure that I would never be able to penetrate his reserve. Once again I was struck by the shifting quality of his looks—his angular features and strong chin—and how dependent they were on light and expression. Only the intelligence in his eyes never wavered.

I had lost my train of thought and groped for the next question. I asked him, almost mechanically, to describe how he remembered the experience of working with Joanna.

"When you design a house for a woman like Joanna, you come to know her very well," he said in a more expansive voice. "All the secrets are unearthed, however indirectly, as you discuss rooms and how they will be used and the atmosphere of each and how they relate to others she has known —other rooms, which served as models for her own." He paused, leaning forward, his hands still clasped: "I soon began to see that she was intensely ashamed of any place where she lived. This remained with her throughout her life, tinged anything she touched, affected any place that became her own. *Shame* crept through the walls.

"At Wakefield," he continued, "you would have thought she would have been immune to it—" He shook his head. "Not at all! The moment the house became hers, it was no longer a joy but something that pressed upon her in a way that was fearful and unhealthy. Nothing was ever right. Nothing ever pleased her for more than a moment. I began to see that this was a woman who would not, who could not rest, in any place she had created. Whatever place she called home would inevitably be the place from which she would want to escape."

I hardly dared speak, fearing he would stop, startled by the acuity and sensitivity of his recollections. "What was she like during that time?" I gently prodded him. "Can you describe her to me, Mr. Brandt?"

"She became very thin. Very thin and very distracted. And yet to David not antagonistic."

"Why do you say yet to David not antagonistic?"

"Because their relationship had deteriorated to a point where they hardly even spoke, where they led almost completely separate lives."

"But then you think something happened to change that?"

"Yes, something that perhaps no one will ever understand. I particularly noticed the change when she returned from that last trip to London, how distant she seemed, how lacking in her usual energy. She had always been moody, of course, capricious—but this was different. Different, and profoundly disturbing."

"And how did it manifest itself?"

"Her need for privacy and solitude became a mania. She developed a near phobia about the telephone—she refused to answer it, and changed her phone number innumerable times, all in the name of privacy. She would write letters—to me, to everyone—as she always had, but would never send them without making a copy for herself first. And she became ill—a respiratory virus that turned into pneumonia."

"Yes?"

"She began to refuse to eat. After her recovery, the doctors attributed her lack of appetite to the aftermath of the illness. But she seemed to flaunt her new emaciated body, to rebel against anyone who encouraged her to eat."

"Please go on."

"She began to exercise—it became a mania. She hired a trainer to come every morning to supervise her workouts."

He paused. "She called me, asking me to design a gym for her."

"And you designed one?"

"I did, reluctantly. Partly because I knew I was creating a room which, for once, would not give her any real pleasure! And yet when the place was finished, she seemed delighted with it."

"Happier?"

"Yes. In fact for a moment, she actually seemed her old self. I remember her walking around the new space, looking almost girlish in her black leotard and tights, and exclaiming in her charming, joking voice, about the new 'instruments of torture,' as she called them—the exercise machines, that is. Her hair was pulled off her face, she wore no makeup, and before I left that day, she went through her paces for me— showing me what she could do on this machine or that. Nothing seemed too hard, too painful, for her to attempt— and in fact her body *did* seem to show the results. She had always been slender, but not without a softness; her body had become lean, very lean and angular, and her face, with its high cheekbones, looked gaunt."

"And what was David's reaction to this?"

There was a long pause. "He did not like it. He was deeply concerned."

"Did he tell her?"

"I'm sure he did—" He hesitated. "But, no doubt, it was hard for David to face what was really happening. For the first time in his life he confronted a situation over which he had no control. She had simply lost her will to live." He leaned forward again, his hands clasped in that familiar gesture, his head bent down so that the light accentuated his wide brow and the cleft in his chin. "There was a desperation in her lack of appetite," he continued, "in the peculiar diets she embarked upon—eating only eggs one week, only juice the next. I had been away a lot during that time, and when I came back and saw her, I was stunned. She was no longer the same woman. She was no longer really interested in the house. Nothing seemed to matter, except . . ."

"Except what, Mr. Brandt?"

"It was about this time that she began to focus on the maze. There had been a vestige of an old maze on the property, but Joanna had it razed. She wanted to begin again. She wanted to create her own labyrinth—a new one, larger and much more complex, with an octagonal design. It exerted an incredible fascination for her, the creation of this maze. She became obsessed with the history of mazes. She studied everything she could—the maze at Hampton Court, Italianate mazes, Cretan mazes, the maze patterns of floors of the great cathedrals. She collected books and medieval chronicles which described the maze that Henry II, according to legend, had built for Rosamund at Woodstock. She loved that story —the story of their trysts, of the king threading his way to his mistress." He smiled ruefully to himself; I thought of the many books on mazes I had seen in Joanna's library and how methodically she had marked them.

"She consulted experts, garden historians," he continued. "She sent me to Thistleton to study the maze there. It was in bad shape by that time; it had fallen into decay. And it was also very different from the plan Joanna eventually decided upon. The maze there had a meandering pattern—no rectangular grid, no central axis. Very much in the style of Capability Brown—a maze without a real beginning, without a real end. It was designed with hairpin turns and created confusion, a vertiginous effect. That was not at all what Joanna wanted at Wakefield."

"In what way?"

"She *feared* disorder," he said decisively. "And by remaking the maze to her own specifications, she felt in control of that fear, I sensed."

"By that you mean?"

"Numbers being the most orderly things of all. She obsessed over the measurements and proportions of the maze —the perfect size, the division of its interior into smaller chambers. She wanted the entrance gate to face east and the overall octagon to be divided into four rooms of smaller octagons; the east and west octagons would be divided in half, with a statue set in each. 'I want it to be as intricate as a chess game,' she told me. The goal—the main statue—would be set in the center of the maze, with a fountain before it. The idea for the statue came from Shakespeare—*The Winter's Tale*, I think. You've already seen it, I'm sure."

I replied that I had seen another of the statues but not yet the central statue with the fountain. "But I had no idea it had to do with Shakespeare," I added, recalling the stone goddess I had seen with Rosalind.

"Yes," he said, looking surprised that I hadn't known. "Joanna chose a statue of a Shakespearean heroine for each 'room.' The rooms, in turn, were to be linked by tunnels of hedges. It was Joanna's idea that the central statue would be reached from the entrance gate by a specific series of turns—three right, three left, five right, five left."

"Did she say why?"

"Those were her lucky numbers. That was all she told me."

"Tell me more about the maze plan," I said, after considering this.

"It was strictly organized, and very complicated. A balance of chaos and order, with the central axis directly through the goal. That was how Joanna wanted it—a Shakespearean treasure hunt through the hedges, in effect."

I continued to reflect on this, almost too absorbed to take notes. "And the chapel on the property," I asked after a moment. "What about that?"

"At the outset, Joanna had it refurbished with some enthusiasm, but eventually she seemed to lose all interest in it, partly because it was a matter of surfaces, of decoration. Decorators finished it off, with the help of Christina von Shouse—the pews were restored, the gilding repainted. I thought it was a travesty—" his tone indicated his distaste, "—entirely Christina's creation."

"During this time did Joanna spend most of her time at Wakefield?"

"Yes. David used the apartment in the city. Joanna, almost never."

"Once the maze was completed, did it continue to absorb her?"

"Yes, very much. She used to walk through it every afternoon—she would stay there and read. I always felt that she saw the passage of her life there, that she had created her autobiography with those statues and their arrangement—a monument to her career."

"Which other women from Shakespeare did she choose?" I asked, still perplexed that no one else had mentioned the specific nature of the statues.

"I don't remember," he replied. "There were about seven or eight, most of them all set in place after my own work was done. I'm sure the idea had to do with her struggle against stage fright. Her identifying with those women, those silent women, made of stone." He stopped abruptly, as if he had said more than he intended. "In any event," he added briskly, "the maze contained something for her that none of us will ever know."

Moments passed. "What did you feel when you first heard Joanna was dead?" I asked, watching him closely.

"Deeply saddened." His voice and demeanor left me no doubt of his grief. "It's impossible to adequately describe the anguish we felt, David and I." He paused. "I, most of all . . ."

"Why *you*, Mr. Brandt?"

He looked at me directly. "Because I had helped rebuild the paradise she could no longer endure."

"But were you *surprised* by her death?" I finally asked.

His expression was grave and faraway. "No," he replied. "I realize now I had actually expected it."

19

The last rays of autumn sunlight had vanished. Brandt moved to the table behind the sofa and silently turned on a lamp. I glanced at him, and then at a bronze statuette of an Indian goddess on the table, her myriad twisting arms thrown into relief by the light. I took a deep breath and turned to a new page in my notebook, relieved and excited that the interview had finally assumed its own rhythm. I was now able to focus clearly on Joanna and her relationship with the man who had—in his own ironic words—restored "the paradise she could no longer endure."

Brandt had not yet mentioned his wife, which I remember finding curious. "Were you married at the time?" I asked him, surprised that the question should be hard to pose. "When you began the work on Wakefield, that is?"

"No," came the brusque response, as he took his seat.

"But you were married later?"

"Yes. About four years later."

"But you have never once mentioned your wife in connection with Joanna."

"They did not get along very well," he answered with some hesitation, his expression opaque. "My wife had her own needs. Her own complexities." Again he paused, only to explain in a low, tense voice, a voice that did encourage questions: "You must understand—Isabelle and I have been separated for six months."

Watching him, I came to my own series of conclusions, partly prompted by the suppressed pain of his expression: He had loved her very much, she was the mother of his son, and she had left him. So my instincts had been correct: The room where we sat was indeed the product of a man's, not a woman's, taste. I thought of Christina von Shouse and her description of Lawrence Brandt—he was dangerously ambitious, she had said, a man who had never suffered. I wondered if this was really true.

"Tell me about Christina von Shouse," I said, glancing up from my notebook.

"What about her?" he asked sharply, his attention having returned to me.

"Her friendship with Joanna . . ."

"It was complicated."

"What do you mean?"

"Christina was very jealous of her."

"Why?"

"I've never been able to fully understand the source of it."

"You've absolutely no idea?"

"No. Except that one succeeded as an artist and the other did not. That one was highly creative and the other a gifted acquisitor." Impatience edged his voice. "That would be enough, wouldn't it?"

I remember feeling his eyes on my pen as I scribbled down those last words, which inexplicably brought to mind Christina's failure to fetch the brooch at the auction. Looking up, I told him about the letter Christina had mentioned to me— the venomous letter that Joanna had supposedly left for David, which was to have been given him after her death.

"I've heard about it," he replied dismissively, "but I'd be reluctant to believe it. Especially if it comes from Christina."

"You don't get along with her, obviously."

"We don't get along or not get along. Christina and her world simply don't interest me." His voice was derisive, his expression disdainful.

I asked him to explain precisely what he meant.

"You must know what I mean—" his look was uncompromisingly direct, "—you, of all people!"

The color rose to my face at this intimation of my affair with Jack. I should have been angry, I realize in retrospect, yet all I could do was change the subject. "I know Joanna wrote many letters," I said, averting my gaze from his as I looked up. "Did she ever write to you?"

"Yes."

"Often?"

"Fairly often."

"Dating from when?"

"From the beginning of the work on Wakefield."

"Do you have those letters?"

"Some."

"What happened to the others?"

"I gave many of them to David, the last ones."

"He told me he has no letters."

Even Brandt could not totally suppress the look of surprise in his eyes. "That's what David told you?"

I reiterated that he had, and that I found it strange. I asked Brandt if he would be willing to let me read the letters he had kept.

"I'll have to think about it," he replied, his expression one of consternation.

"But you must understand how important it is—to the book—that it be right, that her own voice come through!" He appeared unmoved. "Is it possible," I asked after a moment, "that David has destroyed her letters, or at least some of her letters?"

"Anything is *possible*, Miss Rowan," he retorted. "He is the executor of Joanna's estate. David, and only David, has the power to grant permission to quote from her letters. That much I do know." He paused. "And there's something else as well—"

"What is that?"

"There were letters left at Thistleton—letters Joanna seemed to treasure. I remember she told me that very distinctly. I assume David has control over those as well."

I tried to mask my surprise, for it was the first time anyone had mentioned Joanna's having left letters at Thistleton.

The clock struck seven. It was very still and very quiet; I felt depleted suddenly, unable to summon the energy to probe further. When, the next moment, I heard the sound of Frederick's shouting and laughter coming from another room, I remember hoping that the little boy would enter. And indeed, the next instant my wish was granted, for Frederick—freshly bathed and in pajamas—appeared at the door and raced into his father's arms.

Brandt tossed the child about; then the little boy ran to me—I was a stranger, and still the object of curiosity. Frederick had taken hold of my charm bracelet—the bracelet I was never without, which had been given me as a child. Over and over he examined the little charms, looking up at me as he did so with his thickly fringed blue eyes.

"Book," he said, examining the diminutive charm carved of ivory. "Yes," I repeated. "Book." And then, coming to the little gold key, I asked him, "And what's this?"

"Key!" he said triumphantly.

"Good!"

He had come to the charm of a pomegranate, in coral.

"What this?" he said, looking intensely puzzled, but the

next moment, having continued to scrutinize it, he looked up at me and said, with a touching lack of conviction, "Orange."

I laughed. "Well, that's close enough," I told him, touching his cheek. He came to the little gold treasure chest next, its lid studded with a cabochon sapphire. "Box," he pronounced, opening its top and looking inside it.

All the while, I felt his father's gaze. "He likes my bracelet," I said quickly. "People always seem to notice it—it's unusual, I suppose. Even Joanna mentioned it to me the day I met her."

"Did she?" he asked, glancing at Frederick, who was now tugging at his arm. "Come and build the tower," the little boy urged his father, pointing to a ziggurat of colored building blocks on the floor near the desk. Brandt acquiesced, walking in the direction of the tower, which the child gleefully proceeded to destroy. "Frederick!" reprimanded Brandt. "Why did you do that?" Brandt's voice was so stern that the child's eyes filled with tears, his head lowered, and his jutting lower lip quivered pathetically. I wanted to comfort him, but that was not my place, after all! Brandt, however, had already taken his son into his arms, hugged him, brushed a tear from his cheek, and set him on his feet. For a moment the child stood quite still, holding his father's hand as they looked at me together.

I told him it was time for me to leave. "I've kept you long enough," I said, and began to gather my things while Brandt alternately watched me and dealt with his son. Frederick had snatched a piece of kindling from the basket near the fireplace and cavorted around the room, waving the stick.

"Say goodbye to Miss Rowan," Brandt told him, taking his hand. The child approached me; I knelt down and said goodbye to him, ruffling his hair before he squirmed away.

I followed Brandt to the door, pausing to glance at a book that lay on the entrance table: *Mont-St.-Michel and Chartres*, by Henry Adams. Flipping through it, I mentioned to Brandt I had never read the book. "That surprises me," he replied, his tone implying that any educated person would be familiar with it.

His arrogance only made me more determined not to leave without Joanna's letters. "One last thing," I said, putting down the book and facing him. "You mentioned Joanna's letters, the letters about Wakefield."

"Yes," he said, his expression at its most intimidating.

"You must let me see them."

"Why *must* I?"

"Because of my passion for accuracy," I said as lightly as I could, recalling his own words; and then, with utter seriousness, "Because you knew Joanna in a way others did not."

"I'll have to think about it," he said reluctantly, making me realize in that instant that he might actually deny me the letters—a possibility that stunned me, for I was used to getting my way. "Mr. Brandt," I said, with renewed determination. "You *must* let me see the letters. It's the right thing to do."

He looked at me almost quizzically, his eyes scanning my face. "There are two crucial letters," he said after a moment, "And if I let you see them—when will you return them to me?"

"As soon as possible."

"Tomorrow," he said firmly.

"Tomorrow's Sunday," I countered.

"Monday, then."

"Tuesday."

He paused, as if measuring my persistence, one hand in his pocket, the other pushing back his hair. "Tuesday, then," he concluded. "I'll go see if I can find them." I remember how incredibly relieved I felt, and how excited just minutes later when he returned with two envelopes. "Here they are," he said quietly, handing them over. I thanked him.

The telephone rang from a distant room; the nanny, Mary, appeared with a message in hand, followed by Frederick. "I should go," he said, glancing at the message and then at me. "Mary will show you out."

We shook hands and said goodbye.

I followed Mary down the front steps, Dragon bounding behind us. "Frederick's a wonderful little boy," I told her as we walked toward my car.

"Ah, that's for sure," she replied, continuing to watch her charge. "Only it's a pity—" But here she stopped abruptly, suddenly mindful that I was a stranger.

"His mother must dote on him," I said.

"Aye, that she does."

"And his father, too."

"Sure he does," she replied. "It's just that he—" But again she stopped.

The wind had come up, and the half moon was slowly becoming visible in the darkening sky. I walked toward my car, placed Joanna's letters on the front seat beside me, and started the motor. Dragon ran across the lawn, still barking, as I pulled out of the long, winding driveway.

20

As I drove I occasionally stole glances at the letters from Joanna that lay on the front seat beside me, which, now in my possession, I almost feared to read. Even from that vantage point there was no mistaking the strong, distinctive handwriting I recognized from the endpapers of her books at Wakefield Hall.

After a few miles, I pulled over to the side of the road, stopped the car, and took the first letter in my hands. I examined the front, which was addressed to Lawrence Brandt in New York, and then the back, engraved with the address of the Connaught Hotel, London. I opened this, the first envelope, my heart beating fast, my hands almost shaking.

Eight sheets of blue writing paper imprinted with the Connaught's emblem—PLACERE PLACET—were folded inside: sheets of a thin, almost translucent quality covered with Joanna's remarkable handwriting in black ink. Again I noticed the rhythmic fluid loops, the towering capitals, and the gaps between the disconnected lower-case letters:

April 12, 1972
Dear Lawrence—

It was an enormous pleasure to meet you, and I very much look forward to beginning the work, and the initial plans on Wakefield Hall. I sense my house is in very good hands! And so, I think, does David.

My ideas are all intuitive, you see. You have to be able to sleep-walk a little toward the goal. In the past I have been able to do that quite easily—in acting—but houses are another medium altogether, one I've come to rather late in my life. And that is where I'm very grateful indeed to have your eye and expertise. Having merely been an interpreter of others' works, I envy you the idea of actually *creating* space. Decoration seems to me a paltry thing in comparison; I am content to leave that to others. But the ebb and flow of a house, the size and proportion of its rooms and how they relate and connect to one another—this is a challenge indeed, a merging of art, mathematics and aesthetics I find more than fascinating.

You seemed surprised by my insistence on the intrinsic order of the house through its proportions and the geometry of its interior spaces. Is this not what you usually hear from your clients? As I told you last Saturday, I've a horror of houses that overwhelm the intruder with the identity of the owner: I like rather more mysterious rooms, unbefuddled by clutter. A certain austerity and invisible order one might say. I like the idea of the *axis mundi* as well, the ballast of the great cathedrals; the notion that one knows precisely where one stands, between earth and eternity—the central point of the circle, cross or octagon (more of that later).

I had never thought of numbers as being in the least mystical—words had always occupied that place for me —but now that I no longer have words, or at least Shakespeare's words, to keep me company, I might as well find comfort in numbers. That will be your task— to take those numbers and create new and daunting spaces with them. To extrapolate from my primitive ideas and make some *order* of them—order being the most glamorous thing of all.

You asked me to tell you about other places, other rooms that have made an impression on me. The one house I could single out and say that house I loved, that house might be a model, would be Thistleton, the house I mentioned in England. Thistleton belongs to my cherished friend Desmond Kerrith, and is an eighteenth century house of great charm and distinction; in its park there is an octagonal library built as a crenellated, moated tower—my favorite place on earth! It is that tower which has sparked my own fascination with octagons; there is a certain order and serenity to the shape—the circular satisfaction of returning to the place where one started and knowing that place for the first time. Thistleton has a famous yew maze, as well, and a chapel in the gothic style—in other words, it is an arcadian paradise, with unexpected twists and turns and hiding places, a universe impervious to the slings and arrows of what is commonly known as the "real world."

Work on creating and clarifying the spaces we discussed: the double cube drawing room; but most of all the octagonal library, which, as I told you, I covet for myself. (My library is dukedom large enough—so my old friend said . . .) I see it as a room harkening directly back to the tower library at Thistleton—the room that anyone who truly wants to know me *must* visit. My own replica will be a lovely place for all my treasures—

my books, my antique hourglasses, my collection of Elizabethan miniatures (did I mention my Hilliard—the seal of the good Queen, Elizabeth Regina, herself?)

My own octagon should precisely recreate the feeling of Thistleton's—the desk facing east, the window overlooking a rose garden (though in Thistleton's case, the garden lies across the moat). In other words, this room should refer to the other, *should lead to it in fact*—part of my belief that rooms are always rooted in other rooms, always referring to the original, and that original to the original before it (like a story or a play, in other words). Think of Thistleton as the root house and Wakefield as its offshoot. In the progeny, however, we shall correct what, in the parent, I found either lacking or disorderly.

I want you to go to Thistleton and take stock of its rooms. I'm sure my old friend would be very happy to meet a young architect of your talent and promise. I will have Desmond—or his surrogate—show you the library, the chapel, and the maze (now wild and overgrown, I fear). Surely this will inspire you—return, and create my own arcadia!

It is strange that I should have found my own paradise here, in this country, in Massachusetts of all places. When I first saw Wakefield, I remember inwardly exclaiming to myself, "Reader, I married him," with a peculiar sense of recognition and inner peace, as if I had known the house from a lifetime of romantic yearnings. It was only in that instant that I felt I could relegate Thistleton to quite another epoch of my life: as if Desmond's house had been my Thornfield Hall, and this—Wakefield—my tranquil, long-sought Ferndean. Does this confession embarrass you? It shouldn't! For in every other way, I assure you, I am no Jane Eyre, and David no Rochester.

There, now you know everything!

I won't permit myself to reread this letter: I know I

shouldn't have the courage to send it if I did. Excuse its length: you'll learn that what I can't say face-to-face I am often able to express with pen and paper.

Do let me know how the work progresses—and when you would like to go to Thistleton. The sooner the better!

Sincerely,
Joanna Eakins Cassel

P.S. I've enclosed a 19th century edition of *Henry* V from my own collection; it seemed appropriate for you to have it, if it is true, as you told me, that *Henry* is your favorite Shakespeare play. It belonged to Charles Kean —cf. the frontispiece, with his signature—and was given to me by a friend when, at an early moment in my career, I played the French princess. Take a soldier, take a king—take this book from me! As ever, J.

I slowly put the first letter down and unfolded the pages of the second:

March 4, 1983.
Larry—

I write you now about the maze—I have a distinct idea of how to go about it. It came to me in a dream last night with such utter clarity that when I woke up I started. I sat up in bed making some notes and have spent the morning walking about in a daze—pondering how to make real those inchoate ideas which came to me during the night.

I had been thinking of the maze at Thistleton before I fell asleep: its roaming hedges and spiralling shape. All without order. Within it, the single statue of Athena which—as you know—was modelled on me as a young woman. The chaos of that maze did not disturb me then; I was almost attracted to it in fact; but now it does, with a pain and fear I can hardly describe—even to you, my architect and friend. I am at another stage

now—bereft of acting, of Shakespeare's words, I have
become a mute and moated sort of person. Like Lavinia
—that part from *Titus* I always dreaded playing—wandering through this paradise with her arms and tongue
chopped off! Past hope, past cure, past help—as Juliet
would say—

I bring up Shakespeare—as I do incessantly these
days—partly because the dream of the maze last night
was merged with him—the words of his women flooding
through stone. I dreamt of roaming through hedges of
the most specific sort: a great weblike octagonal, divided
into smaller interior octagons; within its central square,
a statue of a goddess in the style of Giulio Romano
which I reached by a series of turns—three right, three
left, five right, five left. But this figure—when I asked
her identity—came not from the Greeks but from
Shakespeare: Hermione from *The Winter's Tale*, dressed
as a goddess (as she is of course in that classical last part
of the play). The queen unjustly accused of adultery by
her husband, Leontes; punished by him, banished. She
spoke to me: but why Hermione, you will ask? That was
my last role on the stage, you see—the role I was asked
to play but never could complete: stage fright overwhelmed me. Onstage I turned figuratively to stone—I
could not move, I could not speak, I was petrified with
fear (*petra*, the Latin for rock . . .) Shakespeare turns
her quite literally to stone, only to resurrect her in the
last act—there she springs to life and *speaks*.

So now you see perhaps why the queer workings of
my mind in its dreamlike state should have turned—of
all the parts—to Hermione. Why she—of all Shakespearean heroines—must stand in the center of my octagon—the octagon referring always to my favorite
place on earth, the room in the tower at Thistleton. But
my Hermione will be truer to the original on which
Shakespeare based his play. For in the root story—
Greene's *Pandosto*—the queen never came back to life;

it took Shakespeare, with his alchemy and his compassion, to do it.

But I—being mortal, and verseless now too—do not have those powers. I cannot command Hermione—as wise Paulina did—to descend, be stone no more, approach. I'll set them in place, my Shakespearean ladies, and then I'll impregnate them with phrases: the pedestal of each will be etched with a quotation of my choosing from her play. It seems only fitting that these statues represent me and my life, that they remain when I am gone, uttering lines I could no longer say onstage . . . A Shakespearean treasure hunt through tunnels of twisting hedges—a challenge to my biographer, no doubt!

Let me now be the audience and stroll among the women I have been! The justice of it pleases me . . .

During my walk today I tried to decide *which* of Shakespeare's women I'll choose; there will be seven—a magic number, the number of the liberal arts. At first I thought I'd use only the banished ladies and lost girls of the last plays—Miranda, Viola, Perdita. The idea of rebirth, of identity refound, I find almost obsessively comforting; the idea as well that even he—Shakespeare—was reduced to silence by that point (I remember what you told me about Frank Lloyd Wright and "powerful emptiness"—surely there's a link). The inadequacy of language, finally! But then, I thought, *no*: I must cast a wider net. Lavinia and Hermione will be among them, of course—one mute, one turned to stone. And Lady Macbeth as well: I owe so much to her, which may be why her quote comes easily: "Things without all remedy/Should be without regard; what's done is done." The rest of the women you will find on the next page, in my plan. Tell me what you think of it.

Find the mason you mentioned in northern Massachusetts and have him begin with Lady M; I'll send him photographs of me in the part, and in the others I decide upon. I want the likenesses as precise as possible.

One last thing: in my dream there was a gate, a gothic gate, and before that gate, a mask weeping streams of tears; below it was a stone engraved with a quote from *Midsummer Night's Dream*. Something to do with "mazèd world." When I awoke, I could not remember the spinning lines—for that was how they seemed to me —nor whether there was anything of that kind in the play itself. I went to the *Concordance*—my treasured book and treasure-trove for anyone who comes later— and found that yes, Titania herself—*myself*, decades ago, when I played her—did use those very words. I want them etched in stone, below a fountain like the weeping mask of my dream:

> The spring, the summer,
> The childing autumn, angry winter change
> Their wonted liveries; and the mazèd world,
> By their increase, now knows not which is which.

The rest is silence—so they say—

Joanna.

I read the letters once, and then again and again, the paper pulled taut in my hands. I can hardly describe the eerie excitement—even the sense of foreboding—that overwhelmed me, the chill as I read the words "A challenge to my biographer!" I read and reread the pages until the moment came when I could almost anticipate each turn of phrase— until it seemed the words were almost my own. Finally, the letters still in hand, I looked up at the darkening sky.

It was the same voice—and yet a different voice—from the first letter to the second, a difference reflected even in the handwriting (the first was clear, shapely, far more regular; the second uneven, rushed, plainly written at great speed). The tone of the first was charming, cerebral, and self-possessed, even at times imperious ("This will be your task")

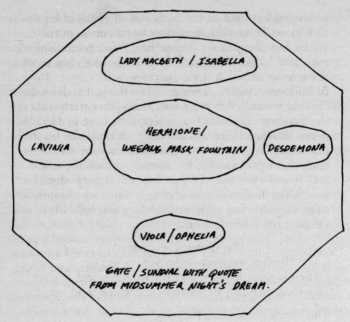

in its insistence, its obsessive insistence, on *order.* ("She *feared* disorder," Brandt had rightly told me.) The second letter, with its quality of literate delirium, appeared to have been written quickly, fluently, with no rereading or editing, the sprinting thoughts often enigmatic and incomplete.

I took up the first letter once more and went through it line by line: her fascination with space, with geometry; the disingenuous tone of "Is this not what you usually hear from your clients?" (Of course not, she must have known.) She calls visitors to a house "intruders" and invests houses with human characteristics: "In the progeny we shall correct what, in the parent, I found either lacking or disorderly." Throughout, the references to Shakespeare: "My library is dukedom large enough" in the first letter, and the merging of his words with hers in the second. And then her mention of the *Concordance* to Shakespeare—"my treasure-trove for anyone who comes later." Was this meant to be a signal to her posthumous biographer?

In both letters were sentences that seemed to have been tantalizingly inserted as clues: this room—her study—should refer directly to Thistleton's, *should lead to it in fact*. Was this also directed to her biographer? And had she begun to compile the folder of memorabilia I had yet to see?

The first letter was full of charm—of that there was no question; but was the tone as guileless as it purported? I was struck by the fluidity of her writing, by the lack of cross-outs or deletions, as if the paragraphs had sprung full-blown; as if she had gone over these descriptions many times in her mind's eye. Or perhaps by that time she was indeed a practiced letter writer: "What I can't say face-to-face I am often able to express in letters." Both Patrick Rossiter and Christina von Shouse had also mentioned Joanna's many letters— yet few, if any, seemed to have survived. Had she destroyed them herself? Or had someone else—David, for instance— and if so, why?

I put the letters down and began to drive, the salient parts of the letters resurfacing in my mind: "sleep-walk a little toward the goal"—this recalled Lady Macbeth, the first of Joanna's great roles, whose nights were rendered sleepless by guilt.

And then her description of first seeing Wakefield Hall: it was intriguingly romantic, even touching. "Reader, I married him," she had exclaimed to herself, recalling that triumphant declaration from *Jane Eyre*. I realized that I, too, had uttered that famous sentence, but to myself, yearning to proclaim "Reader, I married him" as a statement of fact—of my wanting to marry Jack. She was already married when she wrote this, and Wakefield she had come to equate in some way with Ferndean. Ferndean was a tranquil house, the manor that Rochester had escaped to after the tumult of

Thornfield Hall. Why did she equate Thistleton with Thornfield Hall? There was a madwoman in the attic there . . .

And then her description of Thistleton: the crenellated, moated tower—she had mentioned this at length; it was her favorite place on earth. Anyone who "truly wants to know" her must visit it; what clearer signal could there be to me, as the biographer?

And then (for my mind continued to leap) she had sent Lawrence Brandt a book to accompany the letter: her prized edition of *Henry V*. It was beguiling the way she did it, the way she wrote "take a soldier, take a king." Is that how she saw Lawrence; did she in some way equate those lines with him?

Next, I began to analyze the far more disturbing second letter: the dreamlike state in which it seemed to have been written, its way of expropriating Shakespeare's words as her own—her chilling, ironic use of "the justice of it pleases me," from *Othello*. The longing for order and the terrible fear of silence—the hideous image of Joanna as Lavinia "wandering through this paradise" without tongue or arms.

Most of all, it was the maze of statues that startled me: the rationale of the characters Joanna had chosen and what they, and their arrangement, meant to her. "They will be there to gaze at visitors when I am gone, and reveal what I cannot disclose in life." What clues, what message, what secret, lay concealed within the maze and its octagonal web of "Shakespearean ladies"? Which quotes had she chosen from the plays? And was there a significance in the way she had flanked Hermione with Desdemona and Lavinia—was it the idea of three women wronged by men? She had coupled Viola with Ophelia; Lady Macbeth, with Isabella from *Measure for Measure. Why?* Lawrence Brandt had confirmed what I had already intuited about Joanna: She was a very "deliberate person," he had said, a woman who left nothing to chance.

Turning past the East Hampton cemetery, I saw that darkness had encroached on its glassy pond, on its tilting, moss-covered tombstones half hidden by weeping willows.

As I turned right onto the highway heading east, it occurred to me that one sentence, and only one sentence in the letters, did not ring true: "There," she had written him. "Now you know everything!"

21

I found it hard to sleep that night, and when at last I did, my sleep was laced with troubling dreams which, upon awakening, I struggled to remember. Shortly after dawn, I realized it was useless to stay in bed any longer. I sat up and opened Joanna's letters, which lay beside me on the pillow, rereading them once more, as if half expecting that her sentences had not outlived the night. But they had. In the stark morning light, they seemed, if anything, even more disturbing.

Still in my nightgown, I went into the kitchen to make myself a cup of coffee, staring at the circle of blue flames beneath the throbbing kettle. I realized with some trepidation that I had not yet listened to the tape of my interview with Lawrence Brandt. I did so; once, then again. What continued to fascinate me was Brandt's voice—its low, distinctive timbre, his clear diction. Not at all the passionless voice I had expected.

I walked to the window, gazing at the austere cityscape as I sipped my coffee. The telephone rang.

I had expected it to be Jack—it was a little past eight o'clock—but was surprised to hear Christina von Shouse's voice instead. "Hello, my dear," she said in a friendly tone. "You're so difficult to reach. I was told you had taken a leave from your office, and then you're always out in the evening. So I thought I'd try you now. I hope you don't mind my calling at this hour."

Not at all, I reassured her, waiting to hear what could have prompted her call.

"You saw him yesterday, I understand," she began, pausing in a way that suggested she expected me to volunteer Lawrence Brandt's name. But I purposely did not, and so, undaunted, she continued: "Lawrence Brandt. You met with him yesterday in the country, didn't you? And what did you think? Was my assessment correct?"

I was amazed that she knew about my appointment with Brandt, but merely told her that he had been extremely articulate and helpful.

"His wife left him not long ago, you know," was her curious nonsequitur—intended to unsettle me, no doubt. "He was devastated, I hear. But then he should have expected it, the way he treated her! Only Joanna knew how to bring out the best in him. He owes a great deal to her. And to David. They launched his career, without question."

I asked why she felt compelled to tell me this.

"To be helpful to you," she said after a second's pause. "I consider myself the only person who really knew Joanna well. All aspects of her."

I had lived long enough in New York to question such "kindness," and told her that she needn't be concerned: All sides would be carefully weighed. "I want it most of all to be true to life," I added.

"In that case," she replied with a weary laugh, "you might as well give up!"

I asked her why it seemed impossible.

"Because there are some things about Joanna that no one will ever know." She paused. "Except perhaps myself."

"Things you know but will not tell me?" I inquired. "Or things that even *you* do not know?"

"Oh, my dear, there is little or nothing I do not know!" she retorted in her throaty voice.

"I see," I murmured, wondering precisely what she had meant. For the moment, however, I had no intention of letting her know she had piqued my curiosity. "One thing continues to puzzle me," I added as matter-of-factly as I could. "Only *you* seem to know about the last letter which Joanna supposedly wrote David Cassel—the letter to be given him after her death. No one else I've talked to seems to believe that story."

"No one else knows the truth," she replied with icy authority. "Joanna never hid anything from me, you see. She confided in me as she did in no one else." Her tone softening, she added, "There is one thing more—something which I have hesitated to tell you, partly because I myself was not completely certain at the time. Until last week, that is." An enticing pause. "Not only was there a letter, but I have learned recently that a *copy* of that letter still exists. Imagine what it would mean for your book, what it would illuminate, if you were able to find the copy of that letter!"

An uneasy feeling momentarily overcame me as I recalled Lawrence Brandt's description of Joanna's increasing paranoia: "She never sent a letter without making a copy first," he had told me.

"How did you find out about this?" I asked. "About the possibility of a copy?"

"I have—" she paused, "my ways."

"And if there is a copy, who has it? Where is it?"

"Ah, if only I knew, my dear! Wherever it is, it is in a place where David would not be able to destroy it." Then, with a short laugh that heralded a change in tone: "But this is *too* complicated! Besides, this wasn't the only reason for my calling you. I want you to come to dinner. October thirteenth. Black tie. It will be an amusing group."

I said I would check my calendar and let her know. I remember she seemed mildly annoyed by my lack of focus on her invitation; it was the idea of the last letter that continued to engross me.

"The house in England—Thistleton—that made such an impression on Joanna," I asked after a moment. "Where is it, exactly?"

"Hampshire," she said patiently.

"Far from London?"

"Not so far, no. An hour and a half or so by train. I go there several times a year myself—Desmond and I have remained old friends, you see. Of course it is rather sad to see him now —he had a stroke about a year ago, just after Joanna's death. He is only sporadically coherent."

"Do you think it worth my while to go there?" I asked next, having already anticipated her answer; I was only curious how she would phrase it.

"Oh I think you *must*," she said, her tone at once casual and resoundingly conclusive. "I don't think it would be possible to write Joanna's story without seeing Thistleton. Or Desmond Kerrith, for that matter. I knew you would come around to that! But I thought it better not to force it upon you, you see." She paused, as if to let me appreciate the full impact of her thoughtfulness. "I thought it better that you come to that conclusion yourself. I didn't want to seem too aggressive about it." Another pause. "It's *your* book, after all!"

I asked her whether it was possible that Joanna might have left a copy of the letter at Thistleton.

"It's not unlikely, not in the least. It was the place she felt safest, after all. And she was so very close to Desmond—

throughout her life, really. She continued to write him until the end."

I reflected on this before asking her the best time to visit Thistleton.

"Winter," was her unexpected, lulling answer. "Winter—when the park is covered with snow. When the rooms are not milling with tourists. It's a National Trust House now, you see."

"So you know it well?" I asked, wondering whether she would disclose having been Desmond Kerrith's secretary, as Patrick Rossiter had mentioned.

"Fairly well, I must confess," was all she replied. "I've known Desmond for a long time. Since I was a young woman, in London. Everyone knew Desmond then. He had an *inescapable* reputation."

I inquired whether she thought my visiting would be difficult to arrange.

"It would not be easy, but it would not be impossible, either," she replied. "Assuming your introduction is properly made, of course. I would like to think I could be helpful to you there. Especially now, with Desmond's illness. I assume much of the estate's business is in the hands of his lawyers and the conservator of his estate, all of whom I know." She paused, only to repeat: "But of course I'd be delighted to help you in any way I can."

I thanked her, noting two things: her reluctance to reveal she had once worked as Desmond Kerrith's secretary and her eagerness to orchestrate my visit. I said that I would be in touch with her soon, that I would let her know about the invitation to dinner. I asked nothing more about Thistleton, for I had already decided to write Kerrith myself and to ask Christina for help only as a last resort. I said goodbye. "We'll speak," was all she said.

I returned from the surrogate's court to the quiet of my apartment later that afternoon, a copy of Joanna's will, dated

July 10, 1985, in hand. It was unexpectedly short, bequeath-
ing a considerable range of personal possessions—jewelry,
furniture, books, paintings—to her friends (a suite of Biedermeier chairs to Christina, an Augustus John drawing to Patrick Rossiter) and family (to Rosalind, a Burmese ruby ring).

It was the first paragraph, more than any other, that intrigued me:

> I hereby appoint my husband, David Cassel, as executor
> of my will. I give and bequeath to him all my personal
> property, as well as all my letters and correspondence,
> with the exception of those letters and memorabilia
> physically located in the library at Thistleton, Hamp-
> shire, England, which I give to Desmond Kerrith; I also
> appoint Desmond Kerrith as my literary executor with
> respect to those letters and memorabilia. In the event
> that he cannot act as my literary executor, I grant that
> power to his conservator.

I continued to study that telling first paragraph, whose
clauses seemed, in the light of my conversation with Christina von Shouse, so tantalizingly specific: Of all her considerable material possessions, Joanna had addressed the fate of
her letters and memorabilia first. She had granted David
Cassel the power of executor, yet she seemed to have carefully restricted his control by denying him the power over the
letters she had sent to Lord Kerrith at Thistleton. I reread
that crucial phrase: "with the exception of those letters and
memorabilia physically located in the library at Thistleton,
Hampshire, England, which I give to Desmond Kerrith."

I put down the will and walked toward the window, then
back to the desk where the will lay, only to peruse it again,
too excited and nervous to sit still. What was at Thistleton
that Joanna did not want Cassel to control? Had she indeed
sent a copy of that final letter there, the letter Christina had
likened to the hand twisting up from the grave? Or was the
will merely a symptom of a deluded woman, a woman
gripped by psychosis, by paranoia?

* * *

Jack had promised to call at four o'clock that afternoon. At last, shortly before six, the telephone rang. I was cool at first; surely Jack sensed it, for his first words—"Forgive me, darling"—were perhaps too effusive. "I had a meeting that ran late," he explained. "My work."

I reminded him somewhat testily that I, too, worked.

"But that's not how I *think* of you, darling," he told me in a voice at once seductive and admonishing, a voice that begged me to ask him to elaborate.

"How *do* you think of me, then?" I asked, almost reticent to know the answer.

"As the woman I love," he said simply.

"Not enough to live with," I said in a voice edged more sharply than my yearning.

"Soon, darling. I've told you that." He paused. "Trust me to do what's right for us both."

"For us both," I murmured. "Yes."

He asked how I had spent the day.

"Continuing my research," I replied. "On my book."

"Yes of course." Then: "Do you miss me?"

"Yes," I said softly. "Very much."

"How much?" he asked in a voice of a lower timbre, presaging sex.

I ached for him, I admit, but only said, "I'll meet you at the restaurant, at eight."

Here I felt him hesitate. "I can't have dinner tonight—I meant to tell you. Something's come up. A dinner with a board member who's only here for the night." He paused. "I'm sorry."

I felt my anger mounting: This was the second time in two weeks he had cancelled at the last moment. "You could have told me earlier," I said. "I would have made other plans."

"I didn't know earlier."

"I find that hard to believe."

"It's not a story I'd be likely to invent."

"Isn't it? You're pretty good at inventing stories for your wife."

"I see," he said sharply, in such a way that I instantly regretted my words. "I see."

A long, tense pause lay between us.

"I know this is hard for you, sweetheart," he said after a moment, his voice having softened. "I *know* it is, believe me! But you've got to understand my own pressures—my business, my children. You've got to understand that I never, ever mean to hurt you."

I began to cry. "I know that," I murmured, barely able to speak.

"I love you," he said. "Isn't that the only thing that matters? How it is between us?" He paused, adding passionately, "The moment I saw you I felt complete."

I felt a surge of arousal. I told him that I loved him, too, and that it was my need for him, my awful need to be with him, that made his absence so painful.

"I'll come see you after dinner," he said almost boyishly, "If you'll let me."

"I'll *let* you," I said, smiling slightly through my tears.

The next day, I wrote two letters: the first to Desmond Kerrith, asking him to grant me permission to see the letters Joanna had bequeathed to him; the second, an "Author's Query," which I submitted both to *The New York Times Book Review* and *The International Herald Tribune*. "For a biography of Joanna Eakins," I wrote, "I would appreciate hearing from her friends and professional associates, particularly those who corresponded with her or who hold documents relevant to understanding her life and career." This was followed by my name and a box number.

Afterward, I called Rosalind Bennett's office at Goldman, Sachs, with the intention of scheduling an interview with her. I was put through to several secretaries, each of whom addressed me in the neuter, practiced tone of an office executive. Finally, a certain Mr. Crowell—one of two secretaries with whom I had spoken—returned my call, saying that Ms. Bennett would be able to meet with me on the seventh of October, at six o'clock at her apartment, which was located on lower Fifth Avenue. I agreed to the date, made a note of her address, and thanked him.

I realized I had still not responded to the invitation for dinner from Christina von Shouse. I picked up the telephone and began to dial her number, only to pause midway: Something about the invitation made me reticent, a vague and anxious presentiment that seemed totally out of keeping with a simple invitation to a dinner party. It was ridiculous, I told myself. And so I picked up the telephone again, dialed her number, and waited a moment while the maid called Mrs. von Shouse. We exchanged a few pleasantries and then I said, yes, I would be delighted to attend her dinner.

Her last words to me were, as I recall: "I'm so delighted you can come—there will be lots of people you know."

22

Tuesday, 23rd September

An unexpected call from Lawrence Brandt—he's cool, not unfriendly, though, just businesslike. I suspect he trusts no one and am actually rather astonished to hear from him again. Several minutes into the conversation I wait to hear the real reason for this call: he asks about my returning the letters from Joanna (it's the appointed Tuesday, after all). Of course. "I hadn't forgotten," I tell him, annoyed that he should feel the need to call me about it. What I don't tell him is that I find it hard to part with the letters, the pages of which I find strangely intoxicating, comforting—the single most revealing documents of Joanna's life, of her own voice. I merely say I'm grateful to him for having loaned them to me.

I also mention there are a couple of questions I'd meant to ask him: whether she had ever spoken of her life at Thistleton—a time which she had described to others as having been the happiest moment of her life. Yes, he told me (reluctantly, as always). She had alluded to it once or twice. He (Brandt) had always had the impression that her memories of that time, and of that love affair, were too precious to share with anyone else; and that whatever had happened was too painful for Joanna to reveal.

Next I ask him if he remembers the statue, modeled on Joanna, that stands in the maze at Thistleton. Does it still exist? Yes, Brandt says, it does, though the maze itself has fallen into decay; but he's got a meeting in a few moments and doesn't have time to describe it. (This really annoys me.) He surprises me by suggesting instead that we meet to discuss it: he suggests we have dinner on October 13th. I say no, I'm busy, I can't—I say this so brusquely that even I am taken aback. Then I tell him why: I'm going to Christina von Shouse's that night. "Partly as research for the book," I say sheepishly (nonsense, I know!). "Of course," he replies with a cynicism that takes me aback. "Your love of accuracy." In that pause, and in his voice, I feel his disdain for Christina, for her dinners, for her world—most of all I feel his disdain for me, that I should be attracted to that world, the *beau monde* of New York.

I find myself asking if he will be in New York later this month, "should I need to reach him with more questions about Joanna." No, he says, he'll be in Europe—Frankfurt, Paris—though I could always leave a message with his secretary. With his secretary, of course, I repeat. And then I put down the telephone. Even now, as I write this, I am vaguely disturbed by my strong reaction to him—disturbed, most of all, by his ability to make me feel corrupted by New York. To make me feel disappointed in myself, as if I were not living up to my own expectations. In the back of my mind, I tell myself, there is always the conversation with Christina von S. —destroyer of women, cruel to his wife. Her words haunt me, yet they are also comforting—they give me an excuse to rebuff him. He's so proud and intellectually arrogant: his silent treatment when I interviewed him, after all! I don't need this, I tell myself.

Thursday, 25th September

Had dinner with Jack tonight at Paolo's, the Italian restaurant not far from my apartment. (The fact that I order *spaghetti alla putanesca* and gorge myself on it is an irony not lost on me, but is it—I suspect so—on Jack?) It's very late by the time we have dinner—each "special" they've run out of is, of course, precisely the one thing Jack wants. I wear the new black jersey dress Jack brought me from Paris a few weeks ago, a dress only the avenue Montaigne could produce (with its inescapable aura of the *poule de luxe*). Jack compliments me, kissing me passionately when we meet (the restaurant by now is nearly empty). Yet even the warm, safe feeling I experience from his admiration seems to dissipate all too quickly these days. He is preoccupied with Northtech and I find him hard to reach at moments, struggling for conversation, even mildly irked by his habit of scribbling notes to himself on that damn black jotter. Still, when I feel his hand caressing my thigh, I long only for the moment when we go to bed.

He asks about my book on Joanna Eakins as he sips his martini (the sliver of lemon in that wide, shallow glass). I tell him it's going well, although I have uncovered some surprising things. And that the initial premise of the book—the marriage between David Cassel and Joanna—had changed considerably since I began. I go on to tell him that the story seems to exert an "incredibly strong pull on my subconscious." At this, he is barely able to conceal his skepticism (like most men, he has no belief in the subconscious). He asks what my editor and my publisher think of the book. I tell him there's a lot of enthusiasm for it; I also mention the amount I've been given as an advance; the number seems to impress even him. "Well, you've got to do it, then!" he says with sudden gusto (piercing an oyster and wrenching it from its shell at that moment). "Got to be bold. Take a chance."

I mention Christina's story of a last vengeful letter to David Cassel and the possibility that a copy of that letter might exist. And that it is impossible to really know whose point of view to trust—Christina von Shouse's or Lawrence Brandt's, or Patrick Rossiter's. This interests Jack; especially mention of David Cassel, whose career he has long respected, even in some ways emulated. (Likes sense of establishment money, etc., and membership on blue-chip boards.) But he seems perturbed that I might be uncovering things that will antagonize Cassel: he says I should be "careful." What does that mean, I ask him. I feel annoyed.

Then he asks me about Lawrence Brandt—what I think of him, of his house in East Hampton, etc. I tell him that Brandt's house is remarkable, subtle, mention the galleried library and the books. (Do I say this to make him jealous? Perhaps.) I also mention that I went by his (Jack's) house on Further Lane: he wants to know what I think of it— Belleplage, that is. I tell him it's impressive-looking, but totally unsuited to the landscape and very cold, adding that the name seems ludicrous for a house on the dunes of East Hampton. "That's Alice," he says, putting it all on the Wife. But I wonder whether that's true: men never assume responsibility for that kind of thing. Then he presses me for my opinion about Brandt. I tell him that I think he's arrogant but not uninteresting. "He's a talented son of a bitch, though," Jack says, biting into his dessert. I ask about Brandt's wife—whether Jack ever knew her. He said he'd met her once. "And was she very beautiful?" I ask—and he says yes, yes, she was. And that she left Brandt, and that he was devastated. Why did she leave him? I ask next. "Why most wives leave their husbands," he replies. "He was married to his work." I mention the little boy, Frederick. Jack knew about the child. I tell him what Christina von Shouse had told me—that Brandt was a man who had never suffered.

Jack looked up at me and said he doubted that was true: "Why does he work so goddamn hard, then?" A curious response. I hardly touched my food after that, feeling preoccupied without knowing why.

Went back with him to the Carlyle afterward. Windy night, leaves swirling on the street. The doormen all recognize me, which I find dispiriting now—no semblance of the romantic adventure I remember from that first year. I hate this furtive existence and tell Jack so once again. I feel spiteful he is so evasive when the talk veers toward marriage—his response is tender, yet I sense he does not take me seriously.

Still, as he undresses, I marvel at the beauty of his body, its strength and muscularity. I recall the first time we came here —the frenzy and voluptuousness of that winter afternoon. I would have done anything for him.

Memory can intensify, even resurrect, desire. I remember thinking this as he pulled me close—I remember closing my eyes and giving myself to him. I remember wanting to take from him what I found lacking in myself, and momentarily fearing that nothing could satiate my terrible appetite. Not even my ministering to him—a not unselfish act, for there, in its most undiluted form, I felt my power.

Afterward he presses me to spend the entire night with him and leave the next morning. I say I can't (my own vehemence surprises me). What I never dreamt is that he would be so utterly possessive yet so reluctant to change his life to commit himself to me: was I so terribly naive? Again I say, no, I can't. I have to work early the next morning. The truth is that I find it easier to be the one to leave—I so fear his abandoning me! One long, penetrating kiss; goodbye; a walk up dark, deserted Madison Avenue; then I'm home, unsure whether I embrace or dread the silence of my own apartment.

Friday, October 3rd

Card arrived today from Christina von Shouse to remind about upcoming dinner on Wednesday the 13th. Looks very swish: *"pour mémoire,"* etc., on a stiff white card with details (time, place) in calligraphic hand. I immediately wonder what to wear—as I always do. How awful to be saddled with such vanity, and this terrible love of clothes.

Jack's in Seattle again on Northtech business. I will go over my notes on Joanna this weekend and plan questions to Rosalind. She will be a tough nut to crack: is there any feeling there? I'm not sure, although I sense her devotion to David and to Wakefield to be deep, almost obsessive in its intensity. I wonder about its origin. It occurs to me that she will indeed be the one to inherit the house. What does that mean? I'll find out when I ask her just that question—about Wakefield, that is.

The appointment with Rosalind is set for next Tuesday, at her apartment. Six o'clock: for some reason her secretary (the aforementioned Mr. Crowell) felt compelled to add: "And I should tell you that Ms. Bennett is never late."

23

Tuesday, October 7, 1986

I met with Rosalind at the end of the day—in its own way this interview was as indelible as the afternoon with Christina von Shouse, except that Rosalind is rather more touching (to my surprise).

Her apartment is on lower Fifth, in a large, luxurious building. I expected a pseudo-Wakefield English decor (but should have known better) and entered, instead, a curtainless space devoid of color. Everything is white or black: around a black lacquer table in dining room are tall, strict Macintosh chairs. The whole effect is stylish and cold, clearly executed by someone else. R's white Persian cat, curled up on the white leather sofa—and hitherto invisible—suddenly moved, startling me! (R laughing about this as she calls to cat.)

I ask the cat's name.

"Elvis," she says.

"He's very pretty."

"It's a *she*."

Rosalind has cut her hair exceedingly short: from Parmigianino Madonna to Bronzino youth. She wears black: this time, suit of beautiful cut (Italian), which enhances her aura of capability, and high heels which show off her legs and which make her appear much taller. She'd just come from her office, I assume. First time I'd noticed her hands, which are surprisingly ugly and ill-groomed, with ragged cuticles and stains of nicotine; I sense she is rather self-conscious about them. Am also struck by the singular quality of her face—at once exquisite and unlovable. She tells me she has had a "shitty day" and that the market has been "fucked."

She's disgruntled and nervous (though tries not to show it); pours herself a drink (vodka on the rocks), then asks if I'd like some. I say no thanks.

She excuses herself for a moment (goes into bedroom), while I continue to look around. In one corner, there's a chilling study of a dispirited nude, in charcoal. No books, but lots of CD's near a daunting black stereo system: David Bowie, Talking Heads, B52's. Magazines on art deco table before sofa: *Fortune, Business Week, Forbes, Interview, Runner's World*, and *The Wall Street Journal*, of course. (The last anchored with a pair of dark sunglasses and a half-eaten Tiger's Milk protein bar.) I marvel at this type of mind, as well as the capacity to think in numbers and make vast sums of money. Friends on Wall Street tell me she is phenomenally talented at what she does—trading municipal notes— and generally recognized as a rising star at Goldman. The fact that she is Cassel's stepdaughter has not been unhelpful, of course. She returns from the bedroom, eyes brighter, sits down on white sofa, still nursing vodka, and kicks off her shoes. I wonder if she's nervous (this she would be horrified to admit). Picks up her "shades" on top of the *Journal* and holds them, folded up tightly in one hand, watching as I adjust the tape recorder. Then she lights a cigarette and begins to smoke.

Just as I am about to pose first question, the phone rings. She gets up to answer it. Doesn't say hello, but, "Yes," in low, impatient voice. It's her secretary or someone from her office, I gather. During the next few minutes I listen with fascination:

"Tell the bastard to sell."

Pause. Under her breath: "Shit." Another pause. "Of course it's do-able."

Pause. "Okay, sell at fifty." Pause.

"Tell him to leave it to me—unless he wants to fuck it up."

"Okay. Done deal. Just get the paperwork done ASAP. I'll check in later. Gotta go." Slams down phone. Returns. Sits down, curling legs (sheer black stockings) beneath her, proceeds to sip vodka and smoke. Then she looks at me with a cryptic smile, her almond-shaped eyes steely, impatient.

"Everything okay?" I ask her.

"Sure." She's calm, with no vestige of the harsh phone conversation. As if it belonged to another being.

"So where do we begin?" she says, already trying to control the thrust of the interview (which I'd expected she would).

I ask her to tell me her first memory of Joanna.

"Okay," she says, looking up at ceiling, thinking, the next moment turning to me with a querulous, childlike smile. "I was never very good at this."

I ask what she means.

"Talking about the past. Myself. Joanna. You know what I mean. It's like being shrunk."

I smile. "Not quite. You're not lying down, for one thing!" Then, facetiously, "Of course, if it would make it easier . . ."

She rolls her eyes, head bobbing slightly as she begins to reflect. "Okay, okay. When did I first meet Joanna . . .

When I was six or so. Just before she married my father. We
went to see her rehearse—it was Christmastime. She was in
Midsummer Night's Dream at Stratford, that was it. I just
remember sitting in the dark theater, watching her onstage.
For hours. With Christina and her daughter."

I think of Christina's description of taking the little girls to
the theater. "Joanna was in costume?" I ask.

"Yes. She played Titania. You can imagine. It must have
been a dress rehearsal."

"And then you went to see her backstage?"

"Yes."

"And what do you remember of that—being backstage
with her for the first time?"

"A mess. I mean her dressing room was a mess. I remember that."

"Disorder, you mean?"

She nods, stifling a yawn as she stretches out her legs on
the sofa. "Messy. Clothes around, a lot of mirrors. Makeup
all over a dressing table. Cigarettes crushed into jars of cold
cream. She had white cold cream all over her face when we
walked in. I think I was probably scared shitless. She looked
like a ghost."

I try to imagine Rosalind as a little girl, wondering what
she was like before she had embraced this tougher self—the
plump little girl intent on an abacus that Christina had described. "Did you watch Joanna often at rehearsal?" I asked.

"Yes. I'd go there with my nanny. Or with Christina and
Alexandra—her daughter. We'd sit there for hours. Sitting
there, in the darkness, watching Joanna at dress rehearsals."

"And your father?"

"He worked very hard. Didn't see him much."

"When did he die?"

"When I was twelve."

"And you stayed with Joanna?"

"There wasn't much of a choice."

"Until she married David?"

"Right." She smirks. "I came with the marriage, so to speak."

"And were you ever close to her, to Joanna?"

She pauses. "For a moment, maybe." Her expression is both implacable and wounded. "She was one very fucked up woman," she says suddenly. Abruptly moves her legs as she bends over to sip her drink.

"In what way fucked up?"

"In every way. She wasn't exactly the dream stepmother."

I say nothing in response. "But I gather you got close to David?"

"Yes."

"And you came to love Wakefield?"

"It's okay." But here it was hard for her to dissemble—for her attachment to the house is real, and deep.

"I assume you'll inherit the house," I say quietly.

"Probably." A pause. "I haven't really thought about it."

But I continue to prod her. "Joanna had no children, and David's son has been disinherited. Who else would inherit it?"

"You never know. Maybe David will donate it to NYU." Her expression is acid at the mention of one of Cassel's pet charities. "I've never thought about it," she repeats after a pause.

I don't believe this for a moment, and continue to press her: "You mean you've really never thought about it?"

She shrugs her shoulders. "It's just a house. I can buy my own house."

"But not *that* house." The more she tries to deny her feelings, the more I feel her attachment to Wakefield: she has no children, no lover that I know of. Only her stepfather, and the house.

"I don't like accepting things from people. I don't like owing anybody anything," she says after a moment. "I've always made my own money. Bought my own stuff." She seems restless again; as she lights another cigarette, I notice her ring—a large gold ring, inset with a ruby: I assume it was bequeathed to her by Joanna.

I mention the ring and ask her if it was indeed Joanna's.

"Yes," she says warily. "How do you know?"

"I've looked up the will."

"The will," she murmurs to herself, smoking again.

"The letters and the things left at Thistleton which Joanna was so specific about—have you any idea why?"

"None. Except that she was pretty weird those last years. Going after strange men—workmen, David's friends, anybody. Obsessed with the maze. Spending money like crazy. Paranoid about losing control. Irrational. In every way." And then, "Who knows?"

I tell her I know that David and Joanna had come to lead separate lives, that they seemed to have had a falling out at one point. I ask Rosalind if she knows why.

"Maybe he got tired of coddling her," she replies. "You know—the stage fright and all that crap. She wasn't acting anymore, she was just screwing around—with other men, with David's money."

"And so David had affairs . . ."

"Could you blame him?" she says fiercely, with a flash of her dark eyes. "The awful thing is that David really loved her —would have done anything for her—and she just treated him like dirt. Once she got what she wanted, of course."

She pauses, considering this a moment while she drags on her cigarette; then she looks at me slyly: "Maybe she refused to suck his dick. Literally and figuratively." Another sardonic glance. "But I'm getting a little crude for you," she says, baiting me. "Wouldn't want to shock the biographer."

"Not at all," I reply coolly, noting that she looks almost disappointed at my reaction to her swearing. I ask what she means by sucking his dick *figuratively*.

"You know—the wife thing," she replies, raising an eyebrow. "What most women do." She pauses. "That's why I've never been interested in marriage. The idea of being a nurse never appealed to me. Never was the Florence Nightingale type." She smiles to herself, her eyes still upon me.

"But you seem to take care of your stepfather very well," I remark.

"Yes—but that's *my* choice. No one's forcing me to. No contract."

I ask how long after their marriage Joanna and David had begun to use separate bedrooms.

"A year or so," she says, adding, "The dirty secret of most marriages is how little sex there is." Then, slyly: "But that's something *you* should be an expert on, right?"

She catches me off guard—and knows it—with this oblique reference to Jack and his marriage to Alice; the fact that she's aware of my affair upsets me, though I try not to show it. Instead, I carefully pose the next, crucial question. "I've heard Joanna wrote a letter to David, a letter to be given him after her death." I watch her expression as it seems to darken perceptibly. "Is there any truth to that?"

"Only if you believe vicious rumors," she replies at once, with controlled fury. "People will say anything. You know New York."

I resist the impulse to press further, knowing it will only antagonize her and jeopardize my chance of learning more. Besides, her face and her tone of voice are revealing enough. Instead I ask: "And your own relationship with David?"

"Good. Always has been."

"Tell me about it."

"We've always gotten along well. We have things in common—business, the market—things Joanna never understood. Maybe he's proud of my career." Then, under her breath: "Christ." She has knicked her black stocking with her finger; a run speeds up her leg, a ladder of pale flesh from calf to thigh.

Rearranging her legs, she looks up at me with an expression of annoyance—fidgeting gestures, a deep sigh.

I ask what the matter is. "This interview, that's what," she says belligerently. "Haven't you got enough about Joanna?"

No, I say, I haven't. Not yet. "What else comes to mind when you think of Joanna?"

She ponders this, her eyes elsewhere as she distractedly smokes. "Singing for her supper," she says after a moment.

I ask what she means.

"When she married David," she says, "I was fifteen."

The circuitousness of her answer is not lost on me. "It was a very small, private ceremony, I've heard."

"Tasteful." Her expression is spiteful. "That was the word most often used to describe it. They spent a couple of nights in New York before going to Europe. I stayed at the apartment, too. I remember once I got up in the middle of the night to get a glass of water, and I heard them—I mean" her mouth tightens, "I heard Joanna singing for her supper." The last words uttered in a near hiss.

I ask again what she means exactly, even though I'm aware this will exasperate her.

"What do you think I mean?" is her infuriated response. "They were having sex, making love—what else do you want me to call it? And Joanna was making all this noise, moaning, calling his name—a performance like any other." She smiles sarcastically. "A private rendition of As You Like It."

"What did you mean by moaning?" I interject.

Her voice is caustic: "What did you think I meant?"

"Moans of pleasure?" I ask, noting the vehemence of her reaction. "Or—"

"Pleasure, obviously," she retorts. "Or whatever passed for that with Joanna."

"Why did you say singing for her supper?"

"Because that's what she was doing. She married him for money, for security, for all the reasons that women marry, and then—well, she had to do her bit."

"And that included satisfying David in bed?"

"Apparently." She pauses. "The shitty part about it was that David actually loved her. Would have done anything for her. Just like my father! And the moment Joanna knew David was caught, she became restless. She had played that part—

wife of David Cassel—and then she grew tired of it. On to a new part, a new audience."

"Do you think you might possibly be too hard on her?"

"No. Why?"

"Wasn't she kind to you—ever?"

"Sure, she gave me some attention. Told me what to wear. What men liked. Showed me all the jewels her lovers had given her." A bitter expression crosses R's face as she begins to reminisce: "I remember one time—I must've been sixteen —when I came into her bedroom in the city. She'd taken out all her jewelry—boxes and boxes of the stuff on her bed—" here Rosalind slyly imitates Joanna's precise, slightly high-pitched English accent: " 'Come and look, Rosalind, at my treasures. I'll let you borrow them one day.' " R pauses, brow furrowed, as she resumes in her own voice: "Then she held up a bracelet, a necklace, some earrings. 'I only slept with the man *twice*, can you imagine, before he gave me this necklace! You can't imagine the thrill I felt when I opened this box and found—what did he call it?—'Everlasting gems for my ever-lasting love!' She laughed as she threw the necklace on the bed." R pauses. "I remember I felt sick."

Rosalind's gaze has turned inward; a moment passes before I feel her snapping back into her previous self. "But I wasn't her real daughter, after all," she continues brusquely. "You might have thought she would have welcomed a stepchild, especially since—but no, I was always just a burden to her." She lights another cigarette.

"What do you mean when you said she might have welcomed a stepchild, 'especially since'?"

"Don't know. She'd had a child once, a boy, a long time ago—the baby died right after he was born, and I think she always felt guilty about it."

"She told you that?"

"Once. Yes."

"Nothing else?"

"Nothing else." Pause. "She wasn't exactly someone who'd let it all hang out. Her feelings, I mean."

I ask about Christina von Shouse.

"What exactly do you want to know?"

"What do think of Christina?"

"Shrewd. Would have been a good trader."

"You're probably right," I answer, smiling at the idea. And then: "What about your relationship with her?"

"I don't dislike her. But I don't trust her, either. Like a lot of people in this town."

"Explain—"

"Because she used David. Used Joanna to get to him for money. She's always lived beyond her means—would have married David if she'd had half a chance." She paused to drag on her cigarette. "Christina was the only person really close to Joanna," she volunteers for once. "Who really understood her."

"Was she jealous of Joanna, do you think?"

"Who knows? Helped a lot with Wakefield, though—that was part of her bond with Joanna."

"Helped with the decoration?"

"Yes. Among other things."

"And Lawrence Brandt?"

"They never got along—Christina and Larry, I mean."

"Why?"

"Larry thought she was a bad influence on Joanna. Christina knew it—that Larry had told Joanna and David how he felt."

I ask Rosalind how she would describe the friendship between the two women.

"Christina had a knack for making herself indispensable—in Joanna's life, I mean," R considers this a moment, her unkempt hand moving along the run in her stocking. "Joanna couldn't do without her, even though Christina used to annoy her. She even told me that—Joanna did. 'Tina gets on my nerves, but I can't manage without her,' she'd say. There was the way Christina worshiped the acting—the Shakespeare and all that stuff. It fed Joanna's ego. Almost amused her at times to see this woman so subservient. So *adoring*. She liked having that power over her, I guess—just as she did over David."

"What did Christina get out of it?"

"She liked the association with Joanna—a famous woman, a stage actress. Having influence over her. You'd be surprised how some people will suck up to an artist! Christina was just *there*—always there. It began when Joanna was acting—she'd help with her lines, her costumes, her makeup, that kind of thing. She'd gush over Joanna's performances, but she could also be critical. In her own way." R. stops, puts her hand to her mouth as if tempted to bite her nails, but refrains. "I remember once after a performance—can't remember which one—we went backstage afterward, Christina and Alexandra and I, to see Joanna. The first thing Christina said to Joanna was, 'We forgot the *white*, didn't we, Joanna?' I wondered what she meant. I asked Joanna; I remember she looked nervous. 'The white pencil,' she told me, 'I always use it to line the inside of my eyes—it makes them look bigger.' She'd forgotten to do it that night, you see, but there was Christina to remind her!

"And then, another time, I think it was *Hedda Gabler*, we went to see Joanna afterward. For once she was happy with her performance. 'It really *worked* tonight, didn't it, Tina?' she said. 'Yes,' Christina said. 'But can you do it *again*?' I'll never forget the expression on Joanna's face. It was the only time I almost felt sorry for her.

"But in a way Christina's hold on Joanna got stronger after the acting stopped—then she was *really* indispensable! 'If I ever return to acting, it will be because of Tina,' I remember Joanna saying. Then came the New York life with David—you know, Christina helping Joanna with all the things that didn't come so naturally to her." A pause. "I mean, the *plotting* came pretty easily—for men, for money, for fame—but not the other stuff. The houses, the clothes—'That's Christina's domain,' she'd say. 'She's so *refined* in that way.' She was very big on refinement, Joanna was. At least at a certain stage of her life." Here R. smirks; then an aside as she crushes out her cigarette: "No wonder we didn't get along all that well.

"Even with Wakefield, so much of it was Christina," she continues with an uneasy glance in my direction. "The objects, the needlepoint cushions, all the little details." Here R. imitates Christina's throaty voice: " 'We must make it *cozy*, Joanna,' Christina would keep saying. Joanna didn't care about cozy," Rosalind scoffs. "I always felt she just wanted the house to be *grand*, intimidating—like a stage set for a play in which she'd be the star. I mean, she wasn't acting anymore—what the hell else could she do?" She pauses, deep in thought, tearing at a fingernail.

"What are you thinking?" I ask.

"I'm thinking about the two of them—Christina and Joanna. Seeing them in Joanna's study, the two of them playing chess. Seeing who would be first to finish the *Times* crossword puzzle each Sunday. Who'd be the winner." She sips her vodka. "I remember—just a few days before Joanna died, I knocked on the door. She was in her study at Wakefield. Had a message to give her. And there they were, the two of them, going through all the stuff in Joanna's old prop box. Christina folding the costumes, one by one, that Joanna had thrown on the floor. Joanna looked strange, sort of lost. Christina had a weird smile, like the cat who'd just swallowed the canary." Rosalind sat up, straightening her back against the sofa. "Nothing's simple," she said with sudden briskness. "And sure as hell not the relationship between Joanna and Christina. Who controlled who is the question."

I continue to watch Rosalind, noting her skittish gestures. "Did Joanna give Christina a lot of money over the years?"

"Maybe." She looks uncomfortable. "Presents, probably—jewelry, furniture."

"Did David know?"

"Only toward the end."

"And then?"

"The money ended. *Presto*."

"Have you any idea why Joanna felt the need to help Christina in the money department, as you say?"

"Money had no real meaning for Joanna. Once she had it, that is. And maybe she felt Christina had helped her catch David and that it was a way of repaying her."

"How well did you know Christina's daughter?"

"Alexandra?" She looks vaguely surprised at the question. "Well, what was she like?"

"Shy. Christina was desperate for her to become an actress —like Joanna. That's where I do remember the money coming in."

"How?"

"Joanna paid for her to go to college. Amherst. And to drama school. Egged on by Christina, of course."

"And—"

"And what?" she almost sneers.

"What happened?"

"Joanna thought the girl had a little talent, but nothing major. Christina didn't agree—she thought her daughter was God's gift to the acting world. Kept pushing her. I remember once—" here she stops, as if to catch herself from saying something she hasn't intended.

But I press her: "You were saying that you remember once—"

"Christina and Joanna arguing about her daughter. Joanna saying that she, Christina, was pushing Alexandra to a career that might destroy her. That Alexandra might be a good actress, but never a great one. And that she wasn't tough enough—*strength* was the word she used—for the theater."

"Did Joanna ever tell Alexandra this directly?"

"She may have. But then how would I know? Anyway, the girl had real problems. She wound up killing herself."

"What about Christina during that time?"

"What about her?" She pauses. "She seemed pretty much in control, as she usually is. Joanna was the one who was a wreck."

"Did that surprise you?"

"Yes." She lowers her gaze, smoking again. "A little."

"Why do you think Joanna took it so hard?"

"Maybe she felt responsible in some weird way."

I make a note to myself: her account, like Lawrence Brandt's, totally contradicts Christina von Shouse's own description. "Do you think Christina made Joanna feel that way?" I venture. "Responsible, I mean?"

She looks uncharacteristically thoughtful before responding. "No. Not at all. Just the opposite. Christina went out of her way to comfort her. But that's just my gut reaction."

"What about David and Christina?"

She laughs, voice edged with irony. "They tolerate one another, let's say. She doesn't dare show her anger toward him." Noticing my quizzical expression, she adds, "Her anger that the money has stopped."

"Why wouldn't she show it?"

"He's too important in her world. She can't afford to alienate him—socially, I mean. What else does she have?" She looks scornful. "She's never *done* anything. That's her only power, isn't it? To give dinners, to know what's going on. What's new on the Rialto."

There is a pause while I turn over the tape. Then I ask: "Are you going to Christina's dinner on the thirteenth?"

"Probably," she says, shrugging her shoulders.

"Why would you go if you really don't like her?"

"Why not?" Her smile was small, tight and bitter, yet strangely pathetic. "This is New York. You often accept invitations from people you can't stand—you might miss something."

"Like what?"

"Information."

"What kind?"

She shrugs her shoulders, laughing, and says cavalierly, "I just made that up." Pulling her legs tight under her, she adds, "I'll go because I always find it interesting to see her manipulating people."

"Is that her sole interest in life?"

"Would that surprise you?"

"What do you mean?"

"I mean, she likes to control people. Their personal life. Houses, clothes, all of that—the social graces, I think they were once called. Joanna didn't know any of that stuff before she married David—she was a famous actress, and her life was the theater. Acting. That was it. Then she married David and things changed. David was everything that Christina admired." She pauses to light up another cigarette. "But Christina never really made it on that level."

"What about Joanna's stage fright?"

"What about it?"

By now her feistiness hardly affects me. "Well, why do you think Joanna could never conquer it?"

"Not a clue." She pauses, her arms crossed tight across her chest. "Maybe the guilt got to her."

"About what?"

"About her marriage to David. Maybe she was guilty because once again she'd used a man she hadn't any feeling for. Another loveless merger. Difficult to know with Joanna." She pauses again; then picks up *Fortune*, flips through it, and says, "This is how Joanna got David."

"What do you mean?"

She slaps the magazine down on the table. "There was a list of the one hundred richest men in the U.S.—David was on it. She went after him. No dope, Joanna."

"And how did she 'get' your father?"

"No idea. Part of her English period, shall we say—no one was a bigger Anglophile than Joanna! My father was a neurosurgeon, very well known, I guess. Good family, all of that. I just remember him as my father and his coming home at night from the hospital and tucking me in bed, still in his white jacket. Joanna would be at the theater."

"And your mother?"

"A distant memory, unfortunately," she says, uttering the words in a mock theatrical voice. But her bravado is forced; it cannot mask the expression of loss in her eyes. "She died when I was four."

"I'm sorry," I tell her. She shrugs her shoulders. For a moment I pause, wondering whether I should mention that I, too, never knew my mother. But I don't.

"You haven't had an easy life," I say quietly.

"Can't complain. Things happen. I've always got David—he's been good to me."

I thought of my first dinner at Wakefield and the scene around the gleaming dinner table—how gentle Rosalind had been with David, how solicitous toward him, how different from the acerbic, fast-talking creature before me now.

"What about you?" she says suddenly. "Why should you write this book—what's in it for you?"

"I saw Joanna onstage once, and I've always been fascinated by her career, that's all."

"You're sure as hell not doing it for the money!" she says, continuing her scrutiny.

"Everyone needs money." My voice is low; I had anticipated what would come next.

She crunches some ice in her mouth, then looks up: "If you're Jack Varady's girlfriend, you need less money than most."

My stomach tightens; I try to appear cavalier. "Why do you say that?"

"Because everyone knows you're having an affair with Jack Varady. On the Street. Including David. God knows Christina must know." She pauses, swirling some last bits of ice in the glass; for a moment I feel nauseated. "I've had a few little tête-à-têtes with Mr. Varady myself," she says offhandedly. "Don't worry—I'm talking business dinners." A pause. "Never knew he was available," she adds with a sly glance.

Embarrassment overtakes me; she knows it. I wonder if her words are meant to be a warning. "Why should any of this matter to David?"

"He likes gossip, hearing about other people's peccadilloes. Makes his blood rush—especially now, when his life isn't quite so . . . active." Her small, enigmatic smile is edged with an unpleasant prurience.

I tell her it's time for me to leave (it's nearly eight o'clock) and begin to pick up my things.

"I'd like to go to Wakefield again," I say, turning to her, notebook in one hand. "Sometime later this month. Would that be a problem?"

"Not at all. Just tell me when and I'll work it out with David." She seems curious. "What is it you want to see?"

I tell her I'd like to see the grounds again, especially the maze—"take in the atmosphere" is the way I put it. "I wasn't feeling very well the last time," I add, "and I'm sure I missed a lot."

She stands up and only then, with her shoes off, do I realize how small, even delicate, she is—how at odds her manner with her ethereal face and vulnerable neck. Perhaps even she is aware of this, because the next instant, shoes in place, she reassumes her old swaggering self.

She walks me to the door.

"Call me when you've got an idea of the date—when you want to come to Wakefield," she says, standing by the front door. Then she pauses, as if something has suddenly occurred to her: "Do you ride?" I tell her yes, but not very well. "Bring your riding stuff with you," she says. "I'll organize a horse. Show you more of the territory."

I thank her and say goodbye.

"No problem," she replies. Without another word, she shuts the door; I remember the hard metallic sound of the lock sliding into place.

24

The night of Christina von Shouse's dinner arrived.

It seemed that the limestone-and-brick fortresses of Park Avenue had vanquished all the stars that evening—the sky was dark and dense. It was mid-October and unseasonably cold.

I had spent an inordinately long time dressing, and was grateful for the new red dress that I had reserved to wear that night: Even now I can recall the feeling of the silk and the precise, shapely way it was tucked across the hips and the ribbons of red satin that edged its full, billowing sleeves and long skirt. (Curious how a mere dress can delineate an entire experience, even influencing the way it will unfold.) For in that world—the world of New York that I knew—a dress was not really such a trivial thing; or if it was, so were the banners that medieval jousters wore in tournaments or the brilliant flags unfurled by armies marching into battle. (Years later, I would come upon that dress in a locked-up closet and, having almost forgotten it existed, would unshroud it from a plastic bag, overcome by the scent of jasmine and tuberose still emanating from its folds.)

My hair brushed, my diamond earrings from Jack in place, I stood nervously before the mirror for a moment, not entirely displeased. I fixed my lipstick, checked my evening bag, and locked the door to my apartment, taking a taxi from my building to 778 Park Avenue, my apprehension as intense as my curiosity. I was, as I recall, rather late.

The slight, dark-haired maid whom I remembered from the afternoon in August took my cape: Now her dark lipstick and rouged cheeks lent her a doll-like aspect. "Please to find your card," she said with a slight nod, indicating the rows of tiny white envelopes on a nearby console. I found one with my name and opened it. "Blue porcelain," it said: my table. I moved to another console, where the seating arrangement was re-created on a gilt-edged leather table plan, pinwheel-like place cards inserted around it. I was seated next to David Cassel, it seemed, which did not displease me. Tucking the card into my handbag, I ordered a drink from one of the roving waiters and walked into the drawing room.

I felt at once like one who has seen a stage set empty, only to return to find the play in full progress. Competing perfumes scented the air, and the sofas and satin chairs, deserted that sultry August afternoon, were massed with people talking, whispering, shaking hands, and glancing at the threshold where I stood, to ascertain who had just arrived. One glimpse was enough to convince me that this was an "important" dinner: an aura of confidence and self-congratulation already permeated the atmosphere, the sort that accompanies those who know they have accepted the right invitation.

Into this tableau of shimmering conviviality I ventured—I

remember the sheen of blue satin, the touches of malachite, and the ghostly reflections cast by candles into silver trays and objects, all of which were rendered even more illusory by the ceiling's painted sky.

The men, in black tie, had bequeathed unto the women the privilege of color: the rich, challenging colors of couture silks and velvets and the hard glint of precious gems—emeralds, rubies, and sapphires wrenched from the earth, only to be polished, set, and strung into the glittering currency of another breed of "merger." A menagerie of brooches—parrots, unicorns, panthers—glittered from rigid shoulders, bracelets from wrists. I was all too aware of the Faustian bargains these baubles often symbolized; yet that did not seem to prevent the women from wearing their stones triumphantly or the men from regarding these adornments as reflections of their own power, rather than defeat.

Christina von Shouse approached, her neck looped with lustrous gray pearls, her severe black dress all the more stunning in its seeming self-effacement. I could almost hear her mentally assessing my own dress as she kissed me on both cheeks. "Chanel?" she asked at once. I nodded. "Ravishing," she said with a glance that seemed almost inappropriately resolute.

"You must tell me how the book is going," she half-commanded, taking my arm. "Your research." Then, without waiting for me to answer: "I hear you are *relentless*."

I remember smiling to myself at this, before adding, perhaps too gaily, "I feel as if I've opened Pandora's box."

"Well, you yourself said you wanted it to be true to life!"

I nodded, only vaguely remembering my own words. "You have a remarkable memory," I told her.

"Yes," she mused, her eyes circling the room. "I never forget anything." Placing her hand lightly on the small of my back, she turned to me with customary authority and said, "Come. Let me introduce you to everyone," as she led me deeper into the room, her introductions graceful, her rhythm vivace.

I realized at once the extent of her reach, for the guests were not culled from a single pocket of New York society but were creamed from various spheres, the common denominators being money, power, and fame. It was the sort of dinner where identity is telegraphed—either by the names of corporations (*New York Times*, CBS, Drexel Burnham, American Express), or by one's position on the *Forbes* list (several brash tycoons whom money had recently swathed in respectability). The women's banners were culled from another, but no less exacting and fortune-conscious, lexicon: Yves Saint Laurent, Dior, Valentino. Woe to those at such gatherings whose professional or social identity was unknown or ambiguous! Toward those obscure few, New York could be pitiless.

Most of these names, however, I knew, as people were introduced to me by turns. I could almost hear them saying to themselves *Wall Street Journal* (or, in some cases, "Varady mistress"). I heard myself talking and laughing, infused by the hazy warmth of my kir royale; speaking of politics one moment, of a recently published book at another—fulfilling my obligation as a guest, in short, even as I took in the room, its Russian decor at its most splendid, and mused about the relationship of the guests to the hostess.

I quickly realized that Christina von Shouse's relative isolation from any particular group, coupled with her chameleonlike intelligence and the aura of the book on Russian decorative arts to be published *at some point* by Neville Somerfeld, freed her to create this spectacular mix—a connection with the world of intellect, however tenuous, that seemed to distinguish her from other, largely illiterate, Upper East Side matrons who wielded such power in *fin de siècle* New York. Sufficiently glamorous to be accepted by the polished wives of the New Rich, she was also cultivated enough not to be disdained by those with intellectual pretensions (the last group, mainly composed of writers and media stars, who assiduously preserved the illusion of being unswayed by money). Christina was able, thus, to marry several worlds, all the while shielding the *haute* Inner Core from The

Others, as if risk of exposure would somehow diminish the former's status.

Added to this was her powerful gift of decor—the seductive bourgeois touches that duped the richest guests into imagining they had somehow ventured into unconventional territory—but never at the cost of luxury or delicious food. Rooms that are merely grand can be limiting to those with complex social ambitions.

Amid the serious discussions—of Margaret Thatcher, of a *New York Times* editorial on corruption in the Koch administration, of the latest manipulation in the Nancy Reagan regency, of Gorbachev and *glasnost*—there was also talk of the latest Wall Street indictment, the lack of good hotels in Milan, the so-called disfigurement of the streets by the growing number of the homeless, the word on the most recent collection by Christian Lacroix, or the best itinerary for visiting Eastern Europe (that part of the world having recently come back into vogue).

Fillips of conversation continued to float toward me: thus, from an elegant, taut-skinned lady with white hair: "Lending moral support to our pets is so important"; or another—this to do with the liaison between a European woman and a younger man once thought to be gay: "It's about conversion, I should think." At one point I caught the tail end of a discussion about a trip to Paris, the object of the quest being "the million-dollar commode."

I continued to wend my way through the crowd, assailed by the conversations and the voices—and the voices, in many cases, were not pretty. In this way, admittedly, I was and still am something of a snob—voice, to me, is everything, and I find it astonishing that grammar and accent should have been exempt from the fine-tuning accorded decor, clothes, and jewelry. (Here I recalled the acid remark of Russell Heywood, whose decadent figure I had just glimpsed in the crowd: "Why don't they make do with one less Renoir and invest in a voice teacher?") While the ministrations of couturiers and decorators were often able to mask the origin of fortunes made in funeral parlors or in a chain of suburban discount hardware stores called Brass 'n' Tacks, the voices often betrayed origins that had, in every other way, been so painstakingly and expensively concealed.

I stepped up to greet Russell Heywood and Patrick Rossiter, who stood together and whose lively conversation seemed, suspiciously, to halt at my approach. "I'd give anything to know what you two have been saying," I told them, half jokingly.

"Well, you know my motto," said Russell, casting his gaze about the crowd.

"When in doubt, invent?" I suggested with a smile.

"Very good, Elisabeth," said Patrick. "We'll have to have it done up for him in Latin. His crest."

I asked if they had seen David Cassel arrive. "He's over there," said Patrick, pointing to the opposite corner of the drawing room. Cassel sat in the dark green armchair before the fireplace, looking jaunty and appealing in black tie, his hand grasping his walking stick as he focused on the nubile redhead who had just been fetched to entertain him. But then the redhead set off in another direction, leaving Christina and Cassel alone. I observed them speaking together, struck by the intensity of their dialogue and, at one point, by Cassel's visibly unsettled expression. Withdrawing into myself—into the book—I wondered what Christina might have told him that so disturbed him. Still, I continued to banter with Patrick and Russell, asking if they'd seen Rosalind.

"Of course—she's Cassel's date," said Patrick slyly, adding, "You've heard of family romance." He motioned to the heavily curtained window at the opposite end of the room. "She's over there. In black."

Rosalind stood near the deep red curtains, speaking to a man I did not know, her shoulders bare in a long, tight satin dress with a stiff frill-like peplum, her wrists glittering with bracelets; one hand rested on her hip in such a way that I could see the flash of her ruby ring. The black satin seemed to emphasize the slightly mauve tint to her skin, her shorn hair, her long, slender neck.

Now, Cassel himself motioned to me. I made my way toward him, and as I did so, I wondered precisely why Christina had chosen to seat me next to him that evening—for at such dinners, after all, *placement* was paramount. Indeed, to some extent evenings like these were constructed around that one moment when, with a glance to the place card at one's right and left, one knew precisely—and sometimes brutally, too—the true nature of the hostess' regard.

As I made my way toward Cassel, I passed an aging CEO whose previously unassailable status as a trophy guest had considerably diminished with the onset of his dotage and the subsequent eroding of his corporate power. Walking quickly past the stooped, cane-carrying figure, I murmured a greeting —grateful all the while that I had not been chosen to be sacrificed to him that evening: It was an unwritten rule, at dinners of this ilk, that elderly men who had achieved a certain wealth and rank had also won the right to be seated next to a ripe young woman. It was considered one of the prerogatives of old age, just as it was deemed an obligation of youth to grant these aging gentlemen the companionship of younger flesh—at least during dinner. I could say this with some authority, for I had often been included among these Iphigenias of the dinner circuit; I had spent my fair share of evenings shouting into the ear of an aging magnate who had long since ceased to listen (in earlier years out of egocentricity, in later years out of physical impairment) or fending off the withered hand of a venerable billionaire whose libido was not yet entirely inactive.

But now it was the avid David Cassel who grasped my hand; the firmness of his grip, and the focus of his eyes, made me recall our first meeting at Wakefield Hall. "Come join me, Elisabeth," he said. I did so, gathering my skirt about me and saying something cheerful and noncommittal —I asked him about his summer, mentioned that I was delighted to be seated next to him—even though I did not relish the idea of discussing the progress of my research that night. Cassel now appeared to me in such a different light!

He went on to press me about the progress of the book. I hedged, saying only that it was going very well and that my research had confirmed that Joanna's was a fascinating story. "My instincts were right," I told him as blithely as I could, nodding that instant to Rosalind, who had by then discovered us talking.

"Christina's quite a gal," he said distractedly after a moment, tapping the floor with his walking stick, his eyes taking in the roving guests, as if assessing the evolution of the guest list to its present incarnation.

I asked Cassel whether he had met Christina through Joanna or whether they had known each other before. (I was curious to see whether his version would mesh with Christina's.) "Known her for years," he said, barely glancing at me. "She fixed me up with Joanna, you know—didn't she tell you that?"

I told him I had had the impression that their meeting was quite by chance, that he and Joanna had merely happened to be at the same dinner at her apartment.

"Nothing's by chance at Christina's," he retorted. "She knew my marriage had hit the skids. And it went from there." He continued to look restlessly around the room, his impatience palpable—chafing at the notion, perhaps, that it was now necessary to wait for people to come to him. I thought again of the conversation I had just witnessed between Cassel and Christina—what disconcerting news could she have told him, I wondered . . . Suddenly, I thought of the letter. Had Christina mentioned the existence of a copy of Joanna's final letter to him, which he had thought to have destroyed?

Rosalind approached us, greeting me rather coolly, I sensed, as David continued to speak, even to subtly flirt, with me. "Elisabeth asked me if she could come to Wakefield another weekend," she said, trying to catch her stepfather's attention. "To continue her research."

"I don't have any problem with that," he said, with an amiable enough smile.

"How's this weekend?" Rosalind asked, glancing at me as she crushed out her cigarette.

I told her it would be perfect; I could drive up late Friday night. "Okay," she said. "It's a deal."

Dinner was announced; Rosalind began to help Cassel stand up, supporting him with her slender arms. Once more I noticed her ugly hands, so at odds with her stylish dress and diamond bracelets, and that it was only Cassel who seemed to evince in her anything remotely approaching tenderness. Indeed, I remember being startled when they looked at me together—there was something so alike in their expressions that the idea that she was not in fact his own daughter seemed incredible.

I stood up and let them precede me, observing how slowly Cassel walked that night and how much more powerful he had looked sitting down. He had aged considerably over the summer.

Others were filtering in from the library, joining the growing pilgrimage to the dining room. I continued to greet acquaintances, to smile and chat, until I reached the entrance to the dining room. I took one last sip of my drink and set the glass on a nearby table; it was then, as I looked up, that I experienced a rush of bewilderment, happiness, and utter panic: There was Jack, and there, in high-necked pastel silk, was his blond wife, Alice.

I murmured hello: Jack's strained smile and Alice's blank expression met me in response. Unable to read her eyes, I wondered—as I did unceasingly—*whether she knew*. It was exceedingly rare that Jack and I met publicly, for our liaison was not unknown—this was the first time we had ever encountered one another at a formal dinner. As they disappeared into the dining room, I wondered what Christina von Shouse could possibly have intended: It seemed unlikely, with her social antennae, that she did not know of my affair with Jack!

For many moments, I stood paralyzed with confusion and self-loathing, my place card mangled in my hand. My red dress—the dress I had until that moment loved—suddenly felt gaudy, and for a split second I thought about leaving immediately. But pride and competitiveness intervened: I told myself it was Alice Varady, not I, who should feel humiliated. I would steel myself, I would be especially animated, I would hold my head high: I would freshen my red lipstick and make my way toward my table.

Already, the delicate mingling aromas of refined vegetables and meat wafted from the luminous green dining room. Tall candelabras glowed, and the snowy cloth on each of the four round tables spilled to the ground, weighted with agate-handled place settings and embellished by the rich sheen of imperial porcelain. At the center of each table stood a shallow vermeil bowl filled with moss studded with lilies of the valley and blue hyacinths. The room bespoke confidence and worldliness; yet all was underscored by the pressure one felt as the napkin unfolded upon the lap—the social pressure to perform, to amuse, to be an exemplary dinner partner.

I stood by the edge of the blue porcelain table, searching for my place card, my composure still jolted from seeing Jack with Alice. Rosalind had already assumed her place at the next table, one elbow planted near her fork as she swilled the last drops of her vodka. "Can I light up?" she asked me in a strident voice, "or do you think I'm the only evil smoker at this table?" I laughed at her ornery tone and, nervously glancing at her table, told her that it wouldn't be the first time she would be the evil one at the table.

Meantime I searched for my seat, only to find that my place card seemed to have disappeared and that of Leslie Bragg—a notorious fortune-hunting divorcée—had replaced it. I continued to scan the other place cards until I heard a voice—Rosalind, who had been greeting Russell Heywood. "I think I saw you over here, Elisabeth," she said, with a slight thrusting motion of her chin. "On the other side."

I moved to the edge of the red porcelain table and found

my name at last. Puzzled and annoyed, I looked up at Rosalind and Russell, who were still deep in conversation. Was it Rosalind who had changed my place—or Russell, with his love of intrigue? Or Leslie Bragg, with her designs on David Cassel? At that point I was too anxious and tired to focus on the switch and simply took my seat and unfolded the *fleur-de-lis* pleated napkin upon my lap.

I glanced to each side. The place card to my left belonged to Pierre Dufrey, the Swiss industrialist and art collector. I then picked up the place card to my right, starting when I saw the name on it: Mr. Jack Varady. Still incredulous, I read the name again, not knowing whether I should feel furious or elated, not knowing whether I should speak with the hostess herself about it—but surely that would only create more of an imbroglio: Dinner was about to begin. In my consternation, I sipped some water, trying to feign interest in the arrival of the others at our table. It was at that moment, as I looked up, that I caught Rosalind's eyes: In them I discerned malevolence and triumph. No doubt it was she who had switched the place cards. I looked away, almost unable to suppress my anger.

The next instant, I saw a hand on Jack's place card and then looked up to see his intent, golden face: I smiled at him and waited for him to smile back. I meant to welcome and reassure him, even to rejoice at our good luck in finding ourselves together, but in return was met with a reaction disturbing in its ambiguity. I could not read the expression of his mouth or of his intent blue eyes, though I sensed some anger in the way he pulled his napkin from the table and spread it on his lap. The next instant, however, I felt his hand caress my thigh below the table; I began to relax. I even remember the sensation of color returning to my cheeks. All the while, I knew Rosalind would be watching us, and wondered how this would later be recounted to Cassel—an amusing tidbit, given his love of gossip, a titillating accompaniment to a late night brandy, no doubt!

The table was complete now: Pierre Dufrey had taken his

place to my left, kissing my hand before he sat down. I hardly remember the others there, just as I can hardly remember what food was served that night. I only remember that Neil Zinsser, the investment specialist, who sat to one side of Rosalind, mysteriously continued to excuse himself from the table, only to return triumphantly before dessert. (Midway through dinner we would learn that he was bidding on a Tiepolo drawing in a sale at Hutchinson's.)

Fortified by wine and by Jack's caress, I began to talk with Pierre Dufrey, focusing on him with the exaggerated attention produced by anxiety, even as I longed to turn to Jack. Instead, I forced myself to plunder all I knew about Switzerland and the vagaries of the watch business—the industry Dufrey had almost single-handedly transformed by the creation of a disposable watch (a feat which, happily, had been chronicled by the *Times* business section the previous week). We spoke of Geneva and of Berne; whether Saint-Moritz was in fact more charming in summer than in winter; and of Zermatt, where, it turned out, we had both skiied—I told him I had once stayed at the Monte Rosa Hotel, and listened while he countered with his own appraisal of the Hotel Mont Cervin. (The service there was superior, he said, and I ought to try it.) We spoke at length of his art collection, and I even remember evincing a kind of sympathy—peculiar now, to think of it!—as he spoke of the difficulty in acquiring real masterpieces, and the dilemmas of restoring a Turner.

Never once did Pierre Dufrey ask me about myself—what I did or where I was from—nor did it ever occur to me that he would: I had long since mastered the subjugation of the self that was necessary, at least for a woman at such gatherings, to be considered a good dinner partner.

By the time the first course had been cleared (*coulibiac* of salmon, according to my menu card), it seemed to me I had earned the right to turn to Jack. And so, after a sip of wine, I did.

I waited for a moment, for he was still deep in conversation with Pamela Fraser, the wife of the British publishing magnate; I sipped my wine again and took out my compact, pretending to refresh my lipstick. To my left, the main course was being served: I took an inordinately long time serving myself. Jack would serve himself next, I thought, and then he would turn to speak with me! The moment came for him to spear some veal, and while doing so he said something to me in jest—but then, just as quickly, he resumed the conversation to his right. I drank more wine; I forced myself to taste the food; I sat for what seemed like a millennium in silence. I remember staring at the silver and how it seemed to undulate before me. Each time I thought Jack would turn to me, I felt him venture with more energy into the conversation to his right.

At last, Pierre turned to me again, cheerfully picking up the subject we had abandoned. What I said or what we discussed, I simply do not recall: I only remember plunging into a miasma of conversation to my left and unsuccessfully trying to pierce the rampart of silence to my right. Never once did Jack speak with me.

The plates were finally cleared; dessert was served. My humiliation was deep, but so was my will to conceal it: From my laughter, and from the way I had devoted myself to Pierre, anyone would have thought I was having a very good time. Seldom can I ever remember feeling so spent.

Finally, the meal came to an end: It was time to repair to the drawing room for coffee. I had by this time so charmed the Swiss titan that—irony of ironies—he seemed loath to leave my side, even making me promise to let him and his wife know when I next visited Zurich. I said goodbye, and as I stood up, I remember the terrible tension that seemed to inflame my shoulders and back and how my head had begun to throb.

Finally, Jack stood up as well and, having planted his napkin on the table, uttered the only words he would address to me that night, "I think I should go and find my wife."

I walked as lightly as I could into the blue drawing room, where groups of guests, sipping coffee, had already claimed their outposts. I stopped to greet this person or that, my animation intensifying with my confusion. I saw Jack and Alice Varady standing together in a corner, hovering around David Cassel and Rosalind. I noticed how especially animated Rosalind seemed with Jack, how she would tilt back her head, elongating her bare white throat, as she laughed.

At that moment I felt a hand on my shoulder: the hostess, a look of what seemed to be real consternation on her face.

"How can you forgive me," she exclaimed in a low anxious voice. "Someone must have changed the place cards!"

"It was very awkward," I said, barely able to suppress my rage. "I can't imagine how that could have happened."

"Nor can I!"

"It was very awkward," I repeated tensely.

At this she paused, her voice almost sharp, her dark green eyes with that strange, almost somnabulistic gaze I had fleetingly noticed while she was showing me the photograph of her dead daughter: "But we're all adults, surely!"

A tall young man with a noble, thin face approached, and I heard Christina's voice subtly alter to one of relief and *bonhomie*. "This is Umberto Della Croce," she said, turning to me with a radiant smile. She had given his last name a special emphasis, in order to impress upon me the fact that he was scion of the very rich and powerful Italian family. His English was elegant, his manners courtly.

"Come and sit with me here, you two," she said, leading us to a sofa in one corner. Smoothing her skirt as she sat down, she took in the activity of the rest of the room with a swift glance. Having assured herself that her most important guests were occupied, she focused on me and Umberto. Within a minute she had told him all about me—my background, my job. "Umberto is in New York for the next year, learning the ropes of his family's business," she said pointedly, her tone also indicating that it was my turn to converse with him.

I did so, approaching Umberto with the same intensity I had my Swiss dinner partner, even as I was conscious of Jack and his wife still deep in conversation with David Cassel and Rosalind.

Guests began to depart. Excusing herself, Christina stood up and began to accept their thanks and goodbyes, kissing them on both cheeks and offering each a special salutation. Among them were Jack and his wife, who still stood with David Cassel.

I was too proud to leave right away, despite my headache, and continued instead to focus on Umberto (little did he know that my flirtatiousness was hardly prompted by his charms). Whatever he said—his observations of New York, his descriptions of his work—all appeared to fascinate me.

The drawing room, almost empty now, was subdued. I felt a sudden weariness, a longing to be alone, to escape the pseudo-Russian decor and the *faux* sky.

"Don't you ever tire of New York?" I asked Umberto suddenly. "Don't you miss living in Italy?"

Unaware of the change of my tone, his response was cavalier. No, he said, he did not: In fact it was dinners like this that made his new residence so fascinating. "I am—how do you say—a night owl," he added provocatively.

I stood up, holding my evening bag tightly and wanting to be done with the night, wanting to be done with Umberto. I suppose the hurt created by Jack's silence had provoked a certain ruthlessness: Umberto had served his purpose, and now it was time to leave. I extended my hand to shake his, but to my surprise he continued to hold it. "Can we not have a drink together?" he asked me unexpectedly.

I told him as politely as I could that I was very tired and that I needed to be up early the next morning, to work.

The last excuse was of no consequence to him; I should have known better than to use it. "The Carlyle is not very far away," he told me, continuing to press. "We could go there. A quick drink. And then I will take you home."

I was about to say no again. I was about to be firm, almost rude—but then I thought of Jack and the way he had never turned to me, the way he had humiliated me. And then I thought again of Rosalind's eyes. So I smiled at Umberto, a smile of radiant acquiescence meant to signify that he had won a strategic victory. "You have made it too tempting," I said in my most lilting voice. "Yes. Let's go to the Carlyle. But just a quick drink—you must keep your promise!"

We walked together through the drawing room, under the chandelier-lit sky, and to the entrance hall—the entrance which I had entered, shivering, only months before on that July afternoon. Christina von Shouse stood with her severe profile framed by the door, bidding goodnight to the last guests.

Having retrieved my cape, I approached her with Umberto —noticing, at that moment, that her eyes assumed a glimmer.

"So—you have hit it off! How lovely. Now I can feel truly *successful*." She kissed me, and then Umberto, on both cheeks. "Have a good time, you two!" she said gaily as we walked toward the elevator.

We entered the Hotel Carlyle, which summoned up so many memories of languorous afternoons and nights made restless by longing, with Jack.

The dimly lit, smoke-choked Café was busy that night: Bobby Short was singing. I felt people's eyes on us as we entered—I suppose we looked handsome together, Umberto and I, the two of us dressed in our black-tie finery. I only know we were given a table at once and that I drank too much that evening. Red wine only exacerbated my headache.

I doubt my companion felt this, however, for I was, if anything, more garrulous than usual. I leaned on his shoulder, I hung on his every word—I did so in a sort of crazed, intense way that had nothing to do with my real feelings. I know now that I simply wanted him to want me and then, having accomplished that, I could go home.

We stayed until almost everyone else had left, until the Café Carlyle was silent, devoid of Cole Porter's urbane,

ironic melodies. By this time Umberto was, I think, inebriated with my attention, for he pressed me to go upstairs
when we reached my apartment. I came very close to going
to bed with him that night—but I pushed him away at my
door, promising we would see each other again.

The interior of my apartment was dark, the furniture
mockingly expectant. I turned on one light, then another. I
could hardly bear to face the mirror: my face, my body, everything about my physical self suddenly filled me with revulsion. No punishment seemed cruel enough—for Jack, but
most of all for myself.

I ripped the diamond earrings from my lobes and the
bracelets from my wrists and hurled them on the bed. And
with one last glance into the mirror, I took off my once
beloved red dress and threw it in a heap on the floor.

25

Forgive me," said the note that arrived the following day; nothing but those two words, written in Jack's decisive hand, and accompanied by a single mauve-colored rose. The card, engraved with the initials J L V, was thick, hard, familiar; I knew it well, for the same card had often accompanied glittering presents, and flowers, and boxes whose filmy contents were almost indistinguishable from the fragile tissues protecting them.

The note was delivered to my apartment that evening. The numbing effects of the wine and Champagne had long since dissipated; my red dress hung in a plastic bag; my earrings were locked in a drawer. If only hurt and anger could have been so easily contained!

I looked at the note one last time and threw it away.

The following day, another letter arrived—this one thick with pages:

"Darling Liza," it began, as he asked me once more to forgive him. He told me that he and Alice had argued before Christina's dinner, that he was tense, distracted, and *angry at her*—he never meant to take it out on me. His life was in my hands. None of these petty things, he wrote, should cloud the wonderful moments we had known together; it would be a mistake to give a dinner party the power to destroy our love. "These are superficial things—a public facade—compared to our private life together," he concluded. "What you must know, and be convinced of, is how deeply I love you, how much I need you, and how much I want you, even as I write this letter—Jack."

I read the letter several times, reluctant to acknowledge the surge of relief that I had experienced while reading it, how eagerly I drank in his pleas. But the next instant I would remember his coldness at the dinner, his hostile silence. Then unremitting anger, and a desire for revenge, would overwhelm me.

I put the letter in a drawer and never responded.

He called me two days later, early on Friday morning. I remember the rapid descent into safeness that I felt as I heard his voice—how eagerly I wanted to absolve myself from anger, and yet how determined I was not to show it. He asked to see me, his voice imploring, even as I momentarily basked in my power to say yes or no. "You *must* understand how careful I've got to be," he told me. "My wife will turn the kids against me. I've got to make financial arrangements that will protect my assets from her. From her lawyer. Otherwise, she'll take me for every penny I've got. I've got to do this right—for *us*. Don't you understand? Otherwise, there's a nightmare ahead of us."

He begged to see me again—he couldn't sleep, he said, he couldn't eat; I was all he thought about.

The weekend was impossible, I finally said—I would be at Wakefield Hall, continuing my research. I told him I would think it over during the next few days and would call him on Monday with my decision.

26

There was no sense of the previous night's storm when I awakened the next morning in the larkspur-blue bedroom at Wakefield Hall. It was preternaturally quiet; the thrashing rain that had accompanied my drive had vanished like the opaque memory of a discarded dream. I walked to the tall, heavily draped windows in my nightgown, looking out at the burnished landscape and at the hills beyond, a velvety patchwork of autumnal browns and oranges.

I turned away, hungry suddenly. It seemed to me I had filled out a card for breakfast, yet I had no recollection of requesting a specific time—had I? Indeed, moments later, when I called the housekeeper to ask for coffee and toast, her mild surprise only corroborated my own haziness. "Kurt knocked on your door at seven-thirty, which is when you'd asked for breakfast," Olga said. "But you were still asleep! Of course we'll send it up right away."

Breakfast appeared minutes later, accompanied by a note from Rosalind, which I opened warily (her spiteful behavior at Christina's dinner was never far from my mind). "Elisabeth," it said. "I'd planned for us to go riding this morning, but the rain, unfortunately, has nixed that. The ground's still too wet. We'll go tomorrow. I'll meet you downstairs at 10:00. Lunch is at 1:30, dinner at 8:30 (Patrick Rossiter is joining us). Ciao. R."

I began to notice a subtle difference in the way the house appeared to me that weekend; yet the house itself had not changed. There was a febrile, strained quality to the atmosphere that had dazzled me months before—the belabored perfection of a stage set. Perhaps I had noticed this, subliminally at least, during my first visit; now it perplexed me.

I went downstairs to the dining room for a second cup of coffee and tried to force myself to read the *Times*. I heard a voice, then a cat purring, and looked up. Rosalind had appeared, her high rubber boots caked with dirt, her cat loping behind her.

She asked if I had slept well and sat down, legs sprawled, to scan the business section.

All the while, I remember thinking that we were only postponing the inevitable moment when I would ask Rosalind to show me Joanna's bedroom. When I finally did, she responded with seeming equanimity, merely excusing herself for a moment to change her "filthy boots." "Joanna would be horrified to see mud tracked across her carpet," she said, with only the merest suggestion of a smirk.

Joanna's bedroom lay at the opposite end of the corridor from my own. The walls leading to it were lined with moody nineteenth-century portraits of actresses (several of the half-mad Mrs. Kemble as the Tragic Muse; another of Ellen Terry as Lady Macbeth). We came to a pair of tall doors—much taller than any others along the corridor. Rosalind turned the handles; I followed her inside.

"Everything was left just the way it was the day Joanna died," Rosalind announced, with a certain forced nonchalance: "You know—the boss's orders."

The lofty room was painted a pale mauve, a variation of the elegiac lavender of Joanna's library, a color reiterated in the mauve-and-white fabric trellised with green that draped the bed, a splendid *lit à la polonaise* that stood slightly aloof from the whole and yet which was married to the rest through the pattern of its fabric. From each of its four corners a luxurious swag traveled upward, only to be reunited in a circular mauve crown that seemed magically suspended from the ceiling.

My gaze traveled to the shadow cast by the bed upon the fine needlepoint carpet, with its intricate pattern of *fleur-de-lis*, then to the bedspread and pillows embroidered with Joanna's initials. All the while, I half expected Rosalind to sally forth with some acerbic remark, but she did not. Her silence had such a disquieting effect that I was relieved when she eventually excused herself and left.

I heard the door close; I was alone.

To the left stood a tall door that led to a mirrored corridor of closets: mirror after mirror reiterated my reflection ad infinitum.

I passed the last mirrored door and walked into the extravagant bathroom which, like the dressing room, was lined with the same unrelenting succession of floor-to-ceiling mirrors. There was no escaping oneself in this room, no escaping the flaws of age or the evidence of physical imperfection. I wondered about the woman who was obliged to confront this vaguely hostile inner sanctum every day and imagined Joanna here after a dinner party, stripping her face of makeup, or in the morning when, catlike in her black exercise leotard, as Lawrence Brandt had described her, she would weigh herself on the icy metal scale whose weights I now idly pushed back and forth. "The privileges of beauty are enormous," Christina von Shouse had told me months before; yet here, within this mirrored chamber, it seemed likely that Joanna had only felt its pressures.

I stood before the dark green marble sink, with its gold dolphin faucets and untouched soap, and—still lost in rumination—idly opened the drawer below it. What I discovered took me aback: inside, makeup and more makeup lay in chaos. It was not so much the abundance of cosmetics that surprised me—Joanna was an actress, after all—but, rather, the extreme disorder. The little jars, cases of eyeshadows and lipsticks—all the pigments of transformation that Joanna must have come, increasingly, to rely upon—lay in a jumble that seemed so at odds with the absolute order of the rest.

I shut the drawer and left, walking past the mirrored corridor as I reentered the bedroom. Several books lay on the night table to the right; I wondered what Joanna had been reading before her death. I picked up the first: *Shakespeare's Sonnets: The Problems Solved*, by the scholar A. L. Rowse; the second was a well-worn copy of the sonnets themselves. Disappointed, I set the books down; there was nothing telling about them, nothing out of keeping for someone with Joanna's interests.

I walked to the bay window at the far end of the room, with its glorious autumn view of trees, hills, and water. I could so easily imagine Joanna sitting here, on the sofa before the window, intent on the *Times* crossword puzzle, which still lay on the table.

With one last look at the bed—its spiraling folds, its bedsheet embroidered with the huge interconnected initials J E C—and at the deepening shadow it cast across the carpet, I left the bedroom, the door making a hard clicking sound as I shut it.

Rosalind met me downstairs. "Where to?" she said, her voice having resumed its customary briskness. She did not ask me what I thought of Joanna's bedroom, nor did she question me about my impressions. I remember noticing this, and feeling relieved.

To the chapel, I said.

I felt a mounting excitement as we approached the small, neogothic chapel, a feeling that gave way to acute disappointment and bewilderment as we actually entered it. Here again, perhaps, I was influenced by my inability to feel visual things—a painting or a building—calmly. The moment I entered the interior—with its Rossettiesque paintings of maudlin women with serpentine manes and its surfeit of cloying gothic details—I was overcome with revulsion, a sense of spiritual oppression.

Like the main house, the chapel had been built at the turn of the century, but the way it had been restored reeked of such mawkishness, such gaudiness, that it barely seemed related to the rest. Everything about it seemed to mock—mock its owner, mock its purpose, mock the money that had fueled its restoration. The gilding on the pews and vaulted arches was luridly brilliant, the florid religious elements degenerate with gimmickry, and the whole so lacking in subtlety that I looked about in wonder at its lachrymose ostentatiousness.

Rosalind stood at the back of the chilly building, watching me take notes and every so often calling to her cat. "You seem underwhelmed," she finally remarked, approaching me.

"I am," I replied, knowing there was no use in dissembling. "It doesn't resemble the rest of the house at all."

"It was Joanna's idea to restore it—the chapel, I mean. In the beginning, at least. Then she lost interest, so Christina took over. Supervised the work until it was finished."

"And David?"

"He never liked the way it was done. Hated it. And blamed the way it turned out on Christina. He never comes here— never did." She paused, running her hand along the top of a pew. "I remember being here with Joanna after the work had been started. The painters were finishing the gilding over there. She was watching them—closely for once. And then she turned and said—half to me, half to herself—'I've never seen a chapel that inspired so much gilt.' Gold gilt or the other kind? I asked her, sort of joking. And she turned to me and said, 'Both.' " Rosalind suddenly looked uncomfortable, as if she had revealed more than she'd intended, and the next instant resumed her implacable coolness. "Had enough?" she asked me, digging her hands into the pockets of her breeches.

"So Christina took it over," I mused, clutching my note-book as I looked up at the ceiling, all the while wondering what Christina, with her exquisite taste, could have meant by this atrocious decor. The imposition of bad taste on those who know better could only be construed as a circuitously angry gesture—one directed, no doubt, toward David. "And David hated what Christina did to the chapel?" I asked, turning to Rosalind.

"Right," she replied, tapping her foot on the stone pavement.

"He never came here himself?"

"No."

"What about Joanna—what did she think of Christina's ideas?"

"Didn't seem to care. She might have even thought it was funny. Anyway, at the end, *nothing* was sacred to Joanna." She shrugged. "This place least of all!"

I walked to the right side, where something had caught my eye—a portrait bust, deeply recessed in a small alcove that was delicately painted with a stylized motif of blue-and-gold lilies. Above it, a stained glass window in the William Morris style shed its light—a window with the escutcheon of Wakefield Hall, that of double arrows entwined with lilies, and inset with the same motto I remembered from the writing paper: FATE FINDS A WAY.

"That was Joanna's idea," said Rosalind, watching me.

"The window? Or the motto?"

"Both," she replied, adding that the motif had been designed about the same time as the chapel—both had been adapted from the existing gates of the house.

"I see," I murmured, still studying the alcove; there was something distinctive about it—a lightness of touch, a restraint that set it apart from the rest. The bust was Renaissance in style, its face, carved in white marble, that of a young woman; a pair of fluted silver vases filled with lilies of the valley had been placed before it. The expression of the eyes seemed eerily familiar; yet I could not ascertain why, or whether the bust itself was contemporary or antique. I only sensed Rosalind's discomfiture as I continued to examine it and the inscription, carved in Roman letters, that ran along the pediment:

> Give sorrow words. The grief that does not speak
> Whispers the o'erfraught heart and bids it break.
> SHAKESPEARE, Macbeth.

"And who's this supposed to be?" I asked Rosalind, almost facetiously.

I sensed her hesitation. "Christina's daughter," she said coldly.

I tried not to show my astonishment at the idea of this bizarre memorial. "So this is Alexandra," I said slowly. I knew now why the face was familiar: It was the same young woman I had seen in the photographs at Christina's apartment—a more conventionally pretty, though perhaps less striking and intelligent, version of Christina's stern features. I continued to study the marble face, noticing at that moment the discreet bronze plaque below: "Alexandra Williams, 1957–1978."

"Why here?" I asked, turning to Rosalind again.

"It was Joanna's idea," she replied with obvious hostility. "After Alexandra died, she thought there should be some memorial to her—in the chapel Christina had designed. Seemed logical, I guess." A pause before she added, in a disgruntled voice: "Another of Joanna's obsessions."

Her explanation, and the evasive glance that had accompanied it, did not quite satisfy me. "And that's the only reason?"

"Guess so," she said defensively. "She—Alexandra—used to come to Wakefield pretty often. Mostly to visit Joanna—ask her advice, talk about acting. I guess you'd say Joanna was her mentor."

"How did she die?"

"Suicide. OD'd on sleeping pills."

I considered this a moment. "How did Christina feel about Joanna's relationship with her daughter?"

"She encouraged it. Totally. Thought Joanna was a terrific influence on her. Anyway, she was desperate that Alexandra become an actress, so you can imagine how important Joanna was!" She paused. "To Christina's ambitions, I mean."

"And Alexandra herself?"

"I always thought she was sort of scared of Christina."

"What do you mean?"

"Christina pushed her to acting, and maybe the kid was afraid to let it go. Afraid what her mother would say."

"Did you think Joanna knew that?"

"How would I know?" Rosalind looked irked as she folded her arms across her chest; the next moment her eyes assumed an uncharacteristically interior cast. "I'm sure there's a lot that Christina keeps to herself. Who doesn't?" Her voice suddenly erupted with impatience. "Let's go."

As I walked back toward the entrance, I looked down at the stone floor of the nave, with its swirling art nouveau design. I hadn't focused on it upon entering, but now I began to examine the waves of pattern beneath my feet, the progression of which, on closer inspection, formed a cohesive circular design. I stopped to study it. To one side was a medallion, an exquisite depiction of a crenellated tower surrounded by a moat, and under this, unfurled on a blue banner, a single word: *Thistleton*.

I looked up at Rosalind and asked what the design of the floor signified.

"Something to do with that house in England that Joanna was so crazy about. There was a maze there, too. I think the floor's based on the maze."

I realized that this was indeed similar to the pattern Patrick Rossiter had described: the swirling vertiginous paths without a central axis, with the moated octagonal tower-library to the east. I continued to scrutinize the design, looking to see if the goal—the statue of Joanna as Athena that Patrick had described—was also depicted; but it was not.

I asked Rosalind if she had ever been to Thistleton.

"No," came the sharp reply.

"Why not?"

"Because the place meant so much to Joanna," she said, shutting the door.

We left the chapel in silence and began to walk along the boxwood-lined gravel path, toward the maze.

We continued to walk until we glimpsed the hedges of the maze in the distance. There we parted, for I had told Rosalind I wanted to go through the maze by myself. (I did not say that I had brought a copy of Joanna's letter to Lawrence Brandt, with her plan of the Shakespearean "rooms.") She had no objection to this; indeed, she seemed relieved as she set off alone.

After a few steps, however, Rosalind stopped abruptly. "There's something I was supposed to tell you," she said, turning around.

I asked what it was.

"David has left something for you. In your room."

"Something to do with the book?"

"You'll see." She kicked the gravel with her boots, her head bent down, her hands in her pockets, the white cat trailing behind her.

A few moments later, I passed David Cassel's library pavilion in the distance. I hadn't intended to enter it, but by this time I was rather chilled and also, admittedly, curious whether my initial impressions of the place were accurate. I turned the handle to the tall French door and walked inside.

At first glance, I was perhaps even more dazzled than I had been, months before, by the complex textures and colors of the whole, the subtle juxtaposition of the paintings. The familiar Canalettos of Venice glimmered from the walls, their nacreous blues and greens offset by the *chiaroscuro* of Venetian portraits and the feathery lines of allegorical land-scapes.

But now the autumn light seemed to have intensified the atmosphere of masculine order, deepening the patina of the wood and the leather chairs, and rendering more potent the blood-red colors of the Bokhara carpet. The desk had not appeared quite so massive that first afternoon, or the chairs so immense in scale. Everything about the library seemed more powerful, more elaborate, more splendid.

I walked to the Victorian partners' desk in the far corner, whose surface was appointed with a collection of antique letter openers in horn, brass, and ivory. I picked up one shaped like a mythological creature—a centaur, I believe— and absentmindedly held it, continuing to survey the room before setting it back in place.

The wall above was hung entirely with drawings of nudes —primarily Old Master studies in pencil, charcoal, or red chalk. My eyes traveled from one row to another until I came to the last group, at the bottom, and then to a small easel, covered in dark red velvet, which sat on the desk itself. I lifted up the velvet, only to find a charcoal sketch of a young woman, also a nude which, being contemporary, contrasted in style from all the other drawings. It was more intensely sensual, even erotic, in its depiction of flesh. I bent over to examine it, and then, startled, drew closer still. Below the pelvic bone was the slash of a scar—a scar so painstakingly depicted, and so particular in shape, that I knew *it could only belong to Rosalind*. I examined the head, with its chiseled profile, and the long, Mannerist lines of the neck—all impressionistically sketched—and realized that they, too, were Rosalind's.

I felt suddenly enervated. I sat down, my fingers pressed against the desk, as I tried to imagine what the nude drawing of Rosalind, so carefully positioned above Cassel's desk, could mean. *Were they, or had they once been, lovers?* I thought of Rosalind's habitual deference, even tenderness, toward Cassel; her changing my place card at Christina's dinner; her barely veiled antagonism toward me when Cassel had been mildly flirtatious—his "date," Patrick Rossiter had slyly called her. "You've heard of family romance," he had added. Her hostility toward Joanna and her biting account of overhearing Joanna and David in bed; Joanna's use of the word *humiliation* in describing her conjugal life. Even my conversation with Rosalind minutes before, in the chapel, seemed imbued with new meaning: "I've never seen a chapel that inspired so much *guilt*," she recalled Joanna saying.

I closed the door to the library and continued as quickly as I could toward the maze.

I came to the arbor of wisteria, devoid of purple blossoms now—a cold, damp tunnel of bare, gnarled branches through which I passed before approaching the high fence of the hedged-in octagon. I took a deep breath, trying not to think of the discovery in the library—trying only to focus on the maze.

I took the copy of Joanna's letter to Brandt from my pocket and glanced at the plan—four octagons surrounding a central circle, within the overall octagon. The gate swung open; I gazed down the long, twisting path that led to the interior. My heart began to beat fast, and my feet seemed implanted in the ground, incapable of movement: the same vertiginous fear that had gripped me when I had come here alone, on my first visit. This time, however, I continued, reassuring myself that I knew from Joanna's letter the way to the center and back again: a precise sequence of turns—three right, three left, five right, five left—that would take me through the Shakespearean "rooms."

The bronze sundial, first. I read the engraving on the plaque before it—the lines from *Midsummer's Night's Dream* that I recognized from Joanna's letter:

> The spring, the summer
> The childing autumn, angry winter change
> Their wonted liveries; and the mazèd world,
> By their increase, now knows not which is which.

I studied these awhile, running my fingers along the metal surface, noticing, as I did so, that the engraving of the "mazèd world/By their increase, now knows not which is which" seemed smoother than the preceding lines, as if someone had rubbed them again and again. Joanna, perhaps.

Two turns to the right; I came to the first octagon, walled in by towering yew hedges and shared by two statues. From the map I knew they would be Ophelia, from *Hamlet*, and Viola, from *Twelfth Night*; I was unsure only of the quotes Joanna had chosen to accompany them.

Ophelia first—a stone figure of a mad girl with vacant gaze and disheveled bodice, her features eerily reminiscent of the young Joanna's. Tendrils of ivy encroached on her pediment. I drew the vines away and uncovered the inscription: " 'Tis in my memory locked, and you yourself shall keep the key of it."

To Viola next—a sprightly figure in hose and doublet, her plaited hair bound by a feathered cap; "O time, thou must untangle this, not I/It is too hard a knot for me t'untie." I read the lines several times and then walked toward Ophelia, realizing that the two quotes, paired, seemed to form a message: Both were about untying or untangling a secret. I transcribed the lines for each statue onto the map before continuing.

The last of the three turns to the right took me to the first single statue within a smaller octagon. It was the same statue I had seen on my first visit with Rosalind and which I knew from Joanna's design to be the mutilated Lavinia from *Titus Andronicus* (not, as I had assumed on my first visit, an anonymous antique lady). How pitiful were her gaping mouth, cheeks incised with tears, and hideous arms ending in stumps. Her inscription: "She hath no tongue to call, nor hands to wash/And so let's leave her to her silent walks." "No tongue to call"—a chilling way to describe helpless silence; "hands to wash"—here I thought of the delirious Lady Macbeth; "let's leave her to her silent walks"—Joanna, in her own words, "wandering through this paradise with her arms and tongue chopped off." I copied down Lavinia's lines, barely able to look up at her.

I took the first of the three left turns, which led me toward the back of the maze, to the northernmost octagon, with Lady Macbeth and Isabella, from *Measure for Measure*. I approached the statue of Lady Macbeth—I had already seen her as well, without recognizing her, on the day I had come with Rosalind. Here she stood, with twisting hands and demented gaze—the first of Joanna's triumphs and the character whose play, together with *Othello*, I knew best:

> Things without all remedy
> Should be without regard; what's done is done.

The lines had to do with guilt, with the aftermath of the killing of a king, lines all the more chilling in their lack of self-knowledge. I came closer to the statue and looked at its face, so perfectly modeled after Joanna's—the gaze was frightening, the lunatic cross-eyed stare that Christina had recalled her using so effectively onstage, and yet not less frightening than the hands, which seemed to twist together in eternity.

I walked slowly toward Isabella, almost grateful for her sane, chaste face and the ordered lines of her sculpted wimple: "It oft falls out/To have what we would have, we speak not what we mean." Walking from one statue to the other, I realized that the two passages—Lady Macbeth's and Isabella's—also seemed to form a cryptic message. I wondered whether, in Joanna's mind, anything else linked the two characters: Was it significant that one was a wife, the other a sister?

The second and third of the three left turns took me to the statue of Desdemona (not, as I had assumed, to the central circle with Hermione). Desdemona was perhaps the most exquisite of the statues, her hair a mass of coiled curls, her brow unruffled and high, her mouth a sweet repentant curve. I approached the pediment, covered more densely with ivy than any of the others, and drew it away:

Speak of me as I am. Nothing extenuate,
Nor set down aught in malice. Then must you speak
Of one that loved not wisely, but too well.

I knew these were actually Othello's, not Desdemona's, lines; he speaks them shortly before dying. Of all the quotes, this seemed the most eerie—the lines addressed the issue of posthumous fame, of reputation. My hand faltered as I wrote them down.

I began the series of five right turns; once, then again, before arriving at the innermost circle. The hedges here were highest; I entered through the north-facing arch. Within it stood the statue of Hermione set in the midst of a shallow circular pool of deep green water; before it, the tragic "weeping mask" fountain envisioned by Joanna in her dream, its eyes spouting streams of ice-cold "tears." I drew my hand away from the frigid water and looked closely at the statue itself. Hermione was draped in a toga as a classical goddess, her face resembling the mature Joanna's—the same enigmatic expression I remembered so vividly when I had discovered her sleeping in the pavilion that afternoon in London.

The pediment was bare of ivy, the diameter of the pool narrow enough for me to almost, but not quite, touch the stone. I bent forward, scanning the surface for a quote; but there was none. Only the name HERMIONE carved in Roman letters and, below it, THE WINTER'S TALE. I walked around the pediment, thinking that the words might have been etched elsewhere. Still—nothing. I wondered if this was intentional or whether Joanna had simply forgotten to complete the statue; yet that hardly seemed likely for a woman of her exacting nature.

I continued to gaze at the queen, wronged by her husband and condemned to a lifetime of silence: Was this why Joanna had chosen her, yet chosen *not* to grant her words? To leave her mute, as it were, her voice trapped in stone?

I looked at the map again, thinking of the three women in the maze's central section: Lavinia, Hermione, and Desdemona. The first raped, the second and third unjustly accused of adultery by jealous husbands. Three women wronged by men; the reason, no doubt, Joanna had chosen to align them.

I stood up and began the first of five left turns, which brought me to the sundial and, eventually, back to the entrance. With one last glance at the path leading to Ophelia, I closed the gate behind me.

It was the next moment, as I began to walk toward the house, that something occurred to me with startling clarity: Lawrence Brandt had been too glib about the purpose of the maze. Its "mazèd world" was far more than a mere monument to Joanna's career. Together, the statues and their lines were meant to form a message—a message to posthumous audiences and biographers, perhaps.

27

Moments later, I passed a man in overalls—a gardener, I assumed—working by the edge of the gravel path. He was kneeling on the ground, digging up the soil with a trowel. His overalls were scruffy, his face grizzled and thin. When he looked up at me, I remembering noticing that his wire-rimmed spectacles were splattered with infinitesimal drops of white paint and that his clear blue eyes looked surprisingly young for a man whom I guessed to be in his late sixties.

"Cold enough for you?" he asked as I approached, pushing his spectacles up the bridge of his nose.

I said yes, it was very cold—much too cold for late October.

He looked me over. "You're the writer, aren't you?"

Yes, I replied, surprised that he knew. I watched him for a moment before asking what he was planting.

"Black tulips." He took a bulb from a soft brown canvas bag and set it into the earth. "They've got a fancy name, but I call them plain old black tulips. They were always a favorite of Mrs. Cassel's. The maze is full of them—it's a real sight in spring!"

I thought of the statues I had just seen surrounded with black tulips—a mournful, almost disturbing image. "I've seen the maze in the summer and in the fall, but never in spring," I said.

"Reason to come back, then."

"I suppose so."

"So you're the one who's working on the book."

"That's right."

"The book on Mrs. Cassel."

"On Joanna Eakins—the actress. Yes." I continued to watch him, finding something soothing in the rhythm of his work: the digging, the setting in of the bulb, the patting of the dark, covering soil.

"Joanna Eakins," he said almost to himself as he took up the trowel. "Joanna Eakins," he repeated. "That's not the way I knew her—she was always Joanna Darby to me." He glanced at me. "Never could get used to the other names."

"So you knew her a long time?"

"Lord, yes—since she was a kid. Knew her family."

"Did you?" I tried not to show my excitement. "And you are . . ."

"Sam Neely."

I introduced myself, feeling ill at ease with his touching, almost childlike curiosity (in retrospect, I realize with some amusement that years in New York had ill equipped me to deal with guilelessness). His eyes continued to focus on me in their quizzical way; we shook hands.

"And where was it, Mr. Neely, that you knew her, and her family?"

"Call me Sam."

"Where was it that you knew her, Sam?"

"Wyoming. Piney Gulch. Place she grew up."

"Piney Gulch," I remember repeating to myself, as if the very name were possessed of incantatory powers.

"You don't know Piney Gulch, do you?" he asked me, looking up a moment before covering a new bulb.

No, I said. I didn't.

"Ain't a bad place. But it's cold. Darn cold in winter." His brow furrowed, as if he were pondering the degree of that cold.

"What do you remember about her and her family?"

"Different. Kept to themselves. Father wasn't there much."

"And the mother?"

"Kind of—" he paused, struggling for the right description, "moody."

"Anything else?"

"Good-looking. I guess you'd call Joanna's mother good-looking."

"What was her name?"

"Maude. Family name was Gert. Don't know where she came from." I sensed a touch of disdain. "Always real proud of Joanna's father—a builder, called himself an architect. Came from England. The youngest son—so they said." He took a new bulb from the bag. "The mother had airs, though."

"What do you mean airs?"

"Looked down on everyone. Thought she was real fine because she'd married someone from England." A pause. "She sure loved the son—Joanna's brother, I mean. By far her favorite."

"What was his name?"

"Ben. Ben Darby. Year or so older than Joanna. Looked just like her."

"Were they close?"

"Real close—never saw them apart, those two. Ben was

protective of Joanna. Why, in the summertime especially, those two would disappear almost the whole day—walking and hiking. Some people said they did it just to escape the mother! Said she had no business being a mother, said she could be violent. But I never saw it." A pause as he adjusted his spectacles. "Ben sure was proud of his sister—admired her, you might say. Knew she was different from the other girls."

"What else do you remember?"

"People talked because the mother used to send Joanna to the movie theater all day when she was a little girl, all alone, with her lunch in a brown bag—too busy to take care of her, I guess! Joanna'd spend the day like that—movie after movie —Garbo, Bette Davis, whatever was playing. Even when she was little she could do real good imitations."

"And they lived . . ."

"In a cabin. By the hot sulfur springs, by the edge of the national forest. You knew that?"

I shook my head.

"Nice place to grow up if you don't mind being alone," he said.

"Did they come to town much?"

"Not much in winter." And then with a certain look of self-satisfaction: "I always knew Joanna would amount to something."

I asked why.

"Because there was something different about her. Something struggling to be free. Her mother always wanted them both—Joanna and Ben, I mean—to get out. Always talking about the father's family in England. There Maude would be, in the general store, and you'd think she was the queen of Sheba—just because her husband came from England! Even tried to *talk* like her husband. Only wanted the best of everything—but had no money to pay for it! Saying the husband would be back and that he'd settle their bills. Never did, of course. Wanting everyone to know that the father's family came from a place real different than Piney Gulch." A pause. "The husband wasn't there much."

"Think back, Sam," I urged him gently. "Think back on that time—what Joanna looked like."

"Real dark hair, real nice skin. Freckles in the summer. A little plump. Sick a lot. Kind of quiet, but kind of wild at the same time—"

"Wild? In what way?"

"Don't know. Something wild inside, burning to get out." He paused. "Told me once that she never wanted to go to other people's houses because she'd always have to come back to her own." He wiped his mouth with the side of his hand, glancing at me as he continued: "Then the war came, and I lost touch. Went off to the war—" This he related matter-of-factly: "Went off to France, Normandy, Germany, and at the end, when I came back to Piney Gulch, the Darbys were gone. And the next thing, wouldn't you know, I was reading a newspaper one day—the *Piney Gulch Press*— and there was a picture of Joanna, looking all kind of done up. Only now they didn't call her Joanna Darby. Now she was Joanna Eakins. Famous, too. Cover of *Time* magazine— Shakespeare and all—"

"So you were right," I said with a smile. "She had amounted to something."

"Sure had. Always knew she would. So now she was Joanna Eakins, and I thought to myself, boy, she's the first famous person I ever knew. Collected anything I could find about her. Pictures in the newspapers, magazines. Then the way it worked out, I wound up coming East. Doing odd jobs, yard work. One day, about five years ago, I was living up here in Massachusetts then, I heard there was a big house there and that it was being fixed up and that they were looking for people—handyman, gardener. And then I heard—" He paused, aware how intently I was listening. "I heard that the house belonged to Joanna Darby. I mean Eakins. Cassel. And the new husband. So I went there and spoke to this fancy-looking guy—the butler, I think he was called—and applied

for the job. Got the job. So there I was, working in the place
—out of a movie or something—and it belonged to Joanna!
Why, I remembered her with pigtails and here she was, a
famous actress, with silk dresses and pearls. She'd changed,
all right—" he scratches his head, "and yet she really hadn't.
Why, you can imagine how surprised she was when I was
working in the garden one day and I told her who I was."

"And what was her reaction?" I asked, trying to imagine
that incongruous meeting.

"Real surprised—shocked, at first. But then friendly. She
said—and boy, her voice had sure changed, it was kind of
English, the way they used to talk in those movies. She said,
'Why, Sam Neelly, you haven't changed at all!' "

"And so you stayed on at the house, at Wakefield?"

"Sure. Pay was good. Food was good. And Joanna was always good to me. The butler was snooty, but I kept out of his
way." Then he added, with no small pride, "Sometimes I
even called her Joanna, when there was just the two of us.
Never seemed to bother her. She always liked what I did in
the garden. Let me take care of the maze."

"Was there anything odd or unusual that you recall about
her then? Anything at all?"

"Well, let me see," he said, scratching his grizzled chin.
"Those last two years, she changed a lot. Last year, especially."

"In what way?"

"Got real skinny. Seemed kind of like a ghost. Mr. Cassel
was always working, or he'd be with Rosalind. I was helping
with the maze then—heck of a lot of work it was, too. She
liked it just so."

"Did she, then?"

"Sure did. Had to be just right." He stood up, brushed the
dirt from his pants, and picked up the rake that lay by the
border; I remember noticing the large ring of keys attached
to his belt and the harsh sound of the rake as it grated
against the stones.

"There was one day I remember," he continued. "I was

fixing up the paint on the gate over there. She came up to me. 'This is pretty far from Piney Gulch.' she said, 'isn't it, Sam?' She talked real nice, like she always did, but with me I noticed that she'd let a bit of Piney Gulch creep in. Expressions and all. I said, 'Yeah, Joanna, sure is far from Piney Gulch.' And I looked at her and I kept painting and I got my courage up and I said, 'But you've got all of this, Joanna, and you don't look much the happier for it!' And I remember that she kind of smiled. But not a happy smile—a real sad smile.

" 'Well, you know, Sam,' she told me. 'If you've got black clouds following you, it doesn't really matter where you are." And I guess I was surprised, because I said to her, 'What black clouds could *you* have, Joanna?' And she said, 'Something I've done, Sam—something I should never have done.' And then she stopped, like she didn't dare look at me. 'Something bad, something *unnatural.*' "

Sam looked at me with his blue eyes. "Yeah, that was the word she used—*unnatural.*" He shrugged. "Seems like yesterday."

"But she didn't say what it was?" I asked, trying to restrain the nervous excitement in my voice. "Didn't you ask her?"

"Sure I tried to ask her! But her face looked so pained, and so sad. I just remember her leaning against that gate and looking in at the maze with a queer look.

" 'Whatever happened to your brother, Joanna?' I asked her once. But when I said this I was sorry, because she looked real sad again.

" 'He died, Sam,' she told me. 'Drink. Drink got to him. I tried to help him, but in the end no one could really help him—and he was so bright! Do you remember what a bright boy he was? We were together all the time.' I remember I could hardly stand to look at her eyes then—I'd always felt that her brother was the one she really loved. Only person she was ever really close to.

"I could see Joanna drifting into another world with that look she sometimes got, and I said to her, 'It's a shame you never had any kids, Joanna. Maybe it's not too late. Sure would be a fine place for a kid to grow up in!' She looked at me in a way I'll never forget. Her eyes just seemed to pierce right through me—sad, but kind of angry, too. But real sad. And she turned to me and said, 'That would be nice, Sam.' She said this in a real soft voice, almost like it would crack. I tried to keep painting, but it was hard, real hard, because something in her voice scared me.

"Before she left, she said, 'You won't tell anyone what I've said, will you, Sam? It'll be just between us?' And then she came up to me and she put her hand on my shoulder, and I remember it was as cold as a stone. I remember the smell of her perfume, too."

"And Rosalind," I asked, mulling this over. "Was she around at the time?"

"Sure. Always was. Real close to Mr. Cassel, Rosalind. Always thought he had a real soft spot for her. Always said how pretty and smart she was."

"And Rosalind's relationship with Joanna?"

"Kind of . . ." He faltered. "Thorny. Maybe Joanna was even a little jealous that Mr. Cassel spent so much time with Rosalind. The three of them would be together a lot—Joanna, and Mr. Cassel and Rosalind. Why, I remember once—" He paused, stooped over the rake.

"What, Sam?" I watched his expression, recalling the hidden sketch in Cassel's library.

"I was fixing something or other in the house, and the two of them—Joanna and Rosalind—were in Joanna's bedroom. Rosalind was shouting and Joanna was crying and I could hear Rosalind say to her, in a real raw voice, 'You've never cared about David or me. You've only *used* us, the way you've used everyone else!' " Sam shook his head, picking his teeth with a toothpick he had taken from his pocket. "It was terrible—the things I heard them saying that day!"

"Have you any idea what Rosalind meant?"

"Don't know," he replied, shaking his head. "Except that Joanna was always looking for Rosalind to keep David company. Escort him around, fill in at dinners when they had company—company Joanna didn't like, Mr. Cassel's friends. Some folks thought Joanna was jealous of Rosalind, but I always thought she was relieved to have her around—kind of freed her. Know what I mean?"

"And then what happened later that year, the year Joanna died?"

"She went away in June, and when she got back—all during that summer—she seemed a lot worse. Like no one could really help her. And then in September, she died." He continued to rake with long, smooth strokes.

He paused to adjust his spectacles again, scratching the side of his nose. "The house is going to go to Rosalind, you know. When Mr. Cassel dies."

I told him I had heard something to that effect.

"Never did think Rosalind got along with Joanna, but she sure was crazy about Wakefield. Rosalind's pretty cagey, ain't she?"

I asked whether he had seen a woman called Christina von Shouse at Wakefield Hall. He asked me to describe her; I began to do so.

"Yeah, she was here a fair amount," he said, interrupting me. "Always hovering around Joanna. Always pretending to be concerned about her."

"What do you mean pretending?"

"I always thought she was jealous of Joanna, too."

"Why?"

"Because Joanna was rich. Because she had a rich husband and she was famous."

I smiled to myself, wondering how Christina von Shouse would react to this. "Did you ever see a man called Lawrence Brandt? The architect who helped Joanna restore the house? Tall, brown hair, rather conceited?"

"Sure, I knew Mr. Brandt," he said, with a stern, almost rebuking glance. "But I wouldn't call him conceited. He was pretty good to me. He'd go around with me looking at things that needed fixing. A real gent, I always thought. Never asked me to do anything I couldn't.''

I thought this over, then asked, "About the maze, Sam—do you remember Joanna saying anything specific about it? The design, the statues she'd chosen?"

He shook his head. "No—we'd talk about the hedges, mostly. And the flowers, of course—the black tulips, where they should be planted. The only thing I remember her saying—" He paused, leaning on the rake.

"Go on."

"She told me that the maze here reminded her of another house, her favorite house. One in England that also had a maze, with a statue in the middle. Last summer—must've been in July—she told me she'd been back to that house, that she'd left some things there. For the last time, she said."

I watched him closely, never doubting his truthfulness. I was on the verge of asking him another question when I glimpsed Kurt, the butler, watching us from the far end of the path.

"I should go," I said, seeing Kurt walk toward us. I hurriedly thanked Sam Neelly and said goodbye.

After Kurt ushered me inside the house, I was momentarily puzzled, even disoriented, when I saw a package, accompanied by a note addressed to me, which lay on the bed. But then I recalled Rosalind's words—"David has left something for you"—and ripped open the envelope:

Dear Elisabeth:
    Months ago—during our first discussion—I mentioned that Joanna had left this folder of memorabilia. It seems appropriate that you should have it now. I hope it will be useful to you.

                                    Best regards—
                                    David Cassel.

I tore open the brown wrapping; inside was a thick folder of marbleized paper, tied on each side with purple grosgrain ribbons. On its front—just as David Cassel had told me in June—were three words written in Joanna's bold hand: *To My Biographer*.

I untied the ribbons, opened the folder, and looked at the parchment sheet on top, which was written in the medieval style of an illuminated manuscript, with the elaborate first letter of each line picked out in gold:

A SONNET—TO MY BIOGRAPHER:

Excuse not silence so, for't lies in thee
Look in thy glass, and tell the face thou viewest
I may not evermore acknowledge thee,
Since brass, nor stone, nor earth, nor boundless sea
Accuse me thus, that I have scanted all.
But then begins a journey in my head
Even in the eyes of all posterity.
Those lines that I before have writ do lie
Hung with the trophies of my lovers gone,
Making a famine where abundance lies.
Yet this shall I ne'er know but live in doubt;
O let my books be then the eloquence
Whose speechless song, being many, seeming one,
No more be grieved at that which thou hast done.

I wondered if this was a sonnet Joanna had written herself or whether it was by Shakespeare or someone in his circle. There was no indication who had written it—only a fragment of paper, clipped to its back, with these notations in a crabbed hand: R34341, R344203, R34518, R35529, H8554, H85510. I thought of my interview with Brandt—his description of Joanna's latent fascination with numbers—and wondered whether there was a link between the numbers and the poem.

Then I remembered the two books on the sonnets I had

seen on her night table: I scanned the salient lines for clues: "a journey in my head" (the maze and its progression?); "eyes of all posterity" (the consuming issue of posthumous fame); "O let my books be then the eloquence" (the books in her library? books left at Thistleton?) It was, however, the eighth and ninth lines I read incessantly, for they seemed to hold the secret: *"Those lines that I before have writ do lie/ Hung with the trophies of my lovers gone."* Was this a reference to a letter, or letters, she had left with Desmond Kerrith, her "lover gone," at Thistleton?

I put the sonnet aside and began examining the pile of papers and photographs. Tattered newspaper clippings, including advertisements of movies Joanna must have seen as a girl—*As You Like It*, with Olivier and Elisabeth Bergner, *Romeo and Juliet*, with Norma Shearer, *Anna Karenina*, with Garbo. A stack of reviews of her own performances next—many by Kenneth Tynan and J. C. Trewin—as well as a group of carefully marked stage photographs: Joanna as Ophelia, as a hollow-cheeked, kohl-eyed Cleopatra, and—perhaps the most touching, in its suggestion of innocence—of a dazzlingly pretty, sprightly Miranda, with a long thick braid, from *The Tempest*.

I opened a large envelope with personal photographs: Joanna and David at their wedding; Joanna and Christina, sitting at a café together—in Italy or France, perhaps—in summer dresses and large, obscuring sunglasses; a photograph of Rosalind as a plump little girl, sitting in an empty theater, wearing what seemed to be a school uniform, her eyes glassy in their remove, her features uncannily adult.

Tied with a red ribbon in another group were several baby pictures. There was a picture of Joanna as a little girl in braids, as well, her arm tightly around the waist of an older boy—her brother, I assumed, as it was dated 1938. The last photograph was encased in its own envelope and—after the discovery of the sketch in the library—held its own lurid fascination: David, Rosalind, and an unsmiling Joanna together in bathing suits, David's arms clasped around the two women.

One final, unmarked envelope remained inside, this one pertaining to the maze at Wakefield. A scrap of paper lay on top, with the reference to Wakefield once alluded to by Christina: "After the bloody fray at Wakefield fought"; beneath it Joanna had scribbled: "3 Henry VI, II, i, 107." A sheaf of Lawrence Brandt's sketches next, as well as renderings of the gate and photocopies of descriptions of mazes from garden and history books; the name and address of a stonemason; a sheet illustrating different lettering styles, with the simplest Roman type circled; and a sequence of black-and-white snapshots of the Shakespearean statues in progress, their faces slowly emerging from the rough surface of the stone—Lavinia's gaping mouth, Lady Macbeth's stare, Hermione's cryptic smile.

Within the folder was a smaller envelope marked THISTLETON—photograph after photograph of the house and its grounds: a splendid burst of delphinium, a border of yellow yarrow, a pair of stone urns; an aerial photograph of the vast property, with its romantic landscape of follies and temples and its large, meandering maze with the octagonal tower at the edge of the "ruins." A map indicated that the swirling maze could be entered two ways: either by walking across the drawbridge from the rear gate of the moated tower, or from the principal gate to the south. It was, as Brandt had described, a daunting, unruly labyrinth—no order, no central axis.

As I continued to pore over the photographs, it was not so much any specific detail that impressed me but rather the stupefying variety and number of the shots, which suggested, as nothing else had, the full power of Joanna's obsession. I was also struck by the absence of letters; it seemed strange that a woman known not only for her letter writing but also for making copies of her letters should not have included a single one. Perhaps Cassel had riffled through them, keeping some for himself or destroying others, thinking the photographs, memorabilia, and sonnet in the folder innocuous enough.

I returned again and again to the sonnet, copying it down in my notebook, underlining the key phrases, and wondering, as I did so, whether there was a link between it and the passages in the maze.

Patrick Rossiter joined us for dinner that night, and once again the atmosphere seemed subtly changed. Whereas in June he had been expansive, full of stories about his old friend, now he was subdued and quiet (though as ingratiating as ever to Rosalind).

Only by great effort did I manage to eat or keep up with the conversation. I would look at Patrick and think of the maze and its statues; I would look at Rosalind and think of the sketch on David's desk. Was it the imposition of perverse sexual demands that had partly inspired Joanna's posthumous letter to her husband—not, as I had previously supposed, merely neurotic anger? What had actually happened between them? And what was the transgression she had described to Sam Neelly as unnatural?

I noticed with what ease Rosalind assumed the role of mistress of the house, the house she would inherit; how imperiously she presided over dinner, tasting the wine she had chosen and directing the staff. But most of all I noticed how her undercurrent of command seemed to extend to Patrick Rossiter—how he constantly deferred to her.

As I sat through dinner that night, I wondered what Rosalind had said to him, and why.

28

Rosalind drove us to the stables the next morning, the red kerchief at her neck the same color as her lipstick and sports car. She took the curves with a speed and aggressiveness that seemed in keeping with the way she moved and talked and thought. We spoke of many things during that ride—an article on Goldman, Sachs in the business section of the *Times* that morning, and of David Cassel, who had recently been honored for his contributions to the prestigious New York Art Institute. All the while I remember gazing at her profile—the precise curve of her mouth against her anemic skin—and linking it with the sketch of the torso. Never had I met anyone whose ethereal looks belied such *sangfroid*; never had I felt so keenly the weight of her subtly competitive, relentlessly assessing eye.

She had noticed the ring I wore on my left hand—the sapphire ring that Jack had given me.

"Pretty," Rosalind said, with a slight upward tilt of her chin. "From your family?"

"No," I replied, watching her reaction. "From a friend."

"The friend has good taste," came the wry remark. Her left arm was propped on the window, her right hand at the steering wheel. "And what does the friend's wife think," she added, with a mischievous glance, "the long-suffering Alice?"

"I don't know," I replied rather too sharply. "Do you?"

"Why should *I* know?" A long pause, the country vistas spinning before us. "How'd you meet him, anyway?"

"At the Four Seasons one day, at lunch," I replied, aware that our positions were now reversed; yet it seemed prudent to grant her, at least momentarily, the role of interrogator. "He was with an old friend of mine," I added, never mentioning what had flashed through my mind—the visceral recollection of Jack's disturbing presence.

"And then what happened?"

"I saw him a few months later—at the airport in Geneva."

"So Jack seduced you right then and there—first class or coach?"

I smiled slightly. "*He* was in first class, *I* was in coach."

"And he didn't have you upgraded?" she asked, lifting one eyebrow.

"He tried. But I refused."

"How lofty of you," she said acidly. "And how clever." We swung around another curve. "So then what happened?"

"He came and sat with me. In coach."

"And he didn't try to seduce you—not even a little quickie in the loo?"

"No," I replied, by then accustomed to, even amused by, her tone.

We passed beneath some trees, shadows engulfing the sleek red car.

"He'll never leave Alice, you know," she said matter-of-factly as we reentered the sunlight.

Anxiety overtook me; yet my voice was even enough. "Why do you say that?"

"Because she's important to him—for his ambitions in New York. It's an old story. He's got the money, she's got the social clout: the old downwardly mobile WASP name; mother of his children: well liked by the Park Avenue mafia; does all the right charity stuff—"

I thought of the earnest Alice Varady—her Episcopalian disdain for self-adornment, her lunches at the Colony Club, her dogged involvement with tony hospitals, especially Memorial Sloan-Kettering, where she worked as a docent.

"And here he is—" Rosalind continued in the same cynical vein, "—a kid from the wrong shore of Long Island." She paused. "Where's Jack from?"

"Commack."

"What did his father do?"

"He was a contractor."

Her contemptuous smile only confirmed what I had intuited: There was no greater snob than Rosalind. "Where'd Jack go to college?"

"Dartmouth. He worked his way through Dartmouth."

"Of course," she muttered, rolling her eyes. "Why'd I even bother to ask?"

"Why do you say that?"

"Male chauvinism in its purest form. Jockstrap city." She sighed, her mouth forming the small inscrutable smile that suddenly made me recall our first meeting. "Well, he's no different than most men," she said dismissively. "His needs are simple."

"And those are?"

"A climax, a beer, and a ball game. Fairly primitive stuff."

I remember laughing aloud at this—partly out of relief, partly out of nervousness, no doubt.

"I've had dinner with him a few times, you know," she added with a wicked, sidelong glance. "Or maybe you didn't."

I remember her thrill at my discomfiture. "You already told me that—"

"Did I?" She raised one brow, feigning forgetfulness, adding perhaps too vehemently: "He's not my type, anyway."

I glanced at her profile again, wondering what sort of man would be Rosalind's type. "And you?" I asked, recalling the sketch. "There's no man in your life?"

"There have been *many* men. But no man with a capital M."Then, briskly: "Madame Bovary, *c'est moi.* I'm good at falling in love, good at the sex, but not good at the in-between." She shot me another sharp, ribald glance, *"You,* on the other hand, must be good at all three."

"So I'm told," I replied in kind, secretly pleased that my response seemed to disconcert her. "Does David know about me and Jack?"

"Of course. David knows everything."

"And what has he said to you about it?"

"Nothing very much." We took another curve as we passed a barn with green shutters. "It's not your love life that David's concerned about. It's the way you're going about the book."

"What do you mean?"

"The direction it's taking. He doesn't like it."

"You mean he's concerned what conclusions I might draw about him? That I might not present him—or Joanna—in the way he wants?"

"You put the words into my mouth, Elisabeth," she retorted. "I mean the ads you placed in the *Times* and the *Tribune*—that kind of thing. David doesn't think it's dignified. And then the way you were snooping around the help yesterday—"

Kurt had seen me with Sam Neelly.

"It was agreed you'd ask permission before speaking to the staff. And most of all—" She paused. "Most of all, David doesn't like the way you seem ready to believe any rumor that comes your way." Our eyes met. "You know what I mean —that old rumor that's been going around, about Joanna's last letter."

"Then David doesn't know how biographers do their job. *Everything* has to be investigated—even rumors. David is used to calling the shots. But a book isn't a board meeting."

"Obviously, David knows a book isn't a board meeting. That goes without saying."

"Then he should trust me to go about the research in the way I see fit. It's *my* book."

"But Joanna was *his* wife. And David knows everyone in New York—all the players." Her glance was ominous. "That's something you should be aware of."

"And he should be aware that I intend to finish the book. With or without his approval." I said nothing else in response to those vaguely threatening words—"David knows everyone in New York"—which eerily reiterated my father's warning in his last letter.

We arrived at our destination: a cluster of dark red barns with a white clapboard sign in colonial lettering: EASTPOINT STABLES. I got out of the car, wading through drifts of leaves. Two young men waved to us from a distance. Rosalind waved back, quickening her gait as she flicked her riding crop against her calf. I followed her, holding my gloves tight in my right hand.

The horses—tall, shiny-flanked, and fractious—had already been saddled. Rosalind had donned a helmet while a young man from the stables, who had introduced himself to me, handed me a helmet as well. I put mine on.

I asked Rosalind the name of her horse. "Diablo," she said, patting the side of the great dark beast. "And yours is Prince. I chose him especially for you." She mounted Diablo as the stablehand approached me with Prince. I mounted.

"You're a pretty good rider, we were told," said the young man, adjusting the stirrups, which were slightly too short.

I told him I used to ride a little but hadn't been on a horse in a long time. It had been years, in fact—since college.

"This one jumps real well," he said, patting the flank.

"Jumps? But I don't jump."

He appeared slightly surprised. "We kind of had that impression."

I looked ahead at Diablo and at the small figure of Rosalind astride him. Apprehension seized me, though I was too proud to show it. Taking the reins and making a slight clucking noise, I walked to where Rosalind stood. The large dark head of Diablo turned toward me, flashing his huge white teeth.

We walked together across the road along a stretch of white country fence and then, turning left, to a field crisscrossed by crumbling stone walls; from there, down a narrower path that wended its way through the trees. The leaves flickered, silvery in the breeze, the landscape enflamed by the brazen autumn colors. In the distance lay the Berkshire hills, and above us a clear blue sky whose scattered clouds rhythmically continued to join, then disperse.

I began to relax, savoring the quiet and the peace as I gave in to the rhythm of Prince—a high-spirited horse, but quick and sensitive to my commands. I soon began to notice, with mounting uneasiness, how allied he was to Rosalind's horse —how, when Diablo would quicken to a trot, Prince would invariably follow.

I turned to Rosalind and mentioned this half jokingly to her.

"Herd instinct," she retorted. "They're so goddamn dumb, these beasts." She paused, only to add perfunctorily, "Come on, let's canter—you up to it?"

Prince accelerated his pace to keep up with Diablo's while I held on tight, trying only to focus on Prince and his rolling gait, and not on my fear. At last Rosalind stopped; so did I.

"You okay?" she asked me, wiping her brow with the red kerchief.

"Fine," I said, lying.

"You ride well," she said in her cool, appraising way. Then: "Let's go off to the right—we'll hit another clearing, and we can canter some more. All right?"

I nodded. We set off through the woods, pushing aside branches as we rode through the trees, the horses piercing the high piles of leaves with their clicking hooves. The shade was welcome, for the sun was bright that day and exercise had made me warm and thirsty.

A field crisscrossed with vestiges of old stone walls lay ahead. Rosalind waited as I approached. "This is my favorite place. Like it?"

"Let's trot," I said.

"No—canter."

And so we cantered—across the field and through the trees. Rosalind was slightly ahead of me when I saw her jump across a stone wall. I held Prince as he too approached it, forcing him to a walk so that we would avoid the jump. And then I met up with Rosalind again.

"You took that well," I said.

"Thanks," She glanced at me as she mopped her brow. "You should have tried it."

"But I don't jump."

"There's always a first time."

We continued to walk until, once more, we quickened our pace to a canter. But this time Rosalind had accelerated the speed, so the gait was fast, even reckless. I tried to control Prince, to restrain him, but we continued to race across the field until I saw Rosalind ahead, saw her jump once more, saw the stone wall looming in the distance. I tried to halt Prince, but he resisted, whinnying fiercely and nearly bucking me off. The wall lay directly ahead; I held on tightly and desperately, in fear; and then—without my being able to control him—he soared high and we were in mid-air, the wall beneath us.

I do not remember what happened next—only the terror of being thrown, the sound of something hard striking my head, and the pain when I hit the ground, stunned; then utter silence. I lay there for a long time, it seemed, looking for someone, looking for Rosalind. But no one came. Was it simply that trauma had exaggerated the sense of passing time, or had she hesitated before coming to help me? I still do not know—nor did I know why she seemed, purposefully, to have set a course she knew I could not follow.

At last I heard a voice near me saying, "Are you okay, Elisabeth? Elisabeth?" By that time the shock had worn off, and I felt well enough to stand up, however shakily. I had wrenched my neck, and it throbbed. My left arm hurt, too, where I had felt something sharply tear and pull.

My dazed state gave way to anger. I asked Rosalind how she could have possibly led me to a jump which she knew perfectly well I could not take.

"I'm sorry," she replied, her eyes avoiding mine. "I'm sorry. I wasn't—thinking."

I forced myself to mount Prince again. We walked slowly back to the stables in silence.

We returned to Wakefield by one o'clock. I took some aspirin, washed up, and walked downstairs to lunch. My left arm ached so badly that I could hardly lift it, the pain surging through my body. A doctor came; I was told I had ripped a tendon.

I remember how solicitously Rosalind inquired how I was feeling and the effort she made to cater to me during the meal. But in my heart I knew that her leading me to the jump was meant as a signal—a warning not to venture further, not to antagonize or discredit her stepfather, or herself, with the book. All the while I wondered *what* she feared my discovering—Joanna's last letter, most likely. And if so, why? Of Rosalind's motive I was still not certain.

29

Monday, October 27, 1986

Jack called early this morning—was still in bed, arm aching. He wanted to know my decision. I agreed only to see him.

"When? Tomorrow?"

Next Monday, I say. "For a drink."

"Not dinner?"

"No."

"Where?" (He's grumpy.)

I mention the Italian restaurant down the street—Paolo's.

"But I can't make love to you in a restaurant . . ."

I swallowed hard and said, "We have a lot of things to discuss."

"I love you."

"Love is a commitment—"

"I know."

"Do you?"

Odd feeling of peace and also catharsis after this call: secretly glad the visit to Wakefield intervened. Took an aspirin—arm still aching from the fall—and lay in bed for a while, thinking of the folder left by Joanna. The sonnet obsesses me.

A cup of coffee; reread the sonnet; then went to my Shakespeare—my treasured Pelican edition, much marked, from college. I seem to recall a section on the sonnets at the end—look through it, but find nothing resembling Joanna's. Scanned the introduction and find that J's is, of course, an English (as opposed to Italian) sonnet: both styles have fourteen lines, but only the English style has last rhyming couplet. In no other way does Joanna's conform to the usual rhyme scheme (abab cdcd efef gg). Find there is an index of first lines; but this only confirms that there is no Shakespearean sonnet beginning with "Excuse not silence so . . ." Great disappointment. The introduction also reminds me that a sonnet is always *addressed to someone*. Sonnets 1 to 126 (Shakespeare's) to a young man, 127 to 154 to a young woman. This would be a perfect clue if the sonnet were, indeed, one of Shakespeare's! But it doesn't appear to be (though the language *does* have his feeling and cadence.) On the other hand, Joanna—with her expertise—could have aped it. I closed my Pelican, took some more aspirin; felt stymied.

I paced around the apartment, wondering what to do. Decided to reread Joanna's letter about the maze to Lawrence Brandt—the many references to Shakespeare. Did so, searching for relevant phrases, many of which seem even eerier now: "bereft of Shakespeare's words, I have become a mute and moated sort of person"; "verseless now too"; "the words of his women flooding through stone"; "a Shakespearean treasure hunt—a challenge to my biographer, no doubt!" Then comes the line I had—unconsciously perhaps

—been searching for: "I went to the *Concordance*—my treasured book and treasure-trove for anyone who comes later—" Suddenly remembered seeing a copy of the *Concordance* in Joanna's library at Wakefield the first day. The next step: comb through the *Concordance*. Quickly dressed and left for the library.

At the library: took Bartlett's *A Complete Concordance to Shakespeare* from the stacks—huge, beautiful book, with dark green and gold cover, divided into four columns of tiny print. Looked up each line—using both first word and a key word—and found *nothing*. Bitter disappointment. Leafed through it again and discovered—at the end—a separate *Concordance to the Poems of Shakespeare*. Tried the first word —*Excuse*; found nothing. However—miracle of miracles!— looked up *silence*—key word from first line—and discovered the line was from sonnet 101, line 10! Can hardly describe how fast my heart was beating. Went through the same process for the second line: "Look in thy glass—"; my eyes racing down the entry headed *look* until I found the source: sonnet 3, line 1. Continued this process, looking up first word or—if no luck—key word of each line until I came to the last, fourteenth, line. Found—to my astonishment—that the entire sonnet is composed of lines *interwoven from the gamut of Shakespeare's sonnets* and that five—which I underlined—are first lines:

Excuse not silence so, for't lies in thee (sonnet 101)
Look in thy glass, and tell the face thou viewest (3)
I may not evermore acknowledge thee, (36)
Since brass, nor stone, nor earth, nor boundless sea (65)
Accuse me thus that I have scanted all. (117)
But then begins a journey in my head (27)
Even in the eyes of all posterity. (55)
Those lines that I before have writ do lie (115)
Hung with the trophies of my lovers gone, (31)
Making a famine where abundance lies. (1)
Yet this shall I ne'er know but live in doubt; (144)

O let my books be then the eloquence (23)
Whose speechless song, being many, seeming one, (8)
No more be grieved at that which thou hast done. (35)

Was there a pattern to the sonnets Joanna had chosen—a
method to her madness? I read each sonnet again, trying to
find some common theme, but couldn't. Of the fourteen
lines, thirteen were from the first half (addressed to a young
man) and only one from the second (to a young woman). Is
that meaningful?

I imagine Joanna poring over the sonnets, picking and
choosing among the lines that suited her purpose. Creating
her own message from them—but using only Shakespeare's
words, not a single one of her own. I thought again of her
letter to Brandt; she says she's "mute" and "verseless"—like
Lavinia, with her tongue chopped off. Reduced to silence:
"Excuse not silence so"; "let my books be the eloquence";
"speechless song." All refer to muteness—to the terror she
must have experienced; the stage fright. *It's only through
Shakespeare she feels she can speak,* like the seven statues she
has "impregnated" with his phrases! Of all my discoveries, I
find this the most chilling.

Returned from library in a daze; took some more aspirin
(arm very sore). Phone rings. It's Lawrence Brandt, of all
people. He has called—ostensibly—to mention my piece
which finally ran in the *Journal* today, on *Palladio and the
Evolution of the Country House* (Princeton U Press). "Very
well done," Brandt says. This pleases me, more than I'd like
to admit, but only until he adds: "I thought your article was
more scholarly than the book." Another of his backhanded
compliments. "What's wrong with the book?" I ask (defensively, of course). "Too much focus on the objects—the
buildings themselves—and not enough on the cultural currency. The social context." I ask him to explain. "The house
as an expression of social priorities and ambitions—that's
the agenda Palladio's in the middle of. He creates a synthetic
country life for a lot of people for whom this is not the

natural thing. He's a provincial, a rustic—it's only later he gets the juicy Venetian churches." Goes on to link this with Jefferson's idea about buildings as "educating about life." This interests me (though I don't admit it). "There really wasn't enough space to go into all of that," I finally answer, stifling my irritation (partly with him, partly with myself— why hadn't I critiqued the book that way?).

He asked about the book on Joanna. I couldn't resist mentioning the maze and the sonnet (also the sketch of Rosalind and my interview with Sam Neelly—but don't want to go into this on the phone). I ask if I could see him at his office.

"I'll take you to lunch," he says. This makes me suspicious: assume he's beginning to worry about his role in the book and so he's being nice; or perhaps Cassel has put him up to it. I ask if we can do it this week—he says no, he'll be in Paris for work; how's Saturday?

Fine, I say: where and when should we meet?

He mentions a little restaurant he likes—La Touraine. In the eighties, off Madison. He gives the address; I note his arrogance again—the bossy way he never asks if this is what I'd like! Still, I can't possibly turn down the invitation—it's crucial for the research. I agree to meet him there at 1:00.

Saturday, November 1st

Lunch with Lawrence Brandt at La Touraine.

He wears a tweed sports jacket, white shirt; no tie—he looks (this I dread to admit) almost handsome. As usual, he greets me rather brusquely, though he does help me to my seat. At one point I wince—the aching arm. He asks what's wrong. I tell him what happened: riding accident with Rosalind. Furrows his brow; can't tell what he's thinking—

He asks what I would like to drink and joins me in a kir. It's cold outside and the bittersweet taste is warming.

The place is small, charming, with highly polished wood floors, fireplace, and homely windows framed with curtains in a red-and-blue Provençal print. I notice how the owner—

plump, red-cheeked woman—greets him warmly. Almost motherly. They exchange a few words in French; Brandt's grammar is good, but his accent is abominable.

He glances at the menu, then mentions that his father— visiting from St. Louis—and his little boy will meet us there after lunch. Do I mind? Of course not, I say. They're taking Frederick to see the arms-and-armor exhibit at the Met.

"We should order," he says at once, hardly giving me a moment to sip my kir. I order lightly—watercress soup, omelette Parmentier. Wine? he asks. I nod. "White?" Fine, I reply. He orders something quite good. Dry. The food is brought. It's delicious. I watch in wonder as he makes his way through *coquilles St. Jacques*, rack of lamb, *tarte tatin*.

I tell him about the visit to Wakefield—my impressions of the maze, the folder with the sonnet. All the clues point to Joanna's obsession with silence—with muteness, with stage fright. He listens hard. I mention the part in her letter when she talks about Shakespeare being "reduced to silence" in his last plays—*The Winter's Tale* (with Hermione) among them. I show him the sonnet; observes that it shows Joanna's "despair with the inadequacy of language," and wonders whether there's a link between this and Shakespeare's last phase and the fascination, at the end of Joanna's life, with Frank Lloyd Wright (the idea of "powerful emptiness"). I ask him to explain—he does, in the same insightful way in which he explained Palladio.

I resist being influenced by his voice—yet it fascinates. His perceptions, his way of expressing ideas. His habit of smiling slightly by way of emphasis, mid-sentence; then smile vanishes; sometimes his thoughts end with uptilted intonation —one sentence moving seamlessly into the next. The sense of something withheld.

(I catch myself, even as I sip the dry, delicious wine: he's only being charming to ingratiate himself to me. To be presented in a good light in the book. He's very ambitious—as Christina has said—and wants to be well thought of.)

I tell him about Sam Neely. Brandt smiles: Joanna was

"very fond" of him; called him "the last link" to her child-hood. Adds that he knows very little about Joanna's early years—only that her mother was American, her father English.

What about Rosalind? I finally ask Brandt. He seems to draw back. I tell him about the sketch I've discovered in the library—the nude. "They've always been close," he says, meaning R. and Cassel. "But *that* close?" I ask. At this he laughs, but his eyes say, Be careful. I tell him I know Rosalind was jealous of Joanna, but did he ever have the feeling Joanna was jealous of Rosalind? He says no, never. I suppose I believe him—don't press him with any more questions, as I feel that distance again.

Curious that he *never once* has mentioned meeting me in Seattle that day with Jack.

We finish lunch; Brandt's father and son enter restaurant. I introduce myself as LB pays bill. Father—Philip—is very nice, distinguished-looking, with a kindness and gravity about him; the same slightly hooded, intent eyes as his son's. Frederick grabs candies from a bowl near the entrance—jumps around, ducking under table (all of this tolerated with good humor by the *propriétaire*.) I ask what has brought Philip Brandt to New York—says that he'd come to see Larry being given an award the previous day, at Harvard, for achievement in American architecture. This surprises me—Brandt never mentioned it. The father's visible pride in the son. I was amused to see Larry, on hearing his father's praise, reduced to boyish reticence, even embarrassment.

Fathers and sons, I say—they're never objective.

And mothers and daughters? LB asks, turning to me.

Told him I wouldn't know, as I was raised by my father and my mother's sister. And of course they were *never* objective! I add.

Nor should they have been, he says. This takes me aback—don't know why.

Then he mentions my book on Joanna; tells his father—jokingly?—that I'm "absolutely relentless." I say I never think of myself that way. Relentless people never do, he replies, but his eyes are smiling.

I tell Philip that his son was the most difficult interview—the hardest nut to crack. This seems to amuse him; LB only smiles enigmatically.

Brandt asks if I want to come with them to see the arms-and-armor room at the Met. No, I say automatically. I can't. We say goodbye. His rapid stride as he joins his father and son.

I walk home slowly in the opposite direction.

30

I waited for Jack early Monday evening, having finally agreed to meet him at my apartment—the first time we had seen each other since Christina von Shouse's dinner.

"Hello," I said, as coldly as I could. I wanted not to want him, yet I had used his favorite perfume and had chosen my dress and lingerie with care.

It was a late afternoon edged with the furtive dark of autumn.

"Liza darling," he said at once, his arms pulling me toward him. "No," I said, pushing him away. Yet he, rightly sensing within that single syllable a multitude of meanings, did not release me. My heart beat faster, and a shaft of pain, from my injured arm, shot through me as he held me tight.

I could hardly bear to look at Jack, fearing my resolve would melt. I would look at him and see the dangers he had passed—and then desire, tinged with an almost maternal tenderness, would overcome me . . .

"Darling," he said again, his hand beneath my chin, forcing me to confront his eyes. I felt my aching arm. "I know the dinner was painful for you. It was difficult and painful for me, too. But you've got to understand—until the situation is resolved, I can't behave in a self-destructive way. For your sake, for my family's sake. This is a mean, gossipy town—" His voice augmented in intensity: "I don't want people smirking at us, gossiping, peeping-tomming. If we had started to talk—" here I felt his lips grazing my mouth and cheeks, "our body language would have given us away. I couldn't have talked to you without wanting to touch you. You've got to believe me. Darling." Then, fiercely: "Look at me, Liza."

I searched his face for the features of the man I loved—the keen blue eyes, the kouros-strictness of his brow and cheekbones. Blood rose to my cheeks as I began to speak: I told him in strong, unyielding language that I could not bear this any longer—the deceptions, the clandestine meetings, the pain of the encounters with him and his wife, no matter how infrequent. I was no longer prepared to wait, without a deadline. He would have to make a decision—a commitment to me.

"You already know the decision," he replied quietly, brushing strands of hair from my forehead. "It's just a question of when. Of timing." He paused. "I've already made an appointment with a lawyer next week. That's what I came to tell you." He pulled me to him again; I felt the rough texture of his jacket and the smooth surface of his beautiful shirt. I felt myself relax, at once exhausted and exhilarated. "I'm a lonely man in a lonely place," he told me. "Be with me. Stay with me."

I felt my own power to acquiesce or not as he kissed me. Opening his briefcase he produced a small black shopping bag. "For you," he said, his eyes shining with a complex, proprietary pleasure.

Inside was a package wrapped in glossy red paper—I opened it to find a book, a leatherbound and gilt copy of *The House of Mirth*. I smiled gratefully and kissed him, remembering that this had been among the several favorite books I had carried on the plane from Geneva that fateful day.

I opened the cover only to stop in surprise after the frontispiece: This was no book but, rather, an exquisite jewelry box of red leather. My eyes questioned Jack's as I opened the clasp: against the velvet interior lay a poppy-shaped brooch of crushed rubies and garnets, the companion to a pair of earrings Jack had bought me the previous year from the French jeweler Tantale.

"Like it, darling?" he asked me expectantly, almost boyishly.

"Yes of course," I said, glancing at the glittering flower in my hand. "It's beautiful." And then lightly: "But the book would have been enough." I kissed him, my lips lingering on his; inwardly, I was bewildered by my reaction to the present and to the morbid delight underlying it.

I snapped the case shut, sensing from Jack's silence that my reaction had not been sufficiently effusive.

"Liza," he said a moment later. "You don't seem yourself. You seem—" He paused. "Tired, preoccupied. It's the book. You shouldn't have taken it on."

"Why do you say that?"

"I feel your distance from me, darling. I worry about you. I worry about the pressure of the research—whether it's the right career move for you." A pause. "I hope you're not doing it for the money . . ."

"It has nothing to do with money," I said at once, astonished and disturbed by his reaction.

"You don't need to do it for *money*," he reiterated, as if he had not really heard me. "I never want you to worry about money."

I described the singular absorption I felt in working on the book; that it could only enrich my other writing; that the entanglement of relationships and the evolution of character were the most fascinating elements in Joanna's story, and that I sensed I could depict them well. About my conversation with Rosalind and what she had said about Cassel's disapproval, I said nothing. "I saw Rosalind last weekend," I said, adding, "I didn't know you'd had dinner with her."

"Didn't I tell you that?" A pause. "I guess we did—a couple of times last year. Something had come up with Goldman."

"What do you think of her?"

"Tough cookie. Not someone you'd trust. But she's very close to Cassel—he's wild about her, I hear."

I bit my lip. "Did you sleep with her?"

"Of course not," he replied sharply to the question I'd felt ashamed to ask. "She's the last person I'd want to sleep with. I'm amazed you'd even ask me that." He caressed my cheek. "You're the only woman I want to sleep with," he murmured, "the only woman I love. That's why I worry about you—"

"You shouldn't," I said, returning his kiss; once more I said how much the work fascinated me: "It makes my blood rush."

"Makes your blood rush," he repeated, his voice edged with an unfamiliar coldness. "There was a time when you would have used that expression to describe something else." Then, with bulletlike directness: "Us."

"I still would," I said, and looked away.

31

As winter approached, my dreams assumed a dark and sinister dimension.

Windswept, cold, abandoned houses with unending blue corridors pursued me. I would open doors, only to find that some led to infinity while others led to spaces barren of furniture or walls. I would hear a voice and run toward it, only to find that the sound had vanished into wind.

In one dream—rare, because it was peopled with crowds and teeming throngs—I clutched the hand of a tiny child (waiflike in rags), fighting the vortex of strangers, until the moment came when, unable to sustain my grip, the child was lost to me and all that remained was the echo of its voice uttering my name. I searched for the unknown child, calling its name as I struggled against the angry mobs until, at last, I sat down and wept by the edge of a deserted crossroad whose signs were written in a language I did not understand.

I awakened in a sweat and sat up, looking about the bedroom as if to reassure myself that the world of the dream was imaginary. Even so, it continued to replay itself in my mind until, once again, I came to the part where I called the child's name. Suddenly, I realized—how could I have called the child's name when I did not know who the child was? This lapse of logic only served to reassure me of the unreality of the dream, of its absurdity. I remember taking a deep breath, feeling triumphant and relieved, like a cross-examiner who has just uncovered an inconsistency in the testimony of a key witness. It was only then I was able to cast the dream from my mind and get up from bed.

Rosalind's coolness, which I had at first construed as a product of my own paranoia, was indeed real and was accompanied by a sarcasm verging on hostility on the rare occasions when we met; yet she continued to act as emissary for her stepfather. I had grown accustomed to her strange blend of cynicism (toward me) and protectiveness (reserved for David). I had no choice but to deal with her.

In Patrick Rossiter I had rightly discerned a shift of attitude: He was no longer the chatty family friend all too willing to divulge what he remembered of his protégée Joanna Eakins. When, in November, I called him to confirm certain aspects of his recollections—those he had first told me at Wakefield in June—I was astounded to hear him refute many of his original statements, causing me to doubt my own memory and judgment.

I wondered whether Christina von Shouse realized what was happening; in any case, she continued to be helpful. And while I knew better than to trust totally her perceptions—

particularly of Cassel and Brandt—I could not afford to disregard her as a source.

I called her ten days or so after my return from Wakefield and remember the manner in which she asked about the house—as if she were inquiring after an elderly relative or favorite aunt. "And how was it looking, my dear? Was it the way you'd remembered it?" I answered her evasively, only saying I had a few more questions to ask her.

She invited me for a drink two days later, on a Wednesday in mid-November—an eerie reenactment of our first meeting that sultry July afternoon. Devoid of sparkling guests, her apartment had reassumed its silent, but no less powerful persona. Again I marveled at the decor, the aura of which transcended that of the mere *objets de culte* with which, as one acquainted with New York drawing rooms, I was so familiar.

She greeted me at the door of her apartment, dressed with characteristic severity: a black suit that set off her dark, sculpted hair with its bold streak of gray, and a challenging brooch of a unicorn's head pinned to her lapel.

We went into the drawing room and sat, as we had the previous summer, beneath its *faux* sky. She offered me a drink; the maid appeared minutes later with her vodka and my white wine. I asked if I could record our conversation; of course, she said obligingly. She watched, sipping her vodka as I turned on the machine; when I looked up, she was smoothing her hair in such a way that I glimpsed the familiar carnelian scarab ring.

I had already decided not to mention the folder left by Joanna or the sonnet—only the sketch on David Cassel's desk and a few careful questions about Joanna's childhood.

The sketch first: here it was the quality of her response— her expression and tone of voice—that interested me.

"To each his own," was her cavalier reply, coupled with a glance that was not without contempt. "I always thought David to have complicated and insatiable needs. He is not a man of refined tastes in that way. A hamburger and french fries sort of person." She paused, setting down her drink. "So much more of this goes on than you can imagine, my dear!" A knowing laugh. "It would not surprise me in the least—would it you? There was always such tension between them —Joanna, Rosalind, and David, I should say. On the other hand, Joanna never mentioned anything of that sort to me. If something had been going on, I would have known about it."

I pondered this equivocal answer as I made a few notes; then I asked about Joanna's childhood—whether she had ever spoken with Christina about it ("almost never") and whether she had ever met Joanna's mother.

"Ah yes—the *mother*," said Christina with a cryptic smile, settling back into the tufted green armchair. Her eyes had assumed a certain remove. She picked up the lizard handbag from the table at her side and, taking out the gold compact inset with a cabochon ruby, glanced into the mirror as she fixed her powder—a gesture I had come to recognize as signaling the beginning of a new anecdote.

"Tell me about Joanna's mother," I said as she snapped the compact shut.

"There are always telling moments in a relationship which one never forgets and which can irreparably alter a friendship or a love affair," she went on to say. "Or a marriage, for that matter! I think it was the time when Joanna's mother came to visit that seemed to seal David's disgust and disillusionment with his wife. He could not reconcile himself to the fact that Joanna had sprung from *her*—it was that simple. And she of course felt his contempt for her family, his embarrassment over her background."

"Had Joanna ever discussed her mother with you before?"

"Hardly ever. Only that she had once been quite beautiful and had come from a very different sort of background from her father's—the mother's family had a farm, I believe. Joanna's father was English, the youngest of five sons. He had come here from Devon—or was it Brighton?—to make his fortune, and met the mother in the West. They were married almost immediately, to the dismay of his family.

Over the years they had a hard, roaming sort of life. 'It would have been endurable if I had never seen the way other people lived,' I remember Joanna saying, 'but when I did it changed my life.' As a child she longed to escape to other people's houses, at the same time she dreaded visiting them—it was too painful to return to the rage and disorder of her own." There was a pause, before she reflected: "Yes—'rage and disorder,' those were precisely the words she used. A lonely house with only two books—"

"Did she say which two?" I asked, interrupting her.

"Yes—Shakespeare, of course, and a copy of *Bulfinch's Mythology*. Her father's family had sent the books from England."

I made note of this as Christina watched. "Joanna's childhood—" I said, looking up.

She savored her vodka for a moment, setting the glass into its ring of ice before continuing: "Joanna adored her father, but always said he wasn't with them much. A restless, charming man was my impression. At one point she told me, 'When I was a child it seemed a bitter thing not to have a father, like everyone else. But as I've grown older, I can't find it in me to blame him.' The father died years ago. I had the impression the mother eventually moved to Portland."

I asked her to describe meeting Joanna's mother.

"The *mise en scène*," she said, interrupting me with an affable smile. "Of course. It was a lovely day—July seventh of seventy-eight. I remember the date well, because she had come to celebrate Joanna's forty-sixth birthday. David had never met her before—Mrs. Darby, Maude Darby. You can imagine the scene when the car pulled up and the chauffeur opened the door and a frail, woebegone woman slowly made her way out. It was a ravishing sunny day, quite hot, but the mother was dressed in a bulky gray coat, her lumpy shoes scuffed, her handbag—this I always remember—held together with a green rubber band. A visit to the *coiffeur* had turned her hair into a strange, dust-colored concoction. She had lost a few of her teeth. What a pathetic sight she was!

And I must say, when I glimpsed this poor old woman, so much more about Joanna became *instantly comprehensible*.

"I remember how Joanna descended the steps to the car. To this day I remember the mauve silk dress she wore, and how, when her mother appeared, Joanna kept touching her pearl necklace in that nervous gesture of hers. Whatever had happened between the two—the mother and the daughter— Joanna tried in that moment to erase, and to replace it with compassion. But it is not always possible for children to do that, you know—to expunge a whole lifetime of shame and ambivalence with loving-kindness!"

"And David Cassel?"

"Oh yes, he was there—standing at a distance, at the top of the steps. A chilly, formidable figure in a jacket. I wonder exactly what he was thinking at that moment. I wonder at the depth of his disgust. It is quite possible by that time he felt he had been duped in marrying Joanna, that this was not what he had bargained for. She was no longer acting, and now there was this mother. Not what he had bargained for— that is one of his favorite expressions. Perhaps you have already noticed!

"David descended the steps and met Joanna and her mother by the car, shaking the lady's hand and looking askance at her luggage, which was dreadfully shabby. Even the butler looked appalled. But then the help are always the worst snobs of all—it is the only thing they have, after all!

"And then Mrs. Darby spoke. And when she spoke, it was all the more apparent what a disaster the weekend would be. Mrs. Darby had a hideous, provincial American accent—it is hard for me, as a foreigner, to pinpoint its origins, but it did have a dreadful twang that made one cringe. I realized, in listening to her, what an effort Joanna must have made to separate her speech from that of her mother—to speak English beautifully, like an Englishwoman! Like her father."

Christina paused to sip her vodka, wiping the mark it had left on the table with a monogrammed napkin. "Did Joanna resemble her mother—physically, that is?"

"Very little. I must say I strained to see the vestiges of the lost beauty Joanna had described. I think there is always some link to a woman's physical past, even as one ages. Sometimes it is as subtle as a coquettish gesture or a way of arranging the hair. But I could find no such thing in poor Mrs. Darby. She was a frightfully unattractive, unkempt woman with not a hint of *amour propre*.

"I remember later, when her mother appeared at dinner, that Joanna had fixed the woman's hair a bit and lent her some other clothes and a brooch, which was pinned somewhat comically to a dress that seemed too large. She was a timid woman, Mrs. Darby, frightened and shatteringly ignorant—pathetically uncomfortable at Wakefield and completely intimidated by her son-in-law. And of course the path of Joanna's life had meant that there were now unbridgeable gaps between mother and daughter. Mrs. Darby would mention the amount of food or wonder at the number of staff required to keep the place up—all the things one never much thought of at Wakefield, and certainly never discussed." A pause before she added: "There is nothing that makes the rich more uncomfortable than the presence of someone conscious of cost."

I smiled to myself at this pronouncement, then asked if there had been any other guests that weekend.

"No, no one else—only myself. As Joanna's best friend, I would *understand*, presumably. David absented himself most of the time and by Sunday morning, having concocted a spur-of-the-moment visit to New York, left. It was only then that he seemed to show any kindness or warmth toward poor Mrs. Darby. He even hugged her as he left. 'Take good care of my daughter. She's a good girl, isn't she?' I remember the old woman saying. For once David actually responded, out of some vestige of compassion for the old lady. Yet I also recall the deadened look in his eyes as he drove away and the fearsome sound of his Jaguar pulling out of the courtyard.

"At that point Joanna began to relax a bit, as she always did when David left. She took her mother's arm, chatting with her. It was shortly before lunch, as I recall. We took a little walk around the rose garden, Mrs. Darby admiring the flowers, all rare and beautifully tinted and fragrant. Joanna appeared to focus only on her mother, but I knew her well enough to know that her mind was elsewhere—that however much she was ashamed of her mother, it was also unbearably painful for her to see David's callousness toward her, his *horror* that this should be her parent."

She took up her compact again, this time to refresh her red lipstick. "So you see why, my dear—" she looked at me directly, "*why* it meant so much for Joanna to return to the country of her father—to England. To learn to speak properly. And what Thistleton must have meant to her!"

Christina urged me, as she had from the beginning, to go to Thistleton, subsequently calling me once, even twice, a week (often ostensibly for another reason) to inquire whether I had heard from Desmond Kerrith—whether he had responded to my letters and calls. No, I would reply almost wearily. Kerrith had not responded. Then I would wait, trying to discern in the intervening split second whether it was disappointment or triumph that laced the voice on the other end. "You will hear from him, I know—he adored Joanna so!" she told me more than once, adding, "He was rather less than enthusiastic about the marriage to David."

In the first week of December, I received a call from David Cassel's office. After a moment of exchanging pleasantries with his secretary (distinguished voice, elegant phone manner), I was put through to Cassel himself. We chatted for a moment before he asked the question I had been nervously anticipating—whether I would come and see him. "There are some things I'd like to talk with you about, Elisabeth," he said cordially enough. "Matters regarding the book." We agreed to meet at the end of the week at five o'clock, at his apartment on Fifth Avenue.

He had said nothing in the least threatening to me or even remotely critical, yet as that Friday afternoon approached, I found myself dreading the moment when I would enter his apartment.

32

It was the thick, matte red of poinsettia leaves that I first remember of that Friday—the stolid sentinels of Christmas that banked the lobby of David Cassel's building on Fifth Avenue. I had walked from my apartment, my frozen cheeks burning as I battled rush-hour holiday crowds holding tight to packages and hats.

I took the elevator to Cassel's floor, watching as the numbers lit up one by one. I knew he had lived in this building about twenty years, and I had also come to learn—this from Christina von Shouse—that he was displeased by the new group that, in his words, had recently "infiltrated" the building: magnates whose fortunes had not yet acquired the requisite patina.

As the elevator continued to ascend, I realized how quickly my perception of Cassel had changed since our first meeting at Wakefield only six months before. It was his disarming enthusiasm and charm that had seduced me then. The convoluted relationship with Joanna and Rosalind, his terror that I should uncover something harmful to his image— these insidious aspects of his character had only been revealed to me little by little.

In my nervousness I took deep breaths, occasionally smoothing the skirt of the businesslike suit I had chosen to wear. The elevator stopped. The door opened onto a generous foyer dominated by a baroque mirror swagged with boughs of holly and red ribbons. How welcoming and reassuring those Christmas decorations seemed; I momentarily savored the scent of evergreens and the perfume of the paper-white narcissus on the table before me.

I rang the bell. The butler—a short, athletically built Englishman—appeared. I gave my name and followed him into the cavernous, marble-floored entrance hall at the end of which a massive staircase twisted upward to a superior floor.

I handed over my coat and was asked to wait by the bannister which, like the outer hall, was swagged with evergreens. On the wall above were Old Master drawings similar to those I had seen in Cassel's library pavilion and which—by bringing to mind the hidden sketch—only made me more anxious. I turned away, focusing instead on the Renaissance paintings in the foyer: the Italian paintings for which David Cassel was famous. The bowed figures of saints, the beatific faces of Madonnas and angels with their attendant haloes glimmered from their stations in a way that only unsettled me more; even their small primitive smiles appeared alien and tense.

The butler, having returned, announced in a supercilious voice that Mr. Cassel "awaited me" in the library; and would madam like a drink? A glass of water, I said, rejecting the fleeting temptation of alcohol.

I followed him across the vast gallery to the library, with its dark, coffered ceiling and walls covered in red damask. A fire burned within, its flames leaping toward the protective screen. To one side, in a leather armchair, sat David Cassel, his hand gripping the silver hawk-shaped handle of a walking stick.

His manner was welcoming as he slowly stood up. "It's good to see you again, sir," I said, shaking his hand.

"Sit down, dear," he said, jovially enough, making himself comfortable again. He was, as usual, carefully turned out: tweed jacket with a bordeau-colored cashmere vest that matched the silk handkerchief in his front pocket. I noticed his black velvet slippers, with his initials thickly embroidered in gold.

"You'd like something to drink, wouldn't you, Elisabeth?" he asked, leaning forward. "A drink? Tea? What can we get you?" He smiled warmly. I remember how startlingly youthful his eyes seemed.

I thanked him, saying that I had already asked for a glass of water; he was drinking whiskey, I noticed.

I took a seat opposite him and glanced around the room, with its cases of glimmering leatherbound books (like his study at Wakefield, its sole resemblance to a library). The effect of the red and green together with the *quattrocento* paintings was at once impressive and chilling—a museum subjugated to an old man's whims.

The paintings were undeniably beautiful, however. I mentioned them admiringly (partly as a way of procrastinating, no doubt). "They're even more astonishing here than in photographs," I said, gazing at a *Madonna and Child* by Duccio above the fireplace; then, to its right, a depiction of the *Martyrdom of St. Sebastian* by Crivelli, the saint's bluish-white flesh fastidiously pierced with arrows, the glistening drops of blood painted with uncanny realism. But it was the painting directly above me—*Adam and Eve in the Garden of Paradise*—that, even in my nervousness, I found mesmerizing. Its jewellike colors and enigmatic serpent led me to assume that it, too, was Sienese.

I told him what a privilege it was to see these famous pictures here, in this private setting. "Is it really?" he asked disarmingly as he continued to sip his whiskey. "Didn't know you were interested in pictures."

Smiling to myself—he had voiced the same surprise months earlier, when we had first met at Wakefield—I mentioned that my grandmother on my mother's side had known Bernard Berenson as a girl.

"Well, I'll be darned," he said.

I asked about the *Adam and Eve*—its provenance and history.

"There you've got me," he said, affably shaking his head. "Don't know much about that one—it was Joanna's. Found it in London, in a private collection, and the next thing I knew it was hanging here." He flashed his most genial smile and gestured to a marble statuette of a lion on the table to his right. "Not nearly as beautiful as this, though." He patted its rump and looked up. "Roman," he said, "Third century B.C." He took another sip of his whiskey, afterward smiling at me engagingly; at such moments Cassel was so appealing that the idea of a darker side seemed almost ludicrous.

The butler appeared with my glass of water, passing a tray of smoked salmon hors d'oeuvres the next moment. Cassel took two and devoured them, afterward crushing the napkin in his hand. I had a sudden vivid image of him riffling through the folder of memorabilia; greeting Joanna's mother at the top of the steps; his arm around Rosalind's waist—

The fire continued to crackle; the flames leapt.

"So—how's life treating you, Elisabeth?" Cassel asked, his eyes fixed on me, his walking stick upright.

"I'm not complaining," I replied as cavalierly as I could, before adding, "I've been working hard on the book, of course."

"Of course." He set down his glass. "And that—the book —is why we're here. Why I asked to see you."

I told him I assumed that was the reason.

He looked at me, set down his glass, and said definitively,

"I've decided there doesn't need to be a book, and that I was wrong to encourage you to write it."

He had taken me by surprise: In my imaginings, I had expected a long, carefully worded preamble. Not this; not so abruptly!

"I don't understand, Mr. Cassel."

"It's very simple. There is to be no book. I want you to drop it."

"But you authorized the book—you *asked* me to write it!"

"That's right. And I can just as soon bring it to an end."

"I have no intention of dropping the book."

"If it's money—"

"It *isn't* money!"

"If it's money, I'll pay you anything you'd get from your publisher. The rest of the advance."

"It has nothing to do with money. I want to tell the story —Joanna's story." I clutched my hands. "With or without your approval."

"So—" His eyes by this time had abandoned any trace of geniality. "We have come to an impasse. You say you'll go ahead without my authorization."

That was correct, I said.

"I see." He paused. "New York is a small town, Elisabeth. And you have a long and productive career before you."

I resisted the urge to ask precisely what he meant.

"And there are other people, other interesting women, to write about, women whose lives don't present the same—" he paused, searching for the proper word, "complexity of my late wife's."

"It is precisely that complexity which interests me, Mr. Cassel."

"Without my authorization I can't see how you could expect to write this book."

"Perhaps you underestimate my determination, Mr. Cassel. And my resourcefulness."

His face flushed with anger. "So you would persist without

regard to the family of your subject. Don't you consider that irresponsible? Ruthless?"

At this I could barely control my own rage. "I think it's selfish and unrealistic of you to expect me to abandon a book which you encouraged me to write. And I think it reprehensible of you to try to make me feel guilty for wanting to finish it."

"I said nothing about guilt."

"You said it was selfish—you called it ruthless." I remember the leaping flames, and the terse smile of the enameled Madonna and her wizened baby above the mantelpiece. Moments passed. I took a sip of water—my throat was tight and parched—and quietly asked: "Exactly what is it that disturbs you about the way I'm going about the book, Mr. Cassel?"

"Your dependence on gossip, for one thing."

"About the letter? Joanna's final letter to you—is that what you mean?"

"Partly," he replied, glowering at me. "But the letter is a nonissue. There *was* no letter."

I had noticed how he averted his gaze from mine as he uttered those crucial words. "If the letter, or a copy of that letter, does not exist," I asked, "why are you so angry?"

"Because it shows a certain cheapness on your part, a reflection of your way of thinking, that you would give credence to such asinine stories. I don't like the way you've hounded people about it. And I don't like the way you've interrogated the help," he went on. So Rosalind was right—he had heard about my conversation with Sam Neely. "Under the terms of our agreement," he continued, "you were to ask my permission before speaking to any member of the staff. You were not to *hound* them."

"The only person I've 'hounded' is Desmond Kerrith," I countered. "I *have* written him and called him, because I want to see whatever Joanna left at Thistleton."

"She left *nothing* at Thistleton."

"What she left at Thistleton is beyond your control," I said, my heart pounding. "I've seen the will."

"So have I, Miss Rowan," he said gravely, and with such genuine sadness that I was momentarily taken aback. "I don't like people prying into my private life—or Joanna's," he continued wearily. "She was very dear to me." He looked at me almost plaintively, as if expecting me to voice some treacly affirmation of his feelings, the absence of which only seemed to exasperate him even more. "The emphasis was to have been on her career—" his voice had reassumed its hard, drumlike cadence, "not on her private life!"

"The two are inseparable."

"It was to have been a *distinguished* book—not a book where the impression of my late wife's character was formed by the gossip of a handyman!"

"You didn't expect me to be thorough in my research, then—"

"I expected you to be *professional.*"

"By that you mean controllable—"

He jammed his stick on the floor, his face contorted in rage. "So you intend to find these imaginary letters and you intend to finish the book. And I will tell you what *I* intend, Elisabeth." His eyes were coldly fixed upon me. "I intend to make this book difficult, if not impossible, for you to pursue. As I told you, this is a small town—and you're just at the beginning of your career. Both in terms of your work and your private life, I put you on notice: that writing this book in the way I infer you intend to will not be a wise thing to do —not for your career, not for the framework of your life. I don't think I have to put this more clearly than I already have." His fist tightened around the handle of his walking stick. "Make your own choice. But be aware there will be consequences."

"I've already made it, Mr. Cassel," I said, nearly shaking as I stood up. "And now I think it's time for me to leave."

He struggled to stand up as well, his hand still tight around the silver handle. But rage seemed to prevent him from rising, and it was only when the butler came to help him that he finally succeeded, which seemed to infuriate him further.

"Get Miss Rowan her coat," he commanded. "And show her to the door."

I followed the butler through the gallery, the splendid paintings a succession of hostile golden faces, the staircase a twisting blur of black.

Darkness had fallen; it was snowing hard when I left his building.

33

December 11, 1986

Nearly a week has gone by since the meeting with David Cassel.

Those who had agreed to speak with me about Joanna Eakins no longer will; of those I've already interviewed, only Christina von S. and Lawrence Brandt (Larry, I call him now) continue to take my calls.

I can hardly remember feeling so utterly alone.

Met with my editor this morning. I told him about the confrontation with Cassel; then showed him the folder ("To my biographer") with the photographs of the English maze and the sonnet. I told him how the key words haunt me—"journey in my head"; "Those lines that I before have writ do lie/Hung with the trophies of my lovers gone." The idea that

Joanna would, in effect, lead me on a treasure hunt—the goal being Thistleton—from the grave. At this, John half jokingly suggested that the process of researching the book may be as intriguing as Joanna's story itself.

I also told him about the second visit to Wakefield: the ghostly progression of statues in the Shakespearean maze: were these—and the quotes—a message, as well, or merely Joanna's way of struggling against stage fright?

John has been unbelievably supportive and feels—as I do —that I *must* get to Thistleton, even if it means missing the deadline.

December 12th

Jack called me this morning—he'd just returned from Europe. Said he had something to discuss with me—sounded loving but mysterious. Please tell me, I said—I could use some Christmas cheer! Something in his voice made me think he'd met with the lawyer, had told Alice about us.

Asked me to meet him at the Four Seasons at 4:00. Thought this a strange choice at first, but then it cheered me (a public acknowledgment of our relationship?). Jack's a habitué of the restaurant, after all.

Brutal cold this afternoon: leaden sky, wolflike wind that propelled me to the entrance. Checked my frozen face in the powder room; walked upstairs (long, shallow steps) to the Grill Room—Jack in the prestigious corner booth (the one usually reserved for Philip Johnson).

A funereal hour for any restaurant, but especially for this one—pervasive beigeness devoid of milling power brokers. Tables being set by noiseless troops in androgynous uniforms; vacuum cleaner droning. A man at the bar, alone, hunched over his drink beneath the sculpture of bronze stalactites.

Jack stood up: the virile atmosphere of taupe and brown suits him. Thought he looked incredibly handsome—blond hair, beautiful gray jacket, keen smile. No kiss, of course—

not here, in this bastion of restraint! Squeezed my hand; ordered white wine for us both.

Asked me how I was—told him I was well (this with a moment's hesitation, which he didn't seem to notice).

I never sleep well without you, he said. The tremolo in his voice I find so arousing. Told me Alice has been insisting on going out every night. "All those damn charity things." Says he hates them.

But I wonder—I keep thinking of him at Christina's—how at ease he seemed within the will-to-power of the drawing room.

Went on to say he'd always rather be with me. Then leave Alice, I said, and leave that world behind. Nothing in reply; I looked down at the thick white napkin and tablecloth.

Darling, he said. Look at me.

I asked him if he'd seen the lawyer.

These things take time, he said.

I asked if he'd spoken with Alice.

Only shook his head. "You've got to trust me to decide when the time is right—I'm the only one who can make that determination."

Told him he'd said that before; my annoyance exacerbated by his wordy language. Find myself battling undercurrents of anger and—for the first time—contempt. I admire decisiveness and utter commitment; it frightened me that here I saw neither.

He changed the subject. Asked about my work—the book on Joanna. How the research was going.

Told him that it had been very difficult: many of the original sources now refused to speak with me. That Cassel resented my trying to find the crucial letter, which I thought to be at Thistleton. (Described the folder and the messages that seemed to be contained within the sonnet—the clues that led to Kerrith's house.) Told him—with a calmness I did not feel—about the meeting with Cassel. Only briefly mentioned discovery of sketch of nude in the study and that I thought it to be of Rosalind.

I finally admitted that Cassel refused to cooperate with the book.

"I've heard something to that effect," Jack said—this took me aback! His tone is grave, deliberate—it shocks me.

I asked how he'd heard.

"It's a small town. Things get around."

I asked if Cassel had spoken with him about it.

"Don't be ridiculous," he said.

Told him that Cassel knows about us—Jack and myself; Rosalind had told me.

She's a dangerous, bitter girl, he said. And why would I ever believe her?

Had no real answer to that question. Within the Four Seasons—rational light, total order—it *did* seem absurd to believe her.

Jack went on to say he was concerned about me, concerned about the book. "Whether it's the right thing for you to do, at this point of your career."

Told him—tensely—that we'd already had that discussion.

But did you *listen*, darling, he said.

Yes, I did *listen*. (Testily.)

"That's why I wanted to see you today," he said.

I looked at his startlingly blue eyes, Viking coloring, and thought how stupid, how naive, I'd been.

"*Listen* to me, sweetheart," he said. "Unlike you, I know how New York works. I only speak out of love for you. You have no idea how powerful David Cassel is—I should *never* have encouraged you to write this book!"

Couldn't face his eyes. "Don't say that," I said.

But he kept on: David Cassel will use his power against you, he'll discredit you. In publishing, at the *Journal*. Every door will be shut just at the moment in your career when your options should be expanding. There are other people to write about, Liza—

But I *won't* be intimidated! (This, fiercely.)

"But if the family of your subject objects to the book, *why* would you continue? It makes zero sense to me. (My hand in his, tightly.) Isn't it *ruthless* on your part—to persist?"

The word—*ruthless*—astonished me; the same word Cassel used. "I'm only being professional," I said. "I'm only fulfilling my commitment. That isn't *ruthless* at all!"

And what if he sues you for libel?

I'll get through it. (Swallowing hard as I say this.)

"It's for you I worry, sweetheart. For your career."

I gulped more wine; surely his fears were exaggerated. You're taking this much too seriously, I told him.

"You're dead wrong." The expression in his eyes—steely, implacable—frightens me.

Told him I'd suffer the consequences—it's *my* work, not his, after all. "And I'm not your wife!"

Noticed how this made him pause: "But I hope you *will* be my wife one day."

"When that day comes, then we'll see." Another gulp of the soothing Montrachet.

At this he begs me not to do anything "self-destructive": "If I didn't love you, why would I be so concerned?" Caressed my thigh beneath the table; I fight my weakness—I love him to touch me and he knows it.

Darkness by then. People thronging the bar. Jack called for the check—we left the restaurant.

Outside: his car, engine purring. The wind blowing my hair as I button my coat—the fur coat Jack gave me.

I've missed you so much, he says.

He looked so appealing, the neediness in his eyes that always makes me remember the first day we had lunch. I love him; I'm lonely; and it's Christmastime—

I need to think, I said, trying to be strong.

I'll give you a ride—

I need to be alone—

I love you, he said as he shut the car door.

I hailed a taxi home.

34

Sleepless nights followed—no drink could subdue me, no pill lull me to sleep; nothing seemed capable of sealing the Pandora's box that Jack's words had unleashed.

I had come to the sudden, and to me shocking, realization that all the men I had loved I had also feared, and that in my heart the two feelings were fatally equated. Why? I wondered. What was this primal sense of abandonment that held me tight, and breathless? I had loved different men—had loved them passionately, had wooed them and reveled in their caresses—but I had never done this, I knew now, without a grain of apprehension.

Few would ever guess this: It was my own secret, well guarded and impure.

In my mind's eye I incessantly reenacted two conversations—with Cassel in his library, with Jack at the Four Seasons.

Cassel's words, initially so troubling, had left me merely angry. Indeed, the fact that he was so infuriated only seemed to confirm my instincts: There remained something at Thistleton to uncover—Joanna's last letter, most likely.

Jack's warnings, veiled as protective counsel, were more insidious, however, for they had sparked a vortex of self-doubt and guilt that seemed to strangle indignation. The monster-creature of rage—that part of me which would not be silenced—warred with another part which not only doubted its validity, but its right to be angry.

For hadn't my father, too, begged me to abandon the book?

And so the chill feeling in my heart persisted as I continued to dwell on that afternoon at the Four Seasons, with its bitter wind and disturbing pauses, wondering all the time what Jack was really trying to tell me. I had become an archaeologist of sorts, a scavenger of desire, examining and reexamining the shards of a love affair three years old.

A week had passed. A moat of hurt, deepened by Jack's disapproval of the book, stretched between us. When, two days afterward, Jack had called, his voice was gentle, conciliatory, even tremulous. Still, it was not completely possible for him to mask what he really thought. At one point he told me, with a sense of wonder and chagrin (and yet not without tenderness), that I was "obsessed" with the book on Joanna. He said this in such a way that I knew it not to be a compliment—as if obsessiveness, in a woman, had about it a frigid aura of unpleasantness.

Occasionally—at a restaurant or on the street—I would see Larry Brandt. He would listen to me unwaveringly, his hands in his pockets, his hooded dark eyes fixed on me. In the past, I had avoided meeting him; now I caught myself seeking him out. His presence was welcome in a way I could only vaguely understand (indeed, a strange self-consciousness comes over me as I try). It was partly gratitude, I suppose—for his encouragement, his subtle way of directing my mind from the secular world of New York with which I was all too embroiled and which I increasingly felt had almost, but not quite, succeeded in corrupting my sensibility. He would mention a book I should read, an exhibit at the Metropolitan I should see, a film I might like—and all would be exactly right, all would nourish some chord of my inner self which, until that moment, had lain dormant.

If I spoke with him on the telephone, I would put down the receiver feeling content, satiated—not, as I did so often after speaking with others, still ravenous for real communication. With him I had come to feel, as I did with no one else, almost bewilderingly uncensored—I could tell him anything, and wondered at the feeling. The timbre of his voice, the rhythm and inflection of his sentences, the questions he would ask—all of this I drank in.

Yet even at such moments I would feel myself drawing back. I knew Larry was ambitious, and I also knew he would be well served by being shown in a flattering light in the book. And I could not entirely dismiss the derogatory remarks Christina and Rosalind had made about him—a feeling corroborated when I mentioned his name to Russell Heywood one day, only to hear how difficult Larry had been throughout his separation: how unyielding, even "cruel" with his ex-wife (whom Russell knew quite well, it turned out). "He was devastated when she left him," Russell added. "He's still very much in love with her, I hear." At this I was seized with a strange terror, all the while trying to reconcile my own impressions with the judgments of others.

I continued to work on the book, fighting hard against discouragement. And yet discouragement was a companionable enough demon compared to others that began to assail me—self-loathing, guilt, self-doubt. A depression, blacker than any I had ever known, threatened to engulf me. Mazes and tongueless statues stalked my dreams; sleep would seize me at odd moments; and often I would sit at my desk, struggling to concentrate on something which had once excited me, but which now only sparked listlessness.

Every loss haunted me. Everything about my physical self —my body, my hair—seemed hateful.

I lost pleasure in things I had previously enjoyed. The migraines increased; I began to smoke.

In the third week of December, Christina von Shouse invited me to tea. Like conscientious actors, we both played our parts: Christina seemed to listen sympathetically, while I seemed to appreciate her sympathy. All the while she studied me, assessing my reactions and how far I would go in challenging David Cassel. By this time I knew Madame von Shouse to be what the French call a *micmaceuse*—a mischief-maker—but on a grand scale. Her enjoyment of intrigue was both dangerous and pathetic, the paltry substitute for the satisfaction her able mind had never found. I had simply become a new amusement for her.

We sat, as we customarily did, in the drawing room, I on the sofa before the sphinx table, she in her favorite tufted armchair. My head had begun to ache that afternoon, my forehead to throb with fearful intensity. She seemed concerned and asked whether I would like a painkiller or a glass of red wine. To my astonishment, she added—by way of commiseration, I suppose—that she, too, suffered from migraine headaches, and proceeded to produce from her handbag (the lizard handbag which she was never without) a vial of red pills. Would I like to try one? she asked me. No, I said, though I was sorely tempted. A glass of red wine, then? I refused this as well, explaining that a mere sip of wine would augment the pain to a point almost past endurance. "Yes of course," she said, ringing for the maid to bring some tea.

She listened intently as I described the meeting with Cassel at his apartment. I told her that only she seemed to know about the copy of the final letter, adding that Cassel's fury when I had mentioned it, coupled with the stipulations of the will and Rosalind's hostile attitude, had led me to believe that she, Christina, was right: The crucial letter, or letters, lay at Thistleton. As of yet, I also told her, no response had come from Desmond Kerrith.

"You must let me help you, then," she said at once, setting down her cup of tea. "I shall call him for you. Tomorrow, if you like."

This time I did not discourage her from doing so; I had come to a point where even her intervention was welcome (whereas in the past I had been loath even to consider asking her a favor). I simply thanked her.

"But this is no guarantee, you must understand, that Desmond will see you," she replied with a gracious smile. "But we can always try. *Espérons.*" A flash of her red nails as she smoothed a black curl about her ear. "Even if you find nothing there, you must at least see Thistleton, if only to fully understand Joanna's life! What she was *about.*" She described Thistleton's maze and the fascination it held for her dead friend, all the while speaking in a rapid, staccato voice that I had never heard before, occasionally intersplicing her speech with a half-murmured "yes."

"And you must see the tower-library, as well—yes," she said, standing up and pacing before the fireplace, her eyes having taken on an unnerving animation. "It is part of the maze, to the east—yes—but perhaps you know that already. It seems like yesterday we were there together, Joanna and I. That beautiful creature in the tower, kneeling by the trunk of props and costumes—crowns, doublets, embroidered gowns, silk, velvet, ropes of gold—yes—" Her restive hands touched her throat, the mantel, the lapel of her suit as she continued: "I played so many parts with her there—Celia to her Rosalind, Gertrude to her Ophelia, Emilia to her Desdemona. All those words, his splendid words, we would recite them for hours together. . . ." Her voice trailed off; her hands dropped to her sides; the feverish look in her eyes vanished, replaced by a strange, introspective stare.

I asked her to describe the difference between the two mazes—Thistleton's and Wakefield's—as I continued to observe her abrupt shifts of demeanor.

"The maze at Thistleton is infinitely more difficult, more complex. A romantic swirling design, created, they say, by Capability Brown. It is treacherous—now that it is overgrown, even more so!" Then, with somber intensity: "It's a tragedy, really, that Desmond has not kept it up."

I told her half jokingly that if Thistleton's were more difficult than Wakefield's, it must be terrifying indeed. I went on to confess that I had found being in the maze frightening, and even tried to articulate the menacing terror I had experienced while first standing by its gate—the shortening of breath, the feeling of the hedges closing in on me.

"I wonder what Freud would have made of fear of mazes." Christina said with a distracted smile. "That's a phobia I've never heard of. There must be a term for it in German." She sipped her tea. "They have such a gift for labeling different species of anxiety, the Germans."

But her thoughts never seemed to venture far from Thistleton; again I fleetingly glimpsed that dazed look. She murmured almost *sotto voce*, "You must find a way to go there." She leaned forward, her left hand touching her black pearls as she took a final sip of her tea, leaving a broad stain of red lipstick around the rim of the cup. "Unless, of course, you decide not to finish the book—something I would understand, by the way. *Totally.* David can be ruthless, you know!"

I responded in the way she knew I would: I said I had no intention of abandoning the book and that I would be more than grateful for her help.

We parted, as we had in August, at six o'clock. "Until

soon," she said once more, poised by the elevator. She waved; I caught the glimmer of her carnelian ring. It was impossible, from her expression, to know what she was thinking.

35

That week, I received a response to the author's query I had placed in the *Tribune*.

The letter, addressed in a formal, old-fashioned handwriting, was postmarked from France; engraved at the top of the nearly translucent ecru paper was an address on the rue de Varenne, followed by a symbol of a telephone with a number.

4 December 1986
Dear Miss Rowan:

I came upon your "author's query" in the *Herald Tribune* last month. As I am ill-acquainted with the process of contributing to the research of a biography, I hesitated at first to write. It is only after much thought and deliberation that I do so.

I met Joanna Eakins, the actress, many years ago through a mutual friend, Desmond Kerrith, and became a good friend when she was on tour in Paris. As the years passed, we saw one another much too rarely, yet I like to think she held the same esteem for me as I did her. I visited her the summer of her death, at her house in the countryside. It would, perhaps, interest you to hear what I remember of Joanna at that time.

I have no idea whether your plans, and your research, include a sojourn in Paris. If this is the case, do let me know, in the event it is convenient for us to meet.

Respectfully yours,
Liliane de Morbier

I immediately replied, saying I would to come to Paris after Christmas, in the new year; I would call her to set a date. After sealing the envelope, I put on my coat, intending to go downstairs and mail the letter at once. As I waited for the elevator, something—a strange presentiment—made me pause.

I immediately returned to my apartment and, still in my coat, picked up the telephone: I would ask Christina von Shouse whether she knew of Liliane de Morbier. "No," she answered, when I reached her. "Never. It couldn't have been someone important in Joanna's life—otherwise, I should have known about her."

I mailed the letter the next morning.

In those weeks before Christmas, I also heard from David Cassel's lawyers—partners of the old-line Wall Street law firm that had long represented him. The first emissary was tall, thin, and bloodless; I remember thinking of a tough *quattrocento* monk or of repressed Angelo in *Measure for Measure*. Mr. Tarlton tried to be gentle, but when he saw that gentleness would not make me yield, his expression changed and I was treated to the kind of tactics he was, no doubt, more accustomed to using.

He told me that Mr. Cassel, as executor of his late wife's estate, had the power to withhold from me not only the privilege of quoting from Joanna's letters but also the use of any memorabilia that had been entrusted to him (i.e., the folder to the biographer). I told him I was aware of those constraints, but that I hoped to find other documents that were, according to the provisions of the will, beyond Mr. Cassel's jurisdiction. (The letter from Liliane de Morbier had only strengthened my conviction about Desmond Kerrith and Thistleton.) I added that the interviews I had already taped were, of course, still available for me to use.

Mr. Tarlton made it clear that Mr. Cassel was no stranger to lawsuits and that he would not hesitate to use what legal power he could to protect his privacy; did I realize the implications to my life, and to my career? Yes, I said; even so, I had no intention of dropping the book.

The second lawyer, Mr. Norfolk—slight, balding, intense —was far more polished and personable; his message, however, was the same. Relinquish the book, he told me, and Mr. Cassel would make sure that I would "not suffer from having had the courage to make that difficult decision." (This, a feeble attempt to bolster my self-respect.) I asked him why he had used the word *courage*. He smiled indulgently, as if confronted with a recalcitrant child; I remember that his shiny pate seemed to compete with the gleam of the conference room's mahogany table. He had used the word *courage* because "it takes courage to admit one has made a mistake." I told him that was hardly the case; in fact, it was just the opposite. The more anxious Mr. Cassel seemed, the more convinced I was that my instincts were correct: I must see the story to its end.

At this, I felt a shift in Mr. Norfolk's tactics. He went on to say that Mr. Cassel had no wish for me to "endure financial losses," if that was the issue. I would be "reimbursed" for my advance; Mr. Cassel would make certain that I would be "more than well taken care of" for my time and effort. I told him I had no interest in such an offer and that I would finish the book, with or without Mr. Cassel's authorization.

Only to Larry Brandt did I confide my deepest fears, my anxieties, my bewilderment at the mosaic I had only partly succeeded in uncovering and whose cryptic picture, lacking the central motif, I was not yet able to decipher.

We met at the Westbury Hotel for a drink late on the afternoon of December 21—a snowy day with a violent, sluicing wind. I noticed at once that Larry looked rather drawn: It seemed that his divorce was in progress and that it had been a "hard, trying" month. I remember barely being able to confront his eyes as I listened, almost unable to acknowledge how much the end of his marriage to Isabelle had affected him. Instead, I inquired after Frederick, and Philip Brandt, and Larry's work (a housing project near Paris that was nearing completion and that had taken him to France several times that fall).

All the while I remember looking at Larry in the ebbing light, quietly astonished how differently I perceived him since that first day in East Hampton. Even my perception of his looks had changed. Watching him—my impressions partly tempered by my enthrallment with his voice—I thought his massive head, with its wide brows and hooded eyes, handsome.

He asked what progress I had made on the book. I told him that no one acquainted with Cassel would speak with me and that the work was almost at a standstill. My only hope was to go beyond Cassel's sphere—to reach Desmond Kerrith at Thistleton. I brought up the sonnet again, and the Shakespearean maze, and told him how these—together with the letters he had shown me—continued to obsess me.

Only obliquely did I refer to Jack and his discouraging attitude; in retrospect, I wonder *why* I never did. I suppose Larry and I seemed to have evolved an unspoken pact: He would never discuss his failed marriage, and I would never discuss my affair. It was as if these two subjects existed on another, inferior, plane, beneath the bounds of our friendship.

What I *did* tell Larry, as I continued to muse aloud, was that Joanna's life seemed to resist all attempts at coherence. I mentioned the letter I had received from the mysterious Liliane de Morbier and asked whether he recalled meeting a woman by that name.

He did remember an elderly French countess who had visited Wakefield that last summer, he said, a guest he'd met at lunch. He recalled little else about her, and this only because he remembered the name Morbier, an aristocratic name that had, in different guises, played a part in French history.

I said I planned to interview her in Paris; and I distinctly remember the moment (as well as my immediate dismissive reaction) when Larry surprised me and said, "Come in mid-January, when I'll be there." In reply I said something light-hearted, and returned to the book.

I confided having agreed to let Christina von Shouse call Desmond Kerrith on my behalf. "Was that really *necessary?*" he asked. "I think I know Desmond Kerrith well enough to predict that if he doesn't want to see you, no one's intervention will change his mind."

"He sounds like a tyrant."

"He's a complicated man," Larry said, sipping his whiskey. "Joanna was always fiercely protective of him."

"Yes," I replied rather gloomily. "I've been told that. They say he's quite senile now." I finished my wine; Larry called for the check. It was dark; shadowy figures hurried past the windows facing Madison Avenue.

We stood outside, buffeted by the wind, as we said goodbye.

I told Larry how much I had appreciated his help, how I would never forget his listening, and his encouragement.

"Thank you for that," he said, visibly touched.

Several days later, a Christmas present arrived from Larry:

a package of books. Wrapped in florentine paper and tied with gold ribbon, they were accompanied by a note in Larry's boldly vertical and hard-to-decipher handwriting:

December 22, 1986
Dear Elisabeth:

I've enclosed two books for you here, each for a particular reason. The *Henry V*, as you know, once belonged to Charles Kean, and was given to me by Joanna. You should have it now.

The second—*Mont-St.-Michel and Chartres*—is the Henry Adams book you saw at my house in East Hampton. Read it when the world is too much with you, if only to be reminded, in the chapter on Chartres, of "the power of the rose."

My wish for you at Christmas is this: that you find a way to finish the book. There's something at Thistleton you must need to know—read the last quote I've marked for you.

Larry.

I opened the book at once, intensely curious to see what Larry had marked—the moving opening paragraph first, with its thundering description of the archangel poised atop the parapet: "His place was where the danger is greatest; therefore you find him here." I can hardly express how profoundly I was moved by that opening chapter: as if, in that image of the archangel confronting "the tremor of the immense ocean"—*immensi tremor oceani*—I rediscovered everything I had ever loved, or wordlessly admired, and which, until that moment, had been threatened by the world where I found myself.

I came to the last marked page, smiling to myself as I read the passage from Thomas Aquinas that Larry associated with Thistleton: "There is nothing in the intellect that has not been first in the senses."

* * *

Christmas came—the first Christmas without my father. I took a walk in Central Park after lunching with friends, only to return to the quiet of my apartment, with its lonely light and ludicrous luxuries.

Jack was in Sun Valley, skiing with his family. Over the course of three years, I had become all too accustomed to the pain and divisiveness of holidays, to the surreptitious phone calls at odd hours accompanied by the clinking of coins.

He called me on Christmas night, anxious to hear that I had liked my present—an antique pearl bracelet with a glittering clasp of two intertwined *E*'s.

"Are you all right, sweetheart? I love you. I worry about you."

"Do you?" I asked.

"Yes—all the time." A pause. "I met with the lawyer again. This will all work out, darling."

"Will it?"

"But it will take time."

"Yes of course."

And so our conversation continued, littered with pauses and slightly elegiac in cast.

"I miss you, darling," he said moments later, in such an aching voice that I, too, felt moved to say I missed him; it had been an agonizingly solitary holiday.

"Let's go away somewhere together—to Paris," he said. "You told me once that things are always clearer to you in France."

"Did I," I murmured, dimly recalling having said something to that effect.

"Paris, in January," I heard him say again.

I hesitated only a moment, for nothing Jack could have proposed or offered to give me could have tempted me as much as the idea of France. I said yes, thinking of the interview with Liliane de Morbier, and remembering, as well, that Larry had said he would be there. Perhaps in the clear and formal light of France I would somehow find the answer: to the chaos of my life, to the unsolved mystery of the book.

36

What I remember so distinctly is that Paris appeared to me in a different, vaguely less romantic light that January. The dollar was very weak, and the Parisians accordingly triumphant—the shopkeepers on the avenue Montaigne, for instance, and the *antiquaires* on the quai Voltaire, where we strolled our first afternoon.

On Wednesday, I met Jack for lunch at a bistro, on the rue de Trémouille near our hotel.

He told me he'd just come from a meeting at the Bristol, where he'd run into Larry Brandt; Larry was staying there, it seemed. "I asked if he'd join us for dinner tonight." A glance as he unfolded his napkin. "Do you mind?"

"Of course not." I scanned the menu, fighting the realization that we had come to a point where it seemed safer to dine with friends than be alone. "Larry said something to me before Christmas about his being here. In Paris, I mean."

"You should have called him," Jack said.

"I forgot." I sipped my wine. "He's here on business?"

"Yes—some project outside of Paris. He went to Scotland last weekend. A shoot."

"Where shall we go tonight?"

"Taillevent," he replied, looking impatiently for the waiter. "At eight."

After lunch, Jack returned to his Paris office, and I to the research on my book. The beauty of Paris, the distance from David Cassel's New York, the encouragement from Larry, and the truce with Jack—all had contributed to rekindling the pleasure of the research.

The moment the Paris trip had been decided, I had called Liliane de Morbier, and distinctly remember the girlish, slightly high-pitched voice, with its heavily accented but flawless English, that greeted me from the other side of the Atlantic. We set a date to meet.

I remember the feeling of excitement as I left the Right Bank, with its flashy status shops, and walked across the pont de la Concorde to the Left Bank, where she lived; and from there, along the boulevard St.-Germain to the streets of the seventh arrondissement's older, more distinguished neighborhood. Turning right on the rue de Bellechasse, I continued to walk past embassies and private houses until I came to the rue de Varenne. There I turned left, walking a block until I arrived at the address of Liliane de Morbier, pausing to verify that I had come to the right place. In contrast to its neighbors, the building was rather shabby. A newspaper shop occupied part of its ground floor; the heavy, creaking black-green door badly needed paint.

I climbed to the third floor as instructed, and pressed the button on the wall to the right. A light illuminated the dingy staircase precisely long enough for me to reach the apartment. There I waited; rang the bell again. A maid appeared, saying that the countess awaited me in the *salon*. I followed her inside.

I recall the lucid, refined light of those rooms, the sloping parquet floors, the smell of wax, and the frugal flowers. But most of all I remember my first glimpse of Liliane de Morbier: a mothlike, whitehaired creature of a fine-boned prewar beauty—pale blue eyes and *retroussé* nose—who had arranged herself on the central settee and whose childlike feet, encased in thick stockings and black leather pumps, did not quite touch the floor. A child infanta out of Velázquez could not have appeared more innately aristocratic. Twisted around the neck of her antiquated ice-blue silk dress was an extraordinary necklace—a rope of baroque pearls and cabochon sapphires whose bold, even barbaric, style was in striking contrast to her fragility.

She excused herself from standing up as I approached, and extended a frail hand as I introduced myself. Her voice on the telephone had led me to believe that she was a much younger woman, whereas I now guessed her to be about seventy.

We sat together for a first few minutes exchanging pleasantries—the weather, my trip to Paris, my compliments on her beautiful English ("I owe that to my English nanny," she replied in her lilting voice, adding that she had spent a fair amount of time in England; her daughter lived in Gloucestershire.) She asked where I was staying and seemed barely able to conceal her disdain when I mentioned the Plaza Athénée ("It is full of Arabs, is it not?") She asked if I would like some tea. I said I would, very much. She rang for the maid.

I looked around the room—a *salon* of faded, forlorn elegance with tall graceful windows overlooking a severe interior courtyard. Furrowing her brow slightly, she said, "You came to discuss Joanna."

I asked her to explain how she had first met Joanna Eakins —what she remembered of her, and the details of her last visit to Wakefield Hall.

"*Voyons*," she replied with a small sigh. "This will be a test to my rather imperfect memory. But I shall try my best." Her hand touched her throat. "I first met Joanna in the early fifties through my dear friend Desmond Kerrith, an Englishman. You have heard his name in connection with Joanna, no doubt." She looked at me questioningly; I nodded. "They were lovers then, and later great friends—it does not always happen that way. That past lovers remain friends, that is. I had met her during a weekend at Thistleton, his house in Hampshire—a considerably more civilized place than most English houses, I might add! I was spending a great deal of time in London at the time, as my eldest daughter had recently married the son of the viscount Sisley.

"I came to know Joanna better in Paris, however, when she had come with the Old Vic for—how would you say in English?—a short run, at the Comédie-Française. She was in *Antigone*—Anouilh's *Antigone*—and called upon me, as Desmond had told me she might. It was strange—" she paused, "that she should have been gifted in that artistic, histrionic way and yet was also quite mathematical, almost masculine, in her turn of mind. I remember watching her backstage once as she waited in the wings. She would play chess with another member of the company—she was frightfully good at chess, as good as any man—or she would sit alone, working like the devil on a crossword puzzle. It always astonished me to see how she could turn from her actual self to her stage self with such ease. Yet with a strange violence! Onstage she became quite another creature, only partly human. She lived for applause, for an audience—it was to her the stuff of life.

"But I suppose, as I think back on Joanna, that it was another quality that was so memorable. There was—" she faltered, searching for the proper word. "There was about her an atmosphere of *culpabilité*, of guilt, although that is perhaps not quite the correct word." Her brow furrowed, and the fine lines around her pursed mouth became more pro-

nounced. "There was a feeling I always had about Joanna—
comme si elle n'était pas certaine de ses droits sur cette terre."

"As if she were not certain of her rights on this earth," I
repeated, writing down the phrase in my notebook.

"Yes, but it does not sound quite right in English!" She
looked up at the maid, who was setting down a tray before
us; I watched Liliane de Morbier's hands, with their prominent blue veins, as she poured the tea. I added several spoon-
fuls of sugar to mine, noticing, as I did so, that the rims of
the cups and saucers were chipped.

"At the beginning of Joanna's engagement here," she continued, "I saw her quite frequently. She had rented an apartment not far away, on the rue St.-Simon. We would have
lunch together or attend a museum exhibition in the afternoon. This was at the height of her liaison with Desmond—I
remember thinking how radiant she seemed, how serene, as
if that inner torment from which she had always suffered had
relaxed its hold upon her. She seemed, as she never had
before, *à l'aise dans sa peau.*" Her head tilted to one side ever
so slightly. "At ease with herself, would you say—

"It was perhaps due to several things, this change—the joy
in her work, together with the influence of Desmond. A
coming together of the strands of her life. Her eagerness to
learn undoubtedly contributed to her charm for Desmond.
He had a tendency to be bored with women who were to the
manner born. He liked women with—how would you say?—
with a clean slate. But then most men do." She gave an
almost imperceptible smile. "In Joanna he had also her talent, which was stupendous, and her extreme intelligence—a
perfect Galatea to his Pygmalion." She paused to add some
milk to her tea. "And she was of course so wonderful-*looking.*"

I asked whether she had ever met a woman called Christina—now Christina von Shouse—at Thistleton.

"One of Desmond's friends, one of his houseguests?" She
seemed perplexed. "No, I do not recall anyone of that name.
Although I *do* recall a woman called Christina Assante who

was Desmond's secretary. But she was not a *friend*. She was part of the staff—his social secretary, I believe." Her tone of voice registered the full measure of that crucial difference. "That is the only Christina I recall—she was Egyptian, was she not? I remember her as rather thin, severe. Quite well organized."

I mentioned that Christina had become quite well known in New York as a hostess and social arbiter.

"Ah, well—in New York!" came the dismissive reply. "That is altogether possible in *New York*."

I told her that Christina had maintained her relationship with Desmond Kerrith over the years, and added that I had asked her to call him on my behalf.

"I would find it very strange indeed if Desmond's opinion could be swayed by a former secretary. In his own way, he was such a fearful snob—as only the English can be—and so very obstinate besides. He will let you come when he thinks fit, that is my guess."

I asked whether she would consider calling Desmond Kerrith on my behalf. "I will consider it," she said, after a moment. "But I will also tell you that I think it will do no earthly good. There must be a reason why Desmond has chosen to remain silent. He is an extremely *deliberate* person." Her expression changed, hinting of a past relationship I had not, until that moment, discerned—one more intimate than the friendship she had initially described. "I know him all too well, you see," she said with painstaking care. "It was a rather—shall we say—complicated moment in my life. Before the war, before Joanna. My husband—" she paused abruptly, setting down her teacup. "It is all rather in the past." She cast her eyes down.

I found this veiled admission—that she too had been Desmond Kerrith's lover—at once touching and totally believable; I suddenly realized she was probably the French mistress whom Patrick Rossiter had alluded to months before.

I asked if she had seen Joanna after the tour in Paris. "Not as much as I would have liked," she said, with what seemed to be genuine regret. "It was only years later that we met again, in the sixties. We would go together to the *maisons de couture*. Joanna was a client of Balmain at the time, and I of Chanel. Chanel was a friend, a dear friend, whom I later introduced to Joanna. Coco was quite taken with her—she liked intelligent and creative women and was amused by Joanna's gift for mimicry. Joanna had a marvelous way of imitating members of the royal family, as well as certain members of the Westminster clan. The last, as you can imagine, Coco thought marvelously funny!"

"And after that?"

"Years went by, and it was only much later, after she had married David Cassel, that we saw one another."

"What was your impression of Cassel?"

"There is an expression in English—a rough diamond, would you say?"

I smiled. "Yes. That is the correct expression."

"I thought him to be the sort of man she needed, if at times rather obvious. And yet when I visited them at their house in the countryside years later, I was shocked to see the changes which had taken place. Joanna seemed completely devoured by nervousness. At first I thought it had to do with the end of her acting. The stage fright had made it impossible." She paused, her narrow hand grazing her necklace. "There was something quite *malsain* about the whole *ambiance*. Joanna seemed unable to eat, and had devised diets of a strictness and oddity that astounded me. We would sit down to a delicious lunch, and Joanna would be served only a special broth or a peculiar salad. For the first day or so I said nothing about this, thinking that it was merely her way of staying thin—she was not *naturally* thin, as some people are.

"One afternoon, while we were walking through the maze, as we did quite often, I asked *why* she was inflicting this near-starvation diet on herself which, together with alcohol and dieting pills, had already taken a toll on her health. She told me—and this I shall never forget—that she didn't '*deserve*' to eat. I asked what could have possibly brought this idea into her head. I asked about her marriage. I remember looking at her hands—the rings were almost slipping off her emaciated fingers. 'If only it *were* my marriage!' she said with a desperate look. 'If only it were—'

"It was during our strolls that I also began to notice the alarming way she talked about the house, as if she were already dead and buried. 'Strange that Wakefield should have been my wedding present,' she told me. 'And now all of it will go to my stepdaughter, Rosalind. After my death. And David's.'

"On the last day of my visit—a very hot July day—we sat down on a bench before the innermost statue, one of the Shakespearean ladies Joanna had chosen with such care. I remember I took her hand in mine and begged her to tell me *what* the problem was—had her husband been cruel to her? Or was it the stage fright that destroyed her sense of self? At this her eyes almost closed, as if she were in a trance, finally she told me—"

Liliane de Morbier covered her face with her hands; when she looked up it was with the eyes of an old, weary woman: "She had had a child long ago. And she had abandoned that child shortly after its birth. 'There has not been a single day, or an hour since, when I have not thought of that child,' she told me."

I put down my pen; I could hardly breathe; I thought of Patrick Rossiter's description of that episode in Joanna's life —the child had died stillborn, he had told me: Was this the same child or another child? "And the father of the child?" I asked, leaning forward. "Who was it—Desmond Kerrith? And is the child alive?"

"She would not tell me the father's identity—nor would she tell me whether the child had survived. 'My child,' she repeated again and again."

Liliane de Morbier's eyes welled with tears. "Just two months later—the afternoon of the twelfth of September— the telephone rang, and I was told that Joanna was dead. To this day I cannot quite believe it."

She seemed exhausted suddenly, her face drained of color. "Now you see why I finally wrote you," she explained, her hands reaching toward me. "I felt you should know this—strangely, I even felt that Joanna would have *wanted* her biographer to know this."

I told her how much I appreciated her candor, waited a moment to compose my thoughts, then asked, "Did Joanna mention a folder she was compiling for her biographer? Did she ever mention a sonnet she had created to include with it?"

She shook her head. "No, I cannot remember anything of that nature—certainly no talk of a biography. What I do remember—" she paused, "is Joanna being quite absorbed in letter writing. At least that was my assumption. She would disappear into her study in the morning and close the door. I remember seeing her there one day shuffling a mass of cards —index cards—on her desk, grouping each pile together with a rubber band. When I asked what she was doing, she said, 'Trying to make some order of my life, Liliane—so I'm not a nuisance to those who come later.'"

"To those who come later," I murmured to myself.

"That was exactly how she put it."

I was on the verge of asking another question when she said, "This has depleted me, I'm afraid—the sadness of my old friend!" She sat up very straight and said, with unexpected imperiousness, "Perhaps you have enough."

I sensed it was futile to stay any longer, and began to gather my things. Shaking her hand, I thanked her for having contacted me, reiterating that I would be so grateful if she would call Desmond Kerrith on my behalf.

"I will do what I can," she replied. "But you must understand—I saw him six months ago at Thistleton and was dismayed to see how much he had changed. And there is one thing you should know, as well—" She paused in a way that made me apprehensive, and added, in a quavering voice, "You see, Desmond simply has no idea that Joanna is dead."

37

Later that afternoon, after we returned to the Plaza Athénée, Jack and I began to quarrel.

He had spoken with his office from the other room of our suite and then, at length, with his family. The attentive words to Alice, the loving questions to his daughters—all of this I nervously, resentfully overheard. Afterward, he came into the bedroom, planting an absentminded kiss on my forehead and caressing my shoulders—gestures that only succeeded in irritating me and sparking a vague desire to punish him.

"Are you all right, darling?" he asked, setting down his martini and taking up the newspaper.

"Yes of course."

I got up to telephone my editor in New York, ostensibly to tell him about the interview with Liliane de Morbier and her astonishing revelation. All the while I felt Jack listening, his face half hidden by the *Herald Tribune*, its pages crackling as I resumed my place before the dressing table. I lit a cigarette, the smell of smoke mingling with that of the narcissus plants by our bed—a noxious scent that brought to mind the confrontation with David Cassel in December.

I thought of dinner with Larry that night and began to apply my makeup. Anxiety had increased my need for artifice.

Jack had put down his newspaper and was swilling his martini. "So you still refuse to listen to me. You persist in continuing that damn book. Even after I've told you the consequences it might have—for your life in New York, for your ambitions—"

"For *your* ambitions, you mean," I retorted, my nerves aflame. "And I have *listened* to you."

"Not well enough, obviously!"

I rubbed some rouge into my cheeks and proceeded to line my eyes with a dark and sooty pencil.

"Did you hear anything more from David Cassel's lawyers?" he asked, still watching me.

"Only indirectly." I turned to face him, my makeup half completed. "What does that matter?"

"That isn't the point."

"What *is*, then?"

"Really, Liza—"

"Have you spoken with Alice? You haven't, have you?"

"Not yet. I haven't made that determination."

I remember how his verbose language irked me, as if it epitomized everything that was wrong about him. "And when will *that* time come?"

"Soon enough." He threw down the newspaper. "Why do we keep going over this again and again?"

"Because I have to know it's *real*."

"I've told you a hundred times it's real."

"Time is passing."

Edgy silence intervened.

I finished my makeup; he resumed reading. An hour later we left the hotel and wordlessly made our way to the restaurant.

By the time we arrived at Taillevent, the tension between us had abated slightly. I had deliberately chosen to wear a dress Jack did not like and jewelry that was, even for such a cosseted setting, far too conspicuous.

We were shown to a prime table and sat down in silence.

Jack ordered wine—an excellent Pomerol, which the *sommelier* proceeded to open and the two of us to drink in silence. I remember the welcome warm feeling of the wine coursing through me and that I had already succumbed to it by the time Larry Brandt arrived.

Relief overwhelmed me when I saw him. It seemed that he had never looked so appealing, and that the slight ungainliness in his face now appeared almost Lincolnesque, with all the reassuring comfort of a familiar flaw; a flaw which, rooted in life experience, seemed to offset the blond handsomeness of Jack.

We shook hands. Larry sat down, forsaking the wine, at least momentarily, for a glass of whiskey.

Looking around the restaurant, with its tapestries and thick-napped bourgeois splendor, Larry remarked, "It's been years since I've been here." I asked his favorite restaurants in Paris. Larry mentioned several bistros on the Left Bank with which we were unfamiliar—and which, according to him, were excellent.

The headwaiter approached us and proposed what we might eat; we placed our orders with the respect that such a restaurant exacts. I asked, in French, whether it was possible to order a pear soufflé, a specialty of the restaurant—I remembered it was delicious.

We spoke of many things that night, but mostly of the projects that had brought Larry to Europe: the housing complex outside Orléans and the opera house near Hamburg.

These were palpable accomplishments, and I listened with fascination as Larry described their conception and execution.

Jack seemed at once more subdued and yet, at moments, more combative. I remember the unsettling awareness that Larry and I had, over the months, evolved our own code to which, throughout the dinner, I continually felt the need to initiate Jack.

We had nearly finished dinner; Jack, who had received a call from his office, excused himself from the table. I lit a cigarette.

"You shouldn't smoke," Larry said. "It doesn't suit you."

I shrugged, avoiding his disapproving gaze. "I'm sure I shouldn't do a lot of things I do."

"You're wearing too much jewelry. You don't need it." I looked down at the table. "It cheapens you."

"Jack likes it."

"That doesn't mean it suits you," he told me almost harshly.

Jack returned to the table. "Let's get another bottle of wine," he said.

The wine appeared.

We had finished half the bottle when the conversation veered to the relationships between men and women, and from there to the subject of sex. When, I asked playfully, did the two men first go to bed with a woman, and how did they remember it?

We drew lots to choose who would go first. Jack, as it turned out, won:

He'd been going out with a steady girlfriend, in his last year of high school—the daughter of the principal. He had just returned with her from a football game; he was the quarterback. His team had won the game, and by the end of the afternoon he had won her over, as it were, in the backseat of a car he had taken great pains to borrow for the evening.

Next, Larry:

He was in his second year of boarding school and managed

to smuggle his date to his room after a dance (having arranged for his roommate to be away that night). They went to bed together, the beginning of a romance that lasted several years.

I asked him how he remembered that first time. "I was besotted," he replied without hesitation.

It came my turn to speak. Fortified with another glass of wine, I began to tell what I had never told anyone before:

I was twenty, in college; I had never had a lover. Before this time, absorbed in my studies and half in love with several of my professors, I hadn't much been bothered by my lack of experience. But on my twentieth birthday, something changed. I was seized by an intense restlessness, by curiosity, and by shame: that I was still a virgin. (This was the seventies, after all!)

One evening, while struggling to concentrate on a paper I was writing ("the handkerchief motif" in *Othello* being its theme), I suddenly put down my pen. Even if I was not in love, there must be some way to end my stultifying sexual innocence. How to do it was the only question.

I had an old friend at college who was in some ways like a brother. We were the same age; my father was his father's oldest friend. I called him, saying we had to meet as soon as possible. He seemed mystified, but agreed to meet me that night for coffee.

I made my confession: I was still a virgin (which seemed to surprise him) and simply wanted to be put out of my misery. And I was asking him to do it.

He seemed at once amazed and amused by my request. Even so, my instincts had been correct—he very gallantly said yes.

The day of the tryst arrived: a Saturday in mid-January. I remember crossing the quiet courtyard to his dormitory, my boots slipping on the slushy brick paths. The air was icy, the sky an uncommitted color. Everyone else was studying for exams.

We spent the afternoon together; later that evening, after

dinner at an Italian restaurant, he walked me back to my room. I remember feeling stunned, relieved, pleasantly satiated, and sleepy.

I know now that my way had its merits: I'd chosen a friend who was patient and tender, and who never pressed me to sleep with him again. We never did, in fact, so that the memory of that Saturday survived whole and golden.

Here I stopped, so pleasantly absorbed in the memory that I had for a split-second almost forgotten the presence of the two men.

I took another sip of wine and looked at Jack and Larry.

Larry's face had reflected a succession of emotions. He had smiled at the part where I had described writing the paper on *Othello* and the sudden decision to end my virginity. I had also noticed his expression while I described the afternoon in bed—as if he had been trying to imagine me, and the man, and what this had meant within the context of my life.

As for Jack: I had convinced myself that he would find the story funny, that he would tease me, but instead I sensed something quite alarmingly different—the way he gripped his wineglass, a certain tension in his eyes. No doubt I had partly wanted to annoy him—and yet, having achieved precisely that reaction, I felt both triumph and panic.

An uncomfortable silence descended on the table. Jack took my hand, squeezing it hard. "That was some story," he said.

"Come on, Jack," I said, pulling my hand away. "You didn't like it at all. I shouldn't have told it."

"Not at all," he protested, drinking more wine.

"You can't imagine those things going on," I continued belligerently. "Between college kids, I mean. What do you think Amanda's doing?" He flinched at the mention of his eldest daughter. "What do you think's happening at all those parties she goes to?"

"Certainly not what you described."

"Dream on," I told him, my voice rising. "What do you

think the boys are thinking of? And the girls? Or don't you permit them those thoughts? Is it just too sordid, Jack?"

My anger, which until now I had been able to contain, threatened to unleash itself. I caught myself addressing him in a hard, foreign voice even as I felt him growing more remote.

I was too stubborn to retreat verbally, and eventually took his hand instead. Larry changed the subject. I asked him more about his work, and Larry answered in kind, even as he continued to observe us.

The pear soufflé arrived. We ordered coffee.

I sipped the foamy top of my cappuccino, my fingers touching the petals of a rose in the vase on our table. "The power of the rose," I said, looking up at Larry. "The book on Chartres that you gave me—" Then, to Jack: "Larry gave me a book for Christmas. On Chartres and Mont-St.-Michel." I continued to describe the book, at one point hazily quoting Henry Adams on the rationale of the great cathedrals: "Everything subjugated to the desire for light."

"Exactly," said Larry, surprised that I had remembered the phrase: "What someone else called 'vertical ecstasy.'"

"Vertical ecstasy," I murmured, once more fingering the rose's velvety petal. Then, to Jack: "We should go to Chartres this weekend."

"I've never done it," he replied. "Chartres, I mean."

"And if we go," I continued, trying not to notice the way he had put it ("I've never *done* it"), "where should we spend the night? At Chartres, or someplace else?"

Larry said we could drive east, toward Le Mans, and stay at a small town called Solesmes. There was a famous abbey there, he explained, where Benedictine monks still sang the mass. It was very moving, he said; besides, the hotel had an extremely good restaurant.

I asked Jack.

"If that's what you'd like, sweetheart."

Yes, I said.

Larry asked our plans for the next day, and suggested that he take us to the musée d'Orsay.

I said we hadn't been there, but that I'd heard a great deal about the transformation of the *belle époque* railway station into a museum of Impressionist paintings. "Let's go tomorrow, Jack," I said. "With Larry."

"There's no way I can go. I've got a full day. *You* go."

"For just an hour," I pleaded.

"*You* go, Liza," he said in the same insistent voice, motioning for the check. The two men exchanged glances.

"I guess you're stuck with me," I said, looking at Larry.

"I guess so." He smiled slightly.

It was decided that we meet at two o'clock the next day, at the entrance of the musée d'Orsay.

38

On returning to the hotel, I immediately undressed, wanting only to sleep; Jack remained unnaturally quiet as he lay down beside me. I was surprised to feel his arms pulling me to him. Part of me would have succumbed, if only to avoid reproach; the other part resisted. Nothing knifed him more than my unresponsiveness.

He never acknowledged me as he shaved and got dressed the next morning; he never opened his newspaper, which I remember thinking odd. After breakfast he approached the table, bending over to kiss me, his hand twisting my hair into a knot. I turned around to face him, feeling a sudden upsurge of love—strangely touched, even aroused, by the unexpected gesture and its tenderness. I had by then transcended the need to wound him.

"We can't go on like this," he said.

"I know," I managed to reply. "I know."

"I know you're angry, and I understand why you're angry," he continued in the same gentle voice. "But it's poisoning us —don't you see?" I felt his hand beneath my chin, forcing my eyes to face him: "It's poisoning us and our feelings for one another. And I realize it's mostly my fault. You were right —time is passing." He kissed me again, pressing me hard against him, so that I felt his hand at the small of my back, and the edge of his cuff as it grazed my skin. "Darling," he said. "I hardly slept last night thinking about all of this. About us. I've come to a decision. I want to get this all behind us as soon as possible. I've made up my mind." He paused, his eyes scanning my face as he smoothed my hair: "I'm going to talk with Alice and the girls as soon as I return to New York."

Never had he spoken so definitively. I felt compelled to be thrilled, yet thrill was not what I was feeling. "I don't know what to say, Jack."

"Just say you'll marry me." I remember how his blithe, expectant smile touched me, how his clear eyes, with their white-blond lashes, turned on me full force. "Will you marry me, Liza?"

Our eyes met, drawn together by the formidable echo of those words. "Liza," he said, touching my cheek. "You know now how much I love you."

I said yes I did, and that I loved him too.

"But you haven't given me an answer." He enfolded me in his arms. I drew away. Gathering my kimono about me, I walked to the window. "And my book on Joanna," I asked after a moment, turning to face him. "What about the book?"

"That's up to you." A shadow of disgruntlement crossed his face. "But if you really want to marry me—well, you know how I feel about it. I'll be giving up a lot—risking my relationship with my daughters, exposing my family to major gossip and publicity. And I don't think it's unfair to ask you to give up something as well. If you love me as much as I love you, then . . ."

His eyes suggested what I had already divined. "The book," I murmured.

"You said yourself that it's reached an impasse anyway."

"An impasse is not the same as giving up."

"Why would you continue something that could be harmful to you—and maybe even harmful to me—if you really loved me?" He stood beside me now and took my hands in his. "Liza darling, don't you see? If we're committed to each other's future and well-being—well, sometimes you have to make sacrifices. If this book were a matter of life and death, I could understand. But this is something you've *chosen* to do, and which—you've admitted yourself—hasn't gone the way you would have liked. There's no dishonor in deciding not to finish it." He paused. "And you certainly don't need to do it for money."

"It isn't the money."

"What is it, then?" he demanded impatiently.

I faltered, rendered nearly inarticulate by his seeming logic and his scrutiny. "I know it may be hard for you, and for other people—" But then I stopped, pressing my hands to my temples, struggling with the disparity between my romantic imaginings and the reality of this proposal: the idea of a condition being set, of a deal with stipulations. I thought how much I loved him, how his love had changed my life. I thought of being alone again after four years. It was that possibility—being alone again—that finally silenced all other doubts.

Jack's voice was edged with irritation: "Give me your answer, darling," he urged me, adding, in the fervent way that made me recall the glorious first year of our love affair, "You know my life is empty without you."

"You've taken me by surprise, Jack."

"There will be other books," he said with a tender kiss,

"We'll be able to have a life together. No more hiding. A real home and children—"

"I've got to think."

His eyes had changed expression; his voice had lost its earlier buoyancy. I felt, as I almost never had before, my capacity to hurt him. "That's not the answer I would have liked," he said reproachfully.

"I know it isn't," I said, pressing his hand to my cheek. "I'm sorry."

"When *will* you have an answer, then?"

"Sunday," I said, taking his hand. "I'll tell you on Sunday."

He turned to face the mirror, knotting his tie: "If that makes you feel better," he said.

Jack left; I was left alone to dress.

Never had I dreamt that the fulfillment of my desires would be so unsettling. Never had I felt so at sea, so desperate to confide in someone I trusted.

I walked like a somnabulist along the avenue Montaigne later that morning, and then along the Champs-Elysées, stopping at a café for coffee and a cigarette. I sat there awhile, thinking of the marriage proposal, then of the book and its unsolved mysteries—the sonnet, the maze, the idea of an abandoned child . . .

At two o'clock—my head aching, the marriage proposal half suppressed—I hailed a taxi to the Left Bank, wishing I had never agreed to meet Larry at the musée d'Orsay.

He waited by the entrance. He sensed my mood and my chagrin, I think, and met them with a certain gentleness.

We entered the museum, with its glorious ceiling and resounding light, the marble arms of its satyrs, goddesses, and nymphs beckoning from the vaulted central gallery. I remember being affected by the breadth of the space and the whiteness of the light—dazzled by my first glimpse of the museum. Most of all, I remember being surprised by the easing of anxiety—by the surge of inner peace and focus that accompanies the return to the things one loves.

Yet I soon found myself looking to Larry, ready to surrender my first impression—bedazzlement—to his sober assessment. The space was "noble," he conceded, but the way it had been transformed into a museum reeked of "boutique architecture—flashy and tiresome." I protested, saying I liked what had been done, to which he answered, "Wait a few years and come back. It will pall—I promise."

I resisted being influenced by his opinion and yet, undoubtedly, I was; for the vernacular of space and proportion belonged, I felt at least subliminally, to him (just as I had expropriated language and stories for myself). In retrospect, I am struck by the fact that he was so eager to expose me to what he himself did not like—the architecture of the new museum—though he loved the paintings it contained, and passionately, too.

I was curious to see which ones he admired. The sinewy Delacroix of the lion chase was one, as I recall, as were the darker Degas portraits, the nudes of Ingres, and the Tahitian exotica of Gauguin.

We came to a mutual favorite: Manet's immense and enigmatic *Déjeuner sur l'herbe*—the naked woman flanked by the figures of two urbanely clothed gentlemen friends, her flesh pearly white against the inky greens of trees.

"That's how I felt last night at dinner," I said, turning to Larry with a self-deprecating laugh: "naked, before two men."

"I *liked* your story."

"Did you?"

"Yes."

To the galleries with Bonnard, Denis, and Vuillard next. It seemed that Larry had never much liked Vuillard, whose tapestrylike scenes of bourgeois interiors I had always loved, and which he first dismissed as "pleasant." I made him stand with me before one such painting, forcing him to look again at the undulating mosaics of pattern and space. Afterward, he admitted that he had, in fact, appreciated Vuillard in a different way this time; I remember how this pleased me.

He understood sculpture in a visceral way I did not—at least not at that moment in my life—and had the rare gift of being able to articulate its technique and potency. He told me about Rodin and his life and work, and how *The Gates of Hell* had been created: the influence of Dante upon Rodin's only partly realized vision of Inferno.

Moments later we came to a portrait I had never seen, though Larry seemed familiar with it. It was the work of Alexander Cabanel and depicted a certain Madame de Keller. Her hair was black and short, the expression of her dark eyes world-weary and cryptic; a fur wrap was draped negligently about the bluish flesh of her bare shoulders. Whether she was lady or courtesan was hard to tell.

I told Larry she reminded me of Christina von Shouse: "The same look in the eyes," I observed.

"*That* would flatter her, I'm sure." He stood back, studying the painting. "That's how Christina would like to think of herself—as seductive. A femme fatale."

"And you don't think she ever was?"

"No. Never."

I continued to think of Madame de Keller, and then of Christina von Shouse—stylish, shrewd, and sexless—and her friendship with Joanna. "Christina had even more cause to be jealous of Joanna, then," I said, as much to myself as to Larry. "And yet she seems so confident!"

"Between seeming and being lies a world of shadows," said Larry, looking at me in such a way that I felt color rising to my throat and face: "But *you* must know that, Elisabeth!"

I remember how that unsettled me, how I suddenly felt exhausted, as if my eye could absorb no more—though Larry's did not seem surfeited. I suggested that we leave.

"Not yet," he said, in the intimidating voice that, startlingly, reminded me of the first time we had met. "There are some paintings you've got to see." He took my arm so tightly it almost hurt. "Over here—"

And so we made our way to Fantin-Latour, and then to Van Gogh, Cézanne, and Degas. All the while Larry would point out the quality of light in one painting, the influence of photography in another, or a gauzy brushstroke peculiar to one artist's late period. Only when he was satisfied that the tour was complete did we leave.

Outside, the air was bitter cold, the churning Seine deep gray. I turned up the collar of my coat, glancing at the man beside me and feeling rather awkward, as if the sudden absence of paintings had created a void. Larry asked whether I would like a drink, or a cup of tea, or something to eat. I said I would, very much, for I was tired and hungry.

We crossed the street to Le Rapide, a café at the corner of the rue de Bellechasse. The bar glistened with glasses and bottles; beyond it, at small marble-topped tables, people drank coffee and foreign infusions.

We found a quiet table in the back; Larry called for a waiter.

I watched his face as he scanned the menu, recalling the last time I had seen him—in late December, at the Westbury. How much more rested and at peace he looked, how quintessentially American, in this setting, with his tweed jacket and straightforward looks. And yet how at ease —*à l'aise dans sa peau*, as Liliane de Morbier might have said.

A waiter approached our table. I asked for tea and a *crème caramel*, Larry, coffee and a *tarte tatin*. As I took off my gloves, I admitted to having a terrible sweet tooth.

"I'm not sure I believe that," Larry told me with a slight smile, leaning forward.

"Look again!" I said, laughing. "It's only one of my many weaknesses."

The waiter returned with our order. Larry finished his *tarte tatin* in rapid, uninterrupted bites, looking up to wipe his mouth.

"You haven't eaten anything," he said, noticing I had pushed my plate away.

"I wasn't as hungry as I thought." I went on to apologize for having behaved "so idiotically" the night before at Taillevent. "Jack and I have been going through a complicated time, but I never wanted it to spoil the evening with you."

"You don't have to apologize."

I picked up my spoon and absentmindedly began to slice the *crème caramel* into thin, tilting crescents. "He's asked me to marry him," I finally said.

"I see," Larry replied, watching as I lit a cigarette. "You must be very happy, then."

"But in return he'd prefer that I not write the book—the book on Joanna."

His eyes searched mine. "And you've agreed to that?"

"I don't know." I looked away, trying to avoid his scrutiny. "I don't know."

"You must love him very much," he said, in a voice with a harder edge. "Why else would you marry a man who belittles your obsessions?"

I remember holding the scalding cup of tea so tightly it almost burned my hands. "But these things can be worked out . . ."

"If you think they can be worked out," he replied with a forced heartiness, "so much the better!"

"Yes of course . . ." My voice drifted off; I continued to smoke; moments passed. "Your Christmas present meant so much to me . . ."

"I'm glad you liked it," he replied, as if he were not really concentrating. Then: "Joanna would have wanted you to have the Shakespeare."

"Do you think she would want me to finish the book?"

"Only *you* know that."

I told him about the interview with Liliane de Morbier— her haunting description of Joanna's last summer and the revelation about the child. "I don't know whether to believe her," I added. "I don't know whom to believe. I only know I've got to get to Thistleton."

"Thistleton isn't really the issue."

"What *is*, then?" I asked almost angrily.

"*You* know what to do—"

I looked away, thinking of the passage about the senses and intellect he had underlined from Henry Adams. "Adams, again."

"I've already given you my advice."

" 'There must be something at Thistleton you need to know.' "

He smiled as I quoted from his Christmas note; I remember noticing his lean, ruddy cheeks and the faint circles beneath his eyes. "Even if it means giving up Jack?" I asked anxiously. "Even if it means being ruined by David Cassel?"

"You can only be ruined by not being true to yourself. But that's something else you already know."

I took a deep breath and said, "Yes," but not without trepidation, and a longing to turn the questions to him. I asked about his divorce and whether it had been finalized (it had, he replied). And then to a subject we had always succeeded in avoiding: the failure of his marriage.

I asked what his ex-wife was like.

"Very beautiful," he told me with a grave, almost hurtful directness.

"I know," I said almost inaudibly. "I've seen the pictures."

"If only her mind had been as exquisite as her face!" he quietly exclaimed, and with such bitterness I was taken aback. I had always construed his reticence to discuss his marriage as the painful aftermath of Isabelle's having left him; yet now I inferred something astonishingly different—disillusionment and relief.

"But still—you got through it."

"I had my work," he answered. "Work that I loved and that anchored my life. Her own interest in my work was perfunctory—a means toward an end. She was jealous of it, I suppose—she had no understanding of that kind of obsession." He paused, as if reluctant to acknowledge even to himself the full measure of his disenchantment.

"And how did you feel," I asked, "once you had made this decision—to leave her?"

"Bitter at first. But in the end, relieved."

"And Frederick?"

"He was just two."

"Was she—is she—a good mother?"

"Yes," he conceded. "I give her that."

"And your mother?" I asked after a moment. "What did she think of your wife?"

"My mother died when I was twelve," he replied in such a reticent way that his quite obvious pain affected me all the more. I pictured him at twelve, losing a mother he loved— the eldest child, the son, and much adored, no doubt. I remember being tempted to touch his hand, but thinking that the stoical, private man opposite me would not permit it.

He asked me about my own family—where I was born, where I had grown up. I told him I was an only child, and that my mother had died of cancer when I was two. "She was a portrait painter," I added. "She grew up in Boston but used to spend all her summers in Europe. My father met her in London." I paused, fleetingly recalling her photographs—her intense eyes and poignant smile. My mother's death was something I almost never discussed, the only forbidden subject of my girlhood: The confrontation with my father's pain and sense of loss had never ceased to be harrowing.

"You once mentioned that you were brought up by your father," Larry said, "and your mother's sister—"

I nodded. "I adored my aunt; she was very much like my mother, I'm told—"

"And your father?"

"My father died last year," I said, feeling compelled to add: "He died before I reached Geneva." I told Larry how much this haunted me, adding, "My father was a remarkable man."

"And then," he said. "After your father died, you met Jack—"

Guilt made me slow to answer. "No—I'd met him a few years before."

"About the time I saw you in Seattle?"

I thought of that day—his building, the wind, the way he had intimidated me. "No, before," I admitted.

"I see." He sat back, digging his hands deep into his pockets. "I see."

Men in lumpy blue jackets had begun to crowd the bar, downing glasses of whiskey. It was five o'clock. "We should go," I said, picking up my gloves.

He called for the check and helped me with my coat. "Let's walk back to the Right Bank," he said.

We stepped outside. The clouds had thickened.

We crossed the pont du Carrousel and came to the interior courtyard of the Louvre, pockmarked with puddles and ravaged by construction: The top of I. M. Pei's unfinished glass pyramid could be seen rising above the ugly barricades. I asked Larry what he thought of this controversial addition to the Louvre; I thought it seemed awful. He liked it very much, he told me, and went on to explain the historical relevance of the pyramid for the French, and why it was appropriate for "I. M.," as he called him, to have referred to it. And once again I found myself adjusting my vision—this time finding beauty in what I had originally dismissed.

As we walked along the rue du Faubourg St.-Honoré, it began to pour. Larry took off his coat, shielding me from the rain, as I protested.

"Don't be ridiculous," he said.

We crossed the rue Royale and arrived drenched and cold at the entrance of his hotel, the Bristol. I began to say good-bye.

"You can't go back like that! You're soaked and cold!"

I said I'd be fine: "Anyway, I've got to change for dinner."

"What time's your dinner?"

"Eight-thirty."

"You don't need two hours to dress," he said, taking my arm. And then, brusquely: "Come."

We took the elevator to his room; The next moment his

key was in the door; we entered his suite. I remember the preternatural quiet, the gauzy light from windows overlooking the courtyard, and the gun cases from the trip to Scotland propped in a corner. But most of all I remember the long table to one side, with models of the two projects that had brought Larry to Europe.

I took off my coat and shoes, both of which were soaked, while he ordered tea.

The telephone rang: his New York office. He began to speak with an associate, the sleeves of his white shirt rolled up, one hand pushing back his hair as he listened, quickly responding to each question about a measurement or elevation, referring to a stack of drawings on the desk in front of him.

I approached the table with the models of his work—the apartment complex outside of Orléans, and the opera house near Hamburg, whose scope and complexity rather took me aback. The style was strong, tensile, with echoes of the neoclassic; yet there was nothing derivative about it. I was fascinated with the way the buildings penetrated space—how deeply embedded in the ground they seemed, and yet how soaring. I thought them very beautiful, of an almost incandescent self-reliance, and wondered at the mind that had created them—a mind which could see, in emptiness, the possibility of shelter, form, and beauty.

He continued to speak on the telephone while I grappled with an admiration so powerful it verged on the erotic; I hardly dared face him.

He put down the telephone. "The tea will be here in a minute," he said.

I asked about the buildings: how they had come about, and what had inspired them. He told me he had won a competition in Germany for the new opera house and that he was already fairly well known in France, having designed an office building in Toulouse and another outside Lille. "But tell me how you *begin*," I said.

He explained that the process of designing was like anything else creative: at its root was a burgeoning sense of form that gradually clarified itself on paper and was then honed, edited, and perfected by the process of elimination. Not so different from writing, he imagined, although the language of spatial perception was obviously quite different. "But the work and the fortitude required are the same, no doubt."

I confided to him that some of the moments of purest pleasure and peace I had ever experienced had come while writing. "I sometimes feel that the writing is more myself than I am," I said (for some reason that Brontë-esque line had sprung to mind). I remember he did not find the idea unsettling.

The tea arrived on a table covered with thick white linen. There were small sandwiches and scones with cream and other sweets—*mystères* and *religieuses*—for which the French have invented a whole vocabulary.

I poured him a cup of tea, and then one for myself, heaping it with sugar; I remember its sweet, smoky taste, how it almost burned my tongue. At one point Larry set down his cup, looking at me in such a way that I felt compelled to talk, to sally forth with conversation, as I sometimes do when nervous. I told him that Jack and I would leave for Chartres the next day and spend the night at Solesmes.

"I'll call you when we get back to New York to tell you about it," I added. He smiled rather distractedly and seemed on the verge of asking me a question when the telephone rang again. A call from Germany this time.

It was almost seven o'clock by the time he finished. I stood up, leaving my unfurled napkin on the table. "It's late. I should go."

He seemed to hesitate. "Of course—I'll get your coat."

He left, reappearing with my moist coat, and helped me put it on; when I looked down to tie my belt, my hands were shaking. He drew me toward him, my hands in his, holding them tightly before I finally pulled away in silence.

Without another word, I left him, and his room, and the Hotel Bristol.

39

N ever had I known morning to disorient by its very
clarity.

We drove from Paris to Chartres early the next day,
watching as the spires of the cathedral emerged, miragelike,
from the plain. We arrived there at noon, stepping out of the
car into the narrow, winding, deeply shadowed streets.

The looming church beckoned: We passed through its
monumental portals, past the appraising glances of linear
stone saints, and into the cold, unsparing nave, its walls
pierced with wheels of colored light. How many times had I
entered this shrine without having understood the hunger
for light which informed it, and the daring which had put
these soaring walls at risk (the "vertical ecstasy" so vividly

recalled by Larry). I remember looking about, inwardly acknowledging my debt to Larry—for I felt it was partly he, and
the book he had given me, that had led me to the edges of
understanding.

I came upon the other aspect of the cathedral I had forgotten: the labyrinth embedded in the nave's stone floor. Rub-
bing my hands together—it was bitter cold that January afternoon—I followed its coiled pattern, thinking once again
of Joanna and Thistleton and the chapel at Wakefield Hall;
of labyrinths and lives.

I looked up at Jack, hoping that he would see Chartres as I
had—as if that single response could recapture what I so
desperately desired: the man I had originally fallen in love
with, not the near stranger who stood beside me now. But his
response only left me crestfallen: By the splendid rose window, imparting its supernatural reddish-violet light, he
seemed only minimally impressed, indeed almost indifferent.
We went outside: I pointed out the famous portal and the
sculpted figures of the Triumph of Christ. Looking up at
them, he merely nodded, but in such a way I could tell his
mind was elsewhere, on lunch perhaps.

We had lunch at a restaurant nearby, which I fondly remembered from my student days. Jack did not find the meal
very good; we left before ordering dessert.

I bought some postcards, and he the *Herald Tribune*. By
three o'clock we were speeding along the *autoroute* once
more; Jack told the driver to bypass the detour for
Châteaudun in favor of the most direct road to Solesmes.

We drove in silence, Jack focused on the *Herald Tribune*,
while my own thoughts returned obsessively to the decision
that lay ahead.

Was it madness, I thought to myself, to have invested the
book on Joanna with such importance? I did not know the
answer; I only knew that what the book had come to mean to
me was the real question. It continued to exert its awful pull,
as if it had transmuted itself into a labyrinth whose end I had
to reach, however dark the passage. Not to reach that end—

to abandon the book, stillborn—risked a life of inner wandering and barely stifled anger.

We continued to drive through the Loire valley and then through the mute, shuttered towns of the Sarthe—a countryside I knew well and whose roads and towns seemed inextricably bound, that day, with my unrelenting self-interrogation. I thought of Larry, and Jack, and marriage, and the book as I recalled the French towns I had visited long ago: Chinon, Chambord, and moated Chenonceaux; and Fontevrault, with its looted tombs of Plantaganet kings and queens.

We arrived in Solesmes by late afternoon; darkness had descended. At our hotel, La Flèche d'Or, we were shown to a room with a creaking armoire and walls of a faded red toile. Jack thought the room "cramped" and "shabby." I begged him not to change it.

At five o'clock, the hour of the vespers, we heard the bells tolling and walked to the abbaye de Saint-Pierre. I remember the falcon lectern, the shuffling of an old woman's steps, the mauve light, the challenge of the silence. I made the sign of the cross and knelt, hands clasped, in the pew. Monks robed in black filed past us in procession, their voices merged in Latin chants.

I wanted not to think of Jack then, nor of the proposal whose implicit conditions he had set before me, yet both continued to devour my thoughts. To marry him or not; to give up the book for the security of a settled life, with the possibility of children; or to abandon him, to forfeit nearly four years together—for what? For uncertainty, and probable aloneness. For a book that may or may not ever come to be; for the fantasy of another man who might be a mere infatuation, and whose possible darker side had not yet been revealed to me.

Only toward the end of the vespers, as the monks once more filed past, did I glance at Jack. Never had his eyes appeared so blue, his hair so blond, his mouth so pragmatic, his features so chiseled and northern. I noticed how restless he seemed, and fought against acknowledging what I had already sensed was true: What had touched me profoundly had left him unmoved.

Sunday morning came: a brilliant, wintry day. Mid-morning, we made our way to the abbey; again, I genuflected and made the sign of the cross; again, the eerie light streamed through the high arched windows of Caen stone; again, I was immeasurably moved by the chants of the Kyrie Eleison, the Gloria, and the Sanctus. Again, I searched within me for the answer—until that moment, during the Agnus Dei, when I felt a surge of loss, of renunciation, and yet of relief and elation. I began to cry.

Jack said nothing. I think my tears embarrassed him.

We left the abbey and returned to the hotel for lunch.

The dining room bustled with families drinking wine and breaking bread. We sat down, my hands almost trembling, my throat parched.

Then came the question I had once yearned for: "You haven't given me your answer yet," Jack said in a strong, clear voice: "Will you marry me? Will you be Mrs. John Varady?"

I told him I hadn't yet come to a decision.

"When will you?" he asked impatiently.

"Soon," I said, taking his hand. "After we get back to New York."

40

I returned from Paris to find a message from Rosalind's assistant on my answering machine. "Ms. Bennett would like to see you," Mr. Crowell subsequently told me. "For drinks—as soon as possible." I asked the purpose of the meeting and was informed, "I'm afraid only Ms. Bennett can tell you that." We set the time and place.

The Harvard Club was almost empty that afternoon; the sound of Rosalind swirling her drink reverberated strangely. She watched me approach from afar, but never stood up— Cassandra in a gray flannel suit, smoking with metronomic elegance. She looked more polished than I had ever seen her —dark hair perfectly coiffed, flawless red lipstick, lustrous crocodile pumps, earrings crafted from ancient coins.

I sat down. Above us loomed the vigilant heads of elk, with their inscrutable glass eyes and tentaclelike antlers.

Rosalind said hello, raising her vodka, quite at ease within the patriarchal atmosphere of brass, wood, and leather. "A drink?" she proposed, with an assessing glance, her body still motionless. I ordered a glass of wine.

I put down my notebook and the newspaper—*the Daily News*—I had been reading in the taxi. Its lurid front-page story featured the photograph of a coed from Queens who had allegedly been raped.

"Paper?" asked Rosalind, raising one brow as she motioned to it.

I made some joke about my "beloved tabloids" and handed it to her, watching as she examined the headline, then the photograph of the homely victim. "She was *lucky* to be raped," Rosalind remarked with a wicked glance as she slapped the paper down on the table.

"Come on—" I scoffed.

"You've got to admit—" she cocked her head, narrowing her almond eyes. "But I wouldn't want to shock the biographer, would I?" She smiled to herself, smugly at ease with her perverse persona, and knowing I was too accustomed to her jaundiced self to bother to challenge her.

I lit a cigarette and asked how long she had been a member of the Harvard Club.

"Five years—the last link with the B-school. Impresses the hell out of the schmucks at Goldman who never made it to Harvard." She smiled with a devastating sweetness that was, characteristically, at odds with her mordant tone. "So—how goes it, Elisabeth?"

"What do you mean?" I wondered what she was alluding to—Jack or the book.

"The book, of course."

"You know better than I—I'm sure David has filled you in."

She dragged on her cigarette, watching as the smoke

whorled between us. The waiter brought my wine. "And your precious Jack Varady—how's he these days?"

"What has Jack got to do with it?"

"Everything. And nothing." She paused. "He met with David, you know. About you. About the book."

Her expression made me nervous. "When?" I asked, setting down my drink. "And how do you know it was about the book?"

"End of December. The twenty-eighth, I think—I always like to be precise with numbers. And I know because David told me—filled me in, you'd say." Her expression was disarmingly clinical, as if she were watching the dissection of a particularly rare species.

"I'm sure it was business," I ventured, with more conviction than I felt.

"They *have* no business together. It had to do with the book. And with the fact that Jack has sort of become David's protégé. Not in business. But *socially*. David's become his social sponsor." She paused. "You must've known that, Elisabeth."

"I can't imagine what they would have in common."

"No? That surprises me. Even David has his weaknesses, and Jack's goy looks don't exactly work against him. Need I say more?" She crushed out her cigarette. "There's nothing more ruthless than a socially ambitious WASP."

"And what exactly is David sponsoring him *for*?"

"Jack wants a place on the board of the Art Institute. It's the hardest board to crack. David's the head of it."

My tension mounted. "What exactly are you telling me?"

"I'm just filling you in—" again that expression, irksomely repeated, "out of kindness. To let you know that they've met. Hasn't Jack told you? Hasn't he explained his relationship with David? I thought it would be—" she paused, "illuminating for you. In light of the other developments."

Our eyes met. "I hear he's planning to leave his wife," she continued. "Sort of like killing two birds with one stone, isn't it?"

I remembered the moment at Wakefield when she had used the same chilling expression: "Killing two birds with one stone." I took another cigarette and began, as best I could, to light it. "I don't know what you mean."

"He gets you as a wife and the book out of his way—and David's. Have to give Jack credit. He's efficient, all right."

"It must delight you to know that this hurts me."

"Not at all. But as you seem so obsessed with the truth, I thought you should know what Jack is about—the Wrong Stuff with the right cock. A lethal combination." She flicked some ashes from her skirt, still watching me.

"I think I should go," I stammered, so consumed with anger—toward her, toward Jack, toward David—that I could barely speak. I set down my wine with shaking hands, stood up, and began to gather my things.

"Elisabeth," she said in a different, almost imploring voice. "Elisabeth—listen to me."

"*Listen* to you?" I looked at her incredulously. "You're jealous and destructive. You'd do anything to ruin my life, the book—anything. You've done nothing but humiliate me from the first time we met!"

"You're wrong."

"No I'm not."

"Hear me out." She paused. "I know things you don't—"

I thought of the sketch in David's study. "I'm sure you do," I retorted. "But they're too sordid for me to want to know about them."

She looked away, biting her nails; a moment passed. "You're thinking about the sketch . . ."

Our eyes met: "Yes."

"It was David's idea—he had it commissioned, I mean. After Joanna died. I'd just had that operation. The hysterectomy. He thought it would be—" she faltered, "a way of getting over it. I would have done anything for him." A pause. Her eyes revealed such fervent tenderness that I looked away. "You said it yourself—a daughter can be closer to a husband than a wife."

A moment passed; I watched her strike a match and light a cigarette—nothing she had said surprised me.

"But we were talking about you," she said. "About Jack."

Something in her tone—an urgency, rather than its usual cunning—made me relent. I sat down.

"It's *you* who will ruin your life," she said in a softer, more compelling voice. "Jack will use you to get what he wants—don't you see? You've lived in this city long enough to know what goes on. It's a simple system, really—everything's based on mutual using."

The clock struck seven. "Why should I believe you?" I finally asked, searching her eyes.

She paused, leaning forward, her demeanor of a gentleness I had never seen before—as if, in that instant, I had a sudden glimpse of the girl David Cassel adored. "Because you know it's *true*," she said. "Why else would Jack have pressured you to drop the book? Why else would he suddenly have decided it was okay for him to leave his wife and marry you?" She paused again, bringing a clenched fist to her mouth. "What more do I have to say to convince you?"

Moments passed. I looked away, toward the far wall, at the eyes of the enigmatic elk. Of Rosalind's motive I was not certain; that she was telling the truth I had no doubt. "How do I know *you're* not the one who's jealous of Jack?" I asked. "Jealous of his friendship with David? Why should I believe you?"

She looked at me with a candor I will never forget. "You don't *have* to believe me," she answered almost wearily. "Just ask Jack."

I left the Harvard Club, my mind, my body, throbbing with confusion and betrayal; the city seemed to dissolve before my eyes. I thought of Jack, of Rosalind, and then of the two men in Cassel's red library forging their bargain, their "deal." My head pounded. I thought of the words of Christina von Shouse, now come to haunt me: "The funereal progression from the *coup de foudre* to the final disenchantment." I wanted to know the truth, I told myself; yet I already *knew* the truth, and had known it for a while.

Looking out the taxi window, I began to cry, overwhelmed with accumulated hurt—the passionate resentment I had until then repressed. I thought of his heartbreaking silence at Christina's dinner, the "concern" for my career, the placating gifts rather than emotional commitment; but most bitterly of all the hard condition that he had set before me— marry him, but give up the book. . . . I thought of the abbey at Solesmes—the expression in his eyes when I had cried; the spiritual desolation of our relationship—

I slammed the taxi door, fantasizing the mournful thrill of lashing out at him.

I called his office without taking off my coat, without thinking what I would say or how I would say it.

"I'm afraid I can't interrupt him," his secretary told me. "He's just gone into a meeting."

"Get him for me—*now*."

Moments later, Jack came on the line: "What's up, sweetheart?" he asked.

For he had no way of knowing the three decisions that had just unknotted in my mind:

I would leave him, and change my life—

I would see the book to its end—

And I would find a way to Thistleton, driven by the obsession that there was something there I had to know.

IV

41

I arrived at Thistleton in the deepest part of winter: Snow blanketed its walks and lawns; frost-covered trees, the spectral sentinels of February, guarded its massive stone entrance.

The air was of an icy dampness known only to England. All sound seemed to have yielded to the elegiac silence that follows the destruction of a tempest. The night before, a fearsome storm had rent the countryside, uprooting vast trees and leaving the landscape in violent disarray.

I arrived shortly after noon, having taken a train from London to the village of Cheltham-on-Exley, which lay less than a quarter mile outside the gates of Thistleton. In my excitement that morning I had neither been able to eat nor to focus on anything except the letter in my hand—the letter from Desmond Kerrith that had arrived two weeks after my return from Paris, and which, in the stunned aftermath of leaving Jack, had had the effect of anchoring me, of redirecting my obsessiveness, of validating my decision to pursue the book.

I will never forget the moment when I came upon that long-hoped-for letter in the stack of mail—how, with racing heartbeat, I had ripped open the envelope to find Kerrith's barely decipherable signature on the thick white paper, the top of which was engraved with the emblem of twin unicorns before a high hedge maze (the same crest I recalled from the bookplate in Joanna's copy of *Far From the Madding Crowd* at Wakefield). Yet I also recall how my initial thrill gave way to bewilderment, even chagrin. There was an inscrutably arbitrary quality to Kerrith's letter—no mention of the intervention of Liliane de Morbier or Christina von Shouse, no mention of my innumerable calls or letters. In a concise, civil tone, Kerrith had merely agreed to see me, without revealing whether Joanna's letters existed, let alone whether he would permit me access to them. My only hope, it seemed, was to go to Thistleton and plead my case face to face.

The following week, I went to England. Larry accompanied me on this trip (a trip that would mark a new phase of our relationship), but only as far as London: He felt adamantly that the journey to Thistleton was one I ought to make alone. Only in that way did Larry press me to go further; in every other way he exercised restraint, wisely sensing that I was still working through the painful process of leaving Jack, and that pursuing the book would be the best way to dispel any lingering hurt or ambivalence. The wounds were still fresh, and Larry knew it.

I passed through the gates and up the serpentine drive, catching sight of the house from a distance, just as I had first glimpsed Wakefield Hall the previous summer. Yet Thistleton was a house of a different scale: vast—like a palace or museum—it did not appear to be a human habitation.

I tried to imagine the impression it must have made on Joanna when she first saw it—how monumental and otherworldly it must have seemed.

I paid for the taxi, walked up the great stone steps and, after ringing the bell, waited outside, shuffling my feet in the cold as I pressed my frozen, gloved hands to my mouth. At last the door opened and a tall, white-haired butler appeared. I was ushered into an astounding space with a noble double staircase and a pale neoclassic ceiling upheld by four towering marble caryatids.

I heard a clattering of footsteps next: the house manager, it seemed—a slight, sprightly woman with an impressive array of keys and the air of a romantic librarian. There was a coquettishness about her hairstyle and blue eyeshadow, and a coyness about her gaze, that seemed at odds with her tweed skirt and the sloping shoulders of her matronly taupe cardigan. She proceeded to introduce herself as Mrs. Alsop. "Welcome to Thistleton," she said vivaciously, with a flutter of her lashes. "This *is* a treat—to have someone visiting us from New York! A treat indeed." I thanked her, and there followed the usual pleasantries about England and the biting weather and my train trip to Hampshire. I noticed the exotic egg-shaped gold charm, enameled in blue and red, that hung from a gold chain around her neck—a touch that somehow seemed in keeping with her eccentric style.

"You must be very cold, my dear—do come in and have a bit of a warm. A spot of tea would do you good, I'm sure." She fidgeted with her keys as she spoke, her eyes taking in the nuances of my outfit (as country women do, with city visitors). I gratefully accepted her offer, for I was chilled and thirsty.

She suggested that we go the "garden room." "Lord Kerrith has just woken up from his nap," she told me as I followed her small, clattering steps down a long, dim corridor. "He isn't quite ready to see you." Then, with a pert smile: "They are getting him ready." I wondered who "they" were, but refrained from asking: I would discover soon enough.

We passed through a multitude of rooms, rooms of a forlorn grandeur, many of whose furniture was covered in sheets, rooms of gilt and damask and marble, rooms peopled with immense portraits and moody landscapes; rooms with baroque ceilings swirling with color and rosy-cheeked Italianate figures. But all was cold and lifeless; the sound of our footsteps echoing through the enfilade of corridors seemed to startle the frozen faces staring at us from the walls.

We turned to the left, down another narrower corridor, which led, I surmised, to the part of the house occupied by the staff; and from there to the garden room—a winter conservatory, small in scale and *fin de siècle* in feeling. Its cheerful shabbiness and human scale came as something of a relief. Worn Oriental carpets lined the floors, and the armchairs, upholstered in a faded puce chintz, looked cozy and inviting. I sensed immediately that this was where Mrs. Alsop and the army of nurses and hangers-on who took care of Lord Kerrith were accustomed to assembling. There were copies of women's magazines about—*Women's Own* and *Honey*—and well-worn, florid paperbacks with curling covers, stacked on tables. Beneath a what-not in one corner stood a few yellow chrysanthemum plants.

I approached the crackling fire to warm my hands and in doing so looked up at the Edwardian mantelpiece, which to my surprise was lined with postcards of New York City—hackneyed tourist views of the Empire State Building, the Statue of Liberty, and Central Park. Still trying to make conversation, I politely inquired whether Mrs. Alsop had a friend in New York.

"Oh, my dear—yes!" she said with delight, picking up some half-finished needlepoint. "That's Mrs. von Shouse who sends us cards from time to time," she continued, alternately chatting and embroidering. "It's very kind of her, isn't it, to remember her old friends here at Thistleton. We knew her so long ago, when she worked as Lord K's secretary—such a very young woman she was. And now she's in New York. And rather a fine lady there, too, from what we hear."

I remember how my initial reaction changed, how as I glanced at the mantelpiece again the postcards assumed quite a different cast. "And she sends you these postcards, did you say?"

"Oh my, yes. But that's not the end of it." She paused, looking up from the needlepoint. "She's so very dear and thoughtful, Mrs. von Shouse is. Always sends me a basket from Fortnum's at Christmastime, with all sorts of goodies. Lovely tins of tea and my favorite creme biscuits." She looked up, proudly fingering the enameled egg charm I had noticed only minutes before. "She sent this, she did, for my birthday earlier this year. Told me it was Russian, very rare. By that famous designer who did all sorts of things—"

"Fabergé," I interjected.

"That's right, Fabergé! Imagine Mrs. von Shouse being kind enough to send me such a lovely thing. Pricey, too, I should think."

"She sends you presents?"

"Yes, and calls quite often, once a week at least, to find out how Lord K is doing. Whether he's had any visitors, and who's coming to see him—" She paused, looking up from her embroidery. "I told her you were coming today, and she was so delighted!"

"Was she, then?" I asked, trying not to reveal my nervousness.

"Yes! She told me she was to London this week, for an auction or something of that sort, and that she would try to come to Thistleton. To surprise you, and show you around the house. You can imagine—she knows the house very well, having been part of the staff herself." Her brow furrowed. "Oh dear, I shouldn't have told you she was coming," she said sheepishly. "Mrs. von Shouse *swore me to secrecy*, she did—she did so want to surprise you. You won't tell her that I mentioned it, will you?"

"No, of course not. I won't say anything," I reassured her, even as a renewed urgency came over me. "What time did she say she'd arrive?"

"I'm not certain." She shrugged, picking up her needle-point. "She told me she would come as soon as she could—in the early afternoon, most likely. And I'm sure she will. Mrs. von Shouse always lives up to her word. She's a very precise sort of person. She never forgets anything." Smiling to herself, she proudly displayed her half-finished canvas: it was the emblem of Thistleton she was in the midst of em-broidering—an enlargement of the crest of unicorns before the maze that I had seen on Lord Kerrith's writing paper and bookplate. Beneath her version, however, the Kerrith motto was unfurled—the same motto I had been unable to trans-late at Wakefield Hall. I slowly repeated the words: "*Intellec-tus merces est cognitio*—"

"Yes indeed," Mrs. Alsop chirped. "That's the Kerrith fam-ily motto—'Understanding is the reward of knowledge.' Lovely, isn't it? I thought this would be the perfect birthday present—a needlepoint pillow for Lord K. He's going to be seventy-five in November, imagine! It seems only yesterday he was so young and handsome!"

I walked to the ice-glazed windows and gazed outside at the deracinated landscape and at the sky, which was a sere, immutable gray; against this stood the white of the snow-covered lawn, and in the distance, a curious army of frost-covered topiaries that were shaped to resemble the pawns of a chess set. Beyond rose the medieval "ruins" and the tower, which I recognized from the photographs Joanna had left; further beyond, the hedges of the labyrinth. Joanna's photo-graphs had shown them at the height of springtime, when the gardens were in full flower—now it was winter, and all was barren.

The topiaries intrigued me; it seemed odd that no one had mentioned them before. Still staring at the bizarre army of pawns, I thought of a town in the Veneto I had once visited —Marostica was its name—where the main square was pat-terned like a chess board and where, following an ancient tradition, the game was reenacted with human combatants.

"And the topiaries," I said, returning to sit by Mrs. Alsop. "Are they very old?"

"I've no idea, I'm sorry to say, but they're very famous. All part of the plan laid out by the original designers in the eighteenth century—" She paused, looking up at the butler, who had entered the room with lumbering steps and who proceeded to set down a tea tray before us. "People come from all over just to see them," she said, fussing with the small linen napkins. "Lord K was always keen on chess— perhaps that's why the topiaries were always so well kept up. A lot of work it takes, you can imagine!"

The butler left, shutting the door behind him.

"And the tower, beyond the topiaries?" I asked.

"It's one of the many little buildings on the property— 'follies,' they're called." She motioned to me to sit down. "There's one that's meant to be a Roman temple. But the most famous one was built like the ruins of a medieval fortress, with the tower still standing. At the edge of the maze. The tower was always used as a library-study, apart from the house." She smiled, adjusting her voice as if to emphasize a special meaning. "Joanna Eakins—Joanna Cassel, I should say—used to spend such a lot of time in the tower. She would rehearse her parts there, learning her lines, trying on her costumes. Lady Macbeth of course, and then, let me see—"

"So you knew Joanna Eakins, then," I said, interrupting her rambling.

"Oh yes, yes indeed," she said decisively, with a proudly intimate glance, as she began to pour our tea. "She would spend whole afternoons there, reading, working on her parts. She kept her old costumes there as well—they may still be there, in the trunk, who knows!" Looking up, teacup in hand, she asked brightly, "Sugar?" I nodded, my mind still on the tower as she handed me the milky tea in the flower-patterned china cup.

I asked Mrs. Alsop how long she had worked at Thistleton.

"Since I was a girl," she answered, stirring her tea in the

exaggeratedly refined way I sensed she affected for visitors. "My parents, and their parents before them, worked here. I came to the estate as a chambermaid when I was seventeen." She sipped her tea, glancing down in such a way that the arc of incongruous eye makeup was harshly visible. "Oh yes, my dear," she continued, setting down her cup. "When Joanna first came here, you can imagine how everyone was curious about her—she'd had that overnight success in London as Lady Macbeth, and then she met Lord Kerrith. And well, you know how these things go . . ." Her look was slyly confidential, even slightly salacious. "I remember that she couldn't swim, and how Lord K had someone come to teach her every morning, very early, when the water was so cold. How she never, ever complained—very determined in her own way. That I do remember very well. A biscuit?" she asked me brightly, holding up a plate.

I took one absentmindedly and tried, in that instant, to imagine the era Mrs. Alsop had just described, tried to imagine what the house had been like years ago, before the illness and old age of its master, when the rooms were glowing and well tended, when the presence of the famous and gifted filled its halls and park. Now all had changed. I had come to ask an elderly man what he remembered of his former mistress. To let me read her letters—the letters which her will indicated were here, "physically located in the library at Thistleton." But now I sensed what I had not fully realized before: that I would have to penetrate a phalanx of nurses, secretaries, and attendants before reaching him.

"We understand you are writing a book about Joanna Eakins," she resumed briskly, interrupting my thoughts as she offered me a tiny sandwich. "Quite a job, I should think." She bit into her own sandwich, leaving an indentation of shocking-pink lipstick on the remaining bread.

Yes, I said after a moment. The research on the book was the reason for my visit: "I know that Lord Kerrith was such an important part of her life. Especially her early life as an actress, in England."

"Oh yes indeed," she rejoined. "But not only that, my dear. Of her whole life, really! She continued to write to him until the very end, until she died in that dreadful way. So young, she was." She sipped her tea again, adding with a conspiratorial glance: "But you must know that Joanna Eakins was quite the letter writer!"

I answered yes, I did know. "I was hoping to be able to speak with him about it, and hoped he might let me read the letters she left him."

"That decision rests in Lord Kerrith's hands," she replied in a lofty tone that might have amused me had I not been so tense. "It depends on his mood," she added, figeting with her many rings. "And then there's Mr. Percy, of course."

"Mr. Percy?"

"The manager of the estate, now that Lord Kerrith is—" she faltered, "rather variable in mood."

"I see." I remember that her manner was beginning to irritate me, as if she were privy to information which she was purposely withholding. I tried not to show it, however, merely reiterating that I had come a long way to speak with Lord Kerrith and that it would be an immeasurable help to see anything I possibly could.

"Oh, I'm *sure* it will work out," she said in a comforting voice, "And then how lovely that Mrs. von Shouse might be here as well, to show you about!"

There was a pause as I dwelled on that last, remotely ominous possibility; I finished my tea. The clock struck the hour; it was two o'clock.

"It must be a huge responsibility to keep up the house," I said, trying to keep up the conversation even as I continued to glance expectantly at the door.

She nodded self-importantly as she picked up her needlepoint again. "You can't imagine," she said. "Especially in the spring and summer, when the public comes through—the National Trust crowds, you know! It can be very nasty at times. In the old days, Lord Kerrith was always so involved, and it was easier. But now—" She stopped, as if something had just occurred to her. "Have you ever seen the book on the house? The book that Lord Kerrith supervised?"

No, I said, I hadn't. "But you *must!*" she answered, and getting up, she went to a small bookcase, where, from the top shelf, she took out a red leatherbound volume with *Thistleton, The House* inscribed in gilt lettering. "It was written over thirty years ago," she said, handing it to me. "Lord K was always so proud of it."

I turned to the first page, pausing at the photograph on the frontispiece of Lord Kerrith himself as a younger man: not at all the effete visage of the Oxbridge intellectual I had expected. His was a brooding, intelligent face, with a prominent brow and a severe but undeniably sensual mouth—the face of a Victorian explorer at home with the exotic. It was not at all difficult to imagine him as an adventurer, a lover of Joanna, a confidant of Winston Churchill.

I continued to leaf through the chapters, entitled "The history of the house," "The household in the Twenties and Thirties," and "The gardens," until I came to the last chapter, which was written by Desmond Kerrith himself. His epilogue was accompanied by a black-and-white photograph of the household staff, a large and impressive group stiffly gathered on the wide stone steps. I looked at the photograph again, more closely this time, and then looked up at Mrs. Alsop—I had recognized a familiar face in the crowd.

I pointed to a slim, dark-haired young woman in a shapely tweed suit who stood in the front row of the photograph, and asked, "This is Christina von Shouse, isn't it?"

"Oh yes indeed!" she cried with a corroborating glance. "That's Mrs. von Shouse. As a young woman, of course."

"What was her name then, when she was Lord Kerrith's secretary?"

"Christina Assante—that was her maiden name." She leaned forward, confidingly, as if to reveal a piquant bit of gossip that was, I had already sensed, her stock-in-trade. "She was Lebanese—she changed the name a bit, I should think! Life is strange, isn't it? Now she's Mrs. von Shouse, and quite the lady in New York, from what I hear." She made a tiny clucking sound and took another sip of tea before continuing, in a naughty tone, "I'll tell you something else—Lord Kerrith was very sweet on her once. But that was just before he met Joanna Eakins."

"Really?" I remember my heartbeat quickening.

"Oh yes! Well, you see, Lord K was quite the ladies' man in those days. And Mrs. von Shouse—Miss Assante, I should say—was an eyeful then. Quite a bit of goods, she was—" She paused, as if to correct her overfamiliar tone: "Very lively, and very intelligent, of course! *Striking*, you'd say. Lovely figure she had. But then he met Joanna Eakins and fell madly in love with *her*. And the next thing we knew, Miss Eakins was here nearly every weekend, and Lord K himself was spending most of the week in London, watching Joanna Eakins at the theater."

"That must have been hard for Mrs. von Shouse," I said slowly, my stomach constricting. "She must have been jealous."

"You'd think so, wouldn't you?" she replied perkily, oblivious of my change of expression. "But no, my dear, not at all! Miss Assante was quite above that sort of thing. In fact as I remember it, she was so very *helpful* to Joanna Eakins. They became friends almost at once. Miss Assante had always been quite the theater fan, so you can imagine how fascinated she was by Miss Eakins. The two of them would spend time together in that tower" her lacquered fingernail pointed to the landscape outside, "the same tower you see there, at the edge of the maze.

"At one point," she continued, "I believe Miss Assante helped organize Joanna Eakins's household in London—this at Lord K's suggestion, I think—and even her clothes. The sort of domestic things which an actress might not be very good at. And then Miss Assante always had such lovely taste. She was so very organized in that way. Oh no, she wasn't jealous at all." She paused, daintily wiping away some crumbs that had adhered to her bright lipstick. "And then before we knew it, Miss Assante moved to India with her husband. Sent us a lovely engraved announcement card, when she got married, she did. I have it in my scrapbook."

"And Mrs. von Shouse kept up her relationship with Lord Kerrith all those years?"

"Yes—"

"And Joanna Eakins did as well?"

"Yes," she said, placing her folded napkin on the table.

"And you're sure that Mrs. von Shouse said she would be here today—"

"Oh yes, quite sure." A look of consternation crossed her face, "But you won't tell her that I spoiled her surprise, will you?"

"No, no, of course not," I replied, setting down my teacup. I glanced at my watch. "It's getting late," I said impatiently. "When can I see Lord Kerrith?"

"It won't be but a moment, I'm sure," Mrs. Alsop reassured me. "I'll ring them up now and see if he's ready."

Moments later, a nurse in a white uniform appeared and announced in a voice punctuated by a trim, professional smile, "Lord Kerrith is ready to see the young lady now."

A fleeting look of concern crossed Mrs. Alsop's face. "Is he—"

"He's quite well indeed," the nurse replied with a cryptic glance.

"Go ahead then, Miss Rowan," said Mrs. Alsop, standing up. "Just follow Mrs. Keighley. And good luck to you, my dear!"

Through the corridor we walked once more, turning to the right when we came to the end, down another corridor this time, one whose very grandeur indicated we were moving to another, superior part of the house.

At last, after passing through a gallery lined with portraits of frill-collared Elizabethan subjects, we turned to the right, to a vast room streaming with light from an octagonal dome, a room whose painted ceiling of a cerulean sky swirled with ribbons and triumphant roseate cherubs. The marble floor glistened, reflecting the light so brightly that I squinted, the radiance almost obscuring the group gathered at the far end, beneath an immense eighteenth-century battle scene swirling with shields, clouds, and satyrs.

Before it, in a wheelchair, sat an old man half covered by a blue plaid blanket. He was encircled by several women in white—his nurses, I surmised—one of whom was knitting and whose needles made an incessant clicking noise that rent the silence. To one side of this group stood a ruddy-faced young man with a pleasant, eager air.

I stepped forward resolutely, and as I did so, the ruddy-faced young man introduced himself as Edward Percy, the manager of Thistleton. We shook hands and exchanged a few words about my trip.

He led me to the old man; with each step I felt myself struggling to relinquish the image of the younger Kerrith in the photograph.

I extended my hand. His own was soft, babyish, plump, and malleable; willingly, I let it go. The lean nobleman, the adventurer of my romantic imaginings, had been replaced by a round gnomelike creature with a glassy stare and a few wisps of white hair combed across his translucent skull; his face was plump and formless, his skin waxen and tinged with yellow. At once revulsed and mesmerized, I continued to stare at him, trying to perceive in his pitiful bent figure the former lover, the peerless mentor, of Joanna.

At last one of the nurses spoke, a red-haired young woman with a thin Celtic mouth and a voice brimming with the compulsive cheerfulness of those who attend invalids. "We've not had a good day today," she chattered. "Yesterday was lovely, but today not at all. He's been a bit cheeky, I'm afraid."

He continued to stare at me vacantly with watery blue eyes, a stream of saliva dribbling down his chin, which the nurse proceeded to wipe off with ostentatious fastidiousness.

I noticed a few spots of dried food on his tie and the way his blanket-covered legs were doubled up against him, so that his legs appeared stunted; old age had transformed him from titan to dwarf. Meantime, I heard the ceaseless clicking of the nurse's knitting needles.

"Miss Rowan has come to ask you about Joanna Eakins," Edward Percy said in the firm, almost strident voice one would use with a recalcitrant child. "Joanna Eakins," he repeated, nearly shouting.

The old man now appeared to focus on me with an intentness I had not thought possible. "Do you know Joanna?" he barked, eyes narrowing.

"I only met her once."

"What did she say?" he bellowed, turning to Percy, his flaccid cheeks drooping.

"I met her only once," I answered.

"She never visits me now," he barked once again. Then, fretfully, to Mr. Percy: "Does she then, Edward?"

Mr. Percy shuffled his feet. "No, sir, she hasn't come in a long time."

I forced myself to continue, trying not to let my voice belie my despair. "Can you tell me something about Joanna, sir?" I said, approaching Kerrith. "What you remember of her?"

His eyes were blank. "She's living in New York—America."

"I know," I murmured, my eyes catching Mr. Percy's before I continued: "But can you tell me what you remembered of her as a young woman? A young woman?" I remember nearly kneeling at that moment, being almost at his feet.

"Joanna?" he asked again, turning to Percy. "Is she asking me about Joanna?"

Mrs. Keighley, the other nurse, nodded. "Yes, sir. She's asking you about Joanna Eakins." She cleared her throat. "Joanna Eakins Cassel, I should say."

"Cassel?" he asked contemptuously. "Cassel, you say?"

"Did you know David Cassel before she married him?" I ventured.

"Never knew a Cassel," he snarled.

I remember pressing my hand to my face, overwhelmed by a longing to escape. Old age had always terrified me, but never more so than at that moment, when I seemed to be casting my questions into a void.

The clock struck three. "Did you know Joanna?" Lord Kerrith asked me.

"I only met her once," I said dispiritedly. "I'm trying to write a book about her." A pause. "A book about her!" I repeated shrilly, my voice escalating to the near shout the others seemed so accustomed to using.

He tilted back his head in such a way that it led me, for a moment, to hope that he had actually understood my question. His blue eyes appeared focused; his pale, sparse brow furrowed as he gazed at me with seeming clarity and asked: "Are you afraid of going to the unknown?"

I looked down at the floor, clutching my hands, unable to speak. Still struggling to answer his question, I stammered, "The unknown . . ."

He nodded. And then, in a surprisingly strong, even exasperated voice, he repeated, "Are you afraid of going to the unknown?"

I stood up unsteadily, wearily shaking my head before murmuring, almost inaudibly, "Yes."

I heard the shuffling of feet and the coughing of nurses; the clicking of the knitting needles stopped. Edward Percy cleared his throat. "Perhaps we ought to continue another time," he said in a polite, tense voice. "Lord Kerrith does not seem at his best today."

"But how am I to know that tomorrow will be better?" I replied impatiently.

"There *is* no way of knowing." Percy's smile was tight and definitive.

"Then I must try again," I said with renewed determination, as much to myself as to Percy. Kneeling once more and trying to control my frustration, I entreated, "Tell me, Lord Kerrith. Will you let me see the letters Joanna Eakins left you?"

He scrutinized me in such a way I almost thought him lucid. "Only when she's dead," he announced in a suddenly august voice. "Only when she's dead. When the statue is finished—"

I turned to Percy: "The statue? What statue?"

"The statue in the maze—here, at Thistleton," came the abashed answer. "I'm told it was modeled after Miss Eakins. After the war. He has been saying this for some time."

I turned to face Kerrith once more.

"Joanna wanted to wait until she's dead," he said.

"But she *is* dead, don't you see." My voice augmented in pitch and vehemence. "She died a year ago!"

"She never visits me anymore," came the peevish nonsequitur. "Does she then, Edward?"

"She's dead. Don't you understand, she's dead!" I cried.

"I told her she should never go to America," Kerrith said after a moment, woefully shaking his head.

A long pause; the nurses coughed again, and Edward Percy folded his arms.

"Where are her letters, Lord Kerrith?" I asked. "The letters from Joanna—"

"She gave them to Marcus." His expression was blank— like that of a lunatic—and his smile childlike.

I turned to Edward Percy and asked, "Who is Marcus?"

"Marcus Holman. The executor of Lord Kerrith's estate."

"Is it possible he has any letters?"

"It's highly unlikely," replied Percy.

"But can you ask him?" I pleaded.

"I can *ask* anything, Miss Rowan," he replied, visibly restraining his impatience.

"Locked away, locked away—" Kerrith said in a singsong voice. "Locked away—"

"Where is the key?" I nearly shouted. "The key?"

"The key, did you say?" His voice had once more become childlike.

"Yes."

"*You* have the key—the letters are the key," he said in a

strident voice; then, with a demented shaking of his head: "She left the words with you—didn't she, Edward?"

"I don't think so, sir," Percy replied sharply, his hands clutched. And then to me: "I think you will agree, Miss Rowan, that this is a fruitless exercise. Lord Kerrith is not at all what he should be today. I doubt speaking with him will get you very far." He turned to the nurses and, in a brittle voice that seemed to have lowered an entire register, commanded, "Take him away now."

I watched as the old man was slowly wheeled away, followed by the white cortege. The two of us—Edward Percy and myself—were suddenly alone in the echoing, dome-lit chamber, empty now save for a few gilt chairs and the splendid paintings.

"Mr. Percy," I pleaded, turning to face him. "I've come a long way to see Lord Kerrith, to find the letters. I know they're here—here, in the library, just a few steps from this room! You yourself can see that Lord Kerrith is hardly equipped to give me permission or not. There must be someone else who can give me permission. Someone else *must* have that power now—"

We stood together, Edward Percy and I, for many silent moments until he finally conceded with a sigh, "I suppose I could ask Marcus Holman. If it were up to me, I'd simply take you to the library and show you where Lord Kerrith has always kept his correspondence." He paused. "I assume the letters are there, in the box he uses for safekeeping. But I don't have that power, and the person who does—Mr. Holman—is in London. I would have to ring him up."

"Do it, then—now!"

"I can only try." He motioned to me. "This way, please."

I followed him through the same winding, portrait-hung corridor through which we had arrived, returning to the small garden room where I had sat with Mrs. Alsop.

Edward Percy excused himself.

The Victorian clock ticked. Standing by the window, I watched as the last rays of sunlight disappeared from the leaden winter sky, thinking of Joanna and her love affair with the man I had just met: his photograph as a young man came to mind, and the book he had written about his famous house. I thought of the photograph of Christina von Shouse —his secretary then—and the notion that she had been rejected by Desmond Kerrith in favor of Joanna: a younger, more accomplished woman.

Confined in the winter conservatory, I waited endlessly, it seemed, for someone to enter. But no one came. Not Mrs. Alsop, not Edward Percy, not even one of the nurses.

I nervously glanced through magazines, my concentration shattered.

The book on Thistleton drew me again. I went to the bookcase from which Mrs. Alsop had taken it, searching the shelves for the leatherbound volume; but it was nowhere to be found. For a moment I thought a sort of madness had seized me: I began to question my own memory, I wondered whether I had actually seen the book or whether it had been a hallucination.

At last, I heard some footsteps—first from a distance, then approaching close by. I stood up, my heart beating fast.

It was Edward Percy, with the answer.

He told me that Marcus Holman had authorized me to see the letters.

I thanked him with all my heart and asked where we would go next. "I assume they are in the library," I said.

"That is correct," he answered. "This way, then."

We left the garden room, turning down an opulent corridor to the right, until we reached a stupendous wood-paneled library with leather-bound books from floor to ceiling and elegant ladders that crisscrossed the towering stacks; the gilt-inscribed spines, arrayed on the shelves, seemed to emit their own light.

At the far end, before an expanse of leaded windows, stood

an ornate Victorian desk. Edward Percy motioned to me; we walked toward it.

"Here," he said, his fingers pressed against its leather edge. "This is where Lord Kerrith has always kept his private correspondence." He indicated the magisterial red leather box at the far end of the desk that was trimmed with gold ormolu and embossed with the Kerrith crest. Percy took a key from his pocket and proceeded to open it.

"You would like to be alone while you read the letters, I should think," he said quietly.

"Yes," I replied, barely able to speak.

"I will be in my office, to the right of the entrance hall, should you need me."

"Yes of course."

He turned and left, pausing as he reached the red velvet portieres flanking the door. "And if Mrs. von Shouse should arrive?"

"Tell her I'm here, in the library," I replied without thinking.

42

I did not open the box immediately but stood by the desk, gazing out the window across the snow-covered park to the field of topiary pawns and, from there, to the crenellated tower by the ruins in the distance. The silence of the vast house pressed upon me—the silence of the countryside in late afternoon, in winter, in England.

Still gazing at the ravaged landscape, I thought of the winding path, and the obsession, that had led me to this room—against Jack's will, against David Cassel's, against my father's.

"The letters are the key," Kerrith had said in a seeming moment of lucidity. Now the coffer stood before me, its catch unlocked.

I lifted open the lid. Old stage photographs lay on top, tied with a red ribbon, some of them inscribed: Joanna as a white-blond Ophelia, with bodice unlaced and expression of piteous disorientation ("To Desmond—Good my lord, How does your honor for this many a day? Joanna"); the portrait of Joanna as Lady Macbeth—the young, mad creature of the sleepwalking scene. How long I gazed at that harrowing face I do not know; amid the silence of the house, and the recognition of my own aloneness, it seemed to affect me so deeply I had to fight back tears.

More early stage photographs by Angus McBean followed: Joanna as a gaunt Electra in a black robe; as the youthful, storm-tossed heroines of Shakespeare's romances—Perdita in *The Winter's Tale*, and Miranda in *The Tempest*. I had already seen a full-length photograph of Joanna's Miranda in the folder she had left; this was a close-up, however, and infinitely more touching in the radiant, limitless expression of the eyes ("To Desmond—O brave new world, that has such people in it!"). I put the picture down, only to pick it up again before examining the last group of stills—these from the mature roles that marked the end of her career: Hedda Gabler, Antigone, the sensual and hollow-cheeked Cleopatra.

In a plain manila envelope were three personal snapshots: Joanna on safari with a tawny Desmond Kerrith, a shotgun propped between them, a slain lion on the ground. Then the two most searing shots: Joanna arm in arm with Christina, standing at the top of the staircase at Thistleton, dressed as St. Joan and Lady Macbeth ("To Desmond—Remember us, the saint and the madwoman!"); and a snapshot, dated May 1985, of a somber, emaciated Joanna clad in black, standing by the gate to the maze at Wakefield.

I came to the letters themselves and took a deep breath. All were addressed to Desmond Kerrith in Joanna's tall, sloping hand, the envelopes neatly slit open, the writing paper in a spectrum of sizes and colors.

I opened one from the seventies in which she described an

art exhibit with paintings from the Hermitage ("Darling
Desmond, you must come see these splendid paintings at
the Knoedler—especially as we never did take that trip to
Russia together! The Caravaggios alone are worth the visit!
Do think about it and let me know"); then another in which
she spoke of Peter Brook's revolutionary production of A
Midsummer Night's Dream ("Never will the play be the same
to me again—the white clean stage, the marvelous speed
with which the action progresses, leaps rather. This is sheer
brilliance! It makes me wish I were younger, and still acting."); and finally one dated March 1981: "Dearest Desmond
—Write me at once—or ring me up at the very least—to tell
me what you think of The White Hotel. I've had the most
extraordinary dreamlike reaction to it, as if it had infected my
whole consciousness for days. The Jungian images of that
opening chapter seem more than murkily familiar to me. I
cannot shake them from my mind, and long to discuss them
with you—I sense you will understand them as no one else
possibly could."

I continued to search, coming upon a letter in which she
described first seeing Wakefield Hall:

> . . . The property is extraordinary—for the States, that
> is—and I know, with work, that the house can achieve
> my own vision. I've met a young man whose work I've
> admired—his style runs to the neoclassic, yet with its
> own strong stamp. His name is Lawrence Brandt—per-
> haps you have heard of him? He is just beginning to be
> well-known here; I predict he will be among the front
> rank of American architects one day. I think he is
> amused by my romantic attitude toward this house—I
> told him that when I first saw it, I felt like Jane Eyre
> coming upon Ferndean. "Reader, I married him" et al.
> Crazy, I suppose! And yet he did not seem put off by it.
>
> What I would like, darling friend, is something that,
> on a much smaller scale of course, approaches the feel-
> ing of your own heavenly universe at Thistleton—a

world apart, a world far from the slings and arrows of outrageous fortune. There, I am infected by Shakespeare again, you would say! It's true; I realized the other day that the years of my life when my consciousness was guided by his, by Shakespeare's, were among the happiest I have ever known. And yet they changed me, too, in ways I cannot quite articulate. Now that I am no longer his vessel I am reduced to my own words, to my own insufficient voice, and to creating my own house, the walls of which will somehow shield me from the rest. From what? you will ask. From myself, most of all—and my own demons.

Write soon, dear friend—

I paused, the letter still in hand, as I reflected on its last paragraph. "My own demons," she had said; *but what were they, and what had caused them?*

I riffled through the last few letters and opened an envelope postmarked September 10, 1984. It was penned on the writing paper I remembered from the larkspur-blue bedroom at Wakefield, the first sheet engraved with the diminutive, Constable-like rendering of the house itself:

Dearest friend,

There is an awful quiet about this place these days, the spring and summer being the worst time of all. The trees seem to press in on me as I walk, and the shadows cast upon the lawns seem so fathomless I shudder to walk through them. I think, as I do incessantly these days, of my childhood: the inky green and the silence of those woods, and the loneliness of that claustral house; my brother and I alone, always alone, in those bolted rooms. The cold was terrifying, and the walls, with their racks of tinned goods, would shake from the wind.

Even now, as I recall the rage and disorder of that house, I feel my mother's rage, the rage directed toward us for what she herself had not accomplished. This I felt with all the keen egocentric guilt of a child, ready to assume all. It would have been endurable if I had never seen the way other people lived; but when I did, it changed my life. I never wanted to leave other children's rooms—they seemed like heaven!—and yet I never wanted to return, for it was too painful to be acquainted with perfection when I would have to return to the rage and disorder of that house—

Yet now my own house—Wakefield—is in perfect order. There seems nothing left for me to do, and the black depression—blackest of any I have combatted in my life—seems to pursue me so relentlessly that I wonder whether I should not simply give in to it. The mind is its own place, and can make a heaven of hell, a hell of heaven . . . I find myself yearning for that undiscovered country—

My maze is almost finished—thank you, dear heart, for your help. Its octagons refer to Thistleton's, of course—the Soanian domed room I've always loved—but with one crucial difference: your maze has one goddess, and mine has many.

I have chosen my Shakespearean ladies and their quotes with great care—Lavinia, Hermione, and Desdemona in the central row together. It seemed right to me, as silence unites them. Tongueless Lavinia, Hermione trapped in stone, and Desdemona, her voice smothered by the hands of a jealous husband. The two sprightly girls—Viola and Ophelia—share the first octagon; one finds her way, one doesn't. It's only Hermione whom I can't seem to make speak (though Shakespeare could—)

Larry Brandt, puzzled by my new obsession, calls the maze a "monument to my career"—perhaps it's best he think that. It's the mutilation of silence that pursues me, the death-in-life of stage fright. Love, and be silent, she said—

What are the roots of these desperate feelings, you will ask—the slow dissolving of the self, twin-born with

disaffection. They began to close in on me years ago—
after we had come to that decision—worsening with
stage fright; worsening still when David refused to let
me have the child—after he forced me to suppress and
kill that little unknown creature! I told Christina I had
had a miscarriage; little did she know. . . . Even now I
can hardly bear to remember the day when I was
ushered into that white room, gleaming with all the
steely apparatus of clinical death— It breaks my heart to
think of it, and of the emptiness which followed, and
which seemed so much a reverberation of what had
happened years before. It has destroyed my marriage, a
marriage whose foundation was always rooted in the
wrong things anyway, but which might have had a
chance *had he let me have that child*—

He loved me for my fame, and when my fame foun-
dered—why, then, the marriage too was broken all to
pieces. Nor was I blameless in that regard— You, too,
possessed such temporal things, but then you had so
much more! I learned from you, and you from me (in
my small way, I like to think). You taught me about
books, and about paintings; you showed me how to
think—how to enrich the life of the mind—even as you
initiated me into other realms—

This David could not do; I was wrong ever to expect
it. Only now do I truly comprehend the guilty words
from *Macbeth* which I uttered with such conviction as a
young woman. All the perfumes of Arabia cannot
sweeten this little hand, and all the money in the world
cannot replace what I myself abandoned, for everything
that's specious. What's done is done, she would say,
even as the echo returns its fatal version—

As I write to you—dear friend, whom I've not seen for
ten years—my hand trails the paper and my body is
paralyzed with self-loathing. I wonder how I will be able
to live from tomorrow, and tomorrow, to tomorrow—

I put the letter down, unable to shake off its imploring voice—the passionate plea to a cherished friend and former lover whom she had not seen in ten years. "Only later in my life—when we had come to that decision—" What decision did she mean? I thought of Liliane de Morbier and her account of Joanna and the child—

I came to the last remaining sheet—a fragment of another letter, it seemed:

> therefore, keep close to heart what I have asked you— and only show the letter after I am dead and buried. Until then, darling Desmond, not a word, and no talk of where I've left it. *Only you know: The letters are the key.* I *am* maniacally secretive, you have always said—I don't deny it. It's so inured in my being and stems, no doubt, from those hard lessons learned in childhood, the font of all anxiety. I fear David and his capacity for— Never mind, why should I burden you with these things? I have never entrusted anything more precious to anyone than what I have entrusted to you—never has a single thing meant so much. To know that you will be there, to make some sense of it, to corroborate what I have writ-ten—to know that you will execute my final and most important wish—only this has given me some inner peace!

"The letters are the key," she had tantalizingly said . . . I had come all this way and risked so much, but I had come too late! Fighting tears, I rested my face in my hands and thought of my father's death and the words that haunted me —*too late, too late*. Even Desmond Kerrith could not help me now, and Joanna's secret would die with him.

I looked up at the marble bust of Apollo. Its vacant, all-knowing gaze seemed to acknowledge my own desperate feeling of failure.

A ghostly silence had descended upon the house; it seemed as if the inhabitants had fled and I was the only being left. I wondered if and when Edward Percy would return.

I took my coat and walked toward the leaded windows behind the desk, staring at the frozen park beyond—its spidery trees and strange army of topiaries. A clock chimed; wind blew; a door in a distant room closed.

It was then I heard the sound of footsteps approaching.

43

She wore black and stood by the double doors.

"I see you found your way to Thistleton," Christina said, walking toward me. "Mission accomplished." I remember how *mission* reverberated—the same word she had used that summer afternoon. "I suppose I should congratulate you, Elisabeth." She glanced at me, smiling slightly as she placed her red coat on a chair.

I asked when she had decided to come to Thistleton.

"You never told me that Desmond finally answered," she replied, disregarding my question. Her expression was pleasant enough, but her voice, implying she had been responsible for Kerrith's acquiescence, had a chastising edge.

"Your name never came up," I said, aware of the resonance of those words. "The fact that you'd written him . . ."

I wondered whether I was right in discerning fleeting anger in her eyes. "Have you seen Desmond yet?" she asked.

"Yes."

"What did he tell you?"

"Very little."

"It wasn't a good day, I take it." Her tone was ironic.

"No."

She looked at me hard, as if she were trying to decide whether I was telling the truth.

"You must know whatever it is *he* knows," I added after a moment.

"Knowledge is power, after all." Her mouth curved into a small, rebuking smile; I remember how unsettling I found it. "I'm sure you would agree with me, Elisabeth."

Her eyes took in the room; she walked toward the bookcase opposite the fireplace, then to the antique globe before it. The hand with the familiar carnelian ring began to spin the huge, glimmering sphere. "Did you find the letter?" she asked with a nonchalance that seemed rehearsed.

"I found some letters," I replied carefully. "But not *the* letter."

"No?" She seemed surprised, but soon recovered. "Ah well," she said, sighing.

"Why should you care so much?"

"It was—" she paused, looking at me directly, "a way of torturing David and being useful to you at the same time. A way of killing two birds with one stone."

I remember how that expression lingered, recalling Rosalind. "Being *useful* to me?"

"Vis-à-vis your research. So that your portrayal of Joanna would be accurate. Like you, I care about the truth. Deeply."

"So you *used* me to find the letter—"

"The letter was the only thing Joanna ever kept from me. I rather resented it, I suppose—" She gave a sigh, her head slightly tilted.

Moments passed; the room continued to absorb her, even to instill her with a new, palpable energy. She walked past the bookcases, her hand touching the rows of leather spines; next to the bust of Apollo; and finally to the central round library table, which was piled with books and inset with drawers.

"A lovely rent table, isn't it," she said, glancing in my direction as her hand skimmed the drawers. "I remember when Desmond had it moved here from a study upstairs."

"You must know this house very well," I observed, still watching her.

"Yes. In many capacities." She had lingered over each syllable of the last word, as if savoring the full range of its connotations. Then she picked up a book that lay on the table, seeming to peruse its pages. "Why didn't you ever ask me about my relationship with Desmond?"

"The fact that you had worked for him?"

"No," she said patiently enough. "That's not what I meant."

"It didn't seem crucial to the story. To Joanna's story."

"Joanna's story—of course." Another pause. "But you might have asked—unless of course you didn't think it *possible*. That Desmond should have thought of me in that way—" Her mouth had the same fixed, determined look I remembered from the day at the auction, when she had been forced to relinquish her bid. "That Desmond should have been attracted to me—as a *woman*," she reiterated.

"I never focused on it," I answered, knowing this would infuriate her.

"I see."

She approached the desk where I stood. I remember the familiar scent of her tuberose perfume and the glittering panther brooch on the lapel of her suit; but most of all I remember that, for the first time, she looked in disarray—her makeup thick and almost haphazard, her shoes scuffed; a small serpentlike run crept up the back of one of her sheer black stockings.

With a glance at the red leather box, she asked: "The letters—to Desmond?"

"Yes."

"What did she say in the letters? Did she mention me?" she asked eagerly, yet in a way that indicated she did not expect me to answer.

The clock struck four; I would have to bide my time before the crucial questions. "Is the house the way you remember it?" I asked.

"Yes," she replied, her bearing suddenly depleted, "quite." She walked toward the broad expanse of leaded windows, gazing out at the landscape.

A moment passed. She seemed distracted, pacing before the windows, at one point stilling her nervous hands as she continued to gaze outside. I thought of the afternoon in December when we had had tea—the sudden disconcerting changes in her voice and demeanor . . .

"Is that the maze and the tower, by the ruins, in the distance?" I asked, knowing exactly what they were.

"Yes—"

"The tower where you would help Joanna learn her lines?"

"Yes—yes—precisely." There was a new, nostalgic lilt to her voice; she was too inwardly focused for me to guess what she was thinking. "We used to spend much time together there, Joanna and I," she continued in an unfamiliar monotone. "I would help her with her lines. I would teach her about his world—Desmond's world. Desmond had me do it. It would be part of my job he said, one of my duties. To coach her, his new lover, in all the things that mattered so much to him. It was another way of pleasing him. I suppose —showing *her* the way to please him. I would have left him then and there if I hadn't loved him so much—but I *did* love him. I would have given my life for him—" She paused, her eyes heavy-lidded. "I would prompt her for all those roles— onstage, and here, with Desmond, at Thistleton."

She turned to me with the same brisk, conclusive look I remembered so vividly from our first meeting. "You would like to see it, wouldn't you, Elisabeth?" Her eyes assumed a new animation. "The tower?"

"Yes," I said, as if the idea had just occurred to me. "I would—very much."

I gathered my coat and followed her from the library to the great hall, glancing a last time at the quartet of caryatids, then at the staircase where Joanna and Christina had once appeared in costume.

Snow had obscured the twisting path, and the wind had come up; the topiary pawns seemed to shiver with frost. I dug my hands deep into my pockets as we continued on our way.

We approached the half-familiar landscape of the ruins. The stones of the crumbling walls glistened with snow; ice blistered within the cracks. I could barely make out the silhouette of the tower in the distance.

The high hedges of the maze loomed before us.

I turned to Christina: "Do you know if the statue of Athena is still there, inside?"

Her expression was scornful. "There's no reason to believe it isn't."

We crossed the drawbridge over the moat. Such excitement, and yet such apprehension, had come over me that I was hardly conscious of my frozen hands, or cheeks, or feet.

I recognized the door from the photographs Joanna had left—its gothic arch and bold iron fittings. To my astonishment, the latch lifted easily, as if the last visitor had forgotten to secure it. We entered the octagonal stone hall, engulfed in darkness save for a single, flickering lamp. The door shut behind us.

Christina pulled a switch on the right. The light from the wrought-iron chandelier crisscrossed the stone-flagged hall with slanting shadows; three slit-eyed sets of armor, inset on the opposite wall, seemed to glower at our advance.

Two lanterns stood on the table by the staircase; she lit one, handing the other to me. "It will be dark," she said sternly.

The hall was furnished in the late medieval style, with deep heraldic colors and unwelcoming wooden furniture. A tapestry of unicorns and courtly ladies covered the far wall, flanked by a pair of tripod-based torchieres. As in the main house, twin staircases led to the upper floors; here they were fashioned of primitive wood, however, with bannisters of twisted rope. At the bottom of each staircase stood a door.

"You are wondering where the doors lead," Christina observed, in an irritated voice, watching me.

"Yes—"

"That is the door to the maze," she said, motioning to the door opposite, by the bottom of the left staircase. "The other leads to the park, back to the house."

"I should have known," I murmured, thinking of the photographs.

"Yes—you should have known." she replied, a touch of derision in her voice, as if to say: "There are many things you should have known."

We climbed to the first landing, its stuccoed walls stamped floor to ceiling with a pattern of red-and-gold escutcheons. I remember the sight of our lean, looming shadows as we ascended the precarious steps—how frightening they looked, like advancing phantoms, and how they seemed to spark a host of lurid fantasies (I would fall; Christina might push me . . .).

We came to the second landing and, finally, to the third and last landing, from whose mullioned windows I gazed at the panoramic view of Thistleton park and its follies: the Roman temple; the rotunda of the chapel; and directly below, to the east, the meandering outline of the maze.

The narrow corridor led to an arched door at the far end. We walked toward it; Christina turned the handle.

We entered the tower-library. The room was austere, its imperfect multipaned windows set into stone, its timbered ceiling stamped with the same heraldic pattern of the staircase. Rough-hewn bookshelves lined the walls; a Jacobean desk stood before the main window facing the moat.

Christina took off her coat, watching as I approached the far window. A box of matches lay by the hearth of the deep stone fireplace; she took one and struck it, lighting the pair of torches by the door. The reflections of the flames undulated upon the vaulted ceiling.

She returned to the fireplace, knelt down, and lit the kindling. I remember the sudden surge of warmth and how it drew me—the cold was insidious, and my hands were still frozen. I stood awhile by the fire with her, watching her face, wary of her mercurial moods, as I planned my next question.

I noticed a large antique trunk below a nearby window. "That's the trunk, isn't it—the trunk where Joanna kept her costumes?"

"Yes," she murmured with a queer smile of delight as she walked toward it. Kneeling on the floor, she lifted the latch of the concave, iron-hatched lid and began to rifle through its contents: doublets, gowns, coronets, and wigs lay within. "This is where Joanna kept her old costumes—the crown, the intertissued robe of gold and pearl, she would say. Sometimes I would come up here by myself, when she was gone. I'd try them on—" Her eyes at once feverish and childlike, she held up a gown of scarlet linen, embroidered with a turquoise collar. "This she wore for Cleopatra"—she struck an imperial stance—" 'Give me my robe, put on my crown, I have immortal longings in me. . . .' Lovely, those words, no? And this"—she held up a brown laced doublet—"this for Rosalind, I think. And this"—a flash of purple—"this for Medea. And this"—layers of black, together with a long, disheveled wig—"this for Lady Macbeth." She folded the costumes and put them away, one by one. The trunk thudded shut.

She rose to her feet, her stare intense and yet unfocused,

extending her arms in the grandiose manner of a performer taking a curtain call, before she gave a deep bow. Her voice had altered, had become curiously matter-of-fact, though her eyes had once again assumed a disturbing brilliance.

She began to pace before the trunk, clutching and unclutching her hands, as if her entire being were electrified by the memories unleashed by this room. "I would prompt her for all the parts I could never play myself," she began in a bizarre, rapid voice, "Except here, in the tower. Here they rightfully belonged to me. *No one*—not even Joanna—loved those words, loved Shakespeare, as much as I did—

"I was Lady Macbeth here, you see, and Desdemona, and Iago too, and Cleopatra once." Her voice took on a new, unnerving lilt: "Such a splendid ruthless part, Cleopatra—so *Italianate*. You *must* seduce him as you do the audience, I said to her. We were talking about Antony. Yes—I will eat no meat, I'll not drink, sir—I'll not sleep neither. . . . 'Was she anorectic, Tina, do you think?' I remember she asked me that. 'What an odd question,' I said. The death scene always terrified her—the asp at her breast. She never got it right, at least *I* never thought so—"

Christina returned to the trunk, once more sifting through the costumes. "We rehearsed Ophelia together here, as well," she said, staring at me as she held up a gossamer white bodice. " 'As one incapable of her own distress.' Lovely, that description, isn't it? Quite unthinkable, that summing-up in the Olivier film: 'A tragedy about a man who could not make up his mind!' 'The secret is that *he hates his mother*,' Joanna said; 'he cannot reconcile himself to the fact that he sprang from this lustful adulteress.' Joanna was touching as Ophelia, but never totally successful as the queen. As Hamlet's mother. I would have been much better—she even told me so. '*You* should be playing this part, Tina,' she said. Yes, I was very good as Gertrude." She looked at me with an unexpectedly sprightly glance: "Would you like to hear me recite her lines?" Assuming a woeful stance, and speaking with majestic diction, she began to recite the speech where Gertrude describes the mad Ophelia's death:

There is a willow grows aslant a brook
That shows his hoar leaves in the glassy stream
There with fantastic garlands did she come
Of crowflowers, nettles, daisies and long purples,
That liberal shepherds give a grosser name
But our cold maids do dead men's fingers call them.

"How beautiful, how sublime," she continued, resuming her own voice. "How long ago it seems—how full of promise my life then. How *hopeful*—" She turned to me again, her eyes with the deadened look of a sleepwalker, before giving a deep sigh that seemed to signal the return to her previous self.

"It must have been difficult for you to watch," I said, my eyes never wavering from her face. "Always to be there, standing in the wings, when you loved Shakespeare so much, when you knew all those parts—"

"You would have thought she would have been grateful, wouldn't you?" she asked with sudden, hostile vehemence. "I was the only steady thing in her life. 'You're such a rock, Tina,' she'd say to me, 'So *selfless*.' I *was*, I suppose—but she never appreciated any of it. I organized her life. I got her through the stage fright. I taught her how to approach those parts, the great parts, in an original way. How to *think* well. How to analyze character and motivation. I brought order and discipline to her life. She never had any real discipline you know—without me she would never have achieved anything." She stood up, twisting her hands together as she paced back and forth from the hearth to the trunk.

Watching her, and fighting apprehension, I carefully chose my words: "It seems to me—from everything I've been told—that Joanna was a good and loyal friend to you."

Christina turned to me with a tight, disconnected smile: "Does it then, Elisabeth? Of all the observations you've made, *that* is the most naive of all—" Her laugh was harsh, her voice contemptuous: "What could you *possibly* know about it?"

I knew I had to hold steady, to keep probing, if I was ever to know the truth about their "friendship." "It must have been amusing for you to have watched me go about the research," I said. "Planting the idea about the copy of the letter—the last letter to David—when you knew all along it would probably never be found."

She smoothed a dark curl about her ear, her voice deliberate, her eyes cool and assured—the polished woman I remembered meeting that first July afternoon. "We all have our weaknesses. Even you, Elisabeth—it's not every girl who takes up with a married man, is it, then? Not exactly something to be proud of—"

"You speak from experience, after all," I replied angrily.

"That goes without saying. I told you that first day—I am a *collector* of life experience."

"You invented the story about the copy of the letter, didn't you? *Was* there a letter?"

Her glance was evasive. "A letter, yes . . ."

"You knew about me, about Jack. You invited me to your dinner knowing full well he'd be there—"

"You never asked."

"And then you changed the place cards, didn't you, so that I would be seated next to Jack, so that I would be sure to be humiliated . . ."

Her eyes confirmed my accusation.

"Why would you take such pains?" I asked, moving toward her. "What was in it for you, Christina?"

"Because it mattered to Joanna so much—" came her harsh reply. "That you portray her the way she wanted. That you present her in the right light, for posterity. It was the only thing she ever cared about: her career, her reputation, her fame—"

"You must have been very jealous of her to have taken such trouble. Jealous of her fame, her acting, her lovers . . ."

She turned to me with a look I shall never forget—never had I realized with such terrifying certitude that *rage will out*. "She was the most selfish, spoiled, narcissistic creature I have ever known, remarkable for one thing only—her monumental self-absorption." Her slow, implacable coldness gave way to fury. "Playing still another role until the day she died —that of the abused wife and tortured artist! She cared for *nothing* but herself. Even after her death she could not rest content. She could not die without inflicting pain upon everyone else. Without controlling everyone from beyond the grave—*you*, most of all! Even when she no longer had the pleasure of witnessing her treasure hunt—"

She seemed to collect herself and walked to the mantelpiece, her hand incessantly stroking the stone. The next moment, as if possessed by new determination, she began to walk toward me, only to stop abruptly, as if her thoughts had been arrested in mid-flight. "She ruined my life," she said, turning to face me with disarming calmness. "She destroyed everything I had ever loved, took from me everything I ever wanted—

"First Desmond she took from me—how disdainful she was when she came to Thistleton and met me. What lust she feigned for him when she never cared for him an instant, when she simply *used* him, as she had used everyone else. How she played up to him—Galatea to his Pygmalion, another role to win another rich man. How contemptuous she was that I, his mistress, should have been his secretary— when *she* was an actress, an artist! What was she, after all, that she should have been so proud—did you ever know the wretched family she came from? Did you ever see her mother —a vile, common alcoholic? And her talent—what of that? Her talent never sustained itself, it never grew, it spent itself in her greater talent—her talent for destruction. She made Desmond ashamed of his love for me, she made him feel that I was beneath him. Beneath his dignity—*infra dig*, she would say, in that haughty way of hers—

"And then she married David Cassel. You would have

thought, wouldn't you, that she would have owed me one then, that she would have helped me. With money, if nothing else. I introduced them, after all. I *arranged* that marriage. I helped her with all the frivolous things that mattered so much to her, the things for which she had tossed away her career and whatever talent she had: the house, the furniture, the clothes, the jewels. All the things for which she had no intrinsic taste, no refinement—only lust for the things money could buy. It was the only time Joanna felt any lust— for money, for acquisition. Her lust was never for men. She never liked men. She laughed at them behind their backs, even when she had just come from making love to them. 'Men,' she said to me once, with a laugh. 'They're so completely unaware of their own absurdity.' She *used* men again and again and again. For money. As a game. Like the chess she loved to play for hours and hours. But no—when I needed money, the two of them, David and Joanna, made me grovel for it. Made me feel beholden to them. Another of their sycophants." She paused, the sturdy hand with the carnelian scarab ring touching her throat. "But that was not enough for Joanna—no. Even that was not enough."

She took a deep breath, before her voice lowered in pitch. "Then, out of sheer malevolence, out of envy, she took hold of the one thing I had which she did not—*my child*. She killed the one being who made my life worth living—my daughter, my Alexandra."

Her daughter, her daughter, I remember chiding myself. I had followed all the obvious insinuations she had so carefully planted yet had quite disregarded the one skein that had seemed, until that moment, nearly superfluous: the death of her daughter.

"She led Alexandra on. She encouraged her to become an actress when it suited her," Christina continued. "But when it seemed Alexandra might surpass her own achievements, Joanna told her that she hadn't the 'fortitude' to become a great actress. She shouldn't have any 'illusions', she said. 'If I was cruel, it was only to be kind,' she told me. Even then the words had to come from Shakespeare!

"Two months later, my daughter killed herself—dead at Wakefield, in the same room where you stayed, the blue room upstairs! *The memory of that morning will never let me rest.*" She nodded her head. "I could not wake her up. I could not wake her up, her head upon the pillow—" She paused, eyes stunned, as if still clutched by the trauma of that discovery. "My child, my little girl—You cannot imagine what I have endured, you cannot imagine what it is to lose a child . . ." She looked away, her eyes welling with tears; only the most inhuman creature would not have felt her pain. I knelt down by the fire, shaking, holding my face in my hands.

She continued, her voice newly resolute: "But even then Joanna was not satisfied! The guilt she should have assumed herself she inflicted on me instead. She implied I had failed as a mother. She blamed me implicitly for my daughter's death. I wanted to kill myself, you know—I wanted to kill Joanna—

"Then, one morning several months after Alexandra's death, we were in the chapel at Wakefield together. The morning they had come to install the portrait bust of Alexandra, the memorial that was Joanna's idea, as if it could possibly compensate for what she had done! It was there, in the chapel, that she told me in her twisted way, trying to appear sympathetic I suppose, that the first child she had lost—years ago in Scotland—was not stillborn. She had abandoned the child, her child with Desmond." She turned to me with a savage, taunting stare. "Did you know that, Elisabeth?"

"Yes."

"And will *that* be in your book—or isn't that in keeping with the pretty picture you intend to paint?"

"I told you long ago," I said wearily, standing up. "I only want it to be truthful."

"Then we have that in common, Elisabeth," came her sardonic reply. "I too want it to be truthful: the mirror up to nature, didn't you once say? The idea that I should disencumber Joanna's biographer of illusion, as she did my own Alexandra—that has been one of the few joys of my existence." She drew herself up in a rigid position: "How naive you were—how *little* you know of life!"

"Time is on my side . . ."

"I, too, have time. A lifetime of *nothing* but time." She took up her red coat, stopping by the arched doors to face me. "And I promise you this, Elisabeth. One day I will find Joanna's child and tell that child what she was really like—not the misunderstood heroine of your imagination, but a greedy, calculating monster, incapable of love or any human feeling!"

I heard her descend the steps; then the clanging shut of a door. I walked to the far window and watched as she slowly made her way through the park. It was snowing; the paths were white; and the only touch of color was Christina's coat.

The red coat was no more. I turned from the window and sat down listlessly at the writing table, burying my head in my hands. Exhaustion overwhelmed me. Each muscle felt inflamed; my head throbbed.

With every gust of wind I looked up anxiously at the door, fearful that Christina would re-enter: the strange, multivoiced creature I had just confronted, draping herself in Joanne's costumes as she recited borrowed lines. She would prompt Joanna for all her roles—for those onstage, and those here, with Desmond Kerrith, at Thistleton; no one loved Shakespeare as she did. . . .

I only wanted to know the truth, I had told her; yet I had never dreamt the truth would be so wrenching. . . .

Christina had succeeded in her revenge: She had destroyed the Joanna of my imagination—the haunted face of the pavilion; the touching voice of the letters; the tormented artist described by Patrick Rossiter. In her place was a greedy, ruthless creature: demon more than goddess; a Medusa—

For this monster I had risked my job, my reputation; I had disregarded my father's final wish. All this—for what? To portray a woman so manipulative she had planned every detail of her posthumous biography from beyond the grave, controlling her biographer as she had controlled her husband, her lovers, the daughter of her "friend"; a woman wholly obsessed with her fame. Using me as she had used them—

A sense of loss and self-hate came over me; then resentment, aloneness and despair. I stood up and walked to the window, looking across the frozen moat before I turned the latch and pushed the window open, feeling the ice-cold air upon my face. My hand upon the windowsill, I gazed at the icy ring below, surrendering to a morbid set of calculations— how far the jump, how deep the moat, how thick the surface of the ice, what shape the body would imprint upon it . . .

I turned away and closed the latch.

Outside, the light had begun to wane. It was very cold. I approached the fire to warm my hands; the height and acrid color of the flames had subsided.

The three stags' heads mounted on the stone wall above the mantel stared at me with curiosity, even triumph. I thought of Kerrith—a shrunken old man in elegant captivity —and the futility of our meeting. What nonsense he had spoken . . . The letters were locked away, he had said; but he was incoherent. *You* have the key he had said. The letters are the key. *She left the words with you.*

I gave a deep sigh, gathered my coat, and began to put it on; a last glance at the stags' heads. "The trophies of my lovers gone," a phrase from Joanna's sonnet, came back to me. Another tantalizing fillip she had strewn in my path, and which now only sparked my anger.

I took the sonnet from my coat pocket and held the parchment by the fire, hoping the flames would leap up and destroy it. A chapter closed, a road not taken—

"The letters are the key," Kerrith had said; but I had never found the letter. I gazed at the poem once more, seeing words less than the calligraphic pattern of black and gold pen strokes . . . It was in that drifting moment of submerged thought—the very instant when I was about to put the sonnet away—that I looked again at the column of thick raised gold; in that hallucinatory second, the first letter of each line glimmered, then surged into a single vertical motion, as if forged into three words by the light:

Excuse not silence so, for't lies in thee
Look in thy glass, and tell the face thou viewest
I may not evermore ackowledge thee,
Since brass, nor stone, nor earth, nor boundless sea
Accuse me thus, that I have scanted all.
But then begins a journey in my head
Even in the eyes of all posterity.
Those lines that I before have writ do lie
Hung with the trophies of my lovers gone,
Making a famine where abundance lies.
Yet this shall I ne'er know but live in doubt;
O let my books be then the eloquence
Whose speechless song, being many, seeming one,
No more be grieved at that which thou hast done.

"Elisabeth my own" read the acrostic. "Elisabeth my own." I reread the three words again and again, as if uncertain that Elisabeth was my own name. But it was; she had included the sonnet in the folder to me, the biographer; she had asked David specifically that I write the book. "Her final wish," he had told me. What had she meant—that I, the biographer, was *her own?* Was this mocking message her final clue—a way of showing that she had succeeded in controlling me?

I stood utterly still, hardly breathing; the room and everything in it had vanished; time halted; I was trembling . . . I dared not arrive at the conclusion—I fought it—that the other self had already grasped . . .

In the mind's eye of that intuitive self, the sonnet merged with my father's last letter—suddenly his rigid, punishing disapproval of my decision to write Joanna's story assumed a new meaning. "*Now I fear for you,*" he had written with an oddly impassioned vehemence. What had prompted that seemingly irrational fear—was it the fear of a discovery, the fear of a revealed secret?

Then a stroke had felled my father's voice, and he had died and left me alone, unable to tell me the truth himself. "I wish I could speak," he had rasped to the nurse. "I need to speak with my daughter!" What would he have told me had I not arrived too late? What would he have said to his only child, his daughter?

I sat down, still holding the sonnet. She had chosen the Elizabethan style, not the Italian. She collected miniatures of Elizabeth R, Elizabeth Regina, Rosalind had told me, Elisabeth Rowan, that first day. The folder to me, the "biographer"; the octagons that led to Thistleton; the maze at Wakefield, with its carefully charted path to the center . . . Again and again I asked myself *why*: why this labyrinthine way, and was it out of kindness or cruelty?

I sat down by the hearth, thinking of the details of my birth and upbringing: my father's reluctance to discuss the details of my birth or to speak of my mother—a silence I had always attributed to trauma and grief. The lack of my birth certificate, which my father had explained as the result of a fire that had occurred when I was three, and which had destroyed his early papers and memorabilia.

And then I thought of my father's family, and my aunts, and the strained silence that invariably accompanied my questions about my mother. I had assumed they had not liked her . . .

My father's character, certain of its traits—now these, too, came back to me: his love of Shakespeare; the silence that greeted me when I told him, on the telephone from boarding school one day, that I had bought a record of Joanna Eakins as Electra—how I wished I'd seen her in that role! I had asked him if he had ever seen Joanna Eakins onstage. Only once, in *Macbeth*, he had replied with a strange brusqueness. I asked him to describe her performance, and remembered how he faltered, strangely inarticulate for a man whose verbal ability was formidable.

I had chosen not to listen to him. I had gone to Wakefield that June afternoon instead, drawn to the house and its maze. "A monument to her career," Larry had called it; yet I had rightly sensed the maze was much more—a message to me, her biographer, Elisabeth her own . . .

I knelt by the trunk and opened its lid. The costumes lay inside, emitting the pungent scent of lavender. With each gown, each doublet, each cape, each crown, I thought of the statues in her maze. In the light of the sonnet, each quote she had chosen assumed a chilling resonance: Lady Macbeth's woeful, guilty "What's done is done"; Ophelia's cryptic " 'Tis in my memory locked / And you yourself shall keep the key of it." . . . I held a crown in my hands, thinking of Lady Macbeth, then of Hermione—silent Hermione, the wronged queen, the role that had frightened Joanna more than any other, the role that had triggered the final siege of stage fright. She had no quote, strangely; the mother trapped in stone, only to come alive in the last act. "Shakespeare made her speak," Joanna had written; but she, mute and verseless, could not.

There came a moment when even my anguish and confusion seemed spent, when my bewilderment and anger gave way to pity for them both. For Joanna, pursued by her own demons; for my father, who had loved me so and whose love —and that I never questioned—lay at the root of his fear that I should write Joanna's story.

I closed the trunk and walked to the window, pierced by regret at that moment, more than confusion or anger—the regret that I had never really known the man who was my father or the woman who was my mother. Nor had I ever known Joanna: I had seen her for a few minutes, in the pavilion—

Only the statue of Athena, sculpted in her likeness, had survived; the image of Athena from a childhood book that had pursued me since the first visit to Wakefield—Athena bursting fully armed from her father Zeus' skull. She had not left that photograph—only a motto: "Fate finds a way."

I would go into the maze and find Joanna as a young woman; from Athena I would know the truth.

A fine, dry snow was falling, a scrim through which I passed; the full moon flooded the sky with opaline light. I crossed the drawbridge, holding tight to the lantern I had taken from the tower. I came to the high Palladian gate and found it opened easily.

I had entered the silvery underworld of Thistleton—its delphic silence and ghostly lavender light. No order here; yet no terror, either. The unruly hedges did not seem as high, nor as daunting, as those at Wakefield. I wondered why; I had expected them to be treacherous.

I arrived at what seemed the central path to the interior, its wintry carpet dusted with hoarfrost. A pair of urns, one tilted, one cracked; cold had been the culprit. A bench, abandoned . . . skeletons of flowers no longer in bloom but possessed, even so, of an eerie wintry beauty: tall stalks of yarrow, their crowns glistening with frost.

The light of the lantern flickered. I turned down a path wider than its offshoots and walked past a border thick with sleeping flowers, now shivering and silver. I thought I discerned a shadowy figure rising from a pedestal; I ran toward it, my heartbeat quickening at my first sight of the Athena— the only aspect of the maze she had kept from me.

There she stood—lonely, apart. She wore a helmet and a shield, the aegis, carved with coiled serpents. I gazed at the lifelike stone girl, reaching up to touch her tunic, her spear, her shield, half expecting her lips to part in speech, imagining in my delirium that she had come alive to clasp her arms about me. Her eyes, focused and yet unreachable, stared at me—the same expression I remembered from the moment Joanna had awakened. That day she had spoken to me; now I *had come too late.*

I knelt down and placed my frozen hands on the pediment: "Speak to me!" I cried, with all the pain and despair I remembered from my father's deathbed. He could not speak then; nor now could she . . .

The last rays had disappeared; the statue's face was barely visible. She had left me the sonnet, her eyes seemed to say: three words, *Elisabeth my own*, created from all of Shakespeare's. I continued to gaze at the stone face, to circle her, to implore her for the truth. I thought of the path that had taken me to this forsaken place; then—with bewilderment and anger—at the clues she had provided: "If I was cruel, it was only to be kind." What *was* she then—tender muse or inhuman creature? I turned away in rage.

The silence and mauve light brought to mind the abbey at Solesmes and its bittersweet moment of truth and recognition. I took a step, then another, realizing only at that moment the hard truth of my journey: The maze she had created—the maze that had ensnared me—had also set me free.

I returned a last time to the Athena. In that moment her silent, knowing smile seemed to merge with a succession of other faces: that of the figure awakening in the pavilion; of wistful Hermione before the weeping mask fountain; of silent Lavinia; of Joanna; of my mother.

Epilogue

Three years have passed since that day at Thistleton, time enough for pain to yield to forgiveness and compassion. How fateful and ironic, in retrospect, the motto of that English house: "Understanding is the reward of knowledge." Even now I marvel how completely the shock of that realization, once so intense, has been obliterated— like the pain of childbirth which, I am told, is finite and forgotten.

Indeed, the discovery that Joanna Eakins was my mother seems less startling to me now than the subsequent realization, which dawned on me months afterward, *that I had actually known it all along.*

Now it is springtime—late afternoon on the last Saturday

of May—and the view from my window is one of lawn, lilacs, trees, and water, of newly planted pear trees and rose bushes about to bloom. How far away New York seems at this moment—how remote that venal atmosphere of rumor and darkly charted ambitions, how lacking in allure my life with Jack, how distant the world of David Cassel and Christina von Shouse.

The light is still radiant and the house tranquil as I finish my day's work. Before me lies the swelling manuscript of my new biography—a life of Mary Shelley—and, in a nearby cabinet, all the folders, notes, and transcriptions for the book on Joanna.

Only yesterday an auction catalog sent by Russell Heywood brought me back to that extraordinary year of awakening: "Furniture and Works of Art from the Collection of Christina von Shouse," it proclaimed. On its cover, that memorable Russian table, supported by three marble sphinxes; within its glossy pages, all the effects of her apartment I remember so vividly, now wrested from their setting and entombed by the light of a studio: the diminutive statue of Peter the Great, the sketches of the tsar's villa at Tsarkoye Selo, the malachite inkwell, the set of imperial porcelain. The secret life of objects, indeed—

I often recall our meetings in that drawing room—Christina leading me through Joanna's life with her layered glances and recollections, and our final confrontation in the tower when she claimed her dead friend's roles and costumes —the descent into Joanna's selves, the descent into Shakespeare. Only later did I realize that the bizarre shifts in Christina's voice and bearing—from grandiosity to despair, from manic excitement to listlessness—were symptoms of breakdown, of illness.

Christina von Shouse has moved to London—a recluse, from all accounts. The few who have seen her say she is being treated intermittently at Maudsley, the psychiatric hospital; her collection is being sold to pay her bills. In the grip of her psychosis, she is said to assume not only Joanna's persona but the roles she once played, continually repeating entire passages, entire scenes, word-perfect. At such moments her only lucid speech is, in fact, Shakespeare's; nothing else she mutters makes sense.

A pitiful end, indeed, for the self-possessed woman I remember meeting that summer afternoon! The transcription of that conversation lies here, on my desk, together with a framed copy of the sonnet and my book on Joanna, which was published last year.

I never returned to see Desmond Kerrith after our meeting (though his question—"Are you afraid of going to the unknown?"—continued to haunt me). It still astounds me to think he was my real father; and that, even so, I should have virtually no feeling for him. After the manuscript was completed—in May 1988—I merely sent him a copy of the galleys with a note, knowing he was not equipped to read them.

The following week I received a call from Marcus Holman, the executor of Kerrith's estate, in London. Mr. Holman asked to see me immediately; he had a letter for me, he said. I asked him to send it; he said no, that was impossible. He would come to New York to deliver it himself. I asked—unnecessarily, I realize now—whom the letter was from. It was from Joanna Eakins, he told me. She had entrusted it to him the last summer of her life, with this provision: that I be given the letter five years after her death or immediately following the completion of the manuscript—whichever came first.

I met the august Mr. Holman—a white-haired gentleman with a noble voice—on a windy March day, at my apartment. How, now, to describe the moment when he handed me a thick white letter addressed "To Elisabeth Rowan" in black ink; the moment when I first saw my name written in her hand; the moment when I ran my finger across the red wax seal embedded with a swirling *J*—

The *J* split in two as I opened the envelope:

Elisabeth, my own—

The time has finally come for me to speak, if only I can find the courage. Know that I ask for your understanding, dearest Elisabeth—not your forgiveness!—as I set down the words I have spent a lifetime avoiding—

I conceived you; I bore you; four days after your birth, I abandoned you.

Not a single day, not a single hour, has passed that I have not been haunted by your face, your name, the memory of your birthday; when I have not thought of that irrevocable moment when I clasped the charm bracelet around your wrist. Know that I have suffered, know that I have endured a lifetime of hellish silence even as I tried to create my spotless heaven at Wakefield Hall! Not a day has passed when I have not asked myself, *why?* Just as you must now, with rightful hurt and indignation—

For my career, I told myself at first, the career to which I clung, thinking that without it *there was no one in me*. A child would threaten that monstrous side that longed only to create, that only existed when mirrored by an audience. I could not live the way my mother had; I feared it.

And so I gave you up on the seventh of March, four days after your birth. Desmond knew your adoptive parents; it was he who arranged it, but I who struck this bargain—Norman and Claire Rowan would never disclose I was your mother, nor would they ever acknowledge our having met.

Two years later Claire died; Desmond and I were no longer lovers; and Norman and I were left, alone, on each side of the Atlantic—he with my child, I with his letters describing you. I would write him and ask if I might read the stories you had written; I asked what you were like and which books were your favourites; I asked to see your handwriting, I asked about your voice. To my letters and questions Norman responded with all the compassion he had always shown—never doubt how much he loved you!

The years passed, and as they passed, I would say to myself: this year I will meet Elisabeth, this year I will tell her, this year I will beg her forgiveness. But it was always the idea of facing your rightful anger which terrified me. Only a child who had suffered as I had could so have dreaded the anger and hurt of her own—

I married David. I tried to content myself with other people's children—with Alexandra, the daughter of Christina von Shouse. But that, too, only ended in trauma—the unimaginable morning of her suicide—and, with it, a new terror: the realization that truth can destroy, as well as illuminate, and that surviving it is, to a great extent, a question of one's mettle.

Toward that end I would test you: if you could see me as *I really was*, if you were strong enough to find your way through the labyrinth of my life, then you could withstand the bitter truth.

I asked David that you be my biographer. (I wanted you to know, yet was afraid for you to know; this seemed the safest way). I knew that whatever had happened between David and myself—and I was never blameless in that regard—he would be decent enough not to deny my last wish. Time was running out.

I set about to leave you clues; all would lead from Wakefield Hall to Thistleton, from my later years to the roots of my career and my first great love, in England. Still fearing these were not enough, I decided to create the sonnet—it seemed appropriate to use Shakespeare's words when my own were insufficient.

Then—only this past June—you appeared in the pavilion. I had known the day would come, had always known it was inevitable, like the lover's pinch of Cleopatra, which hurts and is desired. There you stood as I awakened, your blue eyes and clear voice so like your father's; and never had my talent as an actress come into play as it did then, as I fought against revealing my own shame and heartbreak. Cowardice and self-loathing only intensified my last, and perhaps my most chilling performance—

Now the day is yours. Be to your own child what I could not be to you; know that it is possible for mother-hood and the interior self to coexist, and that you will be the richer for it—

Darling Elisabeth, my hand falters—I fear my voice will fail me—*I beg your understanding one last time*—

Promise me this:

Go to the statue of Athena at Thistleton and see the hopeful young woman I once was—

Grant my Hermione her words. Make her speak those five lines of the fifth act, as I could not—

Know yourself, as I never did!

Remember me—

                                                            Joanna.

I held the letter, weeping. To see, in her hand, and to hear, in her voice, all that I had intuited from my long journey filled me at once with inexpressible sadness and bittersweet relief. Again and again I read the letter, poring over her words, touching her handwriting, listening to her plea for forgiveness, even as I grappled with my own maelstrom of emotions. . . . Bequeath to death your numbness, for from him dear life redeems you—a line from *The Winter's Tale* . . .

I looked up at Marcus Holman and asked if he had known the truth.

"Yes," he replied quietly. "It was I who arranged the adoption."

I walked to the window, fighting tears. Moments passed. I asked how the letter had come to Marcus Holman; how and when she had left it with him.

"It was in early July, in London—the last year of her life," he told me. "She looked quite unwell. It was something of a shock to see her; I had known her for such a very long time, after all—since *Macbeth*, since those early days with Desmond. She told me she had something precious to give me— something more important than anything she had ever entrusted to anyone before. She told me what it was—the letter —and asked that I promise to be here, with you, when you opened it. Then she said . . ."

He hesitated; I begged him to go on.

"She said that knowing I would be here with you when you read the letter was the only thing that gave her peace—'I have never known such peace before,' she told me with a sad smile." He looked at me with his wise, furrowed face: "She had me promise that would I answer *all* your questions."

My questions! During the past several years I had done nothing but ask questions, as I continued to decipher all the clues she had so meticulously left—the Elizabethan miniatures, the portraits of Elizabeth Regina, many inscribed with "ER," my own initials; the numbered references—play, act, scene, line—to Elizabeth in Shakespeare; the sequence of turns to the center of the Wakefield maze—3, 3, 5, 5—the numbers of my birthdate . . .

"The only questions that remain are unanswerable," I finally told him.

"Yes. Of course—that is only to be expected."

We shook hands; he embraced me; we parted.

I went to see David Cassel not long afterward, with a copy of the galleys. The rooms of his apartment were filled with early spring flowers, just as they had been decked with Christmas greens that December day. The same butler greeted me; the same *quattrocento* paintings followed my progress from the walls—their expressions less inscrutable this time; and David Cassel himself, looking considerably more feeble, sat in the same armchair in the coffered library. ("How's life treating you, Elisabeth?" he growled again.) Rosalind, severe in a perfect beige suit, stood beside him. The two of them looked exceedingly tense, as if they were steeling themselves for another confrontation with the biographer.

First, I told them what I had discovered—the riddle of the sonnet, and the arrival of the letter from England. David's eyes appeared almost childlike in their shock, eerily reminding me, at that instant, of Desmond Kerrith. As for Rosalind—only fleetingly did I detect a trace of emotion in her eyes: Was it fear, perhaps, that I might lay claim to Joanna's estate and to Rosalind's beloved Wakefield Hall? The next instant, when I announced I had no desire to claim any of Joanna's property, I noticed her relax.

In a quavering voice, David said: "You know, Elisabeth, I never meant to hurt you. But you've got to understand— Joanna meant so much to me! More than anyone will ever know. My only desire was to fulfill her last wish."

"Her last wish"—the echo of those three words! I told him that Joanna had left me with a last wish as well, and that it was partly in order to fulfill it that I had come to see him.

"Ask away," he said at once.

I explained the reason for the incomplete statue of Hermione, why Joanna could never bring herself to utter those five lines of the fifth act—the same lines from *The Winter's Tale* I had chosen for the epigraph of the book. I asked that they be carved upon Hermione's pedestal at Wakefield.

"Tomorrow," he said. "Just tell me what they are."

I did not need to read them. I had recited them to myself so many times it seemed they were my own:

> You gods, look down,
> And from your sacred vials pour your graces
> Upon my daughter's head! Tell me, mine own,
> Where hast thou been preserved? Where lived? How found
> Thy father's court?

He bowed his head. Rosalind looked away, clutching her hands. Only after many moments did we continue to speak.

Finally, I approached Cassel to say goodbye; for many moments he held my hands in his. Wordlessly, we said farewell.

Rosalind escorted me to the entrance hall, past the winding staircase into the foyer. I remember the reflection of her strict, seraphic profile in the mirror as she pressed the elevator button—how it inexplicably brought to mind the day at the Harvard Club, the day she had forced me to confront the truth about Jack . . .

"Let's try to get together one of these days," she said, in the way that people do when they know such a meeting will never come about.

"Yes, let's," I replied, my thoughts wandering to our first meeting. How imperious she had been, how forbidding; how strangely skittish and unsure of herself now.

"The day we went riding," I asked. "The jump—why?"

"I only wanted to protect him . . ."

"From what?"

She cast her eyes down and stammered, "It's just that—" before she fell silent, as if unwilling to divulge a secret.

The elevator door opened. I stepped inside, turning to face her as I said goodbye; only at that instant did I catch the astonishing expression of her dark, clairvoyant eyes—Rosalind, and only Rosalind, had known who I was, from the very beginning.

What of Larry, since Thistleton? Never was anyone as understanding, as compassionate as he as I went about reconstructing my life with my new, hard-won knowledge. Never did he pressure me or try to influence the tone of my book. "Only *you* will know what is right," he would say.

Our love for one another has grown, but not in the way I once associated with love. Ours had begun with friendship and admiration, after all, not with desire. The thrill of infatuation, the violent aftershocks of longing—these I never knew with Larry. I had always been seduced by his mind—and to no small extent aroused by his passion for his work—and yet, when we came to be lovers, that too surpassed my expectations. To my astonishment, what I experienced with him was hitherto unknown to me: the imagination he encouraged me to exercise elsewhere seemed to extend to our bed.

We were married a little over a year ago, on a Friday in April, in a little church near Langeais, in the Loire valley—the two of us alone, our only witness the concierge from the hotel where we were staying.

The next day we drove to Normandy, and from there to Mont-St.-Michel—it seemed fitting that we begin our married life there, braced by the winds of Brittany (the "tremor of the immense ocean" recalled from the book Larry had given me). The spring tides had just rushed in; a new moon lit the sky; together we climbed to the rocky parapet of the abbey, watching as the waves advanced.

The following Friday, having returned to New York, we drove to the house in East Hampton with Frederick. The next morning, Saturday, I went downstairs to tell the news to Mary, Frederick's nanny. She was in the laundry room, sorting and folding the little boy's clothes, a copy of People magazine tucked in the front pocket of her apron.

Her cheeks were flushed; she had been working since early morning. After greeting me perfunctorily, she continued to fold the clothes, stacking them in piles.

"Mary," I said, walking toward her. "I've got something to tell you."

Her bright blue eyes were momentarily curious, if wary. "Oh? What is it then, miss?"

"Mr. Brandt and I were married this week, in France."

She barely glanced at me. "Were you, then?" she said in her thick Scottish accent, only the merest suggestion of surprise crossing her face. Then, with more than a touch of resignation: "I suppose I should be calling you Mrs. Brandt now."

"I suppose so," I replied, smiling to myself.

"Have you told Frederick?"

"Mr. Brandt is speaking with him now."

"He'll be too little to understand," she said, her voice edged with a wistfulness, even hopefulness, that did not escape me. "Does the other Mrs. Brandt know?" she asked, beginning to separate a pile of small socks.

"Yes." Her silence continued to trouble me; I knew she was reticent to pose the question on her mind. "Are you wondering how Isabelle—Mrs. Brandt—reacted to the news, Mary?"

She nodded.

"She didn't seem surprised. She said she knew how much Frederick liked me, and that I would be good to him." I paused, still hoping she would respond. "I hope you know that's true, Mary."

"I'd like to think so, miss," she said, averting her eyes from mine. My heart went out to her, for I knew how much she loved the little boy, how much like a mother she had been to him, and I could so easily understand her apprehension— that I would usurp her place in Frederick's life and affections.

She remained with her back turned to me. "Mary," I said, placing my hand upon her shoulder. "I know how good you've been to Frederick—how much he means to you. And I know the idea of his having a stepmother may not be easy for you at first! But I love him too, just as I love his father—and I'll do everything I can to see that his life with us is very happy. I hope you know that."

She was silent, her head slightly bent, her hands suddenly still, as if she were fighting tears, fighting loss.

I drew my hand away and walked slowly upstairs, to the room where Larry and Frederick were speaking.

Only a few days ago, while Frederick was playing with a friend, I heard him brag, "I have *two* moms—one who's in the city and one who's here, in the country, and who makes up stories about my pirate ship." An hour later, his friend having left, Frederick appeared at my door while I was writing, his toy sword trailing on the floor, his boasting having given way to a child's quiet anxiety. Next came the question I had already anticipated: "Why do I have two moms when all my friends have only one?"

I put down my pen, took him on my knee, and hugged him. "If you had something you loved very much—a toy boat, or a car," I said, trying to reassure him, "—wouldn't it be better to have two of them, not just one?" He nodded, but even then I am not sure he was totally convinced. Once more, looking into his searching blue eyes, I struggled to explain, but finding no words that would suffice, I simply sighed and hugged him again: "There are some things you will only understand when you're a grown-up boy, Frederick —one day you *will* understand, I promise!"

And it has touched me very much to see how carefully and thoughtfully he has helped select the first toys and clothes we are preparing now for his sister—

We are expecting a child in November, and have already named her Miranda.

FINIS.

ABOUT THE AUTHOR

FRANCESCA STANFILL was born in Oxford, England, and grew up in New York and Los Angeles. A graduate of Yale University, she wrote for *The New York Times* before completing her first novel, *Shadows & Light*. Her articles have appeared in many publications, including *New York*, *Vogue*, and *House & Garden*.

The author lives in New York City with her husband, Peter Tufo, and their two children. She is currently at work on a new novel.